Sonja's Run

Sonja's Run

Colonel Cut
and the
Romanov Rubies

RICHARD HOYT

FORGE®

A TOM DOHERTY ASSOCIATES BOOK
NEW YORK

SONJA'S RUN: COLONEL CUT AND THE ROMANOV RUBIES

This book is printed on acid-free paper.

Book design by Nicole de las Heras

A Forge Book
Published by Tom Doherty Associates, LLC
175 Fifth Avenue
New York, NY 10010

www.tor.com

Forge® is a registered trademark of Tom Doherty Associates, LLC.

Library of Congress Cataloging-in-Publication Data

Hoyt, Richard, 1941–
    Sonja's run / Richard Hoyt.—1st ed.
        p.   cm.
    "A Tom Doherty Associates book."
    ISBN 0-765-30615-8 (alk. paper)
    EAN 978-0765-30615-9
        1. Russia—History—Nicholas I, 1825–1855—Fiction.   2. Americans—Russia—Fiction.
    3. Photographers—Fiction.   4. Women poets—Fiction.   5. Kidnapping—Fiction.   I. Title.

PS3558.O975S66   2005
813'.54—dc22

                                                                                    2004056319

First Edition: February 2005

Printed in the United States of America

0   9   8   7   6   5   4   3   2   1

This novel is for my agent and good friend,
Jacques de Spoelberch.

I still remember that amazing moment
You appeared before my sight
As though a brief and fleeting omen,
Pure phantom in enchanting light.

—FROM "TO ***,"
ALEXANDER PUSHKIN

The Correa Manuscript

ONE HUNDRED FORTY YEARS AFTER THE DISAPPEAR-
ance of the Romanov rubies from the Siberian mountain
Monko-seran-Xardick (Eternal Snow and Ice), a ruby-
encrusted tiara was placed before bidders at Sotheby's in
London. The rubies, cut and polished in Hong Kong in the late 1850s,
were identical to gems found today in the Vostochny Sayan Mountains
west of Lake Baikal in Siberia. How the rubies got from Monko-seran-
Xardick to Hong Kong remained shrouded in mystery and conjecture.

In April 2003, a Lisbon antiques dealer, João Correa, found a hand-
written autobiographical manuscript in a sea captain's desk tracing the
fate of the rubies to a dramatic incident at a Christmas party thrown by
Tsar Nicholas I in 1852. The authors were Sonja Sankova, the half-
Chinese daughter of a much honored Russian poet, and Jack Sandt, an
American daguerreotype artist and pioneer documentary photogra-
pher. Now regarded as the Matthew Brady of Asia, Sandt's daguerreotypes are today found in museums throughout East and Southeast Asia
and Australia.

Sankova and Sandt took turns writing episodes and chapters in the
third person, drifting at times into the first person. *Sonja's Run* is here
edited and rewritten in modern American English. The inclusion of a
subtitle, *Colonel Cut and the Romanov Rubies,* is a convention of
nineteenth-century romantic adventures.

BOOK ONE

Colonel Cut

ONE

On the Eve of Christmas

EUROPEAN DIPLOMATS AND VISITORS WERE NO LESS eager than Russian social and military elites to attend the annual Christmas Eve party hosted by Tsar Nicholas I. Fancying himself a patron of the arts, the Tsar also invited the best Russian writers and artists to the party. In 1852, as in previous years, the gala affair was held in the grand ballroom of his winter palace on the river Neva.

The Pushkin scholar and lyric poet Mikhail Sankov, the widely acclaimed bard of the Urals, was a guest each year. In December 1852, however, Sankov was slowly dying of a debilitating lung tumor. He extended his regrets, saying his coughing and hacking would be distracting to the Tsar's other guests.

In his place, the Tsar's chief of protocol extended an invitation to Mikhail's daughter, Sonja Sankova, a diminutive twenty-four-year-old Eurasian beauty and herself a poet of growing reputation. Sonja was more political than her father, and her verse was regularly published in the Hamburg political *Neue Rheinische Zeitung*, edited by the economist Karl Marx, who lived in London, supporting himself as a correspondent for the *New York Tribune*. When Prussian officials put *Neue Rheinische Zeitung* out of business in May 1849, Sonja continued publishing her poems in underground newspapers published by European radicals.

Sonja was ordinarily not given to social gatherings, grand or otherwise, but it was unwise to say no to the Tsar. Besides, did poets not write from a palette of experience? And did not Sun Tzu, the famous Chinese military strategist, say one should know one's enemy?

Sonja accepted. Mikhail's friend, the tweedy mathematician Arkady Migalkin, a cultivated gentleman, agreed to escort her. It was known, but unstated, that the charming Arkady ordinarily preferred the company of men.

IN LONDON ON THAT NIGHT OF CHRISTIAN JOY AND GOODWILL TO-ward men, Jack Sandt's hansom cab rattled over the streets and past dark alleys. With the horses' hooves clip-clopping on the stone cobbles, he passed a confusion of filthy wretches, cripples, and urchins lurching in the shadows like desperate, intoxicated crabs. The night air was choked with smoke mixed with a bone-chilling fog that rolled silently across the city. Prostitutes with dark, tragic eyes lingered under flickering gas lamps. One of them, skinny as a rope, with the whitest skin Jack had ever seen, halted for a moment, tracking his carriage as though she could somehow tell in passing that he was a stranger in their midst on Christmas Eve and wondered why he was there. There was no mistaking her unasked question: Why would anybody come to London who didn't have to?

Jack leaned out of the window and looked back. What did she dream of when she went to sleep in whatever dark alley or barren room was her lodging for the night? That someone like him would step from his carriage, as though heaven-sent, and rescue her from her wretched existence and take her to America? That she would then have food to eat and a humane man to take care of her? How he wished that he had the time and the light to pose her properly so that others too could see the emptiness in her eyes.

Charles Dickens had described this London in his stories. Here was the disease and the terrible poverty that had filled Karl Marx's European letters to Horace Greeley's *New York Tribune*. His rage was elemental. The grasping pursuit of profit in the industrial revolution had enfeebled a generation of men, deformed their children, and rendered their women unfit to bear children. A ghastly sight it was. Such desperation!

Three years earlier Jack had stumbled onto a remarkable stretch of nuggets on a creek emptying into the headwaters of the Feather River in Northern California. Rather than squandering his small fortune on prostitutes or risk his gold being stolen in the frenzy of the gold rush, he retreated to San Francisco and banked the bulk of it in a Wells Fargo Bank. With the rest, he bought a daguerreotype camera and returned to the Feather River, where he recorded images of resolute miners standing by their sluice boxes, and prostitutes posed in their boudoirs, looking out at the viewer, their ambiguous eyes forever frozen in the moment. He was a light chaser. He pursued the light and the shadows.

Jack was stunned by the power of his images. Look back, curious viewer, see these adventurous men with their great beards and trousers held up by suspenders and these ambitious women with much-prized bosoms and corseted waists assembled in this time and place to seek their fortunes. Here is what the gold fever looked like on the Feather River in California in 1849.

Following his adventure in the California gold rush, Jack read Alexander von Humboldt's *Central Asia*, the account of the German naturalist's 1843 journey into the Urals and then onward to the Altai Mountains and the Russian border with China. What did these Cossacks and Asians really look like? Jack wanted to freeze them in time so that the truth of their existence might not be lost in the retelling of the tale. And beyond that lay China and the mysteries of the Orient.

Jack was convinced that Asian princes, potentates, and sultans would pay well for a daguerreotype of themselves. They were wealthy, and their egos could not resist the flirtation with immortality available in a mirror image of themselves. This is me! This is what I looked like! Jack arranged to have his Wells Fargo deposit transferred to a Barclays Bank in the British crown colony in Hong Kong. With this bankroll, and by taking daguerreotype images and writing—for he was also skilled with a pen—Jack proposed to support himself.

As the hansom cab rattled and banged through the streets, Jack wondered what Karl Marx looked like, and beyond that about the troubled Russia of which Marx wrote in his letters to the *New York Tribune.* Jack liked Marx's passion. He carried with him a bottle of Ned Piper's Kentucky bourbon whiskey for a celebratory toast.

THE CELEBRANTS OF THE NATIVITY—PRINCES AND PRINCESSES, barons and baronesses, favorites of the court, and Russian officers in their splendid dress uniforms—had traveled to St. Petersburg from as far away as Vladivostok on the Sea of Japan and Sevastopol on the Black Sea. As the snow fell softly in the long winter's night, the Tsar's favorites assembled in a spacious ballroom of the Winter Palace that had crimson walls, a gilded ceiling, and elaborately carved, gilded door frames. The sumptuous buffet, lit by the flickering yellow light of gold chandeliers, included all manner of game, fowl, and seafood. A chamber orchestra of clarity and skill played Christmas music, and a boy's choir sang joyous carols, their clear soprano voices rising to the heavens.

The guests were refined and polite, although the Tsar's illegitimate half brother, Colonel Peter Koslov, arrived saturated with vodka, a condition that had temporarily rendered him indifferent to notions of propriety. Koslov commanded Detachment One, the infamous gendarme unit popularly called "the Wolfpack" for its striking gray uniforms with crimson trim and tunics.

The Romanov crown had long asserted ownership of the many deposits of gold discovered in the empire. In 1820, children in Siberia were found to be playing with emeralds. Shortly thereafter, yellow, blue, and rose crystals of beryl were discovered in the Urals and Siberia. The Russians eventually mined amethysts near the village of Mursinsk and crystals of smoke, pink, and transparent topaz from Alabaska in the southern Urals. Then more gems were discovered: rose tourmaline from Sarapulsk, also near Mursinsk; aquamarine in Nertchinsk, eastern Siberia; Jasper throughout the Urals; and rubies in the mountains west of Lake Baikal. Tsar Nicholas I claimed all these gems as the rightful property of the Romanov crown.

Nicholas placed Koslov and the Wolfpack in charge of transporting the precious stones to artisans who turned them into jewelry and adornments. Later, he gave the trusted Wolfpack the additional duty of expelling Jews from Russia's borders and suppressing the increasingly frequent rebellions of serfs.

Preceded by tales of barbarity and savagery, the Wolfpack was given wide clearance as it traveled about the empire. In fact, Peter Koslov so loved the knife as an instrument for meting out rough justice to recalcitrant serfs that he earned the disquieting sobriquet "Colonel Cut." Koslov was a powerfully built man in his midforties; his cool blue eyes were pools of hubris. If he chose to drink too much, he drank too much. Nobody dared challenge him.

Circulating through the many guests, Sonja and Arkady found themselves at the punch bowl near a half dozen sycophants gathered around Koslov. Talking far louder than he had to, Koslov told his enthralled listeners of the exploits of the storied Wolfpack. He was the head wolf, he said. The dominant male. He collected the Tsar's gold and emeralds and rubies, assembling a treasure of unimaginable beauty. No band of thieves dared challenge the Wolfpack.

The Wolfpack also tended the Tsar's flocks, ensuring that they did not stray. Koslov's audience was apparently charmed by his tales of brutality. Eyes wide, respectfully hushed and impressed, they hung on every word. A clever and resourceful man was Peter Koslov.

Koslov stopped his self-indulgent monologue to focus on Sonja, admiring her petite figure as though the bespectacled Arkady Migalkin didn't exist—or anybody else for that matter. Colonel Cut liked what he saw, and he was a man who took what he liked. Ears. Women. It made no difference. Both were perquisites of power and the authority of the crown.

Stepping to one side, the better to appreciate Sonja's figure, he said, "I speak of transporting treasure for the Tsar. In truth, there is no gem to be found in all the empire that is as grand as you, little one. Such beauty. You stop a man from breathing. No mere gold or emerald or ruby can do that."

TWO

The Blow

 JACK SANDT AT LENGTH ARRIVED IN SOHO, A DIStrict peopled with impoverished European immigrants, continuing on to 28 Dean Street, where Karl Marx, the *New York Tribune*'s European correspondent, lived with his wife and five children. Marx's wife, Jenny, met him at the door to their diminutive flat, and his driver helped him store his daguerreotype equipment and supplies in a cramped space inside the door.

Marx's flat had two tiny rooms. One, into which Jack's luggage was momentarily stored—taking up far too much space—served as the bedroom for the entire family. The second was a combination kitchen, living room, and study where Marx wrote the articles for the *Tribune* that he used to support his family.

Marx was a broad man with a coal black beard and hair and a wide, intelligent face. Jack expected someone with blazing eyes and a fiery countenance. Marx was not. He was an amiable, pleasant man who seemed pleased to meet Jack. In his dispatches to the *Tribune,* it was clear that he was enraged at exploitation of the working class by their bourgeois masters, but now, in his London flat, he was an easygoing, genial host to an American visitor.

The two men moved into the combination kitchen and study, a cramped space walled by piles of books and magazines. Marx said, "Well, the intrepid American daguerreotypist. Here you are at last."

Marx waited while Jenny poured them each a cup of tea, then said, "Here we are. Christmas Eve." He sang softly in English with a German accent, "Silent night, holy night, all is calm, all is bright." He paused, looking amused, then sang, "God rest ye merry gentlemen." He stopped. "A night to love our dear Lord. Did you see all that love in the streets on your way in? The warmth. The caring and sharing."

"Pretty grim stuff," Jack said.

Marx took a sip of tea. "I was wondering what you would look like, I admit." He regarded Jack over the edge of his cup, obviously uncertain of what to make of his American visitor.

Enthralled by Sonja Sankova and unable to take his eyes off her, Colonel Peter Koslov continued with his story of how he had recently personally castrated a young serf for having killed his master's goat. "Took his eggs from him just like that." By way of demonstration, Koslov made a twisting motion with his left hand. "Pitched them onto the snow." That, too, he demonstrated for Sonja's benefit. "Taught him a lesson he won't be forgetting soon."

Sonja was stunned, and it showed.

Koslov cocked his head. Fun to shock the pretty girl. "What? You don't like that story?"

Sonja glanced up at Arkady, then began looking for a way to escape.

Koslov motioned with his hand for her to stay put. "No, please, stay. You're the young poet, aren't you? Sonja Sankova."

"I write poetry," she said. "A legacy of my father."

"I'm told your mother was Chinese."

"From Hong Kong, yes."

Koslov looked amused. "I'm also told that the basis of your poetry is Chinese, not Russian."

"Russian is my mother tongue, so I naturally write in Russian, a wonderful language. My mother gave me the teachings of Lao Tzu, best understood by reading the *Tao Te Ching*. The Chinese believe there are two complementary forces, or principles, that make up all aspects of life. Yin is female, the earth, dark and absorbing. They believe yin is present in valleys, in even numbers, and is represented by the tiger, the color orange, and a broken line.

"Complementary forces? And the other would be?"

"Yang, the male, present in odd numbers and mountains, is represented by the dragon, the color azure, and an unbroken line. Yin and yang proceed from the Tai Chi, the Supreme Ultimate. As one decreases, the other increases. When they are in harmony, they are depicted as the light and dark halves of a circle."

"You have cat eyes. Almond shaped. Almost feline. Tell me, cat-eyed girl, are you set to bare your fearsome teeth? They call me 'Colonel Cut,' do you know that? I bet you do. I am the Tsar's private Satan. Nobody escapes my wrath. Am I the dark side of the circle? The evil yang?" A condescending, patronizing tease was Peter Koslov.

She paused. "In fairness, I should add, my mother introduced me to the teaching of Sun Tzu as well as Lao Tzu."

"Sun Tzu. Different from Lao Tzu, I take it. And he being?"

"The author of *The Art of War*. Being a professional soldier, I'm surprised that you haven't heard of him. In Asia, he is considered a master."

"I can't say that I'm familiar with the gentleman, and neither can I recall the Chinese being especially successful against the British army, or anyone else for that matter. Is my education lacking, in your opinion?"

" 'If your opponent is of choleric temper, seek to irritate him. Pretend to be weak that he may grow arrogant.' "

"Sun Tzu?"

She nodded.

"Speaking of bad temper, have you heard the story of what I did to the serfs at Oblinsk? What would Lao Tzu think? No, I amend that. Tell me what *you* think. Am I arrogant?" Koslov grinned mischievously. He took another sip of punch.

Sonja felt the eyes of the company watching her, waiting for her answer. The orchestra began another song. She said, "I've heard that disturbing account, sir, and I know what you are called. But until proven otherwise, I attribute the story to rumor. I cannot imagine it otherwise."

Koslov looked offended. "You don't believe it? Well, consider it proven, dear lady. The serfs at Oblinsk demanded their freedom. Ninety of them. We had to do something, didn't we? His Majesty had given us a duty. Should I order the serfs shot on the spot? Or perhaps have their testicles removed? I've done that before. All that weeping and wailing and crying out. A kind of music to Colonel Cut."

He held up the palms of his hands. "Or should I be merciful? I consider myself a civilized and generous man. I decided on the latter course. They had heard the stories. They protected their privates with their hands. You should have seen their eyes! But I fooled them. I ordered their ears cut off. Such a sight! I'll never forget it." He smiled at the memory.

"You should have seen those serfs, Miss Sankova. Distraught they were, hands covering the sides of their heads, blooding seeping between their fingers. Yes, they still had their testicles, but what woman would want to have anything to do with an earless man? I saved their ears and dried them. One hundred eighty ears. They look rather like leathery mushrooms. I made a dried-ears necklace that I wear whenever I deal with ambitious serfs. They want freedom? Oh? When they see me coming, I assure you they scatter, and that's the end of that kind of talk." He grinned. "You like that story? It's true. A subject for a poem, I would think."

"I think it's barbarous," Sonja muttered.

Koslov's jaw tightened. He grabbed Sonja tightly by the left wrist. "Say again, Miss Sankova! Remember whom you're talking to! You think it's what? 'Barbarous,' did you say? Apologize. I insist!"

Sonja yanked her left hand from Colonel Koslov's grasp, in the process jerking the inebriated Koslov off balance. As she did, she balled up her fist and slugged him with a roundhouse right cross, delivered with all the strength she could muster. The blow landed with an audible *crack*, like the report of a musket, silencing both music and conversation in the grand ballroom.

THREE

The Nature of Bloodstains

 JACK SANDT RETREATED TO HIS CARPETBAGS AND RE-
turned with a daguerreotype of a forlorn, filthy, cadaver-
ous New York beggar passed out in a pile of trash in an
alley. It was a riveting image, one of which Jack was especially proud. "This is my light, Herr Marx. This is what I see. There is
no lying here. No denying reality. No politics. No rhetoric. It speaks for
itself."

Studying the daguerreotype, Marx was obviously impressed.

"I got interested in daguerreotypes from a man named A. S. South-
worth, whom I met in the California gold rush. A Russian who had
come down from Alaska got me interested in Humboldt. He taught
me to speak Russian as well. I'm not as fluent as a native, but I'll learn
more when I get a chance to speak. In your letter, you said you would be
pleased to sit for me. I hope you haven't changed your mind."

"I'd be honored to sit for you, Mr. Sandt."

"The first thing I have to do is polish the plate. I can polish while we
talk, if that would be all right with you. If there's the slightest imperfec-
tion on the plate, it will ruin the image."

"Certainly, if you explain what you're doing while we talk. Mr.
Daguerre's wonderful invention is fascinating to someone like me."

"I've decided to use a whole plate for your portrait, that's six and a
half by eight and a half inches. They're made of copper, by the way,

coated with silver. This particular one was made by the Scoville brothers of New York. I've added extra silver by a process called 'galvanizing.' I attach an electrically charged wire to a plate and a second to silver, and lower the plate into a solution of potassium cyanide." He put the plate into a vise that he held in his lap, tightening two pairs of wooden wing nuts to lock the plate in place. "The first thing I'll do is sprinkle the plate with a powder of finely ground pumice." He did so. "Then I polish it with this." He held up a wooden blade covered with buckskin so Marx could examine it. "You'll note that I polish in strokes parallel to the edges, first horizontal, then vertical." He began, rubbing quickly, back and forth, back and forth.

Marx leaned over watching him.

Polishing as he talked, Jack said, "Judging by your letters to the *Tribune,* I thought you might grab me by the throat at the door, demanding to know if I was a worker or a capitalist."

Marx grinned. He said nothing, watching Jack polish.

At length, Jack held the plate up, studying it. Then he switched from pumice to jeweler's rouge, polishing the plate with a buff stick covered with flannel. Still alternating his strokes, and without looking at his bearded host, he said, "Four years ago, all the major European powers except for Russia suffered upheavals and rebellions by people seeking justice and a republican form of government. I know from reading your contributions to the *New York Tribune* that you're eager to tell the world about the barbarous Romanov dynasty and its treatment of serfs and Jews."

"I am that, to put it mildly."

Jack leaned forward regarding the German earnestly. "Writers tell. A dag man shows. Would *showing* the world what's happening in Russia be of any service? Perhaps I could help you in that regard."

Thinking, Marx ran the palm of his hand down his beard.

Jack said, "I wrote you a letter of introduction saying I worked for Horace Greeley. That was bogus. A ruse. In fact, I've never met Greeley." Jack held out the plate again, looking pleased. "There, see. It looks nearly black. I've almost got it."

"No? If I might be so bold as to ask, who are you then, if not with the *Tribune*?"

Holding the plate vertically, Jack carefully applied the final strokes. "This will be a vertical portrait. You'll note that these last strokes run parallel to the bottom. That's so that any scratches that I can't see will be parallel to the viewing light and won't cast shadows. I don't work for anybody. I'm on my own."

"I see," Marx said, waiting for the American to finish explaining himself.

Jack said, "On the other hand, Herr Marx, you *do* work for Horace Greeley. I take it you receive letters from Mr. Greeley on stationery with the *Tribune* logo at the top? Even better with a letterhead of some kind that contains his name."

Casually, Marx said, "Why yes, I do."

COLONEL CUT'S KNEE HIT THE FLOOR WITH A THUD AS A SHARD OF broken tooth rattled across the hardwood floor. Blood streamed from his nose and his split upper lip.

Mildly, Sonja said, " 'Attack your opponent where he is unprepared.' "

Koslov made a noise in his throat. The music stopped.

Koslov looked up at Sonja, dazed.

" 'The good fighter will be terrible in his onset and prompt in his decision.' "

Koslov drew his forearm across his nose and mouth. He examined the blood on his sleeve.

"You truly should read Sun Tzu, Colonel."

The room was eerily silent.

Koslov glanced at the Tsar. Had he witnessed the incident?

Yes he had.

If the Tsar frowned, Sonja knew she would be dead within the hour. If he smiled, the party would continue as before. It was yea or nay. Up or down. In a heartbeat, her immediate fate would be decided.

The Tsar burst out laughing, a joyous *har, har, har* at the sight of a slender young woman knocking the hardened Colonel Koslov to the floor. He was hard put to suppress his mirth. "Say, you deliver a hard right cross, Miss Sankova. And a poet too! You surprise me. Are you all right, Colonel Koslov?"

"I'm fine, Your Highness. You're right, the young lady packs a solid blow."

"Perhaps you should enlist Miss Sankova in the Wolfpack. You could turn her loose on the Turks. That would teach them a lesson or two." The Tsar laughed again. He then turned and signaled to the orchestra with his hand. "This is the birthday of Christ Jesus. Music, please." He thus ended the incident. The party was to continue.

Koslov stood and retrieved his handkerchief. His upper lip looked like a split sausage. He breathed softly to Sonja. "For that, pretty one, you will one day surrender your own ears."

"I resist."

"Not this time, Miss Sankova," he said. He put the handkerchief to his face.

"You've gotten blood on your ribbons and medals."

Koslov looked down at his chest.

"They say bloodstains are impossible to remove. A lesson for us all," she said.

"You heard me. I will have your ears." With that, having suffered the embarrassment of having been knocked to his knees by a woman, Colonel Cut left the room to attend to his cut lip and broken tooth. The guests pretended not to have seen the blow or have heard Sonja's remark about bloodstains. Neither did they acknowledge the chip of broken tooth on the floor under the buffet.

FOUR

The Bargain

 JACK SANDT LOOKED ABOUT THE CRAMPED QUARTERS for some free space. "Next I have to coat the plate to make it light sensitive. A smelly job, but it has to be done. Also, I have to do it in the dark. You don't mind if I build a kind of frame tent, do you? It's my own design. It's just large enough for me to sit and do what I have to do. I should be able to squeeze it in here."

"Do proceed, Mr. Sandt. I'm fascinated. And please do tell me more of what you have in mind."

As he began screwing ribs together with wooden wing nuts, Jack said, "Thank you for hearing me out, sir. I grew up on the Chesapeake Bay, where my father worked as an oysterman. I went to California to seek my fortune in the gold rush three years ago and had a little luck. That's where I got interested in daguerreotypes." Having constructed a frame about five feet high, he began stretching black muslin over the ribs. One panel had a small window covered with white paper. "I have a proposition to make that I think you might like. It should benefit us both."

Marx took a sip of tea, thinking. "Those are the best kinds of propositions, are they not? Tell me what you have in mind."

Jack completed the structure, which had a door that hung down from the top rib and buttoned into place. He opened another carpetbag and removed two wooden boxes, one taller than the other. Each box was lined with a blue-green, handblown glass jar containing chemicals. The cover of each had ground glass on the underside and a recessed opening that held the plate. He also had a wooden frame with a sliding panel in front and a removable back.

He said, "The taller box contains iodine crystals. The shorter one has my own formula of bromine and chlorine that I call 'quick stuff.' The bromine enables me to reduce the exposure time. This frame here holds the plate and keeps out the light until it's exposed in the camera. This will be a smelly process, so brace yourself."

Marx smiled.

Jack glanced at Marx. "I want to travel from St. Petersburg to the mouth of the Yangtze River and record daguerreotype images of what I see, a journey that would take me through the Urals and across the Asian steppe to China and eventually to Hong Kong." He placed the two boxes and plate holder inside his makeshift darkroom.

Marx looked interested. "Sort of a modern-day Marco Polo."

"Only I'm not just interested in portraits of kings and noblemen and their pretty ladies. I want to record life as it is lived by ordinary people. Here we go." Polished plate in hand, Jack squatted and entered the square black box, carefully buttoning up the entrance behind him. In the dim light that came through the paper window, he put the plate into position on the lid of the jar of iodine and immediately stiffened.

Outside the box, Marx made a noise in his throat and backed off, putting his arm over his nose. He held up Jack's daguerreotype of the New York derelict, studying it.

Inside, Jack grinned. Raising his voice slightly so Marx could hear him clearly on the other side of the muslin, he said, "Told you it smells to high heaven. I try to hold my breath but I can do that only so long. I get used to it after a while. Ordinarily, I coat the plates two or three weeks before I use them, but in this case I've been at sea and haven't had the chance." Watching the box, he waited, saying, "I've long been fascinated by the travels of Humboldt. That and what I've read about Chinese junks."

"Oh?"

Nearly a minute had passed. Jack removed the plate and examined it. It was a deep orange-yellow. Handling the plate by the edges, he put it in the other lid and placed it over the quick stuff. "Junks are stable and seaworthy, designed to haul cargo and to live on. It's hard work lugging my gear overland, but if I lived and traveled on a junk, why, there would be no problem, would there? They say there are headhunters on the island of Borneo. And Japan will almost certainly be forced to open up to trade with the outside world. That's not to mention all the wonders of China." He checked the plate. It was a deep rose color. He put it back over the iodine. "I want to record all that on daguerreotype images so Europeans and Americans can see what it looks like for themselves." He removed the plate from its second exposure to iodine. He examined it in the dim light. Satisfied that it was ready, he slid the plate into the wooden holder, taking care that both panels were securely in place so no light leaked.

He stepped out of his makeshift darkroom, plate holder in hand. "My plan is to travel to China via the Urals and the Asian steppe and take dags of life in Russia and write about what I see. Unfortunately, Tsar Nicholas has sealed off the interior of Russia to foreigners."

"I see. And where do I fit in?" Marx couldn't help but grin. "I know you have a use for me somewhere."

Jack set up a wooden tripod, tightening its brass fittings. Atop that he fastened his rosewood daguerreotype camera, which had a leather bellows. "This is a Lewis model, out just last year. The bellows makes it compact. The sliding panel on the rear both keeps the light off the plate and speeds up the exposure time. I'll need to surround you with light. If your wife can collect all possible candles and bring any mirrors we can use to reflect light, that would be helpful."

"Jenny!"

"I heard," Jenny said. She and her children had been watching silently from the other room. She was pleased to be part of the process. She set about securing candles and mirrors.

Marx shook his head in amazement. "Quite a process."

Jack grinned ruefully. "But worth the trouble. A painting has its charm, but there's something about a daguerreotype that's memorable. It's the light, you see. By turns fierce and enchanting. A dag man pursues the revealing light."

"Yes, the light. Reality." Marx pursed his lips. "A revolutionary concept."

"I can guild a daguerreotype with chloride of gold or color it with a Newman kit." He stepped aside for Jenny Marx, who had an armful of lamps, candles, and mirrors.

Marx cocked his head. "You still haven't answered my question of where I fit in. Let me guess. I take it by your reference to letterheads that you want me to help you forge *Tribune* documents with Horace Greeley's name on them. Is that your idea?"

Jack beamed. "There, you've got it. So that I might take daguerreotypes of real people, not the fanciful drawings tainted by politics. Yes."

"Do you have any idea of the dangers involved in a trip like that?"

"I have two Colt revolvers and a fifty-caliber Sharps with a Maynard strip and linen cartridges. That and a brace of derringer pistols. I learned to shoot when I was in California. Got a lot of practice."

Marx grinned. "There'd a Yiddish word for what you have in mind. *Chutzpah!*"

"I'll need bogus *Tribune* press cards and a personal letter from Horace Greeley saying I'm going to take daguerreotypes of the wonderful way the Russians have developed the potential of their frontier. From these, Greeley's artists can do line drawings for his newspaper. All nonsense."

"I see."

"Greeley will never know. How can he find out? You want the world to know the truth. I want that, and I want adventure. We both do what we have to do to get what we want. No risk for you. I stake everything I have, including my life."

"You've got a lot of nerve, Mr. Sandt, I'll grant you that."

Jack said to Jenny, "We'll need light on both sides of your husband." He waited while she got candles and lanterns in place. "I propose to spend the winter here in London and leave in the spring when the thaw begins on the Continent. What do you think, Mr. Marx? Will you help me out?"

"Mmm. An interesting proposition, I must say."

Frau Marx stepped back. All the lights she had were in place. She glanced at Jack, her face asking if that was enough.

"I think that will do it, thank you, ma'am. Now then, Herr Marx, I want you to sit up straight, please. Chin up. I'm recording your image for posterity, remember. I want you to sit perfectly still, absolutely rigid for at least ten seconds. If you move, it will blur the image."

Karl Marx got comfortable on his chair. "By the way, regarding your proposal, yes, Mr. Sandt, I will help you every way I can. What Horace Greeley doesn't know, won't hurt him." Marx took a deep breath and let it out slowly. "I believe I'm ready." He froze, holding his breath.

Jack Sandt slipped the plate holder into the rear of the camera and quickly removed the sliding panel. He watched the second hand of his pocket watch.

SONJA SANKOVA HAD A LARGE GASH ACROSS HER KNUCKLES. THE bleeding knuckles throbbed. Her hand was swelling rapidly. It had never occurred to her that slugging somebody in the face was as hard on the hand of the assailant as on the face of the victim. She opened and closed her hand, wincing from the pain. She willed herself not to massage her knuckles. She held up her bleeding hand, examining it. "Hurts," she said to Arkady.

Arkady said, "I bet. You need some ice and maybe some stitches."

Struggling to control her trembling hands, Sonja picked up the crystal glass dipper with her good hand and poured herself another goblet of punch. Raising the goblet with her bleeding hand, she took a triumphant sip, chin held high. She had made an enemy of Colonel Cut. Nobody congratulated her on what she had done. In fact, she was an immediate pariah.

Knowing she was in mortal danger, Sonja Sankova excused herself on the grounds that she needed to tend to her throbbing hand. As a middle-aged manservant and a pretty young maid escorted her down the hall toward the ladies' comfort room, Sonja knew it would be folly to return to the party. The maid started to follow her inside, but Sonja declined her help.

"It's okay," she said. "I'll be just a moment."

Once inside the comfort room, Sonja plunged her hand into the glass basin of cold water that was intended for washing. A gilded ceramic ladle hung on the edge of the basin. The cold water eased the throbbing somewhat, but as the minutes passed and Koslov had time to think about his humiliation, Sonja knew, her situation would grow more dangerous. If she was to survive the night, she had to act quickly. Her hand could wait.

She broke the ladle in half. She folded her hands at her waist as though cradling her swollen hand and hid the broken half of the ladle under her forearm. She stepped into the hall. "I feel nauseated. I believe I need a breath of fresh air."

Still accompanied by the manservant and the maid, she went down the hall. When she stepped outside, she discovered that the softly falling snow had been replaced by a blizzard. A howling wind whipped snow through the streets. She said, "I have pain medicine in my carriage that I keep for my father. It will work quite well with my hand."

The manservant said, "You'll need your wraps, Miss Sankova."

"The wraps can wait. I need relief from the pain." She strode through the snow in the direction of the stables. As she did, the maid, looking concerned, returned inside, presumably to report her intention.

The manservant, at her side, said, "Better to have a boy fetch your carriage, Miss Sankova."

She ignored him.

Guests did not enter the stables. That was the turf of the stable boys who took care of the guests' carriages. Ignoring form and protocol, Sonja plunged forward into the dank and smelly stable.

Perhaps sensing what she had in mind, alarmed, the manservant said, "Please, Miss Sankova. It is forbidden for you to leave the grounds."

She pulled the broken ladle from beneath her forearm and put the broken end at his throat. "I'll have a carriage, a good one with strong horses. I want it now or I'll cut your throat from ear to ear. I mean it. Tell them."

Feeling the sharp edge of the broken ladle, the manservant shouted instructions to the stable boys.

While the stable boys rushed about retrieving a sleigh, the manservant said, "Please, Miss Sankova, this is foolish. You cannot run from Colonel Koslov. He will pursue you to the ends of the earth."

"We'll see," she said.

Moments later two wide-eyed stable boys produced a sleigh hitched to two white horses and led them out into the whirling snow. Sonja Sankova leaped into the sleigh and grabbed the reins and the whip. She cracked the whip over the horses and she was away.

Behind her, the manservant called out, "Good luck, Miss Sankova!"

As she plunged into the blizzard, Sonja smiled grimly. Knowing that he himself would be dead within the hour, punishment for allowing her to escape, the manservant had wished her luck. The rebellion was growing.

As Jack Sandt began packing his gear to go, he picked up a back issue of the *Neue Rheinische Zeitung*. Interested, he began flipping through the pages, although he couldn't read the German. He stopped at a line drawing of a young Eurasian beauty.

Watching him, Marx said, "She is a Russian poet, a regular contributor. Her name is Sonja Sankova. She is half Chinese. Her father, Mikhail, is a lyric poet who grew up in the Urals. An interesting pair, those two. I met them once at a gathering in Cologne."

"She's beautiful," Jack said. "Those eyes. Can you imagine what a daguerreotype would do for her?" He groaned softly.

"She lives near St. Petersburg. Maybe you'll bump into her."

Jack smiled wistfully. "That would be nice, but unlikely. Is this her poem?"

Marx stood beside him looking down at the journal. "Yes, it is."

"Would you translate her poem into English for me. I'm curious."

"Certainly," Marx said. "No reason why not, as long as you understand that it will necessarily lose some of its power after being translated from Russian to German and then into English." He read the poem to himself, thinking about the English, then recited it for Jack.

BEAUTIFUL GEESE
One November morning when the sky
was as cold as an iceman's eye,
I went walking all alone, my boots crunching icy diamonds.
My reverie was broken by a distant, plaintive crying out.
What was this? I wondered.
I looked about.
I heard the lament again.
It was coming from above me, in the thin blue sky.
Geese. Yes.
I looked up and saw their crooked, hopeful V.
They were flying north, not south!
North? Into the winter wind?
I thought surely they are confused,
surely they will turn around.
Whatever will happen to them?
They flew on,
their cries growing dimmer with each passing minute.
So grand they were. So high. So beautiful.

Jack suddenly remembered something. He dug out the bottle of Ned Piper's whiskey. "I thought we might have a late night drink to celebrate."

"Celebrate the birth of the Christ child?" Marx didn't look enthusiastic. "You saw prostitutes and suffering wretches on the streets outside. That scene remains unchanged for three hundred sixty-five nights a year. Now on one night, December 25, it's joy, joy to the world, everybody love his brother." Marx made a noise in his throat.

Jack uncapped the bottle. "Nothing to do with the Christ child.

I propose to drink to peace and goodwill toward men. That part of the sentiment is worthwhile. And also to justice and fairness among men, maybe not so popular with the people who run the factories."

Marx snagged two cups from the cupboard. "Well, yes, Mr. Sandt. I can drink to that. And to your work in Russia. May you emerge healthy and with some honest images that will make people feel some compassion about the lives of common people."

Jack poured generous measures. He raised his cup to Marx's. "That, sir, is something worth a toast on Christmas Eve or any other night."

Jack Sandt and Karl Marx touched cups and drank Ned Piper's best.

"And to the crooked, hopeful V of Miss Sankova's beautiful geese," Marx said.

Jack poured another measure for his host and for himself. "Yes, certainly. To Sonja Sankova's geese."

When they finished that round, Jack and Marx had another and yet another, until Ned Piper had worked his Irish magic, and they were three sheets to the wind, imagining the many daguerreotypes the adventurous Jack Sandt might take of the desperate wretches in the Urals and Siberia. The light! The light! The dag man and the intellectual both sought the light.

FIVE

To Emulate the Running Hare

SONJA SANKOVA HAD REALIZED AS SHE LEFT THE Christmas party that the Tsar would soon be having second thoughts about the wisdom of allowing her to go unpunished. No young woman knocked Peter Koslov to his knee in front of the Tsar without the story spreading by word of mouth across the empire. The mythic retelling of the rebellious blow was the kind of seed that the crown could not allow to sprout.

In the darkness of the winter night, she took her ailing father to an abandoned country house where they could spend the winter. There she would care for him. Perhaps his lungs would clear. Such things were known to happen.

Several days after they had moved into the house, they learned that Arkady Migalkin had been found murdered. His murderer had removed the ears from his corpse.

Colonel Cut was sending her a message.

As the spring thaw approached, the dying Mikhail Sankov told his daughter that he wanted to be buried in the Urals where he was born. Would that be possible? Yes it would be, she said. She would take him to the Urals herself, Colonel Cut and his Wolfpack be damned.

Sonja's father had begun life as a serf owned by a titled Russian in the Urals. When he was a teenager, his master assigned him the task of guiding a visiting Belgian, Viscount Jacques de Borchgrave, on a trip to hunt grouse. De Borchgrave took a liking to the boy, who was an orphan, and bought his freedom, taking him back to Belgium to be educated.

Owing to the extreme length of their mutual border with Russia, and the vast expanse of Siberia to the north, the Chinese maintained a diplomatic mission in St. Petersburg. The thirty-three-year-old Mikhail met Mei Ling, whom he later called Mimi, at a reception given by the Tsar for her father, Chan Bao, the newly appointed Chinese ambassador to Russia.

A Russian poet simply did not ask a beautiful sixteen-year-old Chinese girl out on a date. The Chinese considered daughters of little value other than as objects of barter. Chan, tipsy from the Russian vodka, noticed that Mikhail was infatuated by his daughter. He couldn't take his eyes off her. Mistakenly believing that Mikhail was somehow a favorite of the Tsar and so a worthwhile connection, Chan casually asked Mikhail if he would like Mimi for a wife.

Mikhail, stunned by the unexpected offer, found it impossible to say no. He said *da!* Yes, he would like very much to marry Mei Ling. Eager to please, the gallant father introduced his daughter to her husband-to-be.

The issue of their marriage, little Sonja, spent most of her childhood in Brussels, where her father taught Russian language and literature. Sonja learned to speak French and English in school.

The Sankov family spent the summers in St. Petersburg until eventually the crown, which had seen Mikhail's growing reputation as a poet, offered him a teaching post in the capital city.

Mimi died when Sonja was seventeen, and Sonja regarded the *Tao Te Ching* as her mother's legacy. It was not a religion by the reckoning of the monotheistic Christians, Jews, and Muslims, but rather a kind of philosophy rooted in the shifting forces of the masculine and feminine that Lao Tzu observed around him. The masculine and feminine were both inherently necessary and, in proper balance, good. Too much of one, especially the dominant and dominating yang, was not good. Too much yang, in fact, had yielded the obscene Romanov dynasty.

After her mother died, Sonja devoted herself to her father, traveling with him to London, Paris, and Berlin. The teenage Sonja began developing her own considerable abilities as a poet. But while Mikhail was a lyric poet inspired by memories of his beginnings in the Urals, Sonja Sankova was rebellious and political.

Sonja was aware that she compared all men to her father, and in her mind they inevitably came up short. She had had her suitors, but in the end none had captured her fancy enough to marry. No reason to think that the daughter of a freed serf and a Chinese girl should have a conventional imagination.

Also no reason to think that because Russians had not participated in the republican uprisings in 1848, they would not eventually triumph and rid themselves of the shackles of the Romanov dynasty. Sonja Sankova regarded herself as part of the vanguard of revolution. It would happen, she was convinced, but not without courage and sacrifice.

She was also aware of history's lesson that violence begets violence. The question was clear: Could the Romanov crown be brought down and the serfs freed without such upheaval and passionate excess that the violated themselves became violators? She had seen this happen in families. Was there any doubt that it happened in nations as well, the dubious irony of violent revolution?

Sonja Sankova believed that it did.

JACK SANDT WAS STUNNED BY THE AWESOME BEAUTY OF ST. Petersburg under a mantle of snow. Everything was white and above that a cloudless, forever blue sky. But the drama lay in the gilded domes of the Eastern Orthodox church that poked into the blue. Gold, gold, gold everywhere. Dazzling gold. Gold had been struck in California three years earlier, lots of it, but Jack thought it must be nothing at all to a country with gold enough to cover the exterior of its church domes.

Jack had brought a brace of .44-caliber cap-and-ball Colt dragoon revolvers with 7.5-inch barrels and weighing two pounds, ten ounces each—a real load but worth it. Jack also had rolls of Maynard strips, detonator pellets enclosed in a strip of fabric so they could be successively fed into firing position by action of the lock. He also had a supply of the recently developed "cartridges" made of linen and containing powder and ball. Both strips and cartridges were for a .50-caliber breech-loading Sharps rifle with peep sights. In addition to that he had two .44-caliber derringer pistols that could be secreted in one's clothing.

The Russian authorities told Jack that the crown restricted travel in its vast Asian interior; permission from local officials was required to move from one town to the next. Travelers were required to obtain something akin to a new passport at every stop. Jack knew what that meant. Excuses would inevitably be offered for delay. Palms would naturally be extended by way of speeding things up. In short, an impossible pain in the behind.

Jack met with representatives of His Imperial Majesty, giving them his forged *Tribune* credentials and a letter from Greeley, carefully forged by Karl Marx, requesting permission for him to travel in the interior on behalf of the newspaper. Three days later Jack received a letter granting him an interview with Count Vladimir Chermerkov, minister of the interior.

SONJA SANKOVA WAS FIVE FEET TALL AND WEIGHED BUT NINETY-SIX pounds. She knew Colonel Cut would be pursuing a young woman and her ailing father, so she had her hair cut short and donned trousers. With a fur hat covering her head and ears plus trousers and a heavy winter coat, Sonja could well pass for a boy—at least casually or at a distance. To the casual observer, Sonja and Mikhail were a boy and an ailing old man—the boy's grandfather perhaps.

To get Mikhail to his Uralian origins alive, Sonja would have to stop periodically so that he could recover his ebbing strength. Also there were telegraph wires strung from St. Petersburg to Moscow; she had to be careful in the extreme, traveling minor rivers and detouring through remote villages. After Moscow, they would go to Yekaterinburg, then south.

The Russians had built a series of winter stations along the country's many rivers to give travelers an occasional respite from the bitter cold. These stations were wretched and dirty, hardly more than hovels. While the stations were oftentimes disgusting to enter, it was either accept refuge there and thaw out or slowly freeze to death. The peasants who kept the stations had all heard of Mikhail Sankov and were eager to do whatever they could to help, although some, fearing retribution from the Tsar, pretended not to know who he was.

Mikhail stared forward into the distance, his haggard, hollow blue eyes twisted from the pain of the tumor growing inside him. Mikhail's friends had provided him with a huge supply of laudanum, made from the juice of the unripe poppy, which blunted but did not eliminate his pain. He rode in a dreamlike stupor, reciting poems by his beloved Pushkin. Mikhail felt Pushkin was to Russia what Shakespeare was to England; no Russian with soul was ignorant of Pushkin.

In the first week of their circuitous travels Sonja met a laundress who heard that she had knocked Koslov cold. A village store clerk believed Koslov had been carried off on a litter to receive medical attention. A stable boy, not knowing he was speaking to Sonja, said he had heard from a waiter who was there and witnessed the incident that Sonja Sankova was the most beautiful woman in all of Russia. "And she hit Colonel Koslov with a right uppercut that sent him to the floor with a resounding crash and teeth flying everywhere. Taught him a lesson right then and there with the Tsar watching. Can you imagine? I'd like to meet her one day and tell her I'm on her side."

Sonja repressed a grin, but said nothing.

A week into her odyssey, with a snowstorm having passed and the warming sun rising to her left, Sonja pushed on, her breath coming in great white bursts in the frigid morning air. Peter Koslov had scoffed at Sun Tzu. What could a Chinese know about fighting? There was one of Sun's suggestions that seemed to fit her situation perfectly:

At first, then, exhibit the coyness of a maiden, until the enemy gives you an opening. Afterward emulate the rapidity of a running hare, and it will be too late for the enemy to oppose you.

The horses clip-clopped over the ice and frozen snow at a slashing pace. *Clip-clop. Clip-clop.* Did the Tsar listen for the distant hoofbeats?

Was he aware of their presence, however weak and tentative. Did he hear them growing louder? *Clip-clop.*

Sonja Sankova turned the horses into the biting wind. The horses pushed steadily forward. *Clip-clop. Clip-clop.*

The Charming of Count Chermerkov

JACK SANDT ARRIVED AT COUNT VLADIMIR CHER-
merkov's impressive St. Petersburg offices with properly
shined shoes and his beard trimmed and two heavy carpetbags containing his daguerreotype gear. The amiable
count, a silver-haired man in his late fifties with muttonchop sideburns,
wore spectacles with wire rims and smoked a pipe. He spoke English,
but Jack was determined to conduct the interview in Russian to show
him he knew enough to survive.

After bidding Jack to sit and ordering tea, Chermerkov looked outside for a moment, thinking. He had a grand view from his office—the
gilt on a fabulous dome of an Eastern Orthodox church glistened in
the afternoon sun. Sitting opposite him, Jack felt like a presumptuous
bumpkin.

Chermerkov lit his pipe and released a puff of sweet-smelling blue
smoke. He took a sip of tea and said, "Tell me about your newspaper, Mr.
Sandt. What is your position and what do you propose to do in the interior of our country? This is a vast and sometimes dangerous territory.
Also, if I might add, is this an official assignment from your paper?"

"I work for the *New York Tribune,* sir. I'm a daguerreotype artist. A
dag man. I take daguerreotypes that artists later draw to illustrate the
news. My editor is much taken with the possibility of developing the interior of America purchased by our third president, Thomas Jefferson.

He thinks it might be instructive for our readers to find out what Russia has accomplished with its own interior. He has heard of your many gold and silver mines and your iron and other minerals. He feels our own frontiers likely have similar deposits."

Chermerkov smiled. Jack knew it was because of his lousy Russian.

Jack pushed forward in Russian nevertheless. "I have an English-Russian dictionary."

"What is your editor's name? Should I know about him?"

"Horace Greeley is his name. I can't imagine you'd know anything about him here in St. Petersburg. His mind is on money. Always on money. You know how editors are." Jack paused. Quickly, he said, "A fine man nevertheless. Honorable."

Chermerkov suppressed a smile. "Shall we continue in English? Good for me to practice my English, what with having to deal with London."

Jack assumed Chermerkov was calculating the effect his daguerreotypes might have on potential investors in the mineral-rich Urals and Siberia. There was hope.

"What is it you have there?" The count motioned toward the box Jack had brought, with daguerreotypes stored in slots to protect the surfaces from damage.

"Some samples of my daguerreotypes, so you'll know I do professional work." Jack slipped an image from its slot to show to Chermerkov.

The count was obviously impressed, so Jack showed him some more. He had selected the images carefully to eliminate anything that might be considered political or controversial. He wanted to come off as an obsequious bootlicker, trembling before Chermerkov's power. "If you would like to look at them, I'd be honored. But if you could please hold them by the edges, sir. They scratch easily."

Chermerkov picked up one of the dags. "These gentlemen appear to be workers."

Jack said, "Gold miners in California."

"I see. Rugged looking." He held up another daguerreotype by the edges. "Mmm. And this?"

"Those are oystermen posing by the dock at Baltimore in the state of

Maryland. Would you like me to capture your image while we talk, sir? Perhaps your wife and family would appreciate it?"

Chermerkov puffed on his pipe, vanity doing its duty. "A daguerreo-type? Of me?"

"Yes, sir. On the off chance that you would honor me, I have brought my camera and the necessary chemicals. We have excellent light coming through this window. Enough for a very nice portrait, I would think. We could talk while I work."

Having completed the drill of polishing and preparing a four-and-a-half-by-five-and-a-half-inch plate for exposure, Jack Sandt set about arranging a pose for his subject. "Just as you are would be fine, sir. There behind your desk. Once you find a pose you're comfortable with, you'll have to remain motionless for at least ten seconds."

Chermerkov twisted the bottom of his sideburn with his left hand and took another puff on his pipe. He set the pipe on the desk and sat up straight.

"Look over my shoulder, please."

Chermerkov did.

"Now then, sir, I'm ready. If you could just take a pose, I'll count to ten."

LATER, WHILE JACK WORKED WITH HIS CHEMICALS IN HIS DIMINU-tive tent, Chermerkov ordered a fresh cup of tea. While he waited, he said, "Are you married, Mr. Sandt? Do you have a family?"

"I'm single, sir."

"The reason I ask is that you propose to travel in areas inhabited by Tatars, Cossacks, and other violent people. You put your life at risk. Under the circumstances, the crown can do nothing to guarantee your safety. You'll be on your own."

"I understand that there will be risks, sir. I'm prepared for that."

"Can you shoot?"

"Yes, sir, reasonably well. I learned that in California."

"No lady friend? No family or intended to worry about your safety?"

"No, sir. I somehow never came across a woman I liked well enough to marry. Or one that liked me."

Jack emerged from his tent, carefully holding the count's daguerreotype by the edges. "Here you go, sir."

Count Chermerkov looked pleased. "That's very good, Mr. Sandt. You do good work."

"Thank you, sir. You're a good subject. Handsome and virile, if you don't mind my saying."

Chermerkov liked being flattered. He read the letter from Greeley again. "There's also the question of the time involved. Travels this ambitious in scope will take months if not years to complete. We're talking vast distances here and hard travel. In the winter, you can find yourself in places so cold that mercury freezes. In the summer on the steppes, it gets hot enough to fry eggs on stones."

"I can take whatever time is required. A year, two years. It makes no difference. What matters is that I observe the full range of the Urals, Siberia, and the steppes. I want to record daguerreotype images of your successful ironworks and factories." Had Jack laid it on too thick? He felt a flutter of anxiety in his stomach.

Chermerkov furrowed his brows slightly. An untoward thought had crossed his mind as a dark cloud on a sunny day. "Have you any ambitions of being a writer? Perhaps keeping a journal or some such."

Jack said, "I have an interest in flowers. I collect and press flowers so I can paint them later on. I'd like to produce a portfolio of flowers I encounter along the way if that would be acceptable to the crown, sir. I would be pleased to share my collection with your botanists." He found it hard to assert an abiding interest in flowers without laughing out loud. His gambit was that a totally unexpected lie would be more believable than an obviously duplicitous assertion.

"A portfolio of flowers?" Count Chermerkov looked amused. "Very well, Mr. Sandt, I will give your request further consideration. Mind you, at this point I can give no guarantees. We'll see." He cleared his throat, signaling that the interview was over. "You will be hearing from us shortly."

SEVEN

In Pursuit of Light

 THE DYING THROES OF THE RUSSIAN WINTER STILL gripped the landscape. A thick, heavy fog obscured the road. Sonja Sankova and her father rode in silence. It began to rain. As it hit the snow, the rain froze into a thin sheet of ice. The horses' hooves made a rhythmic *crunch, crunch, crunch* on the icy crust. The bare trees were covered with ice, and in the distance, she could hear the pop and crack of limbs breaking under the weight.

Sonja continued her flight along the top of the bank of the river, cutting across the flat tableland to another bend in the river. Five or six versts later, as the sun came out, a mere sliver on the horizon, she pulled out of the track to avoid some tree stumps.

Suddenly the horses flailed at nothing, and the *vashoc* plunged over the edge of the bank that had been hidden by an overhang of snow. Down Sonja and Mikhail went at a horrific speed, crashing down the steep bank to the side of the river. Sonja slammed into the side of the *vashoc,* nearly dislocating her shoulder.

Wincing from the pain, she pawed her way out of the deep snow. Seeing that her father was under the *vashoc,* buried in snow, she pawed frantically with her mittened hands. "Papa, Papa, Papa!" she cried as she dug. At last, she scraped away some snow from his face, which was nearly purple from the cold. "Papa!"

"I'm here, Sonja. I had a little space to breathe. I'm okay." He smiled weakly. "I amend that. I'm still alive."

Sonja continued digging until she was able to pull him from under the sledge. When at last she got him free of the *vashoc*, she built a fire so he could thaw while she set about rescuing the horses, which were belly deep in snow. After that she had to retrieve and repair the sledge.

Sonja wasn't strong enough to pull the horses out. She had to dig them out with her hands as she had her father, and this she did. The horses, understanding that struggle was useless, remained surprisingly patient while she dug. After nearly an hour of digging, she freed the last horse. Although she was trembling from near exhaustion, there was no resting for Sonja, who still had work to do.

She hitched the horses to the rear of the sledge and pulled it backward out of the snow and ice. Although her fingers were so numb from the cold that they could hardly move, she fixed the broken sledge with rope.

Recovering from the crash had taken the better part of two hours. With the sun dangerously low to the west and a bone-chilling cold setting in, Sonja faced the task of finding a path to the top of the embankment. That and finding a station. If she didn't find a station, they would have to spend the frigid night in the *vashoc*, wrapped in blankets.

So exhausted she could hardly sit straight, she picked up the reins, the cold air cutting through her lungs with each breath. She sighed, popped the whip over the backs of the horses, and they were off again along the base of the bank. Twenty minutes later, she came upon a winding trail that led back to the plateau.

Sonja and her father were sheltered in their journey by members, friends, and sympathizers of a disorganized resistance to the Romanov crown—if "resistance" was an accurate word—who had arranged for a number of writers and poets to say their good-byes as she took Mikhail Sankov home to the Urals.

One of those Mikhail would not be seeing was Nikolay Vasilyevich Gogol, who had died on March 4. Mikhail had been an admirer of Gogol's novel *Dead Souls*, in which the souls of dead serfs were sold along with their master's land. Mikhail had always thought Gogol had resisted the Tsarist regime and patriarchal Russian way of life. But he fell under the spell of a mad priest, Father Konstantinovskii, who convinced him to burn his sequel to *Dead Souls*. Gogol fell ill. He refused to eat. Konstantinovskii poured spirits over his head and applied hot loaves to his body and leeches to his nose, after which the maddened Gogol died.

Mikhail heard this news as he and his daughter set off for the Urals. Leeches to his nose? With such medicines Sonja thought it no wonder Gogol was driven mad. Her father sank into an immediate gloom, wondering how it was that life had turned out so wrong for poor Gogol.

Another acquaintance he would not be seeing was Fyodor Dostoyevsky, who was in exile in Siberia. After an auspicious start with *Poor Folk* in 1846, Dostoyevsky had published four novels that were less well received, but Mikhail was convinced he had a promising future.

Sonja glanced back over her shoulder, half expecting to see the Wolfpack bearing down on her. Nothing. She turned around and rubbed her sore shoulder. She squinted her eyes against the frigid air that cut into her lungs with each breath.

Mikhail said, "I miss your mother. I miss the smell of her food cooking. Foolish not to appreciate all the sights and smells and sounds. They're so grand. Even this ice storm. The sound of the horses' hooves crunching on the ice. A pleasure to be here. Such a gift. You should remember that. Only when you are about to lose them do you fully understand the treasures of life."

"A gift, truly," she said.

"If you get me home, you should continue on to China. You have family there. You can start a new life. Enjoy every day. Write your poetry. Make your language take wing and fly so that your readers will know and see."

THE CROWN ISSUED JACK SANDT PAPERS BEARING THE STAMP OF His Celestial Majesty Tsar Nicholas I that compelled local and regional officials to give him such permissions and assistance as he might require in his travels. In addition, Count Chermerkov arranged for a driver and a guide from the St. Petersburg post office to accompany him as far as Oslanskoi station on the Tehoussowaia River in the Urals. Jack wondered, as he received this good news, if Chermerkov's portrait might not now be hanging in his office for his visitors to admire. Such a handsome, intelligent man was the count.

Thus prepared, Jack set off, a passenger in a horse-drawn *vashoc*, a long, boxlike contraption placed on a sledge. Jack's *yamstchick*, or driver, was Nico, a small, knobby man with a bony face and a hard, muscular body. Nico had a stolid, phlegmatic personality, saying little.

The traffic was such between St. Petersburg and Moscow that deep ruts called *oukhab* were cut in the road, causing the sledge to pitch into the holes with such ferocity as to rattle his teeth. The determined Nico attempted to keep the sledge atop the center ridge, but it was virtually impossible for the horses, dragging it at a good speed, to keep it from pitching into one *oukhab* or the other.

Bump, bump, bump! Whack, whack, whack! Jerk, jerk, jerk!

Out there, light waited.

Bump, bump, bump! Whack, whack, whack! Jerk, jerk, jerk!

EIGHT

Legacy of the Tao Te Ching

SONJA SANKOVA AND HER FATHER, WRAPPED IN A single wool blanket, sat before the warming fire into which the snow plummeted and melted as dreams into time. Her father sat, mute, in the warming glow of laudanum. As the days passed, Sonja felt herself becoming increasingly sentimental. Mikhail told her that memories, not rubles, were what made a man wealthy. At the end, no man of heart remembered owning a gilded carriage. For Mikhail, the small memories that made up his poetry—the thin blue sky on a cold morning, the feeling of setting out across river ice on skates, the rich, earthy taste of a baked potato—those were all little jewels in the rich treasure of life.

Mikhail told his daughter that he was a wealthy man because he had had the good fortune to meet and marry her mother—when, as everybody knew, ten thousand and more things could have gone wrong. He said he might well have met a spiteful, envious, ambitious, or embittered woman, ruled by disappointment and incapable of appreciating the small joys offered up each day. He had not. He had genuinely loved his Chinese bride; for that he would die enriched with wonderful memories.

Sonja was aware of the ambiguous feelings many Russians held for her father. It was difficult for the aristocracy to believe that such a talented writer as Mikhail had begun life as a serf, and they comforted themselves by the fact that he was an orphan. After all, was it not possible that a baby born of good Russian stock had, by some awful misfortune, ended up as a serf in the Urals?

Sonja's talent was also troublesome. Never mind that the Chinese had first invented gunpowder and movable type. What had they done with either invention? Where were the Chinese writers and poets? There were none—at least none the Russian intelligentsia had acknowledged. Sonja had inherited her talent from her father, simple as that.

The ambiguity of poetry was at the heart of its subversive qualities. This vexed and perplexed the Tsar and his many toadies, who preferred clear-cut blacks and whites. It was also one of the reasons poetry was popular among dissident intellectuals. Who was to accurately deduce the true meaning of a well-crafted poem? The charming and lyrical could easily mask the lethally rebellious.

Mimi Sankov had told her daughter stories about growing up in Hong Kong, and she had taught her the wisdom of Lao Tzu to be found in the *Tao Te Ching, The Book of Changes*. Educated loyalists knew the Greek and Roman and European myths, but the Tao? To Romanov loyalists, the Tao at the heart of her poetry was mysterious and foreign, and therefore threatening.

Mimi had said Sonja's father intuitively understood Lao Tzu's definition of a wise man:

The sage holds in his embrace the one thing of humility and manifests it to all the world. He is free from self-display, therefore he shines. He does not assert his qualities, therefore he is distinguished. He does not boast, therefore his merit is acknowledged. He is not self-complacent, therefore he acquires superiority. It is because he is free from striving that nobody is able to strive with him.

Sonja later came to understand that the elegance of the unostentatious man whom Lao Tzu called the "sage" was best rendered as the English word "class." The man without class lived by the delusion that by buying what he assumed were the accoutrements of class, he could somehow separate himself from the commonplace. Alas, a man who thought class was for sale would never have it. Worse, he would most often never understand why.

Colonel Peter Koslov was yang gotten out of control. Sonja's father had a measure of yin, which partly accounted for his poetic imagination. She had a measure of yang, which is why she had been so bold as to strike the odious Koslov at the Christmas party. Perhaps it was because Koslov had feared the yang in her that he had pushed the confrontation. But she had not backed down, and now there were consequences.

She was convinced that the desire for freedom and a republican government was yin, matched against the yang, twisted and grotesque in its proportions, of the Romanov dynasty.

Sonja emerged from her reverie. Her father had been yanked about all day by the icy thumps and bumps. His eyes were closed. He was either asleep or dead. She was afraid to wake him for fear it was the latter. If he died before they reached the Urals, she would straighten him out and deliver his frozen body to Bagodat. The yang of his body would join the yin of the earth.

NINE

Gentleman in a Scarlet Tunic

SHAKEN BUT STILL DETERMINED TO PUSH FORWARD, and armed with his letter from the crown, Jack Sandt arrived in Moscow in a driving snowstorm to obtain the remaining, minor provisions for his trip into the vast interior. He bought several flints capable of starting fires in the coldest weather; Russian boots, coats, wool shirts, and other cold-weather gear; maps; three blankets and a tarpaulin; and salt, salted meat, tea, a metal pot and plate, a fork, and a spoon. Jack knew it would be foolhardy to be separated from his rubles; for his money he bought a leather bag that he could sling over his shoulder.

Jack then toured the city, starting with the expanse of the great square in front of the Kremlin, where the domes of St. Basil overlooked the Moscow River. On the second day after his arrival, the city began a festival celebrating the seven hundredth anniversary of the founding of the city. On the opening day of the festival, Jack's local contact, Count Kafelnikov, invited him to witness a series of tableaux vivants. His Imperial Majesty would be there, Jack was told. It was a wonderful opportunity for an American visitor. Thinking they were making rather much of his connection to an American newspaper, he nevertheless said yes. Perhaps they just wanted to see a total fool close up.

Jack was glad he took advantage of the opportunity. This was his introduction to a world that had been beyond his imagination. He still regarded himself as a wide-eyed American bumpkin, but he did his best to appear worldly as he was taken to a large hall inside the Kremlin walls where an elaborate feast was given before his Imperial Majesty and most of his court. The idea of the tableaux vivants, something entirely new to him, was to depict life as it had been lived seven centuries earlier—including antique furniture, armor, and plate. The models, clothed in costumes of that bygone era, posed in dramatic little scenes.

Jack knew there were wealthy people in the United States, but for the most part they kept their advantages well hidden—keeping to themselves in secluded estates for fear of stirring the resentment of the masses whose labor kept them in luxury. There was obviously no such restraint in Russia. In Russia, whatever the crown desired, the crown received.

After the company tired of wandering around looking at the tableaux vivants, they all settled into their seats to enjoy a program of symbolic sketches elaborating on the theme of history and the founding of Moscow. So attuned was the assembled company to the power of the Tsar that all eyes secretly watched His Imperial Majesty, looking for clues as to how they should receive the entertainment. One of the members of the Tsar's immediate party included an officer in a gray uniform with a scarlet tunic and trim. It was a startling get-up, gaudy in the extreme. Jack wondered who on earth he could be.

In due course, four beautiful girls made their appearance representing the four elements, earth, fire, water, and air. Suddenly, people in a pit just in front of the girls onstage began removing the dresses from the young ladies above them.

This was wonderful! The Tsar seemed amused, so they all applauded, including the officer in the wild outfit.

One comely young lady, kneeling on one knee on a rock, was jerked from her place and turned feet upward on the floor.

They all instinctively laughed. His Imperial Majesty, obviously eager to see the rest of her anatomy, hushed the laugher.

The lady was separated from the remainder of her costume and, blushing, again took her place on the rock.

At the intermission Jack learned that the unusual officer was Colonel

Peter Koslov, commander of the Wolfpack. Jack had no idea what the Wolfpack might be. He was hesitant to press the question because the mere mention of the officer appeared to make his informant nervous. The gray uniform was fitting enough for the commander of the Wolfpack. But the scarlet tunic was startling. Out in the American West it was well known that the deadliest snakes were usually the most brilliantly colored, as though to warn their victims of the danger. It was as though nature responded to some curious logic. The poison wasn't just to kill prey. Poison kept predators at a distance. What was the point of being poisonous if predators didn't know it? Some snakes had rattles at the ends of their tail. Jack remembered one particular lizard, the Gila monster, that was especially gaudy.

As Jack saw it, the colonel's unstated message was as clear as a colorful reptile: *See my scarlet tunic. I am lethally poisonous. Avoid me.*

TEN

Supper with
Ivan Sergeyevich Turgenev

JACK AND HIS RUSSIAN COMPANION LEFT MOSCOW AT six o'clock in the morning and an hour later came upon the cathedral with five domes in a village with fourteen churches and several other public buildings. This was Vladimir, picturesque in the extreme with the towers and domes of the Eastern Orthodox church. Jack's Fahrenheit thermometer reading was twelve degrees above zero, so this was not the time for daguerreotypes. On they galloped through snow and wind, reaching Nijni Novgorod at nine o'clock the following morning. Jack was determined to deliver his credentials to the governor, Prince Onkifovich, said to be a distant cousin of the Tsar, and to take a stroll through the ancient city remembered by Russians as the place where Ivan the Terrible committed some of his most horrific cruelties.

They stopped at a sort of inn on the banks of the Volga in the lower town. The proprietor led Jack up a narrow, crumbling flight of stairs and showed him a flat of filthy pens or private boxes that had been partitioned from larger rooms with inch-and-a-half boards. There were huge cracks between the boards. There was neither bed, mattress, pillows, nor sheets. A guest simply curled up on the boarded bottom and covered himself with whatever he had brought with him. Jack secured one space for himself and another for Nico.

Since Jack was free until late in the afternoon, he strolled through the upper town, his breath coming in great frosty bursts, visiting some of the many churches, several being very ancient.

He returned to his lodgings late in the afternoon, changed clothes, and packed daguerreotype essentials into two carpetbags.

Nico drove Jack through a driving, blinding snow to the governor's residence, a palatial mansion in the upper part of town. Nico was taken to the servants' quarters, and Jack was ushered into the mansion, where Prince Denis Onkifovich had gathered a party of nine to greet him, including a writer, Ivan Sergeyevich Turgenev, who was about Jack's age. A slender, elegant man, Turgenev was soft-spoken and obviously of a good family. His friend Mikhail Sankov, a poet born in the Urals who was dying of an apparent growth in his lungs, had also been invited but was late. He had either died or was delayed by the storm that had settled in over the area.

Prince Onkifovich was a courtly gentleman of about sixty, a slender, balding man with a handsome, neatly trimmed beard and mustache and wearing spectacles. The princess Onkifovich, about twenty years his junior, was a matronly lady with a pleasant face, her body thickened from the trials of having borne five children. The three couples who rounded out the party were local merchants and their wives.

Prince Onkifovich and Turgenev carried most of the conversation. Two of the couples, obviously awed by Turgenev's literary reputation and curious to learn about Jack, listened intently to the conversation, occasionally nodding or putting in a *"Da"* to express their agreement.

Although reserved and self-effacing, Turgenev had much natural charm and charisma. As they sipped tumblers of cold vodka, Jack said quietly, "Do you mind if I try my hand at capturing you on a daguerreotype image, Mr. Turgenev?" Quickly, he added, "As a gift for our host."

Turgenev, upon hearing the request, was flattered. "Yes, certainly. I'd be pleased to sit for you, sir."

A manservant arrived to announce that dinner was ready; they agreed that after they had eaten, Jack would make Turgenev's portrait. In the meantime, if they were fortunate, the poet and Pushkin scholar Sankov and his daughter would arrive.

They settled around a handsome cherrywood table for a meal of roast venison studded with cloves of garlic, roast potatoes, a cabbage salad, and French red wine. The prince and Turgenev were curious as to his background, and with the prince's wife translating whenever Jack got into trouble, he told the Russians that his parents had emigrated to America from Holland, and that he had left home at an early age, eventually winding up at the gold rush in California. "And you, sir?" Jack said. He knew Turgenev had to be from a moneyed, perhaps even titled, family.

Turgenev thought a moment. He took a bite of venison, then said in Russian that he was born in Orel, about two hundred miles south of Moscow, and grew up on his mother's estate of Spasskoye. He said, "I'm curious. What can you tell me of the issue of slavery in the United States?"

Jack said, "I don't like it. It is a great evil tearing the country apart. We're headed for deep trouble over the issue."

"Hmm," Turgenev said, looking thoughtful.

Onkifovich said, "It was at Spasskoye that Ivan Sergeyevich learned firsthand the system of brutalities meted out to the serfs."

Looking momentarily alarmed, Turgenev glanced at the couple in attendance.

Onkifovich raised his hand as if to reassure him. "It is okay, Ivan Sergeyevich. We're among friends here."

The subject of the serfs was obviously a touchy if not dangerous subject in polite company, and they avoided it for the remainder of the meal. As they adjourned to the drawing room, where the household help had assembled a variety of candles and lamps, Turgenev said, "Why do you want to go to Siberia, Mr. Sandt? To take daguerreotype images. Can that be true?"

"I want to go to Asia and make a record of the people there and the way they live. I want to buy a Chinese junk and live on it. I don't need earth under my bed at night."

The princess said, "And have you been told the prospects of what lies ahead?"

"Yes, I have," Jack said. "A difficult journey. Inadvisable, I'm told." He paused. He shook his head and gave them a self-deprecating grin.

Onkifovich said, "You're quite mad. No offense."

They all laughed. "So I've been told many times," Jack said. "But then I'm an American. Perhaps we're all a little touched in the head."

As he polished his plate, studying Turgenev, he said, "You will pardon an ignorant American, but tell me about your writing, sir."

Onkifovich said, "Ivan Sergeyevich first drew the attention of the critics in St. Petersburg and Moscow for his narrative poem 'Parasha,' but lately he has been writing vignettes or sketches of country life, especially the relationship of the serfs and their owners. His narrator, an intelligent, sensitive gentleman, travels about hunting, which is his passion, same as Ivan Sergeyevich. He stays in the background and observes, letting the reader deduce what he will from the hunter's travels and encounters. They are brief and understated episodes, but compelling and memorable. They go to the heart of what owning human beings does to people."

Jack finished the buffing. "And these have been published where?" he asked.

The princess said, "In various magazines. Ivan Sergeyevich wrote most of them between 1847 and 1851 when he was living in Europe and the French countryside. They are called sketches from a hunter's notebook, or a hunter's album. They're translated several ways in English."

Onkifovich said, "I have extra copies that I will give for you to read on your travels."

"If they're truly extra, I would be honored," Jack said. "I will record one image of Mr. Turgenev and one of you and your wife."

As Jack Sandt emerged from the darkness of his developing tent, the prince and his wife, eager to see the result, looked over Jack's shoulder at the daguerreotypes, one of Ivan Turgenev, one of themselves.

Turgenev was more than pleased. "Very good work, Mr. Sandt. A miracle Monsieur Louis Daguerre has delivered to us all."

"Very nice," said the prince.

"You should consider them payment for the hunter's sketches," Jack said.

The prince's wife said, "A fair exchange."

Onkifovich held up the daguerreotype of Turgenev, admiring it. "It's too bad that Mikhail Sankov couldn't make it. His daughter Sonja is accompanying him. A man of action as well as an artist, you would have appreciated meeting her, I'm sure. A match for a woman of her spirit."

The entire table, watching Jack, grinned broadly.

"Tell me about Sonja Sankova."

The princess told him about the buying and educating of the serf Mikhail Sankov by the Belgian viscount, of his marriage to the daughter of a Chinese diplomat, and of their precocious daughter Sonja, who knocked Koslov to his knees at the Tsar's Christmas party.

Jack's mouth dropped. "Cut the ears off ninety serfs! My God!"

His hosts and their guests watched him, saying nothing.

"And Miss Sankova dropped him with a hard right hand. I like that."

ELEVEN

Rewriting the Script for Women

SONJA SANKOVA DROVE THE SLEIGH THROUGH A HARD, cold, gusting wind that pushed the snow out of the blackness in great billowing, swirling rolls. Sonja knew her horses were about to collapse. She let them take their time. The poor beasts rushed forward knowing hay and rest must surely be near. The prince and princess Onkifovich would see to the animals. She hoped she would make it to the prince's house in time to see Ivan Sergeyevich.

Tonight Mikhail Sankov would visit Ivan Turgenev, who was very much alive, not insane, and not in exile. Although he kept his narrators at a remove from their observations, he was clearly a soulful writer, and his observations of the life lived by serfs were impeccable. He father admired him greatly for his intelligence and cool passion.

Sonja regarded individual Russians as puppets in a barbarously scripted, endlessly repeated pageant that was predictable in all its characters and in all the acts of their lives from youth through old age. There were scripts for serfs. Scripts for peasants. Scripts for landowners. Scripts for nobility. Scripts for the royal family. Scripts for men. Scripts for women. Deviation from the essentials of the accepted script or an attempt to play an unassigned role was deemed dangerous by the crown and so forbidden. Russians were famous for retreating into nonthreatening interior worlds of theoretical mathematics and chess.

As each word changed the dynamics of a poem, Sonja thought, each decision altered the script of one's life. What better Russian woman to rewrite her personal script than a poet who understood the power of symbol and metaphor? In publicly stepping out of her assigned role, Sonja had announced that it was possible to rewrite the script. She would show that it could be done.

For Sonja and her father, each sunrise was a triumph. But their survival carried a larger meaning, she knew. It was important to the morale of those who sheltered them and who had a vision of a more civilized Russia that Sonja live, with her ears intact, to tell the tale of her fateful encounter with Colonel Peter Koslov. She had challenged this symbol of the barbarity of the crown and she would survive. It could be done.

Sonja glanced at the pocket watch that was her father's and would be hers upon his death. The storm and their exhausted horses were causing her to run late. Her father sat numbly in his zone of laudanum. She wanted for him to be able to say a proper good-bye to Ivan Sergeyevich.

TWELVE

The Lesson of Oblinsk

JACK SANDT WAS FLATTERED BY THE SUGGESTION THAT he would enjoy meeting Sonja Sankova. He told his hosts that while he was visiting Karl Marx in his London flat, he had seen a drawing of Sonja in a back issue of the *Neue Rheinische Zeitung* and had read her poem "Beautiful Geese."

Turgenev said, "A grand poem."

Jack said. "A line drawing is not as revealing as a daguerreotype, but she clearly has extraordinary eyes."

Onkifovich grinned. "Only her eyes!" To which the entire table joined him in laughter.

Jack was embarrassed in spite of himself. "It was a drawing of her face."

Onkifovich laughed. "I was just teasing. I have a copy of the magazine."

Turgenev said, "Her mother is Chinese. She's a young woman of remarkable courage, what you would call spirited. Independent."

"Charming, is she?" Jack asked.

Looking amused, Onkifovich interrupted. "Charming? That hardly covers it, if I were a man your age." He sighed.

Pretending to be offended, his wife said quickly, "My husband has good taste in women."

To which they all laughed.

Turgenev said. "Cheer up, Mr. Sandt, perhaps you will come across Sonja and Mikhail later in your travels."

"I would like to know about her," Jack said. "Also more about this Colonel Koslov."

Onkifovich said, "Sonja is a slender, delicate young woman. Dark, curly hair, unaccountably fair skin. The best of both races, it seems. She was raised almost entirely by her father, but has Chinese relatives of substance throughout Canton Province and Hong Kong. In Singapore too, if the stories are right."

The princess said, "When Ivan Sergeyevich said she is spirited, he is understating the facts. It is dangerous for us even to have her at our house. As for Koslov, tell me, Mr. Sandt, what do you know about the Tsar's gendarmes?"

Jack shrugged. "I've heard of their existence, but not much more than that."

Onkifovich said, "His Imperial Majesty has set up a special Corps of Gendarmes which functions as political police. They suppress revolts of serfs and see to the expulsion of Jews. The country is divided into gendarme districts, each commanded by a general. There are special gendarme detachments at strategic towns, fortresses, and ports. There are two such detachments near St. Petersburg, one at Kronstadt on the Baltic Sea, and another at Tsarskoye Selo just south of the city."

The princess said, "Colonel Peter Koslov, a personal favorite of the Tsar and highly trusted, is officially assigned to Tsarskoye Selo. In fact he roams all of Russia as the commander of the Wolfpack, a special unit assigned to the dirtiest of chores and supervising the suppression of uprisings wherever they occur. It's carried on the books as Detachment One, but nobody calls it that. It's the Wolfpack. Koslov is notorious, a genuinely evil man. The Wolfpack has murdered thousands of Russian citizens from the Baltic Sea to the Sea of Japan. Last summer the Tsar called upon Koslov to put down an uprising of serfs at Oblinsk. He decided to teach them a lesson."

Onkifovich interrupted, looking grave. "I told you about Koslov's removing the ears from live serfs. The details are loathesome."

"It's sickening to imagine," Jack said.

The princess chewed momentarily on her lower lip before saying, "Those who chose not to live without ears took their own lives. Those with the courage to live did so with carved wooden ears that they strapped to their heads with a kind of leather harness."

Jack paled.

She said, "Colonel Koslov dried the ears and strung them into a kind of necklace that he carries with him. This is just one barbarity. He is known to have blinded serfs, and cut off their hands, and had them skinned alive, depending on their transgressions. All of Russia knows him as Colonel Cut."

Jack inadvertently swallowed.

"Since the Christmas party Sonja and her father have been hiding on a farm in the country. Mikhail is dying. He was born in the Urals and is known as a poet of the Urals. He wants to be buried there. Sonja is determined not to flee the country until she has granted him his wish."

"And what about Koslov?"

"Koslov has been telling his friends that since Sonja finds the taking of a serf's ears so deplorable, that will be her punishment for slapping him in front of the Tsar. She thinks she is beautiful. Let her contemplate the mirror without ears. Instead of writing the poem honoring the Tsar, she wrote a chapbook of poetry, *In Russia,* that contains a poem about the incident, ridiculing Koslov."

Jack said, "I'm sorry I've missed her."

The princess said, "Sonja and her father are fugitives traveling from village to village. She is small, not five feet tall. We're told she has cut her hair short and is traveling as a boy. All Russians who know about the incident at the Christmas party are wondering if they will make it to the Urals before Koslov overtakes them. Where Sonja is, Koslov won't be far behind."

"The darkness chasing the light."

"That is it exactly. For your own safety, it is best to stay well clear of Colonel Cut, Mr. Sandt." The princess obviously felt great sympathy for the father and daughter.

Onkifovich said, "Nobody is betting on their success."

The princess said, "Never mind that my husband is a cousin of the Tsar, we put ourselves at risk even inviting Mikhail and Sonja to supper tonight. But they were in the area, and we couldn't resist introducing her to you. The outside world needs to know what is happening to us."

"I would have taken her image so people could see exactly what she looks like," Jack said.

Onkifovich grimaced. "All Russians with heart respect Mikhail and Sonja. On hearing the story of de Borchgrave's freeing of the young serf, Ivan Sergeyevich used de Borchgrave as the model for the narrator of his hunter's sketches. Ivan Sergeyevich later bought a boy's freedom himself."

Jack looked at Turgenev. "You did?"

Turgenev nodded.

Jack bowed, showing his respect for what Turgenev had done. He had heard of Americans doing the same thing for blacks.

Later, as Jack rose to leave, Turgenev shook his hand gravely, looking him straight in the eyes. "You might try arranging your journal in a series of linked vignettes. See what happens."

"Well, yes, sir, I'll take your advice," Jack said.

"I'm not suggesting that you should somehow attempt to emulate my sketches, but they might be useful as a matter of form. You have to follow your own vision. You have a talent, Mr. Sandt. A shame to waste it entirely on illustrations." He paused. "Think of an emotion."

Jack blinked. "Love."

"Yes, love. Or hate. Pride. Envy. Lust. Pain. Tell us about it."

Jack felt intuitively that Ivan Sergeyevich Turgenev was destined for literary greatness, and felt humbled by the attention.

At the door Prince Onkifovich pressed the copies of the magazines containing the hunter's sketches into his hand. "I promised you these. Reading for your travels, Mr. Sandt."

Jack cleared his throat. "Say, you wouldn't happen to have an extra copy of *In Russia,* would you?"

The princess looked concerned. "We do. And you can have it, Mr. Sandt, but you must never let it be found on your person."

THIRTEEN

A Brief and Fleeting Omen

WITH A COPY OF SONJA SANKOVA'S CHAPBOOK OF
poems and the magazines containing Turgenev's hunter's
sketches in hand, Jack Sandt finished his good-byes. Light-
headed from the vodka, he set off for his filthy lodgings in
a howling wind, with the snow swirling and billowing down the street.

Later, as Nico put the horse and sleigh away, Jack stood at the edge of
the street, savoring a moment alone in the storm. The bone-chilling
cold was hard enough on him, but he wondered about Sonja Sankova,
out there somewhere taking her father home to be buried. He knew that
his friend Karl Marx would appreciate this story of courage in spite of
barbarity. He thought of the many Russians out there secretly helping
the fugitives as a way to nurse the flame of hope. Sonja Sankova had lit
a spark with one well-struck, well-deserved blow. Those helping her
could not in good conscience let the spark be so callously snuffed.

Koslov had removed the ears from ninety human beings for the offense of demanding simple dignity. Now he proposed to do the same to
Miss Sankova. Did Jack have a dog in this fight. Yes, he did.

From out of the storm a single sleigh approached, pulled by a brace
of exhausted horses. A boy, well bundled against the cold with a scarf
around his mouth and nose, popped a whip over the backs of the animals. At his side a hollow-eyed older man with a long, gaunt face was
bundled in a blanket.

As the sleigh drew near, Jack saw that the boy had almond-shaped brown eyes and pale copper-colored skin.

Sonja Sankova saw a man get out of a sleigh and stand alone watching as the driver unhitched the horses and led them away. The man stood in the snow watching her draw near. She could make out the features of a tall, good-looking man, about thirty years old.

Sonja's father broke into a fit of coughing, which he suppressed with the back of his arm. She gripped him tightly in her left arm without taking her free hand off the reins or her eyes off the stranger.

As her sleigh passed the man, she watched him. He had blue eyes.

In Russian with an English accent, he called, "You need to rest your horses."

Should she look back, making clear her interest and curiosity? She saw no reason why not. He likely thought she was a boy. Where was the harm?

She turned.

Jack knew faces. The boy's eyes were not male at all. They were female. He sprinted up the edge of the street, then slipped on the ice. He hit the ground hard, but scrambled awkwardly to his feet. "Miss Sankova! Sonja!" he called. "Wait, wait! Please!"

He continued running after her, doing his best not to slip again, and feeling vaguely foolish. What would he do if he caught up with her?

She heard her name called, and pulled back on the reins.

She turned. The man was running toward her.

"Miss Sankova, wait!" he called.

He knew her name. He recognized her. Alarmed, she popped her whip over the backs of the exhausted horses.

"Wait for him," her father said.

"He called my name. What if he's one of them?"

Mikhail said, "He's American. I heard plenty at the American embassy. I know the accent."

Jack yelled, louder. "I am Jack Sandt. Ask Prince Onkifovich."

He knew the prince? She wanted to wait for him.

He slipped again and landed hard.

Should she wait or shouldn't she? She wanted to. She also knew it was foolhardy to trust instinct when their lives were at stake. Finally, she said, "We can't take a chance." She snapped her whip over the backs of the horses.

As she pulled away, she looked back. Obviously exhausted, he stood watching her through the snow, his body slumped in disappointment. Sonja liked his face very much. She thought momentarily of stopping to let him catch up, but decided she couldn't risk it. Her father came first. She had promised to see him to the Urals before he died. She was going to honor her word. Later maybe she would find someone with whom to complete her personal circle.

To herself, she murmured softly, " 'I still remember that amazing moment.' "

Her father perked up. "What was that?"

"Nothing, Papa."

"I heard you, my little darling. Pushkin. Finish it for your romantic old father. A gift in a cold winter storm."

Her face flushed.

"No need to be embarrassed. It's good for the soul. Please."

> *. . . You have appeared before my sight*
> *As though a brief and fleeting omen,*
> *Pure phantom in enchanting light.*

Mikhail thought a moment, then added, "A poem from him to her or from her to him. It works both ways. I agree."

FOURTEEN

To Ride Sweet Winds

 CURSING HIMSELF FOR HAVING LEFT THE PARTY TOO soon, Jack Sandt ran down Nico in the barn that served that block of Nijni Novgorod. Nico had unhitched the sledge and was giving the horses a well-deserved ration of hay. "Hitch them back up," Jack yelled.

Nico looked bewildered. "Again, sir?"

"Quickly, quickly," Jack said. "Here, I'll help." He grabbed the harness off its peg on the wall. "Where I grew up everybody learns how to harness a horse."

Nico's mouth dropped. He'd never had an employer help before.

Then Jack remembered something. "Be right back, Nico. Finish it off and get it on the street."

By the time Jack got back downstairs, Nico had the horses hitched and the sledge waiting in the storm. Jack leaped into the back, pulled the blanket around him, and hunkered down as Nico urged the horses onward through the blowing snow.

As they came around the final corner, Jack spotted a man in a gray uniform with a scarlet tunic tending to a group of horses outside Prince Onkifovich's mansion about a hundred yards down the street.

"Sir, gendarmes!" Nico said. He looked back at Jack with uncertain eyes. The very sight of the Tsar's gendarmes had frightened him.

"Pull to, Nico. Don't let them see us."

He pulled the sledge into some shadows. "Wolfpack, sir. They have special uniforms. They are to be avoided. We should be very careful."

They waited in the biting wind.

Suddenly the front door of the prince's house burst open, and the gendarmes came spilling out.

Finally, a tall, angry-looking officer emerged with Prince Onkifovich at his side. Jack could make out their faces by the light of a kerosene lantern being held by one of the officer's subordinates.

The officer was agitated and animated. He glared at Onkifovich. He began shouting. Snow had a way of muffling sound, so it was hard for Jack to make out what he was saying.

Displaying remarkable patience and discipline, Onkifovich said nothing.

The officer shouted louder and louder still, until Jack heard him clearly. "You're lying!" he shouted. "Lying, lying, lying! You're all lying to protect her!"

Onkifovich turned up the palms of his hands, the gesture saying he couldn't help the officer.

"The little bitch!" the officer screamed.

Jack thought for a moment the officer was going to draw his pistol and shoot the prince, but he didn't. He began issuing orders to his men. He mounted his horse, and the Wolfpack rode off through the storm, leaving a half dozen of its members behind, apparently to guard the entrance. Why had they done that? Jack wondered.

When the Wolfpack had disappeared into the swirling snow, Jack told Nico to stay put, then got out and retreated down the street. When he was out of sight of the gendarmes, he circled behind Prince Onkifovich's mansion, scaled a wall, and knocked on a side on a side door.

A servant opened it, recognized him, and looked surprised. "Mr. Sandt!"

"I would like to talk to the prince, please. It's urgent."

He bade Jack to stay put. He stepped inside and returned a few minutes later with Prince Onkifovich, who was looking pale, obviously still shaking from his experience.

Jack said, "I saw a sledge with what I thought was Sonja and Mikhail Sankov passing by my lodgings."

Onkifovich looked surprised. "You did?"

"I was sure of it. Miss Sankova is trying to pass herself off as a boy. Didn't they make it here?"

The prince sighed deeply, looking relieved. "A close call. They likely saw the horses of the gendarmes and continued on their way."

"I saw the officer shouting at you in the doorway."

"That was Colonel Koslov. If I weren't related to the Tsar, my wife and I would be dead by now."

Jack said, "If that was them, Sonja was driving. She's small and slender, very delicate, with almond-shaped eyes and short dark brown hair. A beauty. The man had a terrible, racking cough."

"That could well have been them."

"Her horses looked exhausted. Do you think she and her father can outrun Koslov in this weather with horses that can barely stand?"

Onkifovich looked down the street. "It's hard to say, Mr. Sandt. Sonja is a clever and determined young woman. It's snowing hard enough to cover up the tracks of her sledge. Sonja has many friends who would be willing to hide her and her father."

"She has a chance, then," Jack said.

Onkifovich grimaced. "A chance, but only that I'm afraid. She's smart enough to know that the Wolfpack will run her down if she tries to escape on any of the major roads out of town."

"Tell me, do you know the name of someone who might hide her for the night?"

Onkifovich thought about that a moment, then said evenly, "I like you, Mr. Sandt. Not for a minute do I think you would willingly betray Sonja or her father. I don't intend this to be disrespectful, but I have to think of Sonja and Mikhail. You're a stranger here. One mistake or innocent inquiry, however well intentioned, could get them killed. I wish you all the luck in the world, but I'm afraid it would be irresponsible of me to tell you more. I do hope you understand."

What the prince said made sense. "Yes, I do. I would again like to thank you for a generous hospitality." Then Jack had another idea. "You say Sonja is taking her father back to be buried in the Urals. Where in the Urals?"

"The town he uses in his poetry is fictional, but everybody knows he grew up in Nijni Tagil on land now belonging to the Demidoff family."

"I see." Jack unfolded a blank piece of paper with a *New York Tribune* letterhead at the top. "Do you have a pen, sir?"

Glancing about and seeing no scarlet uniforms, Onkifovich gestured for Jack to step inside. After some hurried instructions to a household servant, a pen was produced.

Jack dipped the pen into the ink and studied the paper; then, taking care that the scrawl of his bad handwriting was legible, he wrote a note to the beauty he had seen in the swirling snow.

Dear Miss Sonja Sankova,

I am the man you saw in the snowstorm in Nijni Novgorod. My name is Jack Sandt. I am an American. I take daguerreotype images. I am traveling across Russia to China. I have heard your story. Your bold stroke inspires all thoughtful Russians.

When I was visiting Karl Marx in London, I saw a drawing of your face in a back issue of the Neue Rheinische Zeitung, which is how I recognized you on the street. Forgive me for being so forward, but let me say it openly and truthfully, you have the most extraordinary eyes I have ever seen or will likely ever see. Knowing of your courage, I want to record your image so that more of your fellow Russians might see what you look like, the better to hold the example of your resistance to their collective bosom.

As you travel to the Urals to grant your father's wish, please remember that I am behind you doing my best to catch up. I swear on my mother's eyes that I will not let Colonel Koslov complete his barbarous vow.

Your mother was Chinese. Perhaps you know about these vessels.
In China, I will buy one and ride sweet winds. If I am fortunate, one
day you will ride with me as my guest.

Your sincere admirer, Jack Sandt

Beneath this Jack made a crude drawing of a Chinese junk with lateen sails. He gave the note to Prince Onkifovich. "You may read it if you
please, sir."

Onkifovich read the note, and looked at Jack, suppressing a smile.
"Well, very bold and passionate, Mr. Sandt! But as I understand it, these
are American traits."

Jack couldn't help but be a little embarrassed. "I suppose I did overdo
it just a bit."

"Please, no need to apologize. We're all of us in love with Sonja just
a little. If I were your age and unattached, I hope I would have the
courage to make precisely the same vow. The idea of Koslov cutting off
her ears makes us all want to vomit. Make no mistake, if he finds her,
he'll have her ears."

"I'll do my best to prevent that. I give you my word."

The princess appeared behind Onkifovich, looking worried. "The
chapbook of Sonja's poems that I gave you was our last copy. Good
thing they didn't find it in our house, or we would be dead by now,
never mind my husband's relationship to the Tsar."

Onkifovich put his arm around Jack's shoulder and squeezed.
"Thank you for your concern, Mr. Sandt. But we mustn't take a chance
on an unexpected return by Koslov." With that, Onkifovich embraced
the American, then opened the door for him. "Godspeed, Mr. Sandt.
We're all with you."

Jack returned to the sledge, and Nico drove him back to his lodgings.
By the flickering light of a candle Jack studied the maps that Count
Chermerkov had given him. The crown wanted to make sure the tax
collectors missed no one, so every outpost was marked, and of course
there were the crown's many mines and *zavods* (ironworks). Separately
Jack had a list of the directors of the mines and *zavods* so that he might

arrange for interviews and tours. After a bit of searching he found it, with lettering so tiny as to be nearly unreadable: Nijni Tagil.

That was where Sonja would be hiding, with Koslov hard on their tail. Jack resolved to join in the chase. If she was out there and still alive, Jack would find her. He didn't mind a little hard traveling. He would continue day and night if necessary. He opened Sonja's chapbook and read the poem.

THE COLONEL AT THE CHRISTMAS PARTY
The colonel cut a grand figure
posing at the punch bowl.
So many medals on his chest,
bronze and gold and silver!
One wondered what on earth they honored.
What great battle?
What stirring action oft told
in grand house and peasant hut
to large-eyed, believing children,
eager for tales of swords and cannons
and dying heroes,
of blood flowing in crimson streams
in defense of Father Russia?
And the ribbons!
yellow and blue and every shade of red,
clearly, the Christmas tree was second best.
But wait!
The colonel, laughing, tells the amusing story
of the day he ordered the ears cut from the ninety serfs
at Oblinsk, surely a lesson well remembered.
He likes the punch. Savors it. He takes another sip.

Jack closed the chapbook. He curled up in the fetal position on the icy floor of his box and pulled his heavy fur coat over him. In his mind's eye, he saw her glance back at him. He could not sleep.

 The Ascent of the Urals

 AFTER NOVGOROD, THE ABRUPT SOUTH BANK OF THE Volga in places rose 150 to 200 feet above the water. Sonja Sankova, determined to make as much distance as possible, passed station after station. Still she pressed on, getting colder by the minute. At two o'clock, stiffened by the cold, she stopped at a station; she was told that the ice was unsafe for the next fifteen versts, and she should leave the river.

After Sonja and her father had warmed themselves over a fire, they traveled on. In less than hour she was forced to drive obliquely up the steep bank. Thirty or forty feet below the summit, the horses stalled, unable to pull the load to the top. She got out and pushed and pulled for all her worth, but still the load was too heavy. Night was coming and her only hope seemed to be to send to the next station, ten versts away, for more horses. She climbed to the top of the bank and discovered a caravan of sledges at a distance, coming toward them. The sledges arrived at dusk and the drivers unyoked three of their horses to drag her sledge to the top of the bank.

With that she was away again, pushing her horses hard against the dying light of the sun. Determined, Sonja peered out from the muffler wrapped around her face. She knew that Mikhail, warmed by the laudanum that eased his pain, passed the time by retreating into the past, likely thinking of her mother.

In talking of his happenstance meeting with her mother, Mikhail had told his daughter many times that human bonding was a mysterious, unpredictable process that existed outside conventional lists of wisdom, rules, and wishes so fervently propounded by scholars, priests, busybodies, self-appointed experts, and the envious. She should never be surprised at the conditions that bring men and women come together. For Mikhail, the cup of life was always half full. Even while dying a slow, painful death he remained an optimist.

Before their friends had smuggled Sonja and her father out of Nijni Novgorod, Prince Onkifovich had had a servant deliver her a note from an American dag man, Jack Sandt. She remembered his face and his eyes. She had glanced back and there he'd stood, watching her disappear into the swirling snow.

Her father believed in Sandt. Sandt was coming. Sandt was obviously fearless, a man of action. Sonja should keep the card with her at all times and believe, he said. She knew that the Turks had a word for such an encounter as theirs. *Kismet.* Roughly, fate, but more than that. For them kismet was a concept that resonated meaning.

Sonja glanced at the note, written on *New York Tribune* stationery.

> *As you travel to the Urals to grant your father's wish, please remember that I am behind you doing my best to catch up. I swear on my mother's eyes that I will not let Colonel Koslov complete his barbarous vow.*
>
> *Your mother was Chinese. Perhaps you know about these vessels. In China, I will buy one and ride sweet winds. If I am fortunate, one day you will ride with me as my guest.*
>
> *Your sincere admirer, Jack Sandt*

Was it possible that Jack was more hopeful of a meeting than she? Sonja doubted it.

Her father, watching her, muttered, "He's back there, getting closer."

"Colonel Koslov? Just hours before I lose my ears. Aren't you the cheerful one?"

He smiled faintly. "You know who I mean. Jack Sandt."

Sonja loved that smile. "Who knows? Maybe he is." She popped her whip over the backs of the horses.

"Sandt. Made to order for Sonja. And he is right. God alone knows the mysterious qualities of desire. Dream along with him. Imagine sailing on a junk. What will it hurt?"

"Oh, please, Papa, spare me." Sonja could not allow herself to count on being saved by some phantom American. She had only herself to rely on. She had set a mission for herself, and she would complete it.

She had forgotten many things about her mother, but one thing she did not forget. Her mother had told her that if she ever got into trouble or needed friends she should go to the British colony of Hong Kong and say she was the granddaughter of the Chinese diplomat Chan Bao. She would discover that she had cousins in Hong Kong, Canton, and Macao, and in overseas Chinese enclaves throughout Southeast Asia, including Singapore, Saigon, and Manila. The Chans took care of their own.

Sonja decided her father was right. Her future lay in China. After she delivered him to Bagodat, she would continue on across western Siberia, the Kyrgyz steppe, and the Gobi to China. Maybe she would one day sail on a junk with Jack Sandt. Maybe not. But her father was right. To dream was to have purpose.

JACK SANDT FELT LIKE A BLOCK OF ICE BOUNCING AROUND IN THE *vashoc*. Nico glanced at his American charge, looking worried. "Hold on, sir. We'll make it yet. It won't be far now."

Jack grinned. "In the United States they would say this is colder than a well digger's ass." He decided to read the descriptions of Turgenev's travels among the "round-shouldered, gloomy" peasants of the Russian countryside. Turgenev's sketches, beginning with "Khor and Kalinych," were subtitled "From the Notes of a Hunter" and were published in 1847 in a journal called the *Contemporary*.

They hit a bump. Trying to read on the bumping *vashoc* was

impossible. Jack closed the magazine and returned it to its canvas pouch. He thought of Turgenev's charge. Love. Hate. Pain. Envy. Lust.

He thought of Sonja Sankova, a young woman of passion and conviction, fleeing from a man who would maim her.

Jack arrived in Kazan in the early hours of the morning two days after leaving Novgorod. In the dim morning light he could see the picturesque Kremlin on high ground commanding the river valley. Nearly half the town had burned in 1844, and even now many parts of the city remained desolate and wretched, the blackened ruins of churches and grand buildings everywhere. The burning of Kazan, Jack remembered, and the eternal rising of life out of death, had been the subject of one of Turgenev's famous sketches. The precise meaning of his piece was ambiguous. Still, he remembered it.

Jack was now on the western slopes of the Urals, and he was anxious to see the mountains, but it was impossible because of the falling snow. They left Malmouish without ever having seen a mountain and reached Perm in the early-morning hours of the third day. The stationmaster doubted that they could reach Yekaterinburg in a sledge, but they pushed on in the black of night in a drenching rain. They were now in the mountains, and if all went well they should cross from Europe into Asia in another twenty hours.

They left Perm at three A.M. in a downpour with just four horses. How Nico found his way in the blackness was a mystery, but he did it, making twenty-five versts in an hour and a half. They obtained two more horses at the next station and continued on over the objections of the locals, who said they needed to abandon the sledge and use a carriage, which they, of course, were willing to sell them. The rain continued and the road got worse. It soon became apparent that the advice to switch to a carriage had been sound, for the horses could pull the sledge only with great difficulty.

Three days later they crossed the summit of the Urals and ate breakfast at the first station. A thick fog and heavy rain obscured the country. It took them fourteen hours to cover the remainder of the road to Yekaterinburg, located at the head of the valley of the Issetz.

SIXTEEN

The Splendors of Yekaterinburg

JACK SANDT THOUGHT THE APPROACH TO YEKATER-
inburg, the so-called capital of the Urals, was nothing
short of grand. Yekaterinburg was built on the banks of a
long, beautiful lake, flat as glass and extending for several
miles until it disappeared serenely behind the forested ridges of the Is-
setzskoi. Several rocky mountains covered with pines and larch rose
above the town, and on one stood an observatory that Nico told Jack
was used for magnetic observations. From a distance Jack could see the
spires, towers, and domes of eight churches plus numerous private and
public buildings, most of which were made of brick covered with con-
crete.

The clerk of the hotel recommended to Jack told him that Colonel
Peter Koslov and the Wolfpack were temporarily billeted there. Koslov
was conducting business of the crown with Granilnoi Fabric, where the
Russians cut and polished the many gems and precious stones found in
the mineral-rich mountains.

Jack decided to slow down his pursuit of Sonja on the off chance that
he might get to meet the storied Colonel Cut personally. He wondered if
Yekaterinburg might not contain the seeds of a story that would please
his friend Marx.

The Gornoi-Provlenie, or General Board for the Direction of Mines,
was headquartered in Yekaterinburg, the center of the mining district

in the mountains. Since Yekaterinburg was also the center of the manu-
facture of shot and shells and the casting and boring of large guns, an
artillery officer, General Lev Karensky, was chief of the Gornoi-Provlenie.
A second general of artillery—holding his appointment from the minister of war and so independent of Karensky—was in charge of supervising and inspecting all arms made in the Urals.

Jack reported to Karensky with his letter from the crown. Karensky
assigned a serious middle-aged man to show Jack the highlights of
Yekaterinburg and its manufactures, including the Granilnoi Fabric.

With Nico helping carry his daguerreotype gear, Jack set off for a
tour of the town. Their first stop was a large, elegant mansion on the
slopes of the mountain rising above the city and with a view of the town
and the Urals. The lake below disappeared into the haze to the north
and west. The mansion contained extensive gardens with well-planned
greenhouses and hothouses and a lovely promenade open to the public
in summer. Jack's guide said the owner had risen from peasant beginnings to become a wealthy entrepreneur, only to be banished from the
Urals and have his property confiscated for the crime of flogging some
of his workers to death.

His was not the only mansion in Yekaterinburg. The town was filled
with splendidly furnished residences containing lofty, spacious rooms.
It was the fashion of the houses on these grand estates—owned by merchants and owners of the mines—to have attached conservatories filled
with choice collections of tropical plants and flowers.

Jack was taken to a house with extensive greenhouses. The lady of
the house, a willowy, sloe-eyed beauty, instructed a servant to show
them the results of her husband's hobby. One hothouse was well
stocked with orange and lemon trees. Some of those were blossoming,
giving off a wonderful perfume; others were in full fruit. In another
glass enclosure there were plums, peaches, and cherries. In still a third
hothouse, there were more than two hundred varieties of flowers with
blooms of every color imaginable—scarlet, crimson, orange, deep purple, and yellow.

Jack had never seen an orange tree and was amazed to find them growing in the Urals. The wife was quite proud of the oranges and posed with a slender, languid hand cupped beneath an orange.

Later, Jack's guide told him that the wives and mistresses of the wealthy gentlemen of Yekaterinburg had their dresses imported from France and England. So too French wines and champagnes, French and Italian cheeses, truffles, and other culinary luxuries found in European cities. At their elegant balls they danced to the music of chamber orchestras imported for the occasion.

And did they have fancy balls every night of the year? At this latitude the winter nights ran to eighteen hours long. He asked his guide what they ordinarily did to occupy themselves.

"They play cards," he said.

"Cards?"

He grinned broadly. "They love it. They're famous for it. Everybody in Yekaterinburg plays cards. The rich. The poor. Men. Women. They play with enthusiasm."

Jack furrowed his brow. "Really?"

He laughed. "In New York you have newspapers and periodicals of one sort or another plus literature, and you have the freedom to discuss anything you want. In Yekatrinburg, we have only cards. If you leave town without seeing somebody playing cards, I'd be surprised."

After finishing their tour of the streets occupied by these mansions, Jack, Nico, and their guide went to the government's steam-run mechanical works on a high embankment in the center of the town. Here lathes, planers, hammers, and machines for punching, drilling, grooving, and slotting made cannons and shells, and copper coins as well; and gold was smelted and cast into bars.

Jack's guide then took him Granilnoi Fabric, owned by a Prince Asimov, a first cousin of His Imperial Majesty. At Granilnoi Fabric craftsmen carved tabletops and precious objets d'art from a fabulous variety of jaspers—deep green, dark violet, gray, dark purple, cream, and a ribbon jasper containing reddish brown and green stripes. Jack saw deep pink orlite with yellow and black veins being made into classically designed semitransparent vases. He saw elegant little boxes, lacquered and painted with miniature portraits. The cost of the labor would prevent these elegant crafts from being made in the United States or, he assumed, the rest of Europe, but here it was another story.

He saw an artisan putting the finishing touches on a paperweight that was a beautifully executed bunch of amethyst grapes. He saw a man carving exquisite, highly detailed flowers on a jasper vase for which he was paid three shillings eight pence a month plus two poods, or seventy-two pounds, of rye flour to make into bread. None of the workers were expected to eat meat. Married men fared slightly better. He saw a man carving the head of Ajax on a brooch in high relief, the cream-colored head on a dark green background. He was paid an additional two poods of black flour for his wife and one pood for each of his two children. For similar subsistence wages, he saw artisans carving topaz, amethyst, emerald, aquamarine, and other stones into jewelry and objects as required by His Imperial Majesty. Peasants ran machinery on twelve-hour shifts for a daily ration of black bread and salt, plus a draught of *kvass,* a kind of beer made from rye.

Little wonder that Turgenev had asked what Jack knew about the conditions of the serfs. And Jack was beginning to appreciate what he had assumed to be Karl Marx's hyperbole. No damn wonder Marx sounded hysterical.

Jack took the necessary time to capture a daguerreotype image of the worker bent over his table carving the brooch. The guide watched with pride, believing Jack was taken by the quality of the worker's craftsmanship, which was true. What Jack really had in mind was placing his daguerreotype of the orange trees beside the daguerreotype of the worker, with a cutline saying what he was paid for his labor. She imported French orchestras for her parties. He worked for bread, salt, and enough beer to give him something to look forward to.

While Jack buffed his plates, his guide gave him a running account of the gems available to the artisans at Granilnoi Fabric.

When Jack finished processing the images, his guide murmured with much pride, "You might be interested to know Granilnoi Fabric has been chosen to make a new throne for His Imperial Majesty. His Imperial

Majesty has decreed that it will be made only of gems found in Russia as a demonstration to the world of our vast resources."

Jack blinked. "Really?"

"We have the finest, most experienced craftsmen in the world gathered here. You've seen them for yourself."

Jack wouldn't quarrel with that claim. "They do beautiful work," he said.

"His Imperial Majesty has declared his wish that it be the most beautiful and valuable throne ever made. Prince Asimov has decreed that all craftsmen chosen to cut and mount the jewels be paid an extra pood of flour each month and awarded a medal. They've been working on the designs for the better part of two years."

"I see. Wouldn't it be more secure to make the throne in Moscow or St. Petersburg? I would think the isolation would make Yekaterinburg attractive to bandits."

His guide smiled. "It's not to worry about thieves, my American friend. The crown has certainly thought of that. Colonel Peter Koslov is the chief of security. Perhaps you've heard of Colonel Koslov?"

"His reputation precedes him," Jack said.

"I'm told he is in Yekaterinburg this very day."

"I see. When is all this to take place? The crafting of the throne, I mean."

"Two years ago quality rubies in quantity were discovered at the headwaters of the Black Irkout on the eastern flank of Monko-seran-Xardick. The crown established an outpost on Xardick to see that the Tsar's rubies are delivered to the Tsar."

" 'Monko-seran-Xardick' meaning?"

"Eternal Snow and Ice. They're said to have collected a fortune in uncut rubies. If rumor is correct, Colonel Koslov has been ordered to take a special detachment of His Imperial Majesty's most trusted gendarmes to bring back the gems. The members of the Wolfpack wear distinctive gray uniforms with red trim. You might have seen them in town."

"They're billeted in my hotel."

The guide suddenly looked concerned, and said quickly, "I tell you this because you're an American, but I have been indiscreet. I trust you'll not mention you heard of the rubies of Xardick from me." He cleared his throat.

SEVENTEEN

The Rubies of Xardick

 AT THE END OF THE DAY JACK HAD A QUIET MEAL AT
the inn where he had found lodgings. He was about to go
up to his quarters when he noticed that several gentlemen, including a cigar-smoking Russian officer, were
sitting at a round table in a back room playing cards. He poked his head
in out of curiosity and was invited to join. He hesitated, knowing he
had a long day of traveling ahead of him, and he needed to rest. But at
length, not wanting to seem a poor sport—and having recognized the
officer as the one who had been shouting at Prince Onkifovich—he re-
lented and took a seat that was offered him. He was an officer of the
Wolfpack. Was this Colonel Peter Koslov? Yes. Had to be.

Jack did not want to draw unnecessary attention to himself. He just
wanted an opportunity to see Koslov close up. "I'll play for an hour, then
I have to get some sleep," he said. Almost immediately he was given a
tumbler of cold vodka, the accepted greeting to all newcomers to the
game.

Colonel Peter Koslov, sitting opposite Jack, took a modest puff on
his cigar. "And you, sir, are?" he asked in adequate English. He had high
cheekbones and vaguely malevolent, suspicious eyes, although his question seemed amiable enough. Jack noted that the other three players
around the table appeared to regard Koslov with extreme deference.

"Jack Sandt," Jack said.

"A citizen of what country?"

"The United States. I'm an American."

"I see. Sandt. That's a Dutch name is it not?"

"We Americans are a nation of immigrants. There are many people with Dutch names in the United States."

"So it is. And what is it you are doing in Yekaterinburg?"

"I'm a dag man. I take daguerreotype images. I work for the *New York Tribune*, a newspaper. I'm on my way to take daguerreotypes in the Urals and Siberia. Artists will use my dags as the basis for drawings for newspaper illustrations. I'm here with the permission of His Imperial Majesty." Jack retrieved his letter from the crown and handed it to him for his inspection.

Koslov took another puff on the cigar and read the letter.

Jack waited, his mouth dry.

Koslov looked up, studying him with his terrible blue eyes. "This is highly unusual."

Jack felt a stab of anxiety. "Is something wrong, sir? The document is genuine, I assure you."

Koslov looked down at the paper. "No, no. I'm not questioning its authenticity. I'm familiar with the seal and the signature. And I know Count Chermerkov well. It's the contents that I find curious. It says that on order of His Imperial Majesty you are to be given every assistance. Stationmasters are to provide you with fresh horses as necessary. The directors of *zavods* are to give you tours of their factories and mines and help you secure guides and provisions. Magistrates are to give the necessary permissions to travel wherever you please." He reread the paper and ran his tongue over his teeth. He looked up again. "The Tsar ordinarily does not like foreigners traveling in the interior. Why is it you are an exception?"

Jack shrugged. "I have no idea."

He looked at Jack straight on. "No, no, no. There is more to it than that. I'm curious. Humor me. Whom do you know, Mr. Sandt?"

Koslov still had Jack's paper on his side of the table. Was he not going to return it? "I don't know anybody impressive. I took a daguerreotype image of the count. Perhaps he found that flattering."

"He likely was flattered, but what else. Tell me."

Jack knew he should give Koslov something in the way of an acceptable answer. "I told him my editor was interested in developing the American West, which also has rivers and timber and minerals. Gold in quantity was discovered in California three years ago. My editor wanted to see how the Russians were faring with similar territory. There have long been rumors that the Tsar may be interested to sell the territory of Alaska to the United States. Alaska is on my itinerary. Perhaps His Imperial Majesty would like Americans to know more about what's out there. A good salesman, in a manner of speaking."

"These are excellent credentials, Mr. Sandt. Unrivaled in my experience." Koslov handed back the paper. "If I can be of any service to you in your travels, you have only to let me know. My name is Colonel Peter Koslov, commander of Detachment One of His Imperial Majesty's gendarmes."

Jack put his paper back inside his jacket pocket. "I am very pleased to meet you, sir. I assure you, I will do my best to be a thoughtful and respectful guest in your country."

Jack downed his tumbler of vodka and put some money on the table.

With the cigar clenched between his teeth, Koslov dealt them a hand. He put the cigar down momentarily and studied his cards, but it was clear that he was still curious about Jack. "There are some beautiful women in Russia, Mr. Sandt. Perhaps you will find yourself one." He smiled. "If you are to catch the spirit of our country, you should certainly learn something of our women. They say every man should have a wife to complete his life. Isn't that right?" He looked about the table.

The other players all laughed, but it was clear there was nothing at all amusing about the officer whom they were obliged to please. Jack checked his cards, grateful that he'd had the intuitive foresight to put a limit on his time at the table. The less time he spent in Koslov's presence, the better.

"And your cards? Do you have a good hand, Mr. Sandt?"

"Well, to tell the truth, sir, I don't know for sure. Hard to say. I suppose it depends on the cards the other players are holding. I've played with seamen who say a good player pays attention to the run of cards and rates the value of his hand accordingly. What appears to be an unbeatable combination can sometimes be trumped. And it is often possible to bluff with a modest holding."

Koslov laughed softly. "Good point."

It was Jack's turn. He played a card. "When I was touring Granilnoi Fabric this morning I overheard some artisans talking about a new throne that's being designed for His Imperial Majesty. It is to be made here in Yekaterinburg. Quite an honor."

"It's no secret," Koslov said. "Not widely known outside of Yekaterinburg, but no deliberate secret. Under the circumstances, we're trying to be discreet."

Jack said, "Is it true that His Celestial Majesty has selected you to transport the rubies of Xardick to the craftsmen here in Yekaterinburg?"

"Where did you hear that?" Koslov narrowed an eye.

"From a gentleman in the bar."

"I see. What you heard is true. I've been so honored," he said.

"The Tsar would choose only his most trusted officer to transport the rubies. You must serve him well."

Koslov smiled. "I serve at his leisure. Detachment One does its best for Mother Russia."

Jack said, "The craftsmen do extraordinary work at Granilnoi Fabric. I can't imagine that there are more skilled artisans to be found anywhere in the world."

Koslov seemed pleased at the compliment. "That's so, Mr. Sandt. That's why they were chosen to build a new throne. It will be one of the wonders of the world."

Jack wanted to say that the craftsmen would certainly do their best work, what with reward of an extra pood of flour and a medal, but he held his tongue. He checked his hand again.

Studying him, Peter Koslov said, "You say you take daguerreotypes.

I'm naturally curious. You wouldn't mind showing me some images?"

"Not at all. If you give me a few minutes, I'll go to my room and fetch some to show you."

Koslov turned his palm up. "Please."

Jack knew the Russian was double-checking his bona fides. He went to his room and retrieved three dags, one of Yekaterinburg nestled by the lake, one of the lady in her greenhouse, and one of the craftsmen working at Granilnoi Fabric.

On seeing them, Koslov was properly impressed. "Ah, so you are a dag man. And a good one."

"You doubted me, sir?"

"I was merely curious," Koslov said. "I take it you're the young American at Prince Onkifovich's house at supper a week ago. With the writer Ivan Turgenev. I was told the American took daguerreotypes."

"Yes, I had supper with the prince and some guests, including Turgenev. A week ago sounds about right. One day runs into the next."

"Did they tell you about a poet named Mikhail Sankov and his daughter?"

"They told me about a poet named Mikhail Sankov. He and his daughter were expected that night but didn't arrive."

"I see. And what else?"

Jack furrowed his brows. "They said Mikhail was dying of cancer, but nothing about his daughter. An attractive young woman, they said."

Koslov cocked his head, watching Jack.

Jack was aware that the other players were studying him as well. "I don't understand. What is it about the daughter that I am missing?"

Koslov opened his palm and gestured to the other players. "Perhaps these gentlemen will tell you?" He waited, looking about the table. "No?" He waited, then added, "I thought not."

Jack said, "Would you sit for me, sir? I would like to take two dags. One for you. One for Mr. Greeley's sketch artists."

Koslov straightened in his seat and adjusted the medals on his chest. "I would be pleased to sit for you, sir."

EIGHTEEN

On the Tehoussowaia

THE NEXT MORNING JACK STUDIED HIS MAP AND IN-
quired about the fastest way to Nijni Tagil. He was told
there were two ways to get there: the arduous direct
route, by land, as Colonel Koslov was doing; or by the
dangerous Tehoussowaia River, where the ice was breaking up in the
spring thaw. The Tehoussowaia flowed to the southwest before it turned
to the northwest, which meant that Sonja and her father would eventually have to abandon the river and start back up the Urals by carriage or
horseback. It was possible too that Koslov could first ride overland,
across the ridges, a shortcut, and enter the Tehoussowaia farther downstream.

The river was six feet above its previous high, set in 1830, making it
dangerous in the extreme. What with rapids and rocks, traveling the
Tehoussowaia was treacherous under the best of circumstances. The ice
and high water from the melting snow made it even worse.

Jack thought of the card game the previous night. Koslov had no
way of knowing Jack was contesting his right to disfigure Sonja. If
Jack had a good hole card, it was the element of surprise. He could
hardly ride through the Urals alone. If running the rocks and ice was
the only way he could get to get to Nijni Tagil before Koslov, then run
the ice and rocks he would. His guide of the previous day offered to

take Jack to Bilimbawsky, where he could secure a small boat to take him on to the port of Outkinskoi Pristan. There Jack could buy a proper craft and hire an experienced guide for the dangerous trip downriver.

Jack and his companions set off on the road out of Yekaterinburg in a carriage pulled by five horses. They arrived in Bilimbawsky at eight o'clock, after which the director of the mines treated them to a supper of boiled meat and potatoes, with pickled mushrooms. They talked until one in the morning, after which Jack slept on the same sofa on which the Tsar had slept during his visit to the mine.

Outside they could hear the rushing waters of the Tehoussowaia. During a break in the conversation, they listened to the river. The director told Jack it was dangerous, if not outright madness, to ride the river this time of year. Many seasoned river men had thought they were better than the Tehoussowaia in the springtime, much to the regret of their widows and surviving children.

In the beginning, the valley was narrow, with a forest of small pine on one side rising to the summit. There were meadows on the opposite bank of the Tehoussowaia, although Sonja Sankova saw no cattle except near the widely spaced villages. She and her father and their steersman floated for thirty or forty versts in the drift boat before they saw their first cottage. The steersman said there were bears and elk in the valley, although Sonja saw none. This area had once been subject to violent volcanic activity, and in many places the horizontal strata were now turned at a sharp angle. Sonja and her father were swept past labyrinths of limestone caverns on the shore.

They covered thirty-five versts in nine hours. It was snowing and darkness was descending. After passing a mass of rock at a bend in the river, they saw a light from in the forest. They soon came upon the mouth of a small stream, and above that they saw the ironworks. The current was too swift for them to enter this torrent without the help of some locals who appeared and hauled them upstream with a rope.

The steersman helped Sonja with her father. After a twenty-minute struggle up to their knees in water and mud, they were taken to the house of the director of the ironworks and shown an entrance leading to the door, an opening about four feet high and a little over two feet wide.

Sonja thought her guide had made a mistake. She repeated his question. *"Dom nachalnika?"*

He nodded yes. This was the director's home.

Still disbelieving and indifferent to possible pitfalls, Sonja stooped and entered the cramped space, which served the purpose of keeping the howling winter wind from bursting inside when the door was opened. In total darkness, she groped for the door, which she quickly found. She rapped solidly on the wood. She heard voices inside. She opened the door and proceeded into a second dark space, only to be confronted by a dog that growled and barked furiously, baring its teeth. She heard more voices.

A woman opened a second door, letting in light from a bedroom. *"Da?"*

It turned out this was the wife of Boris Kokorev, the director of the ironworks, who followed quickly at her heels. Sonja, intuitively trusting the woman, took a chance and told them who she was.

Sonja and Mikhail Sankov? Kokorev was surprised and pleased. He sent men with a horse and cart to retrieve their luggage, and shortly thereafter a boy brought her some tea and dried apples and pears.

When their belongings were in place, Sonja was able to change into dry boots, but found it hard to change clothes because Kokorev kept popping in and out of the room asking what he could do to help. He was thrilled to have Mikhail Sankov as a houseguest and wanted to do everything possible to make him and his daughter comfortable.

At ten o'clock, Kokorev helped Sonja prop her weakened father at the head of the table, and his wife served them a dinner of boiled venison, declining to join herself until Sonja insisted. In Siberia, a good housewife knows how to make *nalifka,* a kind of cordial made from wild fruit. Madame Kokorcv's version was the color of claret.

She served Mikhail first, waiting expectantly for his verdict.

Mikhail grinned broadly. "Uralian *nalifka*. It is beautiful. So very sweet. Well done! I assure you, it truly warms the soul of a dying man."

Pleased, Madame Kokorev quickly topped off his glass, and they all drank.

"We should all drink too much," Kokorev said. "Good for the spirit. No reason why not."

"No reason at all," Mikhail said, adding quickly, "If it's no imposition."

Kokorev looked astonished. "Imposition? For the great poet of the Urals. Please, sir, you should know my wife and I cherish your presence. We're honored. We have enough *nalifka* in our cellar to last two winters."

Both Mikhail and Sonja accepted a second glass.

Madame Kokorev beamed with pleasure and produced four more bottles, each of a different color. They were soon sampling all the bottles. Their hosts refused to allow Sonja or Mikhail to have an empty glass in front of them.

With each glass they consumed, Madame Kokorev was even more pleased. Sonja could hardly disappoint her, could she? After days of hard travel it felt good to unwind. Kokorev was an enthusiast as well, and so they consumed four or five bottles, getting more and more drunk.

The more Sonja drank, the sleepier she got. Mikhail too was affected by too much drink. Just as he fell asleep in his chair, Sonja's head began spinning. It was time to turn in for the night. As she rose from her chair she saw her father's *Song of the Urals* on a small shelf of books in the room. Following her eye, Kokorev said, "There is nothing like your father's poetry on a cold winter night. He is a beautiful writer. Nothing passes his eye."

Sonja removed the book from the shelf and opened it to the dedication page. It was for her.

Kokorev said, "They say one day you'll be better than him if you aren't already. All of us know the story of the woman who fractured Colonel Cut's jaw at the Christmas party."

She shook her head. "He dropped to one knee. A broken tooth. No broken jaw, I'm afraid."

He shrugged. "You struck the blow with the Tsar watching. Such courage."

"Such foolishness. He pursues me now."

Kokorev looked grave. "We know that, too."

She sighed, grimaced. "It won't be long now, I suppose."

"What won't be long?"

"Before he catches up with us. It's no secret that he's vowed to take my ears for what I did." Sonja was spinning from the *nalifka*. "We should never, ever forget what happened at Oblinsk, Mr. Kokorev. If we let that kind of barbarity go without reply, we lose our soul. I think I'm ready for bed now."

Kokorev scooped the exhausted Mikhail up in his arms. "We will always remember Oblinsk, Miss Sankova."

Sonja nearly staggered when she walked.

Before she went to bed, she got out Jack Sandt's note and reread it. With the room spinning, she slipped into bed and she closed her eyes.

She was on the rear deck of a junk moored in a small cove. A man with her released the anchor, and it hit the azure water with a splash.

THE NEXT MORNING AFTER BREAKFAST, JACK'S HOST INSISTED ON giving him a quick tour of the *pristan,* or port, where workmen were loading flat-bottomed barks each loaded with nine thousand poods (about 162 tons) of bar and sheet iron. The riverboats, made largely of birch, had straight sides and were 125 feet long, twenty-five feet wide, and nine feet deep. Put together with wooden pins instead of nails, they were aged for a year before they were launched. The decks were not fastened to the bark, so that if the vessel sank after striking rocks or ice, the deck floated on, saving the lives of the crewmen—thirty-five were needed for a nine-thousand-pood bark and forty-five for a bark carrying ten thousand poods.

The director secured a small boat and a crew of three to take Jack downriver. At midmorning they pushed off, and a stout current carried them swiftly downstream past forested banks. The sun glistened brightly on the masses of snow and ice in the valley. Two hours and thirty versts later, shortly before noon, they arrived at Outkinskoi Pristan, where most of the barks were built. Here some four thousand men—some of them brought from villages five to six hundred versts distant—worked diligently loading iron to be shipped downstream to Moscow; cannons, shot, and shell made in nearby Kamenskoi Zavod were floated downriver to Sevastopol and the forts on the Black Sea.

Jack watched several vessels being launched, a splendid and amazing spectacle. Twelve men atop each craft sang the instructions in the form of a chant to about four hundred men and women who used long poles to lever the barks into the water. They sang lustily in chorus as they worked, with each verse pushing the bark closer to the river. The first launch he saw took more than three hours of constant levering and singing.

Jack obtained a boat large enough for Nico, himself, and their cargo, plus a crew of five men and a boy. Unfortunately the heavy rains had caused the river to flood, sweeping massive chunks of ice down the river at a horrific speed. The ice slashed the sides of the moored barks as it swept past, causing much consternation at the port. Finally, the captain of a bark loaded with tallow decided to brave the hazards of the swollen river. An Eastern Orthodox priest offered blessings and a prayer for a safe voyage at a launch ceremony, after which everybody got loaded with vodka.

Jack bought provisions at the *pristan,* including bottles of Madeira and rum, on the chance that they would have to seek refuge in the woods from the frequent spring storms. As he was collecting his supplies, he asked the clerk, casually, if a young woman and her ailing father had passed through the port.

"And your name is?"

Jack straightened. "Jack Sandt."

"And you are from where?"

"America."

"Is there anything else you might tell me by way of identifying yourself?" The clerk continued packing Jack's supplies.

"I am traveling across Russia taking images with a daguerreotype. I have it in my luggage if you'd like to see it. I met Sonja Sankova briefly in Nijni Novgorod shortly after having supper with the writer Ivan Turgenev."

The clerk looked about, making sure they were alone. "I had to be sure of your identity. You understand."

"Certainly. We all know the dangers."

The clerk slipped a piece of paper into Jack's hand. Jack looked at it, stunned: it was a drawing of a Chinese junk.

"Miss Sankova left this with me on the chance you would be passing through. She and her father are one day ahead of you, being guided by my brother. Colonel Koslov and the Wolfpack passed through here several hours ago."

"What?"

"There will be numerous villages along the way with boats moored along the river. Colonel Koslov will have to check each of these to make sure Miss Sankova has not stopped there."

"How do I know if I've come upon her boat?"

The young man smiled. "You should look for a splash of yellow paint on the stern. I put it there myself, an upward slash from the waterline."

"And the Wolfpack's boat?"

"It's larger and has a splash of red. My brother put it there while they were buying supplies." He paused, then added, "You should understand, Mr. Sandt, we do these dangerous things because Sonja Sankova is a heroine of Russia. We all want to do what we can to help her. She trusts you. We beg you please do not let her down."

Jack shook his hand with a firm grip. "I will do my best, I promise. And thank you."

Jack turned to his steersman. "Let's go!"

They packed their belongings into the boat. The steersman offered another prayer for a safe voyage, and they were away. As they pushed off, the clerk who had marked Sonja's boat and passed on her message shouted, "Go with God, Mr. Sandt!"

NINETEEN

The Amazons of Ilimskoi

SONJA AND HER FATHER AND THEIR STEERSMAN pushed off in their drift boat shortly before dawn; floating downstream in the darkness, alert for chunks of ice in the water, was an unnerving experience. Several times they bumped, *ka-whack,* into ice, but somehow, miraculously, the wooden hull withstood the blows. With the rising of the sun, Sonja discovered this was the apparent beginning of a bright, sunny day, but the Russian saying was "No morning sun lasts a whole day," and this one didn't. An hour later the dark clouds rolled over the hills of the narrow valley and a downpour began.

The steersman pulled to shore and tried to find shelter under some large pines, but it was no use. After waiting for more than an hour in the pelting rain, they continued on, arriving in Chaintanskoi nearly fourteen hours later. Sonja and Mikhail were nearly frozen from sitting in an open boat and groggy from lack of sleep. They dried out and rested for a few hours and pushed off before sunrise next morning, approaching Ilimskoi at dusk two days later.

Ilimskoi was a small village pleasantly situated at a bend where a winding stream entered the Tehoussowaia River. In the summer when the birch and aspens were in full leaf, and with wildflowers and shrubs in blossom, it was no doubt beautiful. But now it was a wallow of mud, a place for pigs or hippos, but hardly suitable for human beings.

Sonja knew she had to let her father get a few hours of sleep or she would be escorting his body the rest of the way. Sleep was a luxury with Koslov on their trail, but it was dangerous to continue downriver in the darkness exhausted, weakened by hunger and with numbed senses. She also knew it was dangerous to moor her boat directly in front of the village. Better to beach it slightly downstream.

After taking that precaution, Sonja left her father in the temporary care of the steersman, and doubled back on foot, following a trail that paralleled the river. Arriving at the village, she knocked on the door of the most prosperous house she encountered.

An old man answered the knock and ushered her inside. She was met by two huge women nursing young boys—they were hardly to be called babies—who appeared far too old for such an indulgence. One of the nursing women was thin as a twig. The second was tall and rawboned with a horse face. They were joined immediately by a brace of stout ladies with extensive bosoms and tremendous buttocks covered with almost nothing at all, their costumes being skimpy shifts clinging to their outsized curves and extending barely to the knees.

Sonja threw herself on the old man's mercy. She said, "My name is Sonja Sankova. I need help. I am taking my father Mikhail home to die and be buried in the Urals. He is—"

"The poet Mikhail Sankov."

Sonja nodded yes. "I must warn you that we're being pursued by Colonel Cut and the Wolfpack."

The man peered out of the window toward the boat. The women studied Sonja with interest.

Having decided what he would do, the man bowed politely. "My name is Boris Odurov. I would be pleased if you would accept my hospitality. You look exhausted. Wait here and rest. We'll fetch your father for you. Perhaps he would appreciate hot soup. We have barley and dried mushrooms and fresh venison bones for a good stock."

She kissed Odurov on the cheek. "Thank you so very much for your kindness."

"It's an honor, believe me. We've got a bedroom for your father. We'll see that he's made comfortable and given anything he needs. If you're going to see him to his resting place, you need to get some rest yourself." One of the nursing women went with Sonja's father; the one with the horse face took her hand and led her to a small bedroom.

Trembling from fatigue, Sonja sat on the bed and slipped out of her boots, grateful to be out of the boat and to receive a momentary reprieve from the chores of caring for her father.

The woman with the horse face switched her burden from one breast to another. "Are you the one who knocked out six of Colonel Koslov's teeth at the Christmas party, leaving him unconscious for two days?"

Sonja pulled her trousers over her hips. "I chipped one tooth. Cut my knuckle. He was dazed was all. That's likely because he was drunk." She studied the back of her hand. "I still have the scar."

Her host leaned forward. "A scar? May I see it?"

"You want to see the scar?"

"Yes, please."

Sonja felt slightly foolish, but she was aware of the importance the women attached to being able to tell their friends they had seen the scar. "Yes, of course. If you want." She held out her hand for the horse-faced woman, who drew it close and ran her callused fingers over the scar that ran along the top of Sonja's knuckles. She stepped back, her eyes glowing with admiration. "I'll see that your clothes are washed tonight. We'll dry them by the fire. My friend will sit with your father tonight in case he needs anything. You need to rest." She looked slightly embarrassed and gave Sonja a hug with her free arm. "Please don't give up, Miss Sankova. Don't ever quit. We're all behind you."

Sonja said, "Thank you both truly. I don't know how to repay you."

The woman with the large child said, "You've already repaid us. These children will pass on to their grandchildren the story of the night Mikhail Sankov and his daughter Sonja passed through their mother's house on the Tehoussowaia River."

Behind them someone called to the nursing women. The horse-faced woman hurried away, but returned quickly, her finger at her mouth, signaling for Sonja to remain quiet. "The Wolfpack," she whispered.

"Here?"

She nodded, looking grave.

Sonja slumped. This was it, then. Colonel Cut had caught up with her.

As they approached the village Ilimskoi, the steersman moved closer to the shore so Jack could see if there were any boats moored. As they slid silently by under the cold white moon, Jack saw a boat with a splash of red on the stern. Koslov! He continued drifting. My God, a yellow.

The Wolfpack, checking every village along the way, had stumbled onto Sonja.

"We stop here! Quickly, quickly," Jack said. The steersman, also understanding what had happened, began sculling the boat toward shore.

Jack leaped off the boat, uncertain of what he should do next. Was Sonja a captive? Frantic, running, tripping in the darkness, he followed the shore upstream.

Sonja heard a squeal come from the front of the house, followed by male laughter. "Please, I have to go."

The horse-faced woman whispered, "You stay put for now. Irina and Tamara will take care of the gendarmes."

"How?"

"We fight the good fight with whatever weapons are at hand." She tapped herself on the crotch.

Sonja's eyes widened. "Your two cousins are going to entertain the entire Wolfpack?"

"Irina and Tamara are patriots. While the gendarmes' attention is on what's between their legs, you can get a head start. Irina and Tamara can be very entertaining when they're of a mind. They're quite talented in that regard."

Another squeal. More laughter. The horse-faced woman said, "Your father and the steersman are already outside. You go too. Out of the window. Irina and Tamara are doing this for you. Don't let them down. We'll help you back to your boat." She opened the window.

"Our boat is beached downstream past the bend. It has all our belongings."

The horse-faced woman said, "We'll put you on another boat. When you get to yours, simply abandon ours and continue on in your own."

Sonja took a deep breath. Then, as an afterthought, she said, "I need to leave a note for someone. Just in case."

The horse-faced woman sighed. "Okay then, write it. But be quick and then it's out of the window and down to the water for you."

As Jack entered the village, he saw the Wolfpack piling out of a large house, some of them laughing and joking. In the moonlight, he saw Peter Koslov urging them to hurry to the boat. The gendarmes, apparently rousted from a break, did as they were told, however reluctantly.

Watching from the shadows of underbrush, he wondered what had happened to Sonja and her father.

He waited until Koslov and the Wolfpack had pushed off from the riverbank, and then he banged on the door of the large house. After some delay a woman answered the door and showed him to a filthy room, then set off to find the owner. The room smelled of mud and rot and mildew, but after all that Jack had been through, he marveled at the sanctuary that contained four chairs, a long bench along one wall, an armchair, and a pipe long enough to please a sultan.

Exhausted, he plopped down in the armchair. Two women of Amazonian proportions dressed in insufficient costumes paraded into the room—showing no sign whatever of having hosted Colonel Peter Koslov and the Wolfpack. As they passed through, both bosoms and behinds bulging extravagantly, they gave him come-hither looks, coyly arching their eyebrows. They continued on through a second door to an adjoining room, leaving it open, apparently on the chance that he might require their assistance or services.

He wanted to ask about Sonja, but feared the answer. What had happened to Sonja?

A few minutes later, a man named Odurov arrived and called to the Amazons to bring tea, which they immediately did. Then Odurov began firing questions at Jack, speaking Russian so fast that the American had no way of comprehending what he was saying. Jack punctuated the confusion with an occasional "*Da*" or "*Nyet,*" hoping his host would get the idea that he couldn't keep up with his Russian.

Finally, out of frustration, he began asking Odurov questions in English, speaking as fast as he could. Odurov ceased momentarily, then began again. It was impossible. He refused to stop. Then Jack understood the difficulty. He was trying to determine Jack's identity.

"I am Jack Sandt, an American," he said slowly in his best Russian.

Upon hearing this, Odurov stopped jabbering and beamed with approval. He clapped Jack around the shoulders and steered him into another room, announcing that they were to have soup—never mind that it was in the middle of the night. The soup, made of barley, dried mushrooms, and venison stock, was already made. They would drink vodka as well. This all was clearly intended to be some kind of celebration. Of what, Jack wasn't sure.

"I'm concerned about the fate of a young woman and her father," he said.

Odurov said, "*Da, Da.* Sonja Sankova and her father. They are fine. Come, let us drink and enjoy some soup in celebration of their safe departure."

"They're safe?"

"With almost an hour head start on the Wolfpack," Odurov said proudly.

The two damsels with bulging appurtenances reappeared, introducing themselves as Irina and Tamara. Irina, displaying a generous expanse of breast, placed a huge bowl of curious-looking soup before Jack. The bowl had three spoons in it. The lady gave a separate bowl to the talkative host, proposing that Jack share the soup with her and her colleague. This ploy, Jack assumed, was so that both ladies—in bending to eat their soup—could more casually display their vast bosoms.

In his travels Jack had gone hungry for long periods of time. He had come to admire the combination of black bread and salt. But to take soup from the same bowl as these two ladies? No, no, no. Wondering how this curious company had helped Sonja and her father make good their escape, he watched Irina and Tamara put boiled eggs on the table. Jack and his hosts consumed the eggs with slugs of vodka.

Jack wanted to get back on the river in pursuit of Sonja, but he was exhausted. After the soup and eggs, he was shown to a room with a hard bench, onto which he settled, determined to get a couple of hours' sleep before dawn. The door opened and Tamara tried once more to attract his interest. She drifted casually through the room, pausing before the door of her quarters to give him one last chance to respond to the proffered goods.

Jack remained on the bench. He took off his shirt. He didn't want to sleep in wet long johns. He had only two pairs, and he rotated them. He had to wash this pair so they could dry overnight. He said, "You don't see a lot of strange men in these parts, is that it?"

Tamara gave Jack a smile that he mentally translated as saying no, she didn't.

He wasn't about to sleep in wet long johns out of embarrassment. He stripped off the long johns, hoping his boldness would send her on her way.

Upon seeing him naked, she arched an eyebrow and grinned broadly.

Ignoring her, Jack slipped under the quilt. "Tell me what happened to Sonja and her father."

"While my sister and I entertained the Wolfpack, our cousin saw them out of the back and safely into a boat."

Jack took a deep sigh of relief.

Tamara slipped her hand under her shift and exposed one breast, arching an eyebrow as she did. What she displayed was remarkable. Watching him with a trace of a smile, she weighed her breast in her hand and bounced it twice. "Are you sure you don't want to have a good time also?"

Jack found it hard not to smile at her persistence, but he was in no mood to entertain the lady, no matter how eager she was. "Thank you for helping Sonja and her father. I mean that sincerely."

She said, "Believe me, Irina and I were honored to do our part. Besides, it wasn't such bad duty. Even with gendarmes." She gave him a slip of paper. "This is for you, Mr. Sandt."

It was another drawing of a junk.

Surely he should do something to reward the Amazons for their role in helping Sonja and passing on her drawing. "I have a machine that makes special images of people, rather like a perfect drawing. Yes, I do. Would you like me to take your image? You and your friend. The sleep can wait."

"Irina?"

"I'll need all the candles and lanterns you have. I have to have light. I regard you and your friend—"

"My sister."

"You and your sister as freedom fighters. I would like to portray you in your battle dress."

She brightened. "Why that would be wearing nothing at all! Do you want us naked?"

"I . . . well, sure, if you don't mind."

Tamara interrupted quickly. "Naked it is. We will be honored. Just tell us how you want us to pose." Without waiting for his reply, she opened the door and shouted at her sister. Irina popped into the room. After quickly learning what Jack wanted, the sisters stripped without ado and each draped an arm around the other's shoulder. Thus posed, they were a proud and remarkable pair in an opulent, excessive kind of way.

"Like this?" Tamara said, grinning hugely.

"You'll have to remain perfectly still for at least half a minute."

"We can do that. No problem," Irina said confidently. She wiggled her shoulders, sending her breasts bouncing. "What do you think?"

Jack rolled his eyes and groaned in admiration. "No wonder the Wolfpack dallied!"

Tamara grinned. "Besides being a good poet, Sonja Sankova knows how to pick her men. She's a lucky woman."

"I'll still need more light," he added.

"Oops, forgot," Tamara said. She pulled up her underpants. "Give us a few minutes." She grabbed Irina, and the two sisters, thrilled that they were to be captured for posterity in their sensual prime, set off to collect candles and lanterns.

TWENTY

The Healing at Kooshwinsk

THE WEATHER WAS COLD AND CLOUDY WHEN JACK
Sandt pushed off the next morning, his imagination em-
boldened by Sonja's drawing of a junk. *She was thinking
of him, taking the time to leave drawings of a Chinese junk
as she fled Colonel Cut!* Jack could hardly believe it. He felt a surge of energy and determination. This was likely demented infatuation, he knew,
but he didn't care. It was a grand, lovely emotion, and he was determined
to keep his word to her.

It began to snow thirty minutes later. The Tehoussowaia twisted and
turned, snaking through the mountains. After fourteen hours in an open
boat, snowing the whole while, he reached Oslanskoi at nine o'clock—the
winding river took sixty or seventy versts to reach what was only twenty
versts through the mountains. As per their agreement, it was here that
Nico was obliged to return home. Jack paid him and they parted on good
terms. All partings are little deaths, and when Jack was alone, he missed
his Russian friend.

Jack secured a carriage and traveled through deep snow on a crude
road that wound to the southwest through a thick forest along the
side of a ridge that ascended to the spine of the Urals. The ride down
the Tehoussowaia had been a zig. This uphill zag would take him to the
ironworks at Kooshwinsk near the crest of the Urals.

As he rode, Jack began to suffer the effects of an awful cold. He got sicker and sicker with the passing of hours. His knees ached. His sinuses were so stuffed he could hardly breathe. His throat was sore. He had an awful cough. He developed a terrible fever. By the time he arrived at Kooshwinsk, he thought he was about to die.

Seeing Jack's condition, the director of the *zavod* ordered tea and sent a boy to fetch a doctor. A half hour later, the physician arrived. Despite Jack's protestations that he had to continue on his way, the doctor said he risked pneumonia and put him to bed while a bath was prepared. Jack was too weak to resist. He waited, sweating and shaking from the fever. Presently two Cossacks appeared and carried him to a shelf in a bathhouse that was within inches of a kind of furnace that produced steam. He was steamed until he thought he had surely reached the end of his ability to endure. Then the physician, a kindly-appearing gentleman presumably operating on his behalf, flogged him for forty minutes with a bundle of birch twigs, leaves and all, ceasing only when he was as red as a cooked crawfish.

After this, the Cossacks reappeared and sloshed him with buckets of cold water, fairly causing his heart to stop. Would their ministrations never cease? After this startling treatment, mercifully, they carried him back to bed. But was he allowed to sleep? No! The concerned physician, muttering in Russian, was close at their heels, bearing a bottle of physic. He insisted that Jack accept a dose, and Jack was too weak to refuse. All he could do was hope there was method to the doctor's apparent madness. The doctor left, telling one of the Cossacks to give Jack a dose every two hours during the night. If Jack was asleep, he was to awaken him.

After two days of steaming, flogging, cold-water baths, and foul-tasting physic, during which Jack felt like a living corpse, the fever subsided. But just when he thought he had defeated it, the heat and the sweating and shaking returned. His tormentors, undeterred, again took up the steaming, flogging, and cold baths. Such zeal as theirs was unimaginable, and he could only hope they were well-meaning, and not casual sadists. They were apparently bent on curing him even if it meant killing him.

THE RIVER WOUND THROUGH THE DARKNESS WITH BARELY DIS-
cernible meadows on both banks. It was a brisk morning and Sonja settled in, doing her best to help by watching for rocks ahead and for
dangerous chunks of ice. At midmorning, she thought she heard men
singing lustily. Singing in the middle of an isolated river in the Urals? At
first she thought it was her imagination, but no, singing. It was coming
from behind them. She pulled the scarf up over her mouth and nose.

As they passed a wide bend in the river, she saw the source of the
singing, and was relieved to see that it was not the voices of the Wolfpack.

A crew of one of the barks was floating happily along on the deck of a
bark that had sunk after hitting a rock or a chunk of ice. But however
quickly the bark had gone under, the crew members had had the foresight
to grab their stash of vodka, and so were getting loaded on their way
downstream. Such good fortune to still be alive! Now they were singing
robust songs and giving thanks to their Maker and whoever it was who
had thought of decks that floated on when a bark went under in such
treacherous waters.

Seeing Sonja's boat in front of them, the survivors shouted and
waved at her, but shortly thereafter they apparently guided their deck to
shore, and that was the last Sonja saw or heard of them.

At noon Sonja and her father shot a rapids through a narrow gorge;
on the other side, broken masses of rock were covered with flowering
shrubs and bushes; larches, pines, and birches grew out of the clefts.

Late that afternoon they came upon a glade where a simple cross
marked the birthplace of the great-grandfather of Prince Demidoff. The
prince's pregnant great-great-grandmother was being ferried downriver
on a bark containing produce from one of the mines, when the party en-
camped on this site. The child born here was to become a powerful
agent in the development of the mineral wealth of these vast regions,
and the source of the prince's large holdings. On Mikhail's request, they
stopped and had a lunch of black bread, salt, and sweet sap drawn from
a nearby tree. Delicious it was.

After passing through a thickly wooded forest, Sonja and her father arrived at Cynowskoi Zavod, an ironworks that produced wire marketed in Novgorod. It was here, under the protection of the Strogonoff family, that Yermak the Cossack had begun his conquest of Siberia. The battlefields were on the far side of the Urals, but it was to this place and the limestone caverns on the Tehoussowaia that Yermak retreated after his first defeats in Asia.

At Cynowskoi Sonja bought herself and her father a dinner of dried meat and fruit, boiled potatoes, and a pickled cabbage salad. But it was hard for her to eat a good meal without being racked by anxiety over her failure to put more distance between herself and Koslov. She had left several messages for Jack Sandt along the way. Was he back there? she wondered. Was he keeping his word?

The last leg of the journey to Zavod Tourinsk was the hardest for Sonja, who was mentally and physically exhausted. Her father was too weak to sit up in a saddle, so she transported him on a makeshift litter fashioned from two poles—one attached to either side of his horse and with a canvas sling in between. There Mikhail lay on his back, suffering. There was no way to prevent the jerking and jostling as the ends of the poles bounced along the ground. Sonja kept her father well drugged with laudanum.

Mikhail clenched his teeth, determined to endure whatever was necessary to make it to the place he wanted to rest. He winced. He gagged. He vomited. Out of deference to his determined daughter, he refused to cry out.

Sonja could hardly bear to see her father in such pain, and kept him in a constant stupor from her supply of laudanum. With the passing of time she knew that whatever lead she had had over Peter Koslov must surely have been lost. Yet Koslov had not made his appearance. And neither had the phantom hero, Jack Sandt, whose note she found increasingly annoying. Yes, she couldn't stop her daydreams. But if Jack was so determined to help, where in heaven was he?

Americans! Big talkers!

When Jack Sandt's fever broke for good, the director and the doctor invited him to supper. He was pallid and so weak he could hardly walk, but was desperate to resume his pursuit of Sonja Sankova as soon as possible. After dinner, the three men settled around the fireplace to drink some vodka. It was then that the physician told him that Sonja Sankova had left a note for him.

It was written on the same kind of paper and with the same pen as the drawing of a junk that the Amazon at Ilimskoi had given him.

Dear Jack Sandt, Colonel Koslov likely believes that my father wants to be buried in Nijni Tagil, where he grew up. Not so. He wants to be cremated on Mount Bagodat. The people who give you this note can help you find the way.

The doctor said, "Colonel Koslov and the Wolfpack passed through town a few hours before you arrived. You were far too sick to continue then, so we held the note until you were better." He looked rueful. "We too want to help Sonja and her father. We did our best to get you on your way as soon as possible. We apologize if you thought our steam and cold water and floggings went beyond the pale."

"How long ago was that?"

"Three days," the doctor said.

Jack slumped in disappointment.

"I take it you know the story of the Christmas party. You know about Oblinsk and Colonel Cut's vow."

"I do."

The doctor glanced at the director, then said, "Colonel Koslov is a determined, dangerous man, famous for having his way."

"I know that. I do this at my own risk."

The doctor sighed. "I am able to heal such diseases as a cold or influenza and can perform minor surgeries, repair broken bones and such, but my abilities are limited with respect to madness."

"Sonja says her father wants to be cremated on Mount Bagodat," Jack said. "Why is that?"

"It's a long story. You'd have to be a Uralian to understand. Koslov is a European Russian. He looks down on us Uralians. He certainly does not understand our history and passion. If you make it there in time to help Sonja Sankova, she'll tell you why. Because of her sick father, Sonja was forced to go downstream, then cut overland, but there is a shorter route through the mountains if you know the way."

That night the doctor and the director secured the services of a trustworthy guide for Jack, a thin man named Yuri, who told him they would have to travel by horseback to Zavod Tourinsk at the base of Mount Bagodat. Jack had spent a lot of time on a horse in his time, and he didn't mind a little hard riding, but for this trip he was still weak from the fever.

TWENTY-ONE

In the Valley of the Toura

 THE NEXT MORNING, JACK SANDT JOINED THE DIREC-
tor and the doctor for a breakfast of venison sausage,
black bread, and tea. When they were finished, Jack stowed
his daguerreotype gear atop three packhorses, and he
and Yuri mounted up for their journey to Zavod Tourinsk. Jack was so
weak that he could hardly sit atop his saddle, but he was determined
to push on.

Looking up at him, the director took him by his hands and squeezed
tightly. "Godspeed, Mr. Sandt. Eat well so you can regain your strength,
and remember, all Uralians are on your side. If you're successful in
keeping Sonja Sankova out of Koslov's hands, you'll be welcome here
anytime."

The season of mosquitoes was beginning, and there were millions of
them. Yuri had lived in the Urals for ten years and feared nothing except
the dreaded tribe of insects that feed on blood. He said there were no
mosquitoes on the planet that could compare with those winged vampires. He provided Jack with a box made of thin sheet iron that hunters
used to thwart the insects, although there was some doubt as to which
was worse, the mosquitoes or the cure. The contraption was seven
inches long, four inches wide, and five inches deep, and had small holes
punched in the bottom. Jack put charcoal in the bottom of the box and
moist wood over that, causing smoke to billow up. He slung the box

over his shoulder with a leather strap and rode his horse sitting in a
cloud of foul-smelling smoke that burned his eyes.

With each in his private cloud of smoke, Jack and his companion
proceeded east, venturing along a serviceable road into a narrow valley
of the Urals. Unfortunately, the road soon petered out.

SONJA SANKOVA AND HER FATHER SAW BAGODAT RISING ABOVE
them with black clouds collecting around the summit. Within minutes
the clouds swept downward toward them, enveloping the mountain in a
shroud of blackness. Here and there plumes of white opened in the
clouds as though jets of steam had been forced up from below. Soon the
dark clouds were everywhere, rolling and boiling with horrific activity.

Then came the lightning, great jagged bolts, one after another light-
ing up the forest, followed by thunder cracking and popping overhead
in a frightening fury. The rain lashed at the ground with a vengeance.

Sonja dismounted and unhitched her father's litter. She pulled him
under a fir tree and pulled a tarp around them. They waited with the
water slapping hard against them. "We're here. We made it," she said. "A
few hours more. Hold on."

Mikhail started to smile, then succumbed to a racking cough. "A few
more hours. I knew we'd make it. I've never doubted it."

Father and daughter fell silent, listening to the pounding rain.

Finally, Mikhail said, "He will make it, you know. He will."

"Who is that? Peter Koslov?"

"Jack Sandt. The world is full of evil, but there is honor, too."

Sonja smiled and gave him a hug. "Isn't it nice to think so?" The rain
was easing. Sonja lifted her exhausted father onto the litter and lashed
him into place.

As quickly as the storm had descended from the heavens, it retreated
south, leaving them in warm sunshine. These bizarre, sudden thunderstorms were a casual occurrence in the Urals. One minute sunny, the
next darkness, lightning and thunder straight out of a nightmare.

The storm having passed, Sonja continued the torturous remaining versts to their destination—Zavod Tourinsk at the base of Bagodat. They were drenched by the rain dripping off the branches of overhanging trees, but she was determined to finish before her father died.

Sonja came upon a river about sixty feet wide, only to discover that ice had carried away the expected bridge, and parts of it lay in a tangle downstream. She dismounted and strapped her father to the back of his horse like a bag of potatoes. Leading her father's horse, she set out to ford the stream, but when she attempted to negotiate the opposite bank, her horse tumbled back into the cold water, landing on its side, hooves flailing.

Mikhail could do nothing except watch his daughter struggle in the frigid water. Soaking wet and freezing, she again took her father's horse by the reins and this time climbed the bank without incident.

Mikhail said, "Faith, daughter. Keep the faith."

JACK AND YURI PUSHED HIGHER INTO THE URALS UNTIL THE SUN began setting over Europe. While Yuri set up a camp, Jack hiked higher up the mountain to enjoy the sunset. What a glorious sight! Above him the snowy cap of the Pavda was glowing a ruby red, while below him the valleys were all gloom and mist. Soon the entire sky was lit with a brilliant red of such beauty as to render it beyond the ken of any mortal artist. Jack watched, dry mouthed at such incredible beauty. As the crimson ebbed, the air began to hum with the inevitable mosquitoes, and he started back downhill.

A white vapor began to rise in the valleys so that the vista below him appeared like nothing so much as a vast, eerie white lake that was studded with islands that were the tops of mountains. He heard the pop of a musket farther down the mountain.

When Jack got back shortly before ten o'clock, he found Yuri waiting patiently for him, turning a chunk of bear flesh over the fire. The smoke provided some protection from the mosquitoes. They had camped directly in the icy wind, rather than in the shelter of a rock, which he found curious. The wind cut through the heaviest coat. When he momentarily used a tree to break the wind, he quickly understood their logic. The mosquitoes were foiled by the wind. Standing in the lee of a windbreak was to invite the terrible hum of winged tormentors. The best tactic, as the Russians had learned from long experience, was to stay in the wind and keep the fire blazing.

Talking and laughing about the adventures of the day, they enjoyed a fine meal of roast bear and Uralian *nalifka*. At one o'clock, sated with meat and not a little drunk, they wrapped themselves up against the cold and lay around the fire. Sleep did not come easily for Jack. He smelled of smoke and couldn't stop digging at the mosquito bites on his neck, his wrists, and the backs of his hands. At last he made it, although he was awakened once, shaken by a nightmare in which a man with a huge knife was about to sever his genitals.

The next morning the rising sun bathed the mountains and the pine forests in the most beautiful golden hue Jack had ever seen. Still suffering mosquito bites, Jack and his guide pushed on. Traveling the Valley of the Toura past a grand lake of the same name, they arrived two days later at Zavod Tourinsk at the base of Mount Bagodat.

As they came upon the spartan village, they saw that they had arrived on a festival for the workmen and their families. Life was hard in the *zavods,* and when it came time to play, the workers played hard. Almost immediately, Jack spotted Sonja Sankova and her father watching a wrestling match.

The Festival at Zavod Tourinsk

 IN THE SLEDGE SONJA SANKOVA HAD BEEN ALL BUN-
dled up against the snow, and Jack Sandt hadn't seen
much except her face and her extraordinary brown eyes.
Every night he had gone to bed wondering what the rest
of her looked like. Now he knew. At twenty-four, she was seven years
younger than Jack, but she hardly looked her age, being both slender
and barely five feet tall. It was easy to see how, with short hair, trousers,
and a scarf pulled over the lower half of her face, she had been able—
viewed by a casual passerby or at a distance—to pass as a boy.

After so much dreaming and thinking about her, Jack realized he was
reluctant to know the real woman. As a remembered moment, she was
perfect. Yes, the real woman had a remarkable form and face. She had
grit. She honored her father at the risk of being maimed by Koslov. She
was a skilled poet. But what if she was lovely on the outside and somehow ugly on the inside?

A dream was only that, a fantasy. After all his hard travels and remembering that one grand moment in the snowstorm, here was Sonja
in flesh and blood. The man-woman thing was far more complicated
than raw desire.

Each wrestler stripped to the waist and tied a sash around his waist. A
wrestler gripped his opponent's sash with his right hand, putting his left
hand on his opponent's shoulder. On a signal from a neutral party, the

action began, each wrestler bent on throwing his opponent to the ground. The outsized champion, a local giant who relied on brute strength, proceeded to defeat one challenger after another.

Jack was sure Sonja was watching him from the distance. At length a slender young man who was an apparent stranger to the *zavod* challenged the champion. The locals, convinced that the bulky wrestler was invincible, greeted the challenge with laughter. The stranger calmly tied his sash and readied himself for combat. The champion, reveling in his successes, regarded the upstart contemptuously. This was all part of the drama. Where was the fun without a little posturing?

The wrestlers grasped sash and shoulder. The signal was given, and they went at one another energetically. In a heartbeat, the newcomer flung the champion on his back. The onlookers could hardly believe what they had seen! The throwing of the invincible hulk was one story for the vodka when the snow was howling outside. The hulk taken by surprise was even better.

The vanquished champion, recovering quickly from his shock, sprang cheerfully to his feet and challenged the victor to another match. His demeanor made clear his feelings. The upstart had surprised him. He was determined to defend his honor. He would not be defeated again. Again the two wrestlers grasped sash and shoulder, and again they went at it. Alas, the champion landed on his backside once more.

Unable to restrain himself and forgetting Sonja for the moment, Jack stood, joining the enthusiastic cheering for the smaller stranger. These were peasants whose only experience was that brute strength ruled the day. When there was an unexpected break in the iron rule of blunt power, however fleeting, they were delighted.

It was this same craving for the triumph of the underdog over the mighty—surely as much an attraction to Russians as it was to Americans—that had earned Sonja so many admirers.

THE WRESTLING HAVING FINISHED, SONJA'S FATHER TURNED HIS attention to young girls at play. Girls dressed in colorful holiday costumes joined hands and walked round in circles singing plaintive songs, some of them very beautiful. With just days or hours left to live, she knew, her father was taking great pleasure in watching two girls playing a simple game of skill and dexterity. Each stood at an opposite end of a plank about seven feet long and with a block in the middle. One girl bounced, sending her opposite skyward. Up and down they bounced, sending the other yet higher and higher until they were soon flying up three feet or more, a feat requiring great balance and dexterity. The joy of youth was in their delight.

But Mikhail's daughter paid little attention to either the singing girls or the girls bouncing up and down at the ends of the plank.

Jack Sandt was walking straight toward her.

As if in a dream, as though she were somehow standing outside her skin, viewing herself at a remove, she stepped forward to meet him. "The estimable Jack Sandt, I take it. My American hero."

Jack Sandt laughed. "I bet you've been wondering where in tarnation I was, big-talking American. Never fear, sweet lady." He bowed deeply, making fun of himself.

Sonja laughed and relaxed a little. At first blush, she liked him. He wasn't at all disappointing.

"Catching up with you took some doing, that's a fact. I see you're still one step ahead of Koslov, and that's all that matters. And I want to thank you for the drawings of the junk. They kept me going."

"I have to admit, I was worried that your letter was the work of . . ." She paused, trying to think of an acceptable term.

"An infatuated lunatic?"

She laughed again. "Perhaps that's going a little far, although I admit my father was the believer."

"It's possible you were right, of course."

Jack Sandt had a natural, self-deprecating way about him that she found charming. "My father told me to keep the faith. You'd catch up."

"Smart man," Jack said.

"Although you had me wondering, I have to admit."

"Please, call me Jack."

"Jack it is. I'm Sonja. We did our best to make the prince's supper. It was the storm. When Prince Onkifovich brought me the note, he showed us the daguerreotype you took of Ivan Sergeyevich. Very nice!"

"Thank you," Jack said. "I immediately knew it was you passing by. Had to be. I had my driver hitch the horses back to the sledge, and we returned to the prince's house. My driver knew what the crimson uniforms were all about. I doubled back to a side entrance. It was there that I wrote you the note."

Jack glanced at her father. "Your father looks pleased by our conversation."

Sonja looked back at her father, who grinned broadly and applauded. She gave him an oh-you wave of the hand. "He can see we're having a good time and he likes it. He's a sentimentalist and an optimist. He's been waiting for you to show up. Each day he reminds me that you're behind us, struggling to catch up. Won't you join me and my father?"

Jack rose. "Would you like to have a daguerreotype image taken with him? I can do it right here at the festival. The light is good."

Sonja's eyes brightened. "Yes, yes, yes. But we'll have to hurry."

When they got to him, Mikhail Sankov was alive, but barely. He smiled weakly, struggling to keep breathing while Sandt got his daguerreotype box and chemicals to record proud father and brave daughter together before the father began his return to the good soil of the Urals.

Less than an hour later, the poet of the Urals was dead.

 A Plume Above Bagodat

Carrying Mikhail Sankov's body to the summit of Mount Bagodat was no easy task. Sonja and Jack hired a carpenter to build a simple pine casket. The carpenter attached leather handles to help strap it to the back of a packhorse and to carry it up the mountain by hand when necessary.

The locals thought Sonja and Jack were mad, yet they all knew of Sankov's reputation and respected him, even if they had not read his poetry. To his dying breath, Mikhail Sankov, a son of the Urals, a onetime serf, had written poems of the Urals. He was a Vogul in spirit if not direct descent; he wanted to be returned to the Urals—the plume of smoke from his burning body would repeat the Vogul protest. Sankov was a hero. They knew that Sonja was a poet too, but she had grown up in European Russia, not the Urals, and although she was his daughter, for them it wasn't the same.

Sonja and Jack hired four helpers. At dawn the next day, they put the casket in a wagon and began their journey to the base of Bagodat. From there they strapped the casket to the back of a packhorse and started the ascent through a pine forest. When they started it was a warm, sunny day, but these were the Urals, after all, and both Sonja and Jack knew they could expect anything.

An hour after they left the wagon, they thought they heard thunder, but as the sky remained clear and sunny, they thought they must be imagining it. When the mountain became too steep and rocky for the horse, they removed the casket and continued their chore, climbing higher and higher with their burden.

At length they reached the summit, upon which sat an octagonal wooden chapel, about ten feet in diameter, that held a cast-iron urn containing the ashes of Tchumpin, who had established trade with the Russians. Tchumpin's detractors had immolated him, sending black smoke rolling from the summit as a warning to anybody who might have intercourse with the Russians. The Voguls, wild with fury at the Slavs to the west, bitterly resisted the coming of civilization to the mountains, but in the end the tsars overwhelmed them. Mikhail's express desire was that the rains take care of his ashes. In the Urals that was no problem.

As it was Mikhail's wish to be cremated on Mount Bagodat, they set about collecting wood, which they piled atop his body. It took the better part of midday to build a large mound of wood atop the poet. Sonja insisted that she alone be allowed the honor of starting the fire. It was her father's wish. As his daughter and only child, it was her chore. As the dead wood available on the summit had been soaked by the frequent storms, Jack knew starting the fire going wasn't going to be easy. After a long, frustrating struggle during which Sonja nearly expended all of her matches, she succeeded in producing a timid start. They both knelt and wooed the uncertain flame by blowing on it. Soon they saw the first tendrils of orange flame flickering out like an adder's tongue. Slowly the fire gained strength, then burned in earnest, drying the remaining wood in the process. It was still a wet fire, however, and the smoke of hope billowed to the sky. But the flames got stronger and hotter, until finally the fire was burning with a vengeance.

When it was clear that the flames would carry the day, Sonja stepped back and said, "Take him back, Urals. A wonderful man, my father. I loved him dearly."

Jack held her tightly, and they watch the fire rage, a proper pyre.

At the height of the fire's energy they saw a bank of black clouds rolling toward them, with the slanting rays that indicated it was bringing rain. In the valley below them the vapor billowed and swelled in huge surges. They watched the race between fire and storm. As the pile of wood began collapsing into charcoal on the ashes of Sankov's mortal remains, the dark and dreadful clouds drew closer and closer.

When the first large drops of rain hit the embers, sizzling, Jack and Sonja retreated into the chapel. In the distance they could hear the thunder, growing closer and louder by the minute. Soon they were under siege by one of the wildest storms Jack had ever seen. The wind began howling in a rage, slapping the rain hard against the chapel and dousing the embers of Sankov's pyre. Lightning came in great, impossible white sheets followed by a horrific popping and cracking of thunder. Soon the rain came in torrents, leaking in a steady stream through cracks in the roof of the chapel and soaking them thoroughly. Sonja and Jack clung together, and even their Russian companions, who were used to such occurrences, seemed spooked by the ferocity of the storm. It was fearful; there is no other way to describe it. They were in the eye of a maelstrom, a fury. A flash of lightning struck a rock immediately below them, tingeing everything with red and causing the hair to raise on their arms. Another bolt hit a nearby tree. The storm was at once sublime and awful. They sat in silence, mouths dry.

Finally, Sonja said, "His main memories of growing up here were the thunderstorms. So many stories."

"This is for him, then."

She pushed some water off her face with the palm of her hand. "He wanted his body to be burned on Bagodat and for the rain to take care of his ashes."

As suddenly as it had appeared, the storm, having paid homage to the poet Mikhail Sankov, moved on and the sky was a lovely, pure blue.

They collected themselves and descended the mountain, soaked to the bone and cold. The sun, setting over Europe, spread out below them to the west.

TWENTY-FOUR

Celebrations

THE WORKERS AND THEIR FAMILIES CELEBRATED THE
last night of their festival with a huge bonfire in the street,
over which they cooked elk, bear, grouse, and other wild
meats. While the women and children continued with
their singing and games around the fire, the men settled in with their
vodka and *nalifka* to joke and tell stories. The unexpected dethroning
of the local wrestling champion had been replaced by talk of the plume
of smoke that had risen atop Mount Bagodat that day, visible for miles,
that signaled the return to the soil of the poet Mikhail Sankov. The
ironworkers and their families were not to be confused with any sort
of literary community, but they knew that Sankov was a poet and his
daughter was the courageous young woman who had knocked Colonel
Koslov to his knees.

The occurrence of the horrific thunderstorm was not lost on the vil-
lagers. They too regarded it as a proper send-off by the Urals. Its ferocity
would likely grow in the telling.

Mikhail Sankov's skill and influence as a poet would grow with the
passing of time and generations. Where once Sankov had been well
known in the literary salons in Moscow and St. Petersburg, he would by
their reckoning one day become the toast of Paris and London as well.
Whether or not that was true in fact made no difference in the Urals.
Sankov was born of the Urals and had openly identified with the Vogul

resistance to the spreading of Russian influence. He was an orphan and so belonged to them all. The Urals were in his soul. He had known the pain and joy of the people who toiled in the ironworks and had made it the center of his lyric poems.

Above the bonfire and the brooding shadows, a full moon in a dazzling, starry sky bathed the Urals in splendid white light. Somebody began playing an accordion, a prelude to dancing.

Inside, Jack and Sonja sat on the floor of her diminutive room, listening to the singing and the laughter that was a farewell to her father. They had a bottle of *nalifka* and sipped it, slowly, enjoying the sweetness as they regarded one another in the dim light. He had found her. They had buried her father. Now, for the first time, they were alone.

Jack opened the shuttered window, letting the moonlight in. "Well, here we are," he said, slightly awkward. He cleared his throat.

She smiled. "We made it."

"Together, but still strangers," he added.

"I . . ." She started to say something but stopped.

He read her mind. "You were going to tell me that you've never been with a man before." He paused. "In a physical way, that is."

She looked embarrassed.

"I didn't expect anything different. And I wouldn't have wanted it any other way. We just met one another. We've got plenty of time for that."

She was clearly relieved.

"Who knows, if we're lucky, we'll have . . ." He stopped.

She rescued him. "Years ahead of us." She looked chagrined. "If I can say that without sounding presumptuous."

He grinned. "No, no, that's all right. Years a minimum. More like decades, I would think. But it's not good to miss the courtship at the start. We might be on the run, but why should we be denied a courtship? After all that time thinking about you, I was a little scared when I finally met you, I admit. But it turned out I like you, and I like being with you."

"I felt the same way, and I like being with you." She leaned toward him ever so slightly, and he gave her a gentle kiss.

They straightened, looking one another in the eye. He said, "I won't be able to sleep tonight. Me in my room. You in yours."

"Nor will I," she said. "A kind of torture."

"But a sweet and necessary torture." He groaned.

She laughed. "I agree entirely. Tell me about your daguerreotypes."

He said, "There is something about a daguerreotype that's especially dramatic. An artist can cheat. A daguerreotype is a mirror of reality, and the viewer knows it. I've got money waiting in a Hong Kong bank that I want to use to buy a Chinese junk so I can record images of Asia. I want to show how people live. Rich people. Poor people. Everybody in between. When I was in London, Karl Marx thought I needed a partner. He's right. It strikes me that two people of artistic imagination working together could take a lot of striking images."

Sonja shifted on the floor. "A partner sounds like a good idea. Why don't we take your idea one step further?"

" 'We?' "

She blushed.

"No, no. I like the 'we' very much. Tell me what you were going to say."

"I've read that the Chinese bind the feet of little girls to make them smaller. Before we get that far you will likely see for yourself how the Kyrgyz and Kalmyk treat their women. And there are stories of slave traders dealing in women. What if we set about to record the fate of women in Asia with photographs—record the entire experience from Chinese and Hindu brothels to Muslim harems. We can also write. I know some editors in Europe."

"We can sail out of Hong Kong. Didn't your mother say if you ever needed help you should go to Hong Kong? There are Chans there."

She liked that. "There and all over Southeast Asia."

"The doctor at Kooshwinsk said Koslov was heading for Nijni Tagil, where your father grew up. How far away is that?"

She shrugged. "My father said two days perhaps. Maybe three."

"Not much of a head start, and there's no telling what lies ahead. Under the circumstances, it seems best that we travel as man and wife."

"Traveling as man and wife, I agree. To Hong Kong then."

"I think another kiss would be in order." He hesitated. "Until we know one another better."

"Until it's right. We'll know when the time is right."

As before they kissed gently and sweetly.

Outside there was laughter followed by the giggling of children.

"You know, Sonja, I think this is going to work out for us," he said.

"Of course it will, you foolish man," she said. "We just need a little time."

Outside the Uralians danced. A celebration. Inside a celebration too, and sharing of another order.

TWENTY-FIVE

The Nature of Predators

IF THEY WERE TO OUTRUN PETER KOSLOV, JACK AND Sonja couldn't expect to ride a *tarantass* forever. They needed the ability to strike out across open country if necessary. The next morning Jack bought Sonja some riding boots and men's shirts and pants, and had a bewildered tailor fashion her a crude pair of leather chaps. An hour later, they were on their way, leading packhorses with their belongings and Jack's daguerreotype equipment.

Jack had spent enough time in California to learn something about how to ride and take care of a horse, and he passed on what he had learned to Sonja. "The cowboys out west say it doesn't take brute strength to ride a horse. The trick is to respect your mount, talk to him."

"Talk to him? A horse?"

"Or her, if she's a mare. They never use 'it' in reference to a horse. A horse is a he or she. Learn his ways. Give him a little pat of appreciation once in a while. Respect his feelings. Don't use your spurs on him unless it's an emergency. Don't ride him too hard or yank a bit in his mouth for no good reason. And take care of him. See that he's properly fed and watered. And judging from my experience, they're right. A horse knows whether or not a rider gives a damn about his feelings."

Sonja grinned.

"The truth is we need horses more than they need us. There are herds of wild horses out west that are descended from mustangs that escaped the Spaniards. If you treat a horse like I've seen some people treated, they'll balk. A good horse is your friend and partner. He can sense when you're in trouble. If you treat him right, he'll give you everything he's got in an emergency."

When they were a couple of hours out of town, Jack pulled up in a meadow and dismounted.

Sonja looked around. "What?"

"You know how to shoot?"

"Shoot? No. Why should I?"

"Well it's time you learned. With Koslov on our tail, I might need some help somewhere down the line. I want you to be ready when the time comes. I don't know a whole lot about horses, I'll admit, but the truth is I've always had a knack for shooting. I don't know why that is, and I'm not bragging, mind, but I do know how to shoot."

"Teach me," she said, and dismounted also.

First, Jack taught her how to load the shotgun, the Colt pistols, the derringer, and the Sharps. He explained the firing mechanisms. He told her how her breathing could pull off her aim, especially at long range. He taught her some ways to control that. He taught her to hold her right wrist solid with her left hand when she was firing one of the big pistols. And he taught her how to use and adjust the peep sight on the Sharps so she could shoot at a distance if she had to.

Then he gave her some practice using tree trunks for targets. She was startled by how hard the pistols bucked in her hand, and the balls went every which way. The first time she fired the Sharps the recoil nearly knocked her on her rump.

Rubbing her shoulder, she said, "That was hard."

"Don't be afraid of it," Jack said. "If you're afraid, you'll likely flinch, and that'll pull off your aim."

"Hard not to be a little afraid," she said.

Jack grinned. "When your life's on the line, something amazing happens to your body. If you know what you have to do to survive, your body will do what you've trained it to do. You'll do what you've been taught to do under the circumstances. Given a choice between your life and somebody else's, his goes. Also, if you get into a jam, you should remember the motto of the Texas Rangers."

"Oh?"

" 'A little man will whip a big man every time if the little man's in the right and just keeps coming.' "

She gave him a disbelieving look. "Do you think that's true?"

Jack laughed. "Naw. It sounds good, I know. And the fact is, I don't even know if that's their motto. I heard it once in a mining camp from a drunk. The point is good. The little man can win only if he keeps trying. If we don't resist Koslov, he will certainly win."

FROM BAGODAT, JACK AND SONJA TRAVELED SOUTHEAST THROUGH a forest of large pine, birch, and larch, shortly thereafter entering a meadow of wildflowers in full bloom. They concluded that the Urals, after having given her father a splendid thunderstorm for a send-off, were now offering flowers in his memory. Enjoy, Mikhail Sankov had said. Enjoy they would.

The flowers here grew both singly and spread out in a splendor of color. Some meadows were covered with an abundance of pale pink, white, and crimson wild roses; others were carpeted with yellow, white, lilac, and blue anemones.

As the blossoms opened for the sun, so did their life together.

Although Jack and Sonja had been together less than two days, they appeared to be an amiable and complementary match. If they had reservations about the wisdom of such precipitate and unusual matchmaking by a dying man, they suppressed them in a euphoria of optimism and determination. Jack and Sonja, in the heady throes of newness, were at once romantic and realistic. Of course there would be difficulties between them.

Sonja was a quick learner, and turned out to be good on a horse. Jack had no doubt that she could keep up with hard travel, although there was no underestimating the difficulties that lay ahead—especially with

Koslov on their tail. They would have little opportunity to rest as long as they remained in the Urals. If they reached Asia still alive, perhaps they would have an opportunity to slow down and enjoy.

They traveled southeast along the bank of the Baransha River. They entered a thick forest, only to find their path blocked by a profusion of large boulders that had fallen from the steep sides of Mount Katchkanar, which rose high above their flank. They picked their way through the boulders, with overhanging branches nearly scraping them from their horses.

They rode into a dense wood, negotiating fallen rocks and passing among tree trunks with a thick canopy of foliage overhead nearly shutting out the light. They continued on through a dark and dismal forest.

They emerged to face a treacherous slope of rocks and were soon forced to dismount and lead their horses. Having successfully traversed the rocky slope, they descended into a small valley forested with large pines and Siberian cedars, under which beds of geranium and peony in full bloom grew atop a thick mossy turf. A small stream meandered through the center of the valley.

No sooner had they negotiated that obstacle than they came upon a sodden morass that Jack was slow to recognize.

Jack's horse sank up to the saddle flaps.

He grabbed a branch and pulled himself off the stricken horse.

Sonja, riding behind him, quickly pulled up. "Hold on! Hold on! Don't let go."

"I'm okay. See to the horse first."

Sonja tied her mount to a nearby tree.

Its eyes wild, the stricken horse struggled frantically in the muck.

"Quickly, Sonja. Quickly. Fasten your lariat to the horn of your saddle and I'll drop down by the horse."

"And do what?"

"Loop it under his withers to prevent him from sinking deeper."

Sonja did as she was told. Jack let go of the branch. His horse stopped sinking. He had at last found solid footing. Once the horse stopped sinking, it relaxed. A few minutes later, it scrambled out of the muck, eyes still wild.

Only when the horse was on solid ground did Sonja burst out laughing.

"You should see yourself, Jack. You look like you tumbled into the pit of an outhouse."

Jack looked down at himself. So he did. He felt wretched, but he was a sight to behold, it was true. "Next time, you get to ride first," he said. "I get to laugh."

Jack was miserable in his wet clothes but there was little he could do until they found a stream and a good place to camp. Finally they came upon a small lake and stopped. As they turned their horses loose to graze, Sonja set about washing his sodden clothes in a mountain stream. Jack used his line and a fly to try his luck at the grayling. In little over a half hour of twilight, the best time to fish, he caught nine beauties, enough for a supper for a half dozen people. They decided to boil the last of their potatoes for a truly grand supper. They would eat until they could eat no more, then sit by the fire and enjoy the moonlight and dream about China and junks and Asia.

As the sun slipped over the ridge, the mosquitoes began to hum. Fresh blood in quantity had happened their way, and the demonic little vampires were determined to make the most of it. Jack and Sonja quickly built a large fire, for the smoke as much as the warmth and to cook the fish. Their horses, tethered for the night, were likewise tormented by the mosquitoes and looked at Jack and Sonja with obvious longing in their big brown eyes. Jack and Sonja took pity on them and tied them closer to the fire, and soon the horses were unembarrassed competitors for the prized space in the smoke.

Jack squatted beside Sonja as she fried their fish in tallow.

She flipped the fish with a stick. "This is far too much for the two of us."

"If we kept the potatoes much longer, they'd go to sprout. What we don't eat, we'll leave to the bugs. No food goes to waste in a forest like this." Jack poured them each some elderberry *nalifka*. "To China and the far-flung clan of the Chans and the many aunts and uncles and cousins of Chan Bao's lovely daughter."

"To China," she said.

They drank. As they ate, the only thing they could see was the shadows and silhouettes set against the dim reflected light of the lake. They saw silhouettes that moved. Silhouettes with eyes that watched them.

"You see them, Jack?"

"I do." Jack grabbed his shotgun and gave it to her. "See, I told you it would be good for you to know how to shoot." He readied the caps on his Colt revolvers.

"Wolves," she said. "They're waiting for the fire to die down, then they'll make a dash for us."

Their horses knew the wolves were out there too. They became restless and uneasy, snorting and yanking at their tethers.

Jack said, "Don't shoot too early. You can't miss at close range with a shotgun. Just point and shoot and crank the cylinder."

The clouds rolled past the moon and stars, reflecting more light on the lake. They heard a howling in the distance.

Sonja said, "The word is out. That's another pack on the way."

The howling grew nearer. The wolves at the edge of the lake began growling. Jack and Sonja needed to keep the fire going, but they had only so much wood and didn't dare venture into the darkness. They added what wood they had, and the flames momentarily crackled and blazed.

They waited. The howling came nearer and nearer still. The wolves by the lake became more and more agitated.

Listening to this, their horses became more and more agitated.

Slowly the fire ebbed, turning to embers.

The horses began whinnying and yanking at their tethers.

The wolves were upon them in a dash. Jack and Sonja began firing at will. The corpse of one wolf slammed into him, nearly knocking him down. The remaining members of the wolfpack retreated into the darkness.

TWENTY-SIX

To Prepare a Proper Supper

No more howling. No more growling. The malevolent shadows by the lake disappeared. Jack and Sonja had killed three wolves, and they saw trails of blood leading into the night, evidence that they had wounded more. Sonja was clearly confused about something. "Did you encounter wolves when you were in California?"

He shook his head.

She said, "Hard to believe they would give up after one charge. That's not the stories I've heard. They had us outnumbered, which is why they attacked us in the first place. Now they should be regrouping. We should be hearing them yipping and yelping and calling out to one another."

Jack put his finger to his lips and turned his head, listening. "Total silence. You want to know why they're not yipping and yelping?"

She nodded.

He cleared his throat. "Maybe somebody is coming. A more formidable number than just us."

"We shouldn't ignore the possibility," she said.

He turned his head again, listening. A faint voice in the distance. "Hear that?"

"Yes, I did."

Quickly, Jack picked up their canvas bucket of water and doused the fire. It took a few moments for their eyes to adjust to the light of the moon; then, with Jack leading the way, he and Sonja circled through the forest, climbing a slight ridge as they did. Ten minutes later, they came upon an outcropping of rock that enabled them to look down on the valley leading to the meadow where they were camped.

They saw a file of mounted figures progressing slowly up the valley. The lead rider held a torch. Even in the pale light, his gray uniform was clear. He was riding point for the Wolfpack.

"It's them," Jack said softly. "Him."

"What do we do?"

Jack frowned. "If we run, we likely won't get far. Koslov will know from the signs of our fresh camp that he's closing in. Why take a chance on one of the Wolfpack horses breaking a leg in the darkness when they can easily run us to ground in the daytime? In the morning, when he can see us, he'll run us down."

They fell silent, watching the distant, lethal progression of the Wolfpack up the narrow valley.

"Ambush them?" Sonja asked.

Jack frowned. "Two against twenty. They're professional. We'd never last."

"I'd rather go down fighting than surrender. I will not yield to his sickness. No!"

Suddenly, Jack thought of something. "You ever eat almonds, Sonja?"

"Once, at a party in Brussels. They were good."

"Nice aroma."

Sonja looked puzzled. "So?"

Jack grabbed her by the hand. "Quickly, quickly, back to camp. Hurry!"

As they ran, she said, "What do you have in mind? What are you going to do?"

"Serve the Wolfpack a nice supper."

They half slid down a steep pitch, plunging through a thicket. "Run, run," he urged.

"Supper?" she yelled, breathing hard.

"You'll see. Don't stop. Faster, faster."

At length they arrived at their campfire, gasping for breath. Jack started digging into the saddlebags of the packhorse that carried his daguerreotype gear. "Quickly now. Get our gear packed while I finish supper for our guests. They'll be hungry when they get here."

Stashing their belongings in saddlebags as fast as she could, Sonja said, "Our guests? What are you talking about?"

"I don't want anybody saying that Jack Sandt is not a thoughtful and generous host. No sir, I am an American. We Americans are a hospitable people. Famous for it. We treat our guests right. Fried fish. Boiled potatoes. *Nalifka.* Such a fine supper it is. Hah, here it is!" He pulled a brown bottle from one of the saddlebags.

Watching him, still packing, Sonja said, "And that would be?"

"This would be potassium cyanide. I use it as part of a process to add extra silver to my daguerreotype plates."

"You mean cyanide, the poison?"

"Bad enough that I have to put up with the fumes when I work. I certainly wouldn't want to eat any." Jack grinned. "When the Wolfpack gets here, the food will still be warm. Koslov will know we're not far away. He'll conclude we're at his mercy. They've been riding hard. No time to stop for a decent meal. The fish are beautifully done. Why not camp here and enjoy a good supper prepared by his quarry? No rush."

Jack unscrewed the lid to the bottle, holding his face back to avoid the fumes. "Hoo, this stuff stinks. If I spike their food with enough to kill them, it will taste bitter, and they won't eat it. The trick is not to overdo it."

Sonja immediately understood what he was up to. "Add just enough to make them sick."

"There, you've got it. Koslov will get the best fish. He's the commander, after all. Nothing but the best for the commander. When he finishes that fish, it's gonna be a long, long night for him, guaranteed. No way in hell that Colonel Cut will feel like vomiting and riding at the same time. If he spends a couple of days puking, it will give us a chance to gain some time."

Sonja finished her chores and gave him a hug. "Oh, you resourceful, treacherous man. Quick thinking."

Jack gave her a brief kiss. "You like those qualities in a man?"

"Under the circumstances, I like them a lot."

He arched an eyebrow. "Husband material, you think?"

"Don't get carried away with yourself. We'll see."

"We'll leave them a spread they can't resist."

"We've got some black bread left and a jar of pickled mushrooms."

"Let's give them everything we've got. Make it look irresistible."

Sonja squatted by Jack as they tended to their chore of poisoning the supper. They experimented with one of the smaller fish first, gently lifting the crust of the skin to add a few carefully measured drops of potassium cyanide. By the time they got the largest fish, beautifully fried, they knew how to do it right. Working quickly, but carefully, they laid a beautiful, poisoned spread.

As he mounted his horse, Jack called out, "*Bon appétit,* Colonel Koslov." Jack and Sonja, grinning at their ploy, hoping fervently that it would work, rode off into the moonlight, leading their packhorses. They had survived another day. Life was grand!

TWENTY-SEVEN

The Baroness Hosts a Ball

THERE WAS NO SIGN OF THE WOLFPACK BEHIND them the next day. While Koslov and the gendarmes recovered from the poisoned supper, Jack and Sonja rode hard, extending their lead. They had not eaten for close to two days, having squandered the last of their food on poisoning the Wolfpack. At dusk, their stomachs growling, they came upon the picturesque Lake Chirtanish, which Jack's map told him was a few versts northwest of Maias, a gold- and silver-mining *zavod* on the Maias River. Maias, located at the foot of a mountain known as Ilman-tou, was what folks out west in the United States called a jumping-off place, meaning the leap from civilization into the unknown. This was the last settlement in the southern Urals.

As they rode on toward the *zavod*, Sonja told him that Lake Chirtanish was famous in the Urals for being a double lake.

"A double lake? What do you mean by that?"

"I mean a lake on top of a lake. Over the millennia, a mountain lake was covered by a thick matted mass of decaying vegetation, somewhat like peat. A second lake formed over the peat. Hence a double lake."

They arrived in town at dusk. Jack presented his papers to the youthful director of the *zavod*, an enthusiastic Russian about thirty years old wearing wire-rimmed spectacles and muttonchop whiskers. Once he had gotten used to the sight of a woman dressed in men's clothing, which they assured him was necessary for hard traveling, he gave them a lengthy dissertation on the many wonders of the area. He began with an explanation of the wonderful double lake, saying it was known throughout the world, and told them about the gold and silver mined there as well as the many gems—beryl, tourmaline, garnet, and topaz. All of these, he said, were sent to Yekaterinburg, where they were cut into gems by the craftsman at Granilnoi Fabric.

In addition to that, there was something else.

"The baroness Marya Borisovna is sponsoring a ball tonight and the two of you are invited."

Jack blinked. "A ball?"

He smiled. "We may be isolated here at Maias, but we observe the finer social customs. Most of us have never met anyone from America. We would be honored by your presence. No, more than that. We insist upon it."

" 'We'? If the baroness is sponsoring the ball, shouldn't she deliver the invitation?"

"No, no, no. I have full authority to extend the invitation, believe me."

Jack was uncertain.

"The lady is my mother," he said. "Believe me, she will be disappointed if you don't come."

"I see."

"Our officers and their ladies will be dressed in their finest. It is an event not to be refused, I assure you."

With an invitation like that, how could they refuse? There was one problem, however. Jack said, "My wife and I have no clothing appropriate for a ball. Also, we need to eat something before we do anything."

The director stepped back, eyeing Sonja. "I'll have some venison and boiled potatoes and a cabbage salad prepared for you immediately. Will that do?"

"That sounds wonderful," Jack said.

"As for the clothes, your lovely wife is about the same size as my niece. We'll find something for both of you. You will be my guest for the night. My wife and I have an extra bedroom."

Jack and Sonja were escorted to the director's house, where they were quickly provided with a lady's gown and gentleman's suit. Thus properly attired, they were taken to the baroness's residence, an elaborate mansion on the hill overlooking the settlement. The director had gone ahead to help his mother with final preparations, so they arrived alone, uncertain what to expect.

They were escorted into a large room where a most remarkable couple was receiving the guests.

The lady, presumably the baroness, who was about sixty years old, had outfitted herself in the costume of a girl of twenty. She wore a pink dress, matching pink gloves, and yellow shoes, but it was her jewelry that was most astonishing. A rope of purple glass beads with cut facets and a rope of green beads in the shape of drops were wound together and piled gaily on top of her head—the beads being of a type that might once have festooned a chandelier. A heavy red glass ornament dangled from a chain around her neck. She wore bracelets decorated with yellow glass that matched the glass that studded the tightly cinched girdle on the exterior of her dress.

The chest of the uniformed gentleman at her side was covered by the most bizarre collection of medals Jack had seen. There were so many medals with colorful ribbons of all the primary colors attached to his tunic as to render his torso seemingly impenetrable by musket ball.

The director of the *zavod* popped seemingly from nowhere to introduce them. "This is my mother, Baroness Marya Borisovna, and my father, General Yevgeny Pavlov. These are our guests, Mr. Jack Sandt and his wife, Sonja."

The aging face of the baroness was plastered with powders and paints of several hues of pink and red, rather as though they had been troweled on like a thin layer of colored mud.

Sonja curtsied and Jack bowed deeply and kissed the lady's hand.

The lady was thrilled. "We are very pleased to have a guest from the United States of America. Good for you to take your independence from the English."

Jack was relieved that there were guests behind them so that Sonja and he had an excuse to move on.

It was a most remarkable start to a ball in that the guests, once received by the baroness and her husband, retired immediately to adjoining rooms that were separated by sex. Perhaps twenty-five men occupied one room; close to thirty girls and women had gathered in the other. The women, dressed in brightly colored Chinese silks, looked like a bed of tulips. They were about as animated as tulips as well, for they sat mute, solemn flowers staring at the floor and ceiling as though awaiting the scythe. Meanwhile in the room next door, the men, many of them bedecked like Christmas trees with their many medals, knocked back large quantities of vodka and *nalifka*, growing louder by the minute. It was obvious they were talking and joking about the charms of the tulips next door, perhaps speculating on the night ahead. They didn't merely laugh, they guffawed, braying like inebriated donkeys, indifferent to the effect their raucous carrying-on was having on the poor women.

In short, the women waited nervously for the music and dancing to begin while the men bolstered their courage by getting drunk. Although each sex obviously craved the attentions of the other, their contrasting emotions were extraordinary. While this was a ball, a place for high spirits, one would have thought it was the eve of battle.

The baroness had assembled what Jack supposed was a form of chamber orchestra for the occasion. Having ascertained that all her guests had arrived, she raised her gloved hand, a signal that it was the time for the dancing to begin. The musicians, including three violinists, a cellist, and a gentleman on a harpsichord, began playing. Jack didn't think they were bad, but he hadn't heard a whole lot of music outside of fiddlers at a square dance.

The ladies immediately began licking their lips, clearing their throats, and smoothing the wrinkles from their dresses. Sighing, they smiled nervously and filed uncertainly into the larger room. The gentlemen, some of whom appeared nearly incapacitated by alcohol, lurched bravely into the chamber, ready to display their social graces.

The baroness had detailed a couple to break the proverbial ice by dancing a beautiful Russian dance representing the caprice of two lovers. The company watched politely and applauded lustily.

Following this, the baroness and a handsome, athletic young officer performed a spirited Cossack dance in which the remarkably clad lady, seemingly transformed, leaped around the room with astonishing grace, jumping and bounding with an energy one would have thought unimaginable. Jack was sure he wasn't the only spectator who wondered when the pile of beads on her head would topple onto the floor. But no, they stayed firmly in place. He thought she was surely courting a heart attack by such exertions, but when the dance was finished she seemed ready for more. Never mind that the baroness was living in an isolated outpost in the south of the Urals, that was no reason to endure a totally barbarous existence. If civilization was to be found in Europe rather than Siberia, she would bring civilization to Maias. This was a ball, time to dance.

This obviously wasn't the first ball to be held in Maias, and the party knew its cues. After the baroness and her partner had retired from the floor, the tulips suddenly began smiling, radiating joy, or at least masking their uncertainties and anxieties.

The inebriated gentlemen, determined in their mutual resolution to endure the trial ahead as one, rose to their feet, ready to proceed. They took to the floor, some perhaps more nimbly than others.

Thus encouraged by the Cossacks, Jack said, "Would you honor me with a dance, Miss Sankova?"

"I would be delighted, Mr. Sandt," she said. "I thought you'd never ask."

"I like the baroness's spirit," Jack said.

"So do I," Sonja said. "She will not yield to the coarseness. The music plays. Never mind the passing of her youth, the baroness Marya Borisovna dances!"

As Jack twirled her around the room to a graceful waltz, he whispered in her ear, "Pretend this ball is for us. The beautiful Sonja Sankova wishes to announce her engagement to the handsome American, Jack Sandt."

"Well, of course. Our own engagement ball in the southern Urals, complete with a chamber orchestra," she said. "Isn't it wonderful that life has such nice surprises?"

BOOK TWO

Ali

ONE

In the Chapel of Kamenskoi Zavod

A DEEP SADNESS OVERCAME JACK AND SONJA AS THEY took their last look at the crest of the Urals that was the border between Europe and Asia. Sonja felt sentimental because she had just laid her father's ashes down on Mount Bagodat, and it was there, at the festival, where Jack had gotten a chance to talk to her at last. Whether out of misguided emotion, madness, or the vicissitudes of the human imagination, Jack and Sonja had joined together in casting their fortunes to the wind. There was no turning back.

The southern Urals were formed of pine-clad hills, and wooded valleys lay ahead, and after that the vast steppe. As they looked over the vista, Sonja said, "We've only been together for days, but it seems like years have passed. I can't help but think what would have happened if you hadn't had the potassium cyanide."

"And it's hard for me to forget the baroness," Jack said. "She was telling us to live! Enjoy!"

"If I am to die, I——" Sonja stopped.

"Go ahead, finish," he said.

"If I am to die out here on the run for what I did in St. Petersburg, I want it to be . . . I want it to be as your wife. I don't want to——" Again, she halted.

"You don't want to die alone. Already, I can read your mind. I feel the same way," he said. "We can marry now and save our wedding night until later. I have no problem with that."

She gave him a lopsided grin. "Is that an official proposal then? Are you asking me to marry you?"

He laughed. "If you will say yes, it is exactly that. If you will say no, then it isn't a proposal. I'll save it for later."

"My answer is yes, without hesitation or reservation. I'm so much in love with you, I can hardly stay in my saddle." Having said that, Sonja looked embarrassed.

"Oh, you provocative little thing, you. It's going to be a long, long time to our wedding night." He groaned.

Sonja liked that. "Control yourself."

"Let's go find ourselves a priest." Jack put the horses at a gallop.

Ninety-one versts later they arrived at Kamenskoi Zavod at a little after noon and quickly found the residence of the director, a burly man with bushy eyebrows and wearing thick spectacles. The crown had given the director of the *zavod* civil and religious duties including the administration of justice, the signing of birth and death certificates, and performing civil marriage ceremonies.

The director was happy to meet an American and his intended bride. "Yes, of course we have an Eastern Orthodox chapel, for this is a pious and God-fearing community. Our chapel is small, but surely one of the most beautiful in this part of Russia." He was obviously curious about why Jack and Sonja would want to complete their union in such an isolated part of the world, but beyond an initial furrowed brow, he said nothing.

His wife, a plump, matronly woman with a happy countenance, seemed to find nothing remarkable about the circumstances of their arrival and request to be married. A marriage between an American journalist and a Russian girl at Kamenskoi Zavod! Life was never so coarse as to exclude love and commitment. She was thrilled. Even Jack's papers excited her. Officials and magistrates of the empire were enjoined by the Tsar to assist him in every way possible. Jack had been to St. Petersburg. He had been to Moscow. The lady could tell by Sonja's polish and her easy movement from Russian to English that she was educated. She would have been shocked to learn that Sonja's father was a liberated serf.

She was filled with excited chatter as she gave instructions to her servants to set a table for her guests. The director and his wife and Jack and Sonja enjoyed a meal of roast grouse and boiled potatoes before the marriage ceremony.

Jack had been raised Roman Catholic, but in a casual way. His mother regarded the Bible as a form of inspired literature, not as literal truth. She said some of the great novels and poetry of the Western world were based on stories from the Bible. And she taught him never to look down on other religions or scorn them. There was no point to judging religions. In the end, who really knew?

Despite her interest in Asian philosophies and religions, Sonja was officially Eastern Orthodox by faith. Both Jack and Sonja signed papers attesting to their date and place of birth and their citizenship, and that they were free to marry.

They were surprised and pleased by the elaborate gilded interior of the tiny chapel. Gold, gold, gold. Everything was covered in gold—delicately fashioned angels, cupids, and saints, and the arched ceiling that rose to God's heaven. They were to take their wedding vows at the foot of a suffering gilded Christ on the cross, a splendidly executed piece of religious art. Yes, Kamenskoi Zavod was isolated and out of the way, but what a lovely place to be married. No majestic cathedral was more holy or sacred than this intimate little chapel.

The director and his wife insisted on donating cheap rings for the couple. The marriage ceremony was quick and to the point, ending with the usual questions of both man and woman.

"Will you take Sonja for your wife, Jack Sandt?" the priest asked in Russian.

"Yes, I will," Jack said. "I love her dearly." His mouth was dry. His heart was thumping. He was in love. He could hardly believe this courageous little beauty was to become his wife.

"Will you take Jack Sandt for your husband, Sonja Sankova?"

"Yes, I will," she said softly, and squeezed his hand. "I want to spend the rest of my life with him."

It was done. After the briefest courtship on the run from Colonel Cut, Jack and Sonja were man and wife.

The marriage finished, Jack showed the director and his servant how to operate the daguerreotype. Jack and Sonja posed for one daguerreotype at the sweet little chapel where they had been married. The bride held a bouquet of wildflowers.

Jack and Sonja bought a carriage from the director. With a carriage, they could take turns sleeping while they pushed forward; there would be no rest for the gendarmes pursuing them on horseback. Jack and Sonja spent another hour in the company of their hosts, and, having received their blessing, they left in their carriage. It was dark; Jack put the horses at a gallop.

As he did, he said, "I will do my best to be a good husband, Mrs. Sandt."

"We did the right thing. We will be good together," she said.

They descended a steep hill in the blackness and crossed an aged bridge over the Kamen River, hooves clattering against the wood, the rumble of the wheels echoing up from the water. Once on the other side, they ascended a similar steep hill, and traveled to the next station, nineteen versts distant, in an hour.

Never mind their strange courtship, they were in love, and now they were Mr. and Mrs. Jack Sandt. They leaned against one another as they fled the Wolfpack. They wanted one another passionately, but the question of when they would get an opportunity to consummate their marriage went unspoken. Neither wanted an awkward, fumbling union in their carriage, or a hurried, coarse coming together on the ground, exhausted, with buzzing bugs and the hooves of Wolfpack horses thundering in the distance.

They had stood before God and proclaimed their commitment as man and wife. To properly complete their state of marriage, they wanted the simple pleasure granted other newlyweds: rest, quiet, a proper bed, and the freedom to dream and plan their lives in peace. For now that would have to wait. Their immediate goal was survival.

They pulled into another station, where they had fresh horses yoked, and were on their way again, newlyweds, big dreamers.

TWO

The Bells of Terra Incognita

THE ROAD WAS NARROW AND IT WOULD HAVE BEEN
dangerous were it not for the bells fastened to the horses
to alert travelers of oncoming carriages. Some carriages
had a bell for each horse. Others had three bells attached
to the lead horse. The resulting clamor was a familiar sound in Siberia,
and at times, late at night and in a dark forest, it was a lonely and melan-
choly ringing. *Hear us. We too are out here in the loneliness and isolation
of terra incognita.*

A few minutes after they changed horses, they heard approaching
bells and were quickly confronted with a carriage traveling in the opposite direction. The driver, wanting to beg, cut in front of them in attempt
to block their way. Jack pushed around the other's horses without a word
and continued on. It took another hour and a half to the next station,
where they changed horses once again. Their new horses were not large,
but were sturdy and well fed, with long, flowing manes and tails.

When the sun began to rise, they could see mists rising over the Issetz
River in the distance. When the sun was well above the horizon, there
stretched before them the vast, awesome plain that was Siberia. The
morning was crisp and invigorating. They traveled first along the high
bank of the Issetz then onto the plain, where farmers were in the fields
tossing freshly cut hay about. There were no fences in the fields. Every village had a ring fence of posts and rails around it, enclosing a tract of land

seven or eight versts in diameter, with a watchman assigned to watch the gate on the road. Within this ring, all the cattle and horses of the village as well as pigs, ducks, and geese were turned out to graze and feed. Each peasant had his own small plot of corn.

They pulled into another station, where Jack showed his papers. They were immediately given fresh horses and were on their way through fields of hay and seed crops, their bells ringing, wheels rattling, and the sun rising high over their heads.

About an hour and a half later they saw the graceful domes and towers of the great Monastery of St. Dolomete at the village of Dolomatou, once a town of importance, now fallen into decay, most of its buildings abandoned. The monastery stood on a rise above the left bank of the Issetz River, near its junction with the Techa River, entering from the south. The walls surrounding the monastery had beautiful towers at the corners, giving it the appearance of the Kremlin. At the eastern end of the enclosure, the grand church rose with a fairy-like lightness to its parts.

Jack and Sonja walked around the walls, finally entering through a large portal, where a kindly monk met them. Peering out from the shadows of his hood, he said, "Good morning, I am Brother Dominic."

Jack introduced himself and his wife.

Doing his best to suppress his interest in Sonja, the monk said, "Won't you come and have breakfast with us?"

Jack glanced at Sonja.

"We would be pleased," Sonja said.

As they started inside, Dominic held back momentarily, the better to admire Sonja's behind moving this way and that in her men's trousers. Noting that Jack had caught him at it, Dominic said mildly, "Forgive me, Mr. Sandt. We serve our God, but we remain men after all. Our pleasures are limited in such isolation."

"I bet they are."

"You have a beautiful wife."

"Yes, she is," Jack said, catching Sonja's eye. "I'm very proud of her."

"We rarely see women," Dominic said.

They were seated at a large, crude wooden table in a great hall. They were joined by eight other monks, who were apparently subordinate to Dominic. A very young monk, a novice hardly in his teens, served them black bread, salt, and tea. Only Dominic spoke. The others, possibly under a vow of silence, remained mute. They were hardly able to keep their eyes off Sonja.

Breaking his ration of bread with his hands, Dominic said, "Tell me, why is it that an American and his beautiful wife have strayed into our path, so far away from the amenities of Europe? One would suppose you two would be living in Moscow or St. Petersburg."

The question had been directed at Jack, but he was uncertain of the best answer.

Sonja said, "We are fleeing for our lives, Brother Dominic."

Dominic cocked his head. "Oh?"

"From Colonel Peter Koslov and the Wolfpack. They are behind us at this very hour."

"The gentleman with the necklace of human ears?"

Sonja nodded.

"I see." Dominic took a sip of tea. "You're not the woman who, if you will pardon my directness, knocked Peter Koslov on his arrogant ass?"

Sonja grinned, but said nothing.

Dominic was pleased. "You are among friends." He looked at his silent colleagues. "Am I right?" They nodded their heads in agreement.

After breakfast, Dominic took them to one of the towers to view the vast expanse. Using his Dutch telescope, Jack was able to make out the tiny figures of men on horseback riding hard in their direction, the capes of their crimson tunics flapping in the breeze.

He gave the telescope to Dominic. Upon focusing on the Wolfpack, Dominic said, "Go quickly. We will delay them. We are monks. To refuse our hospitality would be to spit in the face of God. Very bad luck for Colonel Koslov."

As Jack and Sonja climbed into their carriage, Sonja said, "We are in your debt, Brother Dominic."

"No, no, Mrs. Sandt. It is our duty. As men of God, we are in a great struggle against evil. Colonel Koslov is of Satan sent. We resist his kind. Go now with our best wishes and prayers."

THREE

The Issetz, the Ishim, and the Steppe

WITH KOSLOV IN CLOSE PURSUIT, JACK AND SONJA proceeded from station to station. Nobody in these stations was so foolish as to lie or mislead Colonel Cut, so he would know when they had arrived and when they had left the last station. But which could cover the most ground, twenty-five men on horseback riding without sleep, or one carriage that could travel day and night, its two passengers getting periodic rest? They were in front of Koslov, and Jack had papers with the seal and signature of the Tsar commanding all cooperation. In practice this meant they could change horses at each station.

No station had twenty-five fresh horses for Peter Koslov and his men. If Koslov pushed his horses too hard, they would drop from exhaustion. He could do as he pleased, swear in a rage, cut the ears from everybody who got in his way, shoot people, but the facts remained. In time he would either rest his horses or walk back in defeat. Koslov's other alternative would be to commandeer three or four horses at a single station, one for him and two or three companions. In that case, thanks to the inventive Mr. Sharp, Jack had a way of leveling the contest. His .50-caliber breech-loading rifle was equipped with a peep sight that could be raised or lowered to account for distance. Koslov and his men carried muzzle-loading weapons. Jack could load and fire six or eight rounds of linen cartridges detonated by the efficient Maynard strip to each shot in reply.

Fired from a safe remove afforded by the large caliber, that was a distinct advantage.

For the moment, Jack and Sonja traveled as hard as they could, day and night, hoping their lead was growing larger. They took turns driving the horses and sleeping. It was the duty of the person not driving to keep an eye to the rear using the telescope.

They soon left the Issetz and entered the shade of a deep, thick stand of larch, pine, birch, and poplar. After twenty versts of cool shade they once again were in a deep valley. Then, about eight versts in front of them, they saw spires and domes, and as they draw closer they saw white buildings and the green domes of churches with their golden crosses shining in the sun. This was Shadrinskoi, famous for its vodka and looking prosperous.

On entering Shadrinskoi, they proceeded immediately to the post office, where there was a sign saying they were 2,591 versts from St. Petersburg. Jack presented his papers so he could proceed to the next town, after which he and Sonja took a quick trip to the large market where they bought eggs, salt, flour, lard, soda, tea, pickled mushrooms, potatoes, and cured meat. Their provisions on hand, they were again on the road, which swung back in the direction of the Issetz. They reached the river late in the afternoon. It was now a broad stream that meandered through pastures.

They soon came upon a party of ninety-eight chained convicts, or *zeks*, marching to their banishment. Mounted Cossacks rode in front and on either side of the caravan, watching over their charges. They stopped long enough to learn that the lead group of sixteen men and eight women—all chained as one—were on their way to Nertchinsk in eastern Siberia, a journey of more than four thousand versts, an eight-month march. The remaining convicts, chained in pairs, were on their way to Irkutsk, six months and three thousand versts distant. Behind them a caravan of six wagons pulled their baggage. They counted a dozen women on these wagons and were told these were wives following their husbands into exile.

A party of *zeks* left Yekaterinburg every Monday morning. They marched two days, covering from twenty to thirty versts a day, resting one day in the barracks at each station, usually just outside the village. The stockade wall was made of trees about a foot in diameter, about fifteen feet tall, and sharpened at the top. The prisoners slept in log huts in the center. A single word in reply to a blow from a brutal master was all it took to send a peasant on this long trip into exile. This vast network of stockades, or gulags, was strung along all major routes in Siberia.

Sonja said there were stories of convicts who spent decades in torturous exile, only to return toothless, broken, and mentally crippled. Some were forgotten because their records were lost. Others had nobody to inquire about their safety or location.

Jack and Sonja proceeded through monotonous country, passing a dozen stations before arriving at Bezroukova, and continuing on to Ishim on the sandy, sterile Steppe of Ishim, which was dotted with salt lakes. This was part of the larger Kyrgyz Steppe, guarded by a line of Cossack posts and forts.

They crossed the Ishim River by ferry, then passed a large, mist-covered lake at Kroutoia. After Toukalinsk they arrived at Beokichevo station at dawn and turned northeast to the valley of the Irtiseh, where the sandy plain gave way to good pastures amid stands of birch and poplar.

Later that morning, they reached the station called Chornoye Ozero, or Black Lake, entering the broad valley of the Irtysh River, in places ten to fifteen versts wide, the eastern bank rising more than a hundred feet above the water.

Here on the high bank, looking back, they spotted the Wolfpack behind them again, distant figures riding hard in dogged pursuit. The monks of the Monastery of St. Dolomete and other haters of the crown at stations along the way had done whatever they could to delay Colonel Cut, but he was determined to have his way.

Stopping at several filthy stations run by lethargic, vaguely malevolent convicts, Jack and Sonja followed the river downstream past hundreds of cattle grazing on the banks. They passed Serebrenaia. At Ponstink station, the road veered away from the Irtysh.

They fled. The Wolfpack chased, seemingly as inexorable as time and tide. How much longer could Jack and Sonja stay in front of Colonel Cut? The question, unanswered, was with them always as they fled, both exhausted from a lack of proper sleep.

FOUR

Action in the Swamp of Gorki Ozera

 AFTER JACK AND SONJA PASSED THROUGH KIANSK,
a town inhabited by exiled Polish Jews, they entered undulating country dotted by lakes and swamps and broken
by stands of birch and aspen and great tangles of underbrush. White and yellow nymphaea grew along the shores of the lakes.
They crossed vast carpets of wildflowers; near the villages cattle grazed
amid geraniums, large clumps of crimson dianthus, pale blue and deep
blue delphinium, and scattered red peonies and purple crocuses.

When they entered the Barabinsky Steppe, the landscape suddenly
changed. Gentle hills topped by stands of large timber circled extensive
plains like the boundaries of an immense park. Late in the afternoon
they circled Gorki Ozera, or Bitter Lake, which had thousands of geese,
ducks, and divers swimming on its surface.

The alarmed fowl rose as one from the lake, some of them heading
directly for them. Sonja had the shotgun. She carried it loaded.

"Do it, Sonja!" Jack yelled.

"Do what?"

"Cock your shotgun. Quick, quick."

The first flight veered to one side.

Quickly, Sonja removed the shotgun from its scabbard and cocked it.

"If you're close enough to see detail, aim at the duck's body. If it's
farther away, shoot in front of it."

"In front?"

"Swing the barrel in the direction the duck is flying and pull the trigger."

Steady streams of fowl were leaving the water.

She had the shotgun ready.

"Wait, wait."

A second huge flight of ducks was coming their way about twenty yards high. If they didn't veer as the first had, they would pass directly overhead.

Suddenly the sky above them was covered with fleeing ducks, thousands of them.

"Now!" Jack yelled.

She swung the muzzle skyward and pulled the trigger. The recoil nearly knocked her off her horse, but she was a fast learner. Two Asian black ducks tumbled from the sky and bounced to a rest on the ground.

Sonja was delighted. "Two at once. Yes!"

With the ducks on board the *tarantass* they ascended a hill at the far side of Gorki Ozera. It was then that Sonja, using the telescope to survey the road behind them, suddenly stiffened.

"What is it?" Jack asked.

"Six men riding hard."

"Koslov?"

"It's impossible to tell."

Jack felt a flutter in his stomach, and he knew Sonja was worried too. They pushed on with as much speed as they could muster from their tiring horses. They reached the next station at dusk, with dark clouds gathering on the horizon. They were told there were swamps ahead and a storm was brewing; they should wait until daylight. The explanation for the many swamps was straightforward. It got so cold in the middle of this vast continent that the ground froze solid, not thawing until late in the summer. The horrific thunderstorms in the Siberian spring dumped too much water on the ground for the earth to accept because of the ice just under the surface. Farther north the ground never thawed. The swamps were difficult enough to cross when a traveler could see. At night and in a storm, they were nearly impossible.

"What do we do?" Jack asked Sonja.

"We have no choice. Go forward," she said.

"I agree," he said.

Nobody at the station at Gorki Ozera wanted to risk a worse form of exile by refusing to help an American bearing papers from the Tsar. Jack obtained an extra horse, making seven in all, and hired the help of two men and a teenage boy with ropes to help them negotiate the swamp. Since they had claimed the last fresh horses at that station, if they could make it through the night, they had a chance of regaining their lead.

The first three versts after the station were on firm ground, but then Jack and Sonja entered a thick wood with swampy ground and high reeds and bulrushes surrounded them on either side. Ahead of them the road, literally floating on liquid mud, rose and fell in waves.

Just as it began to rain, the *tarantass* sunk up to its axle. As the workers unfastened the horses, Jack and Sonja could think only of the six riders gaining on them. The workers threw boughs under the hooves of the horses to give them some footing, then pulled them, struggling, from the muck. Once they got the horses on solid ground they attached ropes to the *tarantass* and pulled it slowly up and out of the soupy mud.

In ten minutes that seemed like ten hours, they were out of the trap and on solid ground again, riding hard through a driving rain.

The horses immediately plunged into another patch of mire and sank as before, up to their bellies in mud. Sonja was at the reins, and before she could react, the *tarantass* joined the horses in the muck. Above them lightning popped and thunder rolled through the heavens. The Russians, shouting at one another, again unhitched the horses. The boy mounted one of the lead horses, lashing its head with a strap, but the poor animal, wild-eyed from the storm and the painful beating, was unable to move.

Jack and Sonja heard horses approaching from behind in the darkness.

"To the other side," he yelled above the popping and cracking of thunder.

She understood. They abandoned the *tarantass* and waded across the impasse, waist deep in mud, keeping their weapons above their heads.

The Russians ignored them, concentrating on extricating the stricken horses and the *tarantass*.

Jack and Sonja waited for the riders.

Their helpers urged the horses slowly, slowly from the mud. Each second seemed like an hour.

The riders drew closer.

"Quick, quick, yoke the horses," Sonja called softly to the Russians.

Uncomprehending, they set about their chore.

"Faster," she murmured, the urgency mounting in her voice.

They listened for the riders. Closer they came.

"Is it them?" Jack said softly.

They heard a man shout an order.

"That's him," she said with a hint of resignation. To the Russians she whispered harshly, "Hide the *tarantass*. Hide the *tarantass*. Get back! Get back!"

Jack understood her logic. Here they would make their stand. They had no other choice but to use their momentary advantage.

The two men and the boy did as they were told. If they had reservations, they said nothing, but they had no idea one of the riders was the storied Peter Koslov.

The rain began to come in earnest.

Jack and Sonja waited in the shadows of the underbrush.

Koslov was suddenly upon them.

Lightning flashed, revealing crimson tunics. Thunder cracked overhead.

Colonel Cut and his men plunged blindly into the mire. Surprised, swearing, but having negotiated such swamps before, they urged their horses forward.

Another bolt of lightning lit the ground.

As the lightning flickered overhead, Koslov and his men struggled in the swamp directly in front of Jack and Sonja.

"*Da!*" Jack called.

Sonja fired the .30-gauge shotgun, the recoil rocking her shoulder. She cranked the lever, turning the cylinder, and fired again.

Jack fired a round from the Sharps at a man whose horse rose from the murk just as he pulled the trigger. The gendarme toppled from his mount. Jack grabbed a Colt revolver. Holding one revolver in his right hand, cocking the hammer with his left, he fired six shots, aiming at the torsos of the surprised figures atop the floundering horses. When that revolver was empty, he picked up the other pistol and continued shooting until it was empty.

A bolt of lightning popped directly overhead, and there, standing directly in front of Jack, was Peter Koslov.

"You!" Koslov yelled.

Jack fumbled for his .44-caliber derringer.

As he raised the muzzle, Koslov disappeared. Jack saw only a foot sticking above the horse's back and shot at that. Koslov screamed, and only then did Jack realize that, seeing the pistol, the athletic Koslov, experienced in battle, had dropped down on the far side of his horse, using the beast for protection.

All was confusion. Riderless horses whinnied and flailed about. "Let's go!" Jack called. He thought he had hit Koslov's foot, but wasn't sure.

Jack and Sonja scrambled aboard the *tarantass*. Jack grabbed the reins and slapped a handful of rubles into the hand of one of the Russians, hoping he would not suffer for being innocently involved in the ambush, and they pushed off, leaving Koslov and his soldiers behind floundering in the mud and the blood.

"Good work!" Jack yelled.

"Did you see him?" she asked.

"I think I might have hit him in the foot or ankle with my derringer. He saw me about to shoot and dropped behind the body of his horse. He knows who shot him. He likely won't fancy getting shot with a forty-four-caliber ball at two feet away."

"'Likely'?" Sonja laughed. "My darling husband, you have no idea how he will react. Here is a man whose chief pleasure is torturing serfs. If Colonel Cut catches us, he'll take more than our ears."

Jack and Sonja encountered no more swamps that night. Eventually the storm abated. At dawn they changed horses at another station and continued on their way. For the moment, at least, they had put some distance between their tormentor and them.

FIVE

The Man Who Would Be Khan

AT KRONTIKHA, JACK AND SONJA HAD A MAGNIFI-cent view of the Ob River, a broad mirror reflecting the late-morning sun. The Ob wound in gentle curves from one side of the great valley to the other. The river, 12 to 15 versts wide, was dotted with innumerable islands and was braided into a web of smaller streams that ran between the islands. About 150 versts to the northeast lay Kolyvan, the seat of government before it was transferred to Tomsk, a like distance farther on. Above the high banks of the Ob, a pine-covered plain stretched into the distance as far as the eye could see.

They crossed the Ob on a ferry, an adventure in itself. Muscular young men pulled the ferry along ropes stretched from shore to shore of the smaller streams that made up the larger river. Thus they progressed slowly, from island to island, until they had made it to the far side of the valley. On the other side they turned south, passing through low-lying farmland that had recently been flooded. They came upon Sousounskoi Zavod, a copper-smelting works belonging to the crown. They traveled through thick pine forests that night. The next morning they passed by Pavlovsky Zavod, an abandoned silver mine. The mountains of the Altai were somewhere ahead of them, but they couldn't see them.

Still surrounded by pine forests, they traveled through versts of deep, soft sand, which meant hard work for their overworked horses. Innu-merable small, sandy ravines led down to the Ob, and it soon became evident that they were nearing the steppes that extended to the west from the Ob to the Irtysh—an area inhabited by the Kyrgyz before the Cossacks drove them deeper into Asia. The Cossacks defended their territory with a line of forts from Omsk along the Irtysh to the Bouchtarma River, 2,500 versts distant.

The pine forests thinned, then disappeared entirely. They passed by several monotonous stations. Dreary plains stretched out in every direction. The only trees were found along the watercourses.

Late in the afternoon, they saw an almost mystical, spiritual sight: the misty Altai rose directly in front of them, both awesome and somehow unexpected. As the sun set, they changed horses at another station and continued traveling through the night.

In the morning they came upon the first ridges of the Altai, which extended down onto the plain. They crossed these foothills and returned to the plain until they came upon Kolyvan Lake, lying beneath dark mountains with broken, rugged tops. As they passed along the shore of the lake, shining under the reflected sun, they encountered extraordinary granite forms that had apparently been formed by liquid rock forced up from the bowels of the earth to cool, then forced up again to cool once more, so that it looked like molten metal frozen solid. These huge granite obelisks resembled the buildings of an abandoned city. As they continued around the lake, they saw rocks in the shape of ruined castles and huge towers and rocks that look like gigantic human heads and twisted, snarling beasts straight from a nightmare.

With the lake and the miraculous granite forms behind them, they stopped to water their horses in a small stream at the bottom of a ravine. Suddenly, they heard the clatter of hooves, an ominous sound in a place so isolated. Before they could withdraw their weapons from the *tarantass* they were set upon by a group of horsemen, twenty fierce-looking Asians bearing muskets and swords. They were dark skinned and brown eyed, and had large noses. They aimed their muskets directly at Jack and Sonja.

THE LEADER, A FIERCE-LOOKING MAN WITH HIS HEAD WRAPPED IN a kind of turban, said in broken but acceptable Russian, "My name is Ali. I am Kyrgyz. In the hadith, it is told that the prophet Muhammad promised his followers that one day there would come the Mahdi, the Expected One, to deliver his people from oppression. The Expected One is me, Ali, named for the prophet's brother. It is my destiny to one day drive the Kalmyk all the way to China and the Tsar's Cossacks all the way to the Urals."

He paused, Jack assumed, to give them time to be properly impressed. He pointed at Sonja and said, "And you, pretty lady, are Sonja Sankova. Dressed like a boy! Such a costume."

Sonja glanced at Jack with fear racing through her eyes.

Ali pointed at Jack. "And you are the American, Jack Sandt."

Jack said nothing. Ali had the upper hand. He knew who Sonja was. He knew who Jack was. Let him talk if he wanted.

Ali smiled. "They're saying Colonel Peter Koslov and his men recently encountered some trouble in a swamp in the middle of the night. In a terrible storm as it happened. This was near Gorki Ozera."

Jack glanced at Sonja.

Ali said, "The two of you ambushed them while they struggled in the swamp a few feet in front of you. You wonder how I know all this? The three men who were your guides had their ears removed for their effort on your behalf."

"My God!" Jack said.

Sonja paled.

"You killed four of his men and crippled another."

"And Koslov?"

Ali tapped his ankle. "You got him here, Mr. Sandt. With a pistol. Shattered the bone beyond repair. He saw you clearly. He had met you earlier, he claims."

"In Yekaterinburg," Jack said.

"Now he has two assaults to avenge, getting knocked to his knees in front of the Tsar and getting his ankle destroyed in a swamp. He also took pellets here. From the lady's shotgun." He ran his fingers down his ribs to indicate where Koslov had been hit. "Each of the pellets had to be dug out with a knife. His left ankle will be forever stiff. He's lucky he still has his foot. I know all this from relatives of the doctor who treated him. Word passes fast in the Steppe. There are few secrets."

A .44-caliber round at close range. No wonder Koslov almost lost his foot.

"My cousin was one of Koslov's many victims. For the crime of disrespect, Koslov blinded him, then rode off, leaving him alone on the steppe, where he wandered until he starved to death. That, my friend, was a mistake of consequence. I am an honorable man. What Colonel Cut does to my cousin he does to me." Ali cocked his head, inspecting Sonja. "I like that fair skin and delicate body. Very nice eyes. You need to let your hair grow." He looked back at Jack. "When Koslov's ankle heals enough for him to ride, he'll resume his hunt for your pretty wife, Mr. Sandt. All Russia knows what she did to him at the Christmas party. If the stories are true, he has vowed to remove her ears. He will not rest until all Russia knows he avenged his embarrassment. When he does, he'll have to deal with me." He thumped himself on his chest.

"I see," Jack said. He glanced at Sonja, then back at Ali. "Then what?"

"Then my friends and I will make the gentleman scream for a fortnight. He loves cruelty. He likes the knife. He enjoys torture." Ali smiled. "Colonel Cut knows nothing about torture. He just thinks he does. He is an idiot. He will curse his mother's eyes before we're finished with him. His screams will make the devil cringe. They will make the animals have nightmares in the Urals and the Altai. The Tsar will hear him in St. Petersburg. The Russians need to learn that the Altai and the Kyrgyz Steppe belong to us, not them. No amount of Cossacks or gendarmes will convince us otherwise."

Jack started to speak, but Ali held up his hand, silencing him. "I am told you take images with a machine. You are working for a newspaper in America."

Jack said, "Yes. I'm on assignment for the *New York Tribune.*"

Ali's black eyes bore into Jack. "Assignment? Assignment to do what?"

"To take daguerreotype images of what I see in the Urals, the steppes, and Siberia and write a series of articles for my paper telling what I found. The *Tribune*'s artists will use the images for their drawings."

"For the *New York Tribune*?"

"That's the name of the paper, yes."

"Could you also sell articles to newspapers in London?"

"I hope to."

"And Paris?"

"There too," Jack said.

"Will you succeed?"

"I think so. All of Europe has heard exotic stories about what's out here. People are curious."

"What if you were to write an article about the greatest warrior and conqueror since Ghengis Khan? Would your editor like that?"

"Mr. Greeley would like that very much indeed. Everybody would like to read that story."

Ali laughed, showing white teeth. "You are a very lucky man to be who you are, Mr. Sandt. Otherwise you would already have been dead. You are to take my image for the newspaper artists. I wish to be portrayed on my horse and carrying a Kyrgyz battle-ax."

"If you sit on the horse, there will be movement, which will blur the image. You can pose with the battle-ax, however. That would work."

"Then I will pose. You are to write an article telling the world how the Expected One has arrived in the Altai to liberate the Kyrgyz people from the oppression of the Tsar."

Ah, so Jack did have some bargaining power after all. Count Chermerkov wasn't the only one with an ego. "I could do that, but I won't unless I get my wife back. I'll capture your image and write the article in exchange for my wife."

Ali thought a moment. "Plus similar articles in newspapers in London and Paris as well. I will tell you what to say. If you deviate by one word, your wife dies." He gave his horse a pat on the neck.

"I will have to get to Sevastopol, then book passage to London and on to New York. All that will take months."

Ali grinned. "Months? So? I have plenty of time. It's you who will be in a hurry, Mr. Sandt. I have your wife, and there's nothing you can do about it until you please me. I will require fifty copies of the published newspapers containing a drawing of me and the article. The article will not ridicule me. It will not malign me. It will not belittle me. It will not disparage or otherwise displease me. Otherwise, I will keep your wife and kill you or kill you both depending on my mood at the time." He watched Jack. "You have a choice. You can die now and I ride off with your wife, or you can agree to introduce the world to Ali, the Expected One, and one day I will give you back your wife, and you can produce babies as stupid as you have been for delivering yourselves into my hands. I am an honorable man. I keep my word."

Jack didn't have much choice. "Agreed. I'll have to unpack my gear."

"Get what you need."

Jack started digging for his camera.

Ali dismounted and put his foot on a rock, arched his back, looking into the distance. "I wish to be portrayed like this, the fierce, brave Mahdi with his faithful men behind him. A heroic kind of pose."

"Got it," Jack said.

Ali tilted his head and squinted his eyes, which made him look more like he was trying to pass gas than like any kind of conquering hero.

Ali said, "When you finish, I will tell you what the story will say. You will record it on paper."

ALI, HOLDING THE PLATE BY THE EDGES AS HE HAD BEEN TOLD, WAS pleased with how he looked on the daguerreotype, in which he stood stiffly, gazing into the distance. "Very good, Mr. Sandt! What a wonderful machine!" He showed the daguerreotype to his followers, who beamed with enthusiasm.

To Jack, the dag made Ali look like a totally preposterous egoist. Having packed the other image in its protective box, Jack readied his pencil and notebook.

Ali, seeing he was ready, said, "I am to be known as the Kyrgyz leader, born in a yurt in the most modest of *aouls*, who rose from being a simple shepherd to fulfill the promise of the prophet Muhammad and unite his people in the face of the barbarous Tsar Nicholas I. I am the sworn enemy of all those who abuse and mistreat the people. I am kind and generous. I share with my people. They worship me. They will do anything for me. Out of the generosity of their heart and their great love for me, they give me horses and camels and sheep and cows that I require to feed my army. When my army has grown to sufficient strength, I will drive the Russians back to the Urals, and if it pleases me, perhaps even farther, to Moscow perhaps or even St. Petersburg, where I will liberate the Russian people and join the councils of world powers."

Jack pretended to be scribbling madly, bent on capturing every phrase and nuance.

Ali paused so that Jack might catch up.

"Got it," Jack said.

"My mother was known to be one of the most beautiful women on the Kyrgyz Steppe. My father was a brave and wise man. Russians murdered them both, and I have vowed to avenge their deaths. I first used a battle-ax at age six when I fought off a band of renegade Kalmyk who had invaded our *aoul* bent on stealing our cattle. I was just a boy with no hair on my balls, yet I still killed sixteen Kalmyk. All Kalmyk avoided our *aoul* from that day forward. I was just eighteen years old when a band of Kyrgyz warriors who had noticed my intelligence and leadership and skill in battle stepped forward and asked me to lead them out of their bondage. Let the world know I am a man of destiny."

To Jack, what was remarkable about Ali's rambling fantasy was his utter lack of self-consciousness. He was serious in the extreme. Very solemn. He believed all of his grand vision. What was even more remarkable was that he believed that Horace Greeley and editors in London and Paris would believe it as well. Was Ali demented, or just an extreme example of the human imagination gone wrong? One thing was certain: he was dangerous. And he had Sonja. For the moment there was nothing Jack could do but deal with him on his terms.

Ali said, "Colonel Cut will remember you every time he pulls a boot over his deformed ankle. You've been fortunate to make it this far. For the moment the stations ahead will continue to accept your papers from the crown, but that won't last. We intercepted a detachment of Koslov's gendarmes and the commander told us, under pain of extreme discomfort, that the stations are being ordered to detain you, and the gendarmes at the border are to prevent you from leaving the country."

Jack took a deep breath and let it out between puffed cheeks.

"I will let you keep your weapons and your money. You'll need them to make it safely to Sevastopol and then back to Europe and America. Foolish to deprive you of what you need to get home to write my story. The world will want to know what is happening here. The people I conquer will welcome me because they will know that I have delivered them from evil and will protect them from harm. All I will require is a modest tribute to pay my armies." He motioned with his hand to Jack. "Now go. You should ride hard. There are more gendarmes on the way. There are gendarmes at all the border crossings, but it will take time for them to get the word."

Jack said, "Could I have a moment with my wife, please? I'll need to send some medicine with her. She gets headaches. There's no reason she should suffer."

He frowned. "Oh, very well. Get her medicine and say your romantic good-byes."

Jack took Sonja in his arms and they kissed. Quickly, he whispered in her ear, "I'll catch up. You know me. You know I'll never quit, no matter what the odds. I won't give up. Never doubt that. We'll be together again. I am your husband."

"And I am your wife. I'll keep the faith."

Ali was getting impatient. "That's enough. Find whatever it is she needs."

From their gear in the back of the *tarantass* Jack retrieved a square tin that they used for their medicines. He slipped his loaded derringer into the bottom of the tin and covered it with bottles of laudanum.

Sonja saw what he had done and caught his eye.

He kissed her again, then whispered in her ear, "One shot for an emergency."

"Enough! Enough!" Ali scooped up Sonja and threw her on the back of his horse.

Sonja said, "Do as he says, Jack. Save yourself. I love you."

"I love you," he said.

Ali rolled his eyes. "They love one another! Love! We Kyrgyz don't believe in such foolishness. Marry a man to a woman and they will come to love one another. One wife or two, three. What does it matter? All of a man's wives will love him if he has power and wisdom and takes proper care of them."

"I ask you not to harm Sonja. She is a Russian, yes, but she did nothing to your cousin."

Ali said, "That's true, she didn't. I assure you it is not my intention to harm her. When she is in my *aoul,* she will be a gentle little kitten, purring to please her master. When she's served her purpose as bait for Koslov, and you've made me the talk of every capital in Europe, you can have her back. If you're caught before you make it out of Sevastopol, tell them Ali has your woman. Let Colonel Cut get her if he can."

Jack said, "Tell me, if you will, how long do you think it will take for Koslov's ankle to heal?"

Ali thought a moment. "Good question. Weeks, I would imagine. The gendarme commander we captured tells us that when he is able to ride, Koslov has an important mission for the Tsar that will require him to lead a large detachment of gendarmes to the Syan-Shan Mountains near Kossol-gol. That will take him weeks if not months."

"What kind of mission?"

Ali smiled. "You are a curious one, aren't you? To pick up something. The detachment commander was reluctant to tell us exactly what it was, and the poor fellow died before we could convince him to give us the details. If he hadn't been so stubborn, he might be alive today."

"Destined for where? St. Petersburg, I take it."

Ali shook his head. "To Yekaterinburg. No matter. It doesn't concern you. The only thing that matters to you is satisfying me so you can get your wife back, although I find your concern remarkable. She's just a woman. Women are for copulating and making babies and milking the mares. Who cares what happens to one woman, when there are many more women out there to be mounted and make babies and milk mares? Such foolishness!" Without another word, Ali rode off, followed by his Kyrgyz warriors.

Jack didn't care what Ali thought of him. Foolish or not, he yelled, "I'll catch up, Sonja! I'll never give up! Never!"

JACK SANDT DIDN'T KNOW IF SONJA HEARD HIM OR NOT. HE WAITED and soon they were gone. He felt more alone than he ever had in his life. He had lost his beautiful, sweet Sonja before they'd even had a chance to consummate their marriage. Even though he'd done all he could under the circumstances, he felt that he had let Sonja down. Would a better man have come away with his wife? For the moment Jack didn't have the heart to press on.

It was getting dark. He built himself a campfire and retrieved a bottle of vodka from the *tarantass* and sat down to think things through. Soon it got dark and the cold descended quickly. Above him in the starry night the high peaks of the Altai loomed, brooding.

Jack knew he couldn't pursue the band of Kyrgyz warriors by himself. He needed to find a Cossack. He had the money necessary to hire whomever he wanted. His bottle of vodka was empty. He opened another and kept drinking.

The captured gendarme commander had told Ali that Koslov had a special mission to the Syan-Shan Mountains. That was no doubt to retrieve rubies from the headwaters of the Black Irkout on Monko-seran-Xardick. There had to be something Jack could do with that information. But what?

Jack took out his maps and studied them by the flickering light of the fire and soon found Monko-seran-Xardick, the mightiest mountain of the Syan-Shan. That was where the rubies awaited transport to the artisans at Yekaterinburg.

It struck Jack that he had two choices.

His first option was to push on to Europe and America, where he could have typesetters produce bogus editions of the *Times* of London, *Le Monde,* and the *New York Tribune* with Ali's grandiose nonsense above the fold on the front page. Ali was isolated on the steppes and would have no way of knowing the difference. But that plan would take months, during which Sonja would be at Ali's mercy. She could be emotionally and physically destroyed or even dead by the time he got back.

His second option was to find some Cossacks who could help him rescue Sonja. Where there was a will there was a way. Ali surely needed money to arm his fantasy army with muskets. If Jack couldn't spirit her out of his camp, perhaps he could steal the rubies and buy her back.

He had lost Sonja to a madman. He knew what Ali would do to Sonja every night, and the thought of it made him want to vomit. His stomach twisted with rage. He stood and screamed to the stars, "I will not accept this abomination without getting Sonja back. I will not! Ali will not take my wife to his bed without paying a price. He will *not!*"

Sitting before the warming glow of embers, Jack Sandt felt more lost than he ever had been in his life. He wiped the moisture from his eyes with his forearm.

SIX

Into the Altai

 THE NEXT MORNING JACK REACHED THE VILLAGE OF
Oubinskoi, where he sold his *tarantass* and loaded his
belongings onto three packhorses so he could push on
alone, avoiding the stations along the main routes. The
crown relied on Cossacks to block incursions by the Kyrgyz coming out
of the Altai. To find a Cossack guide, he had to go where the Cossacks
were.

Soon after Oubinskoi, Jack came to another broad, deep river, the
Ouba, which, like the Ob, had poplars, birches, and willows on the shores
and was divided into willow-covered islands. On the right side of the valley of the Ouba, the Oubinskoi Mountains rose higher and higher, eventually becoming part of the awesome Altai. Beyond that lay the Kyrgyz
Steppe and the mysteries of faraway Cathay.

Not wanting to stop, he rode without eating. Finally, with his stomach
growling, he knew he had to eat. When the sun was directly overhead, he
stopped long enough to catch three graylings ranging from a half pound
to a pound and a half. The river narrowed as he progressed upstream,
and soon the pine-clad foothill rose to rock-crested mountains three to
four thousand feet on each side. Soon the stream hopped and burbled
over rocks and passed through rocky gorges. As he settled into camp that
night, the setting sun colored the snow of a huge mountain rising high

above him. He checked his map and knew that must be Mount Ivanoff-sky Belock.

The next morning Jack passed through the village of Riddersk on the flank of Ivanoffsky Belock, and then a silver mine from which ore was sent downriver to smelting works at Zmeinogorsk, Barnaoul, and Pavlovsky.

Soon thereafter Jack came on the Grom River, one of the wildest streams in the Altai. *Grom* meant "thunder," and sure enough, Jack heard the river before he saw it. The water, coming from melting snow high in the Altai, thundered and roared through narrow chasms of rock.

At dusk he passed a jumble of amazing boulders, some of them surely weighing twenty-five to thirty tons. How had they come to be there? He couldn't figure it. As darkness fell, he came upon a village of about twenty families living in a meadow nestled among some cedars well above the Grom. The village had several fields of hay growing, and he saw two dozen or more cows grazing as they pleased. On the way to the village, which turned out to be inhabited by Cossacks, he passed several beehives.

A few minutes later, the bearded patriarch of the community stepped from a cabin and welcomed him inside. They introduced themselves, and Jack learned that the patriarch's name was Emil. Emil was dressed in a simple white shirt that hung over baggy blue trousers. He tied the shirt around his waist with a red sash. He tucked his trousers into handsome boots that reached nearly to his knees.

The cottage was immaculate. The floors, walls, benches, and tables had been scrubbed with birch bark and polished until the wood looked new. Emil's plump wife—Jack was not told her name—wore a white linen chemise and a pink-striped skirt. She had tied a red handkerchief into a cap. She wore rough shoes, but no socks. A young woman, perhaps nineteen or twenty years old and similarly clad, looked at Jack with large brown eyes. Jack surmised that she must be the daughter. A visitor! She was excited.

———

Sonja knew that Ali and his warriors had expected her to be a drag on their long journey to their camp. They were clearly surprised when it turned out she could ride a horse nearly as well as they could. To pass the time on the long ride, Ali amused himself by speculating out loud on the likely manhood of anybody who earned his living as a dag man.

Jack had found her once. He would find her again. Her father had told her to keep the faith, and he had been right. To survive, Sonja had to be patient and believe in both herself and Jack.

Ali and his warriors pushed their way through a thick, dense wood, making slow progress through a snarl of nearly impossible underbrush. It was tough going for the horses, which were forced to negotiate decaying trees covered with mushrooms, moss, and ferns.

The Kyrgyz bandits left the thick forest and crossed a stream beside a large pile of boulders that had obviously been pushed down the canyon by a wall of water. But these boulders had rumbled down the mountain years ago and were now overgrown by a tangle of bushes and large plants. The warriors started the ascent of a steep ridge. They climbed for several hours, then entered a magnificent cedar forest, free of bushes and undergrowth, and carpeted by moss.

They climbed up, up, up, their horses laboring hard and lathering heavily. The higher they climbed, the smaller the trees became. The diminutive trees gave way to stunted dwarfs in the ravines, and finally, there were no trees, just lichen and rock.

Late that afternoon, reaching the summit of a barren, rocky ridge, they looked down into the valley of the Koksa, with the pale blue Kaier Koomin Mountains in the distance. As they drew closer, the pale blue slowly darkened, turning eventually to green. The mountain light was blue, crisp, and light. The valley light was yellow, turning the landscape heavy and languid.

An hour later, they reached Koksa Lake, the source of the Koksa River. It quickly turned cold with the setting sun, and they decided to camp near the skeletons of six yurts, conical dwellings favored by the Kyrgyz and Kalmyk, an Asian race from farther southeast in China.

These particular yurts were Kalmyk. The birch bark had been stripped off the ribs, but the Kalmyk, out collecting and drying the fruit and game in the summer, would return in the autumn to cover the yurts with new bark. Here six Kalmyk families would spend the winter, snug against the snow.

With the setting sun, a dark gloom settled over the valleys, while the orange globe bathed the snow-covered peaks in a rosy glow.

At length the Kyrgyz built a fire for the night. Sonja prepared their meal by boiling dried meat and rice that they carried with them in their saddlebags. The Kyrgyz warriors slept rolled up in *voilock,* a kind of felt made of pressed horse or camel hair. Ali had a separate fire some distance from the others so he could enjoy his new woman in private.

Finally, Ali, calling Sonja "Little Kitten," gave her a slap on the butt and took her with him to his fire. He pulled her under his *voilock,* and his hands were immediately on her. Each time Ali took her, she lay back and endured, determined not to cry out or show any response that Ali could interpret as pleasure. For Ali, she would be an object. The woman Sonja Sankova Sandt would save herself for her wedding night.

When Ali was in her, she closed her eyes tightly and concentrated furiously on Jack. Sonja thus fled emotionally, leaving her rigid, unresponsive body pinned as though it existed in another time and place.

She was on the Chinese junk on a gentle sea. She was cooking chunks of fish on a wok above charcoal on the deck. She stirred the fish with chopsticks. She could smell garlic and ginger and green onions. The wind blew through her short hair. Jack squatted beside her and plucked a chunk of fish from the wok with chopsticks of his own.

SEVEN

The Mill on the Grom

THE PATRIARCH EMIL HAD NEVER MET AN AMERI-can. He had heard of America, yes, but he knew nothing about it. He immediately called for vodka, and they took their seats at the family's table. The wife and girl quickly lit candles made of tallow and brought out a bottle, along with some dried fruit and cedar nuts. Emil and Jack began the ritual of drinking and talking while the wife and girl watched at a distance, curious about everything that was being said. They rarely had visitors. And this one, an American!

Jack told the old man that he had never heard of anything as horrific as the roar of the Grom.

Emil grinned broadly and drank a slug of vodka. "Do you remember passing some boulders just downstream from here?"

"How could I forget? They're huge!"

He said, "There used to be a mill about a verst downstream from here where we used to grind the corn and rye. Three years ago there was a terrible storm followed by a deluge. The water poured down as from a bucket. Then we heard a terrible roar. It was deafening. A few minutes later we heard the trees popping and snapping from upstream. Then it was upon us, a wall of water, pushing those boulders down from the mountain. Our houses here were high enough above the stream to be spared, but everything below us was swept away, including the mill."

"What?"

"Those boulders tumbled like pebbles. It's possible to build a mill that will withstand the floods in the spring, maybe not a flood like the one that tumbled the boulders down the valley, but still." He grimaced.

"Why don't you?"

"We don't have the money." Emil didn't sound like he was trying to cadge a donation. He was merely stating a fact.

"I see."

"We endure long winters. Every spring is a triumph. When we are crushed by falling boulders, we do not quit. We endure. We rebuild."

The wife, seeing that their tumblers of vodka were empty, hurried forward to pour them more.

Emil eyed Jack. "But never mind the mill. Tell me about yourself, Mr. Sandt."

"Jack."

The vodka was already having its effect. Emil grinned. "Okay, Jack. Tell me where you come from in America and how you came to be here."

"I'm a dag man, actually."

"Dag man?"

"I take daguerreotype images." Jack could see they had no idea what a daguerreotype was. "If you give me a minute, I'll show you what I mean." Saying no more, he rose and went outside, where he retrieved the box of daguerreotypes from the pack.

He returned inside and slipped out the wedding plate, holding it by its edges. "This is my wife, Sonja, and I on our wedding."

Emil and his wife and daughter stared at the image of Jack and Sonja, hardly believing their eyes.

"Would you like me to take your image as well? It will take a while. I'll have to prepare the metal plate and erect a small tent here in your house. I will want your entire family here by the table. You'll have to remain perfectly still for at least ten seconds."

"We would be honored," Emil said.

With Emil at his side, Jack went outside and retrieved his gear.

Jack sipped vodka as he polished and buffed two small plates. As he worked, he told Emil what it was like to grow up along the Chesapeake Bay.

JACK EMERGED FROM HIS TENT WITH THE TWO SMALL PLATES CONtaining the image of Emil and his family. Holding one by the edges, he showed it to Emil. "You must never touch the surface. Hold it by the edges."

Emil took it, beaming with pride. His wife and daughter quickly hurried over to see the daguerreotype. They smiled broadly. The girl giggled.

"One for you, one for me, is that fair?" Jack asked.

"More than fair," Emil said.

For the first time, his wife spoke. "Thank you. Thank you very much. We are honored. We will hang it on the wall for our visitors to admire."

"You will need to cover it with glass to protect it," Jack said.

Jack decided it was time to tell Emil about Koslov and Sonja and Ali. When he got to Sonja's kidnapping by the Kyrgyz named Ali, Emil raised an eyebrow. "Ali has your wife? The young woman in the picture."

Jack nodded.

"Ali is a famous madman."

"I figured that."

"I know about Peter Koslov as well. Colonel Cut. How is it that Ali let you live?"

Jack said, "I agreed to write an article about him in my newspaper and in papers in London and Paris. I recorded an image of him." Jack removed the dag of Ali from the box.

Emil's eyes widened. "That's him. He pretends to be the savior of the Kyrgyz, but he is a bandit. What he's been doing is promising the chiefs of the smaller *aouls* that they'll one day be given the horses and cattle of the rich *aouls*. He steals animals from the larger *aouls* on the pretext that he needs them for his army."

"He says he is the Mahdi."

Emil looked disgusted. "The Expected One, yes, we've all heard of that nonsense. He pretends he is on a higher mission to unite the Kyrgyz and reclaim their territory north of the Altai. The truth is that he is a thief who bends religion to suit his own purposes. All he cares about is himself. Those Kyrgyz who think he is anything other than a murdering thief are fools. Incidentally, I've heard the story about what happened to his cousin. That's apparently true."

"I see."

"If Ali succeeds in avenging the murder of his cousin, it will enhance his reputation among all the Kyrgyz. He wants to be known as an unstoppable warrior. You understand his motive now?"

Jack sighed. Unfortunately, he did. He said, "What about my wife? What will Ali do to her? He told me he wouldn't harm her."

Emil glanced at his daughter and shook his head. "He's a Kyrgyz. Kyrgyz lie. Your wife is an attractive woman and . . ." His voice trailed off.

Jack said, "Tell me, what if I had an idea that would give Ali all the money he needs to buy muskets by the thousand. Would he yield my wife then?"

Emil raised an eyebrow. "Perhaps. It is hard to say. Ali is no fool. He needs muskets for his ambitions. It would have to be a very good idea indeed, but I would hate to see it happen. He would kill us all."

Jack knew his host had a point there.

Emil was curious nevertheless. "He would cheat you anyway. He'd never stand by a deal. Where would you get this money?"

Jack said, "By stealing rubies destined for the Tsar's new throne."

Emil sat up straight.

"And more than enough money for you to rebuild your mill."

Emil brightened. "Oh?" He paused. "Why don't you just rescue your wife from Ali and steal the rubies yourself? I can get you a dependable Cossack."

Ah, now you're talking, Jack thought. "You can?"

"Certainly. The best."

"I will pay him well. But he has to be good, someone who knows the Kyrgyz and Ali and the ways of the steppe."

Emil waved for more vodka. "My nephew Parsha knows the Altai. He is a good horseman, and he can communicate with both the Kyrgyz and the Kalmyk in their language. And believe me, he has good reason to join you."

"And that would be?"

Emil hesitated, then said, "He hates Ali with a passion, but I think it's best if he tells you why in his own time and his own way—if he agrees to go with you. I guarantee that if there is a Cossack within a thousand versts who can figure out a way to rescue your wife, it is Parsha. He is the best. He is motivated. And you will like him."

Jack dug into his money belt and retrieved some coins, which he slid across the table. Emil looked at the coins and blinked. "What's this?"

"Money so you can start rebuilding your mill."

The Cossack picked up a coin. "These are gold! This is more than enough for us to rebuild our mill."

Jack shrugged. "Then build it. If you earn more by helping me, you can expand your herd or buy yourselves some good stoves or better muskets or whatever. Believe me, you'll earn more than enough money."

"Parsha is in the mountains hunting deer with some friends. They will dry the meat before they return. I'll take you to him, but it will be a long, hard trip."

Jack smiled. "I'm used to long, hard trips."

"And an even longer trip to find Ali. With your wife as his captive, he'll stay on the move until he can lure Koslov into an ambush. That will likely mean going deep into the Altai or one of the other chains of mountains pushing out onto the Kyrgyz Steppe."

"Whenever you feel like starting," Jack said.

"In the morning," Emil said. "Tonight we drink." Eyeing the coins on the table, feeling pleased at his good fortune, he knocked back the remainder of his vodka.

Jack did the same. He didn't have enough money buy off Ali's thirst for revenge, but the rubies destined for the Romanov throne might do anything.

EIGHT

In the High Cholsoun

AFTER A BONE-CHILLING NIGHT, JACK SANDT AND Emil awoke with frost covering the ground. The grass crunched when they walked on it. Dawn was as spectacular as the sunset, if that was possible; the orange light sparkled brilliantly off the crystals of ice. As the frost melted about them, they had a breakfast of tea and dried venison and proceeded down the Koksa River, which they eventually forded, crossing into a valley drained by the Karaguy River.

The valley of the Karaguy River was filled with dense stands of birch, larch, and pine. Here Jack and Emil encountered a certain kind of large black squirrel that Jack had never seen. Some squirrels played in the grass in front of them, scrambling up the trees as they approached; others followed on either side of them, leaping from branch to branch high above, as though they were racing. Emil said their fur thickened in the winter, turning gray, which is when the Kalmyk killed them to make hats and clothing for cold weather.

They came upon the horns of a large stag, but Emil said the deer were now higher up in the mountains, where they had gone to escape the mosquitoes. That was where Parsha and his companions and the Kalmyk hunters had gone to hunt meat for the winter. Emil said even the bears with thick fur couldn't stand the mosquitoes in the summertime, and he was right. Jack doubted if medieval armor could block their eager beaks. He and Emil were forced to sling the odious smoking boxes over their shoulders or be driven out of their minds. Emil told him to bear with it for another three or four cold nights and the mosquitoes would be put out of business that year.

The bottom of the Karaguy River valley was filled with lush grass and picta trees. Ten versts later they came to a branch of the Arkym, coming from the south, where it descended from the Cholsoun Mountains. The wide, fast, surging Arkym—all sound and fury and white water—was divided by an island of rocks that had washed down from above over the aeons and from which a profusion of trees and bushes now grew. It was impossible for Emil and Jack to ford the stream, so they started up the great ravine. Dwarf cedars sprung out of the cracks in the rocks above them. The top of the ridge was devoid of any sort of vegetation. The ravine narrowed to a chasm with what amounted to cliffs on either side, but Emil knew of a trail that hunters took to the hunting grounds, and they followed it.

The trail wound, high, high above the water, which they could hear roaring far below. Eventually they dismounted and led their horses. Jack's mouth turned dry. A wave of anxiety coursed through his stomach as he was caught in the grip of vertigo. He could hardly breathe. He found it impossible to look down. He kept his eyes on Emil's back. How the horses managed to stay on the narrow trail was beyond him. Soon the river was a white ribbon so far below them that it ran silently. On the opposite side of the gorge, rocky crags rose in wild grandeur, looking like nothing so much as huge buttresses propping up the mountain.

Eventually the trail led back down to the river, which was smaller, ice cold, and clear as crystal, flowing through chutes of perpendicular rock. Soon the last of the stunted cedars disappeared, and they came upon a small depression with a lake in the middle, its shores covered with flowers, including a beautiful bed of flowers in full bloom that reached to their saddle flaps—some were blue and white; others were a deep purple or purple edged in white. Among the flowers were the white and pink blossoms that he had seen in the Urals and another variety with deep red flowers on its branches. The lake itself was shallow on the edges, quickly changing into an extraordinary blue, suggesting it was very deep.

They pushed to the top of the mountain, which was devoid of vegetation save for moss and lichen on the rocks. At the summit, Jack paused to check his maps and better understand where he was. The Altai chain ran northwest to southeast. To the north lay the rivers he had mostly recently passed, the Arkym, the Karaguy, the Koksa, the Grom, the Ouba, and all the rest of the rivers, a great vast web of water that fed the Ob. That mighty north-flowing river eventually emptied into the Kara Sea just below the Arctic Ocean. To the south lay the Kyrgyz Steppe and beyond that Tibet and the Himalayan Mountains. Mongolia lay to the southeast and China beyond that. To the west, past the Urals, the rivers draining the European basin, the Volga and the Don, flowed into the Caspian Sea and the Black Sea.

If Emil's guess was right, Ali's camp was likely to the south, in one of the chains of mountains rising above the Kyrgyz Steppe. That's where the Expected One would be taking Sonja.

SONJA RODE WITH HER STOMACH GRINDING WITH HATRED AND RE-sentment of Ali. Her father had once told her that what you sowed you would eventually reap. She would do what she had to do to survive. She would remember Jack and their mutual dream. She would endure. But she would never accept Ali's barbarous treatment of her, never. Nor would she even once go to sleep at night without reaffirming her pledge to one day give Ali the roughest of rough justice that he thoroughly deserved—callous, crude, uncaring revenge.

Sonja knew enough Kyrgyz words to understand that Ali and his band of Kyrgyz marauders usually roamed the headwaters of the Irtysh River, from which he retreated southeast onto the steppes of Mongolia and China when the Tsar's Cossacks pursued him. She was given to understand that Cholsoun Pass was the only way to descend the south side of the mountains, the other routes being blocked by steep precipices.

With Sonja riding beside Ali at the front, the party of warriors negotiated the side of the mountain, traveling alternately on mossy turf and bare stone covered with scattered rocks. Below them the steep slope plunged thousands of feet to the base of the mountain. Above them, crags rose to the summit. After about two hours of slow, treacherous progress, Ali told her they were nearing the pass, which was difficult to spot this high up. They stopped every few minutes to study the terrain.

Suddenly the clouds blackened around the peaks above them, signaling yet another bizarre storm. Ali had spent his life enduring such storms, but Sonja detected a hint of anxiety in his eye. When the Kyrgyz heard the first rumbling of thunder, they began looking about for cover. There was none. The claps of thunder grew louder, startling the horses. The horses wanted cover as much as their riders, and they quickened their pace, a dangerous business on such a steep pitch. Finally, Ali spotted some large stone pillars about three hundred yards dead ahead.

Glancing back, Sonja saw huge streams of lightning descend from the black clouds, bathing the mountains in an eerie glow. They were washed in light every two or three minutes, followed by huge pops of thunder that got louder and louder. Then they were plunged into darkness, followed by an awesome, startling roar, and a furious wind was upon them, ripping up the dwarf cedars by the roots and propelling them parallel to the ground. Whether this was a tornado or just a freak storm was impossible to tell.

A branch slapped Sonja's shoulder, nearly knocking her off her horse. She put one arm around her head to protect herself from the sting of dirt and pebbles. Even more dangerous, the wind hurled stones like musket balls. The fleeing warriors were at the mercy of the wind and of great sheets of lightning that were closing fast.

Alarmed, Ali yelled something to his men.

Sonja didn't have to be told to hurry. She didn't want to be knocked cold by a flying rock or fried by the lightning. Blinded by the maelstrom, the Kyrgyz headed for the cover of the giant pillars. The wild-eyed horses, spooked by the lightning and the ferocity of the wind, needed little urging. They set off at a near gallop that was dangerous in the extreme on such a steep pitch.

Just as they arrived at the pillars, the air turned crimson. A bolt of lightning touched down directly behind them, and the hair rose on her arms and legs. This was followed by a loud crack of thunder directly overhead that nearly knocked them to the ground. Then came a horrific rattle of hail the size of eggs. Cold and wet, they hunkered under the rocky overhangs of the pillars, grateful to still be alive. In a few minutes the ground was covered a wintry white from the hail. The storm rolled on around the mountain, and they could hear only its murmuring in the distance.

After a few minutes the sun shone brilliantly, and they could see the amazing black clouds moving away from them on the spine of the mountains. The incredible storm had fallen upon them and disappeared in the space of an hour or less. They started down the mountain through Cholsoun Pass.

Ali fancied himself a great lover. He was a powerful man, and did not women respond to powerful men? That night, as he did every night, Ali threw her on her back.

Eyes tight, jaws clenched, she saw the junk.

Ali forced her legs apart. He yelled at her in Kyrgyz, something she did not understand.

Jack was at the helm. She was beside him.

Ali slapped her.

They tacked. They ducked. The boom passed over their heads.

He pushed himself into her.

The wind caught the sail and the junk headed to port.

On top of her, slamming hard into her, the frustrated Ali yelled at her.

Jack gave her the helm while he went below.

Ali slapped her again, bloodying her nose. Her tactic was the same every night. She retreated into a trance, indifferent to whatever Ali did to her. This infuriated Ali. He wanted *her,* the beautiful, sexy little Sonja, not just her body. He wanted response, emotion.

Jack came out of the hold with some leftover roast pork from the last island they had visited.

She was totally unaware when Ali finished.

He screamed at her, his eyes wild.

Jack also had some flatbread he had made earlier, and a jug of coconut water.

Ali slapped her again. She didn't move. She didn't make a sound. She felt the warm blood flowing down her face. She received another blow. She tasted salty blood in her mouth.

Finally, the Expected One was finished. Whatever pleasure he had gained was blunted by her total suppression of emotion. He rose from her, disgusted. He kicked her in the ribs, knocking the wind out of her. He spit on her and stalked off.

She lay there, struggling to breathe again. Once again, Sonja Sankova had triumphed.

The pork sandwich tasted good. So did the coconut water.

NINE

Parsha

JACK SANDT AND EMIL STARTED DOWN THE SOUTH-
ern face of the mountain on a trail to the hunting grounds
favored by both Cossacks and Kyrgyz. An hour later, they
came upon another stream, formed by the melting snow,
that plunged down the steep flank of the mountain. They progressed
slowly on the steep, treacherous trail. They came upon the stunted trees.
As they descended the mountain the trees got larger and both the trees
and grass thickened.

Jack saw three huge stags standing in silhouette on a distant ridge.
Beautiful they were.

He stopped his horse. "Look there." He took out his telescope and focused on the stags. They were within range of his Sharps, but they
would likely roll down the steep incline, and it was too close to dark to
retrieve their carcasses.

He gave the glass to Emil for a closer look. Watching them, Emil said,
"What did I tell you? They're up here grazing far above the mosquitoes.
We'll be getting to Parsha's camp soon. You'll hear it before you see it."

"Hear it?"

"Yes."

They continued their descent carefully, leading the horses because of
the loose rocks on the steep trail. The stream beside the trail grew larger
and larger, its volume fed by rivulets on either side. Jack had negotiated

the rocky slopes above a timberline before, but the experience was always unnerving. The smallest slip would send a man or horse plunging thousands of feet down a steep slope. Finally, when the sun was low in the west, Jack heard a sound below them that was far louder than that made by the stream plunging over bare rock.

"What's that?" he asked Emil.

Emil looked back and grinned. "We're here."

They stood at the edge of a precipice where the quickening stream abruptly disappeared, plunging straight down some sixty feet over three levels. Far below them, they could see the water cascading in a grand white lace before it slapped hard into a deep pool. The hunters' camp was back in the trees about ten yards from the edge of the pool. It took them a half hour to get there from the top of the waterfall, as they had to traverse a dangerous, zigzagging trail down the steep pitch.

The hunters began returning just as Jack and Emil reached the bottom. A huge fire marked the center of the camp, and there were deer carcasses hanging from the branches of the trees. The carcasses, frozen solid, remained in the shade during the day. The Cossacks and Kalmyk would cut the flesh into thin strips and dry it in the sun. The hunters all knew Emil, who introduced Jack to them one by one.

At length a huge, bearded man, the largest Cossack Jack had ever seen, standing well over six feet tall, led a packhorse into camp with the carcass of a stag strapped across its back. He bloused his trousers into his knee-high Cossack boots. He had a broad red band around his waist and wore a hooded wool coat.

Emil leaped to his feet and embraced the amiable giant. "Parsha, this is my American friend, Jack Sandt. Jack, my nephew Parsha, the best hunter in the Altai. The best shot, too."

They shook.

Parsha looked amazed. "An American? Here in the Altai?"

"We will have our supper and I will tell you all about it," Emil said.

There was something about Parsha that Jack immediately liked, and he thought the feeling was mutual. Here was a man he could trust to keep his end of the bargain when the going got tough.

Jack had brought several bottles of vodka on his pack animal, and now he broke them out to share with the hunters—there were five in all—while one of them set about cooking the meal. This consisted of hanging a cast-iron pot over the fire and throwing in several chunks of deer tallow. When the fat was melted the chef began tossing in a potpourri of sweetbreads, kidneys, a couple of tongues, chunks of liver and heart, and chopped testicles. When the meat began to sizzle, he stirred it earnestly with a stick. With the aroma of frying meat wafting up, Jack told Parsha his story with his companions listening carefully.

When he had finished, Parsha said, "I know Ali is a treacherous Kyrgyz, but it's true what happened to his cousin. If I were him, I would want justice too. His pretensions of liberating the Kyrgyz from the Russians are all nonsense. He's a posturing, murderous thief leading gullible fools."

"It's almost ready," the cook said. He threw some brains into the stew.

They gathered around the pot. A bitter cold was descending on the mountain. Their backs were cold, but their faces were warm from the fire.

The cook fished out a chunk of meat and sampled it. "Just right."

They began retrieving pieces of meat with their hands, washing it down with vodka.

Chewing on a piece of heart, Parsha said, "My uncle mentioned something about rubies headed for a new throne for the Tsar."

Jack told him what the guide had said in Yekaterinburg and matched that with what Ali had said. "Unless I'm mistaken, Colonel Cut will shortly lead a detachment of gendarmes to fetch the rubies."

"And you propose to do what?" Parsha said.

"Rescue my wife, then steal the rubies."

"Oh?"

"But my wife comes first or no deal." Jack retrieved his wedding daguerreotype from its box and held it by the edges for Parsha to see. "This is her, Sonja, on the day we were married."

Parsha smiled. "Easy to understand why you're willing to risk your life to get her back. She's very beautiful. You should believe me when I tell you I want Ali more than the rubies. Someday I'll tell you why."

Although Jack didn't yet understand Parsha's hatred of Ali, there was no doubting the Cossack's sincerity. "Perhaps we can both get what we want."

Parsha smiled. "When I say I want Ali, you should know the Kyrgyz are not all bad, once you know their ways. The chiefs and sultans of the larger *aouls* hate Ali as much as the Cossacks and the Kalmyk. They may all be Kyrgyz, but each camp is different."

Jack understood what he was saying. Some of the Indian tribes out west were trustworthy in the extreme. Others were not. The best guides were trappers who knew the ways of each tribe and their chiefs.

Parsha said, "I agree with you that it's dangerous to leave your wife with Ali too long. Rescuing her won't be easy, but with a little help maybe we can figure a way. When I say I only want Ali, of course I'd like rubies as well. But tell me, how do you propose to steal the rubies from Colonel Koslov? The Wolfpack is the best unit of gendarmes the Tsar has to offer."

"I have no idea. Perhaps it's impossible. All I really want is my wife back."

Parsha grinned. "Then we take Sonja back. I kill Ali. *Then* we steal the rubies from Peter Koslov."

"We? The two of us?"

Parsha shook his head. "Unlikely the two of us can do it by ourselves. But as Ali's band has grown larger and he has been stealing the animals of larger and larger *aouls*, he has collected powerful enemies. The trick is to find a chief or sultan who has had enough and so is willing to help us out. I'm a Cossack. You're a resourceful American. You had to be to get this far. I can speak the language of both the Kyrgyz and the Kalmyk. Between the two of us, we'll come up with something." He leaned forward, his face earnest. "Sonja and Ali first, then the rubies if we think that's possible. We take it one step at a time. Do we have a deal?"

"We have a deal." They shook. Jack said, "How do you propose we begin?"

"Ali roams a huge territory in the Altai and the steppes. No telling how long it will take us to run him down. Weeks maybe. We've got some hard traveling in front of us. I say we leave at dawn and see if we can't recruit some help."

Jack knew he couldn't retrieve Sonja by himself. He didn't have much choice but to throw in with Parsha. He said, "Do you suppose we could do some hunting before we push off? We'll need some meat for the trip, and I want to show you what my Sharps can do. Maybe it will give you some ideas."

Parsha drank some more vodka. "Sure. I'd like to see your rifle in action. Emil and others can finish drying the meat in camp and take it back."

Jack slept that night with his blanket as close to the fire as he could get without burning himself. He knew that as the embers died down the mountain cold would move in with a vengeance. He was exhausted after the long day's travel, and the meat and vodka had made him sleepy.

Jack fell into a deep sleep.

There was a fire. In the shadows of the flickering fire, bearded Kyrgyz faces. Sonja stood by the fire, looking down. Ali took Sonja by the wrist. He threw her onto the ground. She lay, eyes wide, awaiting her fate. Ali yanked her to her feet and ripped off her dress.

Jack woke up, sweating. Each night he had that same dream, or one close to it. Each time it drove him wild. He could not stand it that Sonja was in Ali's hands, and yet, for the moment, there was nothing he could do but pursue her and each night endure the horror of seeing her in his sleep. She was his wife. She was in the hands of barbarians and at their mercy. And for the moment there was nothing he could do but accept what had happened, and vow never to give up until he got her back.

The fire was down to embers. He put some more wood on, and in a few minutes it was blazing again. It was a clear night, and a full white moon lit the mountain. It was hard to believe he had ever seen a whiter moon. In the thin air, the heavens seemed extra bright, the stars like diamonds splashed against the blackness. Above him the silhouettes of the trees loomed, silent, brooding. Lying rolled up in his blanket near the summit of the Cholsoun Mountains, Jack looked up at the cold white moon and fabulous stars sparkling down on Asia. He could not go to sleep. All he could do was think of Sonja in the hands of Ali. She was out there somewhere, depending on him. He would not let her down.

TEN

What Mr. Sharp Wrought

EACH ASTRIDE A HORSE AND LEADING A PACKHORSE with supplies and daguerreotype gear, Parsha and Jack Sandt set out on a trail carved out of the side of the mountain. The trail led upward toward the smaller trees, so that they looked down on ridges covered with larger forest. Just ahead of him on a narrow trail, Parsha said, "This shouldn't take too long. There's a clearing up ahead where we can wait. We've been having our best luck early in the morning and at sunset. They lie down and sun themselves in the heat of the afternoon."

It was hard for Jack to concentrate on what Parsha was saying because the sheer drop below the trail descended for what looked like thousands of feet. Trying to make sure of each step, Jack was afraid to look up, much less watch for deer. He said, "I want a long-range shot. The longer the better."

"There's a meadow up ahead where we can wait. They do a lot of moving around in the morning," he said.

A few minutes later, they reached a landform covered with large boulders that stuck out from the steep slope. Dead ahead was a forested ridge, and below them still farther, in a meadow nestled in a saddle between their mountain and the next, a small stream trickled through a grassy meadow.

Parsha stopped and squatted, grimacing. "We're late," he whispered, pointing down at the meadow.

Jack didn't see anything. He unfolded his telescope to its full length and studied the meadow. He took a minute, then saw them, a stag and five does grazing in the meadow.

"We'll never get close enough for a shot without spooking them," Parsha whispered. "They can smell you a verst away, and those ears."

"This'll do," Jack said.

Parsha looked disbelieving. "What are you talking about?"

Jack leaned against a boulder, still studying the huge deer through the telescope. How Parsha had spotted them with his naked eye was beyond him. He handed Parsha the telescope.

Parsha took a look through the telescope. "Big stag," he said.

Jack sat down behind the boulder. "Let me explain this gun," he whispered. He retrieved a cartridge from his trousers. "This," he said softly, "is a cartridge." He handed it to Parsha. "It's made of linen. Cartridges are a recent invention made possible by breech-loading guns."

Parsha turned the cartridge in his hand.

"Simple, I know. I don't understand why somebody didn't think of it before. It goes here." Jack opened the breech.

Parsha closed one eye and looked down the barrel. "What are those lines?"

Jack said, "They're called rifling, which is why this gun is called a rifle. It shoots a bullet rather than a ball."

Parsha took another look at the cartridge, running his finger over the bullet at the end. He looked puzzled. His own musket fired a ball from a smooth bore. "I don't understand. It looks like this shape would tumble in the air, making it less accurate."

"The rifling makes the bullet spin. That prevents the tumble and makes the bullet more accurate, not less. An arrow that spins is more accurate than one that flies straight. Same principle."

Parsha believed he had the best. Now this!

Jack said, "Don't ask me about the physics involved, but it works.

Now then, your musket is fired by a matchlock. You load it from the muzzle. You ignite it from the breech. What lights the powder in these cartridges? Is that your next question?"

Parsha grinned.

Jack showed him a strip of detonators. "This is called a Maynard strip because it was invented by a dentist named Maynard. The hammer falls on one of these tiny packets of powder, called detonators, igniting the powder in the cartridge. Each time I cock the rifle for another shot, the strip advances, presenting a fresh detonator. I pull the trigger and the hammer hits a detonator, exploding the powder inside the cartridge. I replace the cartridge. I fire again. While you're busy reloading your gun from the muzzle, I can load and fire six or eight cartridges."

"Say, that is something!" Parsha said. "But what happens when you run out of cartridges?" Parsha arched an eyebrow.

"I save the linen shells and load some more. I have a small press and bullet molds in my pack. All I need is powder and lead for the bullets, same as you. Rapid reloading is just one advantage of my Sharps. The second is an adjustable peep sight. The third is the range."

Jack tapped on the rear peep. "This is a peep sight. You put the raised dot at the muzzle in the center of the circle at the breech and lay the dot on your target, and there you have it. If you screw the peep higher, the muzzle is raised for longer range. If you're shooting at a closer target, you screw the peep lower. You see how that works? No guessing. This fires a fifty-caliber round. The longer the barrel, the more accurate the shot. You fire a fifty-caliber bullet from a rifled barrel this long and you get maximum range."

Parsha used the telescope to take another look at the deer. Watching the deer, he grinned. "You think you can hit that stag from here?"

"Long, rifled barrel. Massive firing load. It's within range."

"Impossible. All you'll do is scare it off."

"You think so?"

"That far away? I don't believe it."

Jack inserted a linen cartridge into the breech and locked it into place. He laid the barrel across the boulder. "Let's give it a try and see what happens. How far away would you say that is?"

Parsha put the scope down and studied the stag far below them, squinting his eyes. "I don't know. Six hundred yards?"

"About half a verst."

"Something like that," Parsha said.

Jack screwed the peep higher and sighted at the grazing stag. He knew where the stag was only because he had studied it through the telescope. At this range it was nearly hidden behind the dot in the middle of the peep. He screwed the peep higher. He said, "After all my big talk, I'm not sure if I can pull it off at this range. We'll see."

Parsha smiled. He clearly didn't believe Jack had a chance. "I'll watch through the telescope."

"Fair enough." Jack sighted in on the stag once again, hoping to score a shot on the animal's ribs just behind his front leg. He took a deep breath. He let it out slowly, concentrating. He stopped breathing. In that heartbeat, when his body was perfectly still and the barrel was unmoving, he pulled the trigger.

The Sharps rocked hard against his shoulder.

"Yeeeeeeee!" Parsha exclaimed.

The recoil of the Sharps had sent the muzzle off the target, so Jack didn't know whether he had scored or not.

Parsha gave him the telescope. He looked down on the meadow to see the stag jerking in the grass.

Jack quickly removed the cartridge, inserted another, and cocked the rifle. He gave it to Parsha. "Your turn, partner. Finish him."

Parsha eagerly grabbed the gun, pleased that Jack was going to share his special gun. "It's ready to fire, just like that?" He was disbelieving.

"Reloaded. Just like that." Jack snapped his fingers. "Dot in the middle of the peep, remember. Aim right at the target. The sights are already adjusted for the distance."

While Parsha sighted in on the stag, Jack watched the wounded animal through the telescope. Legs flailing, it was pawing at the air with its hooves.

Beside him, the Sharps exploded a second time.

In the telescope the stag lay still.

"Good shooting, Parsha! Regular Davy Crockett or Daniel Boone."

Parsha turned the Sharps in his hand. "I don't know who they are, but with a gun like this my grandmother would be a good shot."

"With a *rifle* like that your grandmother would be a good shot," Jack said.

He laughed. "Whatever. Remember last night you were worrying about how we would retrieve Sonja from Ali's band?"

"How could I forget? Hard to sleep."

Parsha handed the Sharps back to Jack and set off down the trail in the direction of the fallen stag. "Stop your worrying. We'll get her back."

"How? Last night you had no idea."

Parsha paused momentarily to dig at his testicles. "Last night, I didn't know about your, uh, rifle."

Jack grinned. "There, you've got it. That's the kind of talk I like to hear."

"Hard to teach an old dog new tricks," Parsha said. The trail started downhill in the direction of the meadow with the dead stag. He said, "I guess I understand how a spiral groove inside of the barrel makes the bullet spin. What I can't figure is how the spinning keeps the bullet from tumbling or makes it more accurate than a ball. A ball seems like the natural shape."

ELEVEN

The Nature of a Precipice

To the south of Cholsoun Pass, Ali's Kyrgyz band rode through the valley of Kaier Koomin. Above them loomed Mount Chesnok (Mount Garlic). To the east, the high peaks of the Cholsoun were dusted with a mantle of early snow. The Kourt-Chume Mountains, south of the Cholsoun's snowy summits, marked the frontier of China. Notwithstanding the Tsar's desire to expand his empire, the Kourt-Chume was a natural and formidable barrier; extending to the valley of the Irtysh, the mountains turned south and ran toward Nor-Zaisan.

Sonja inferred from what few words she had learned of the Kyrgyz language that Ali's camp was located in one of the few passes in the Kourt-Chume that led from Russian territory at the headwaters of the Irtysh into China. Peasants and *zeks* manning the isolated travel stations were more interested in survival than in pleasing Koslov and the Tsar, and it was clear that Ali was bribing them to serve as his eyes and ears. The authorities and bureaucrats in the *pristans* and *zavods* were a more difficult problem for Ali. Not only were they more ambitious and eager to demonstrate their loyalty to the crown, but they had units of Cossacks to guard against Kyrgyz bandits.

Sonja also knew that Jack would no longer be able to use his papers from the Tsar in his travels. It was well known in Russia that poorly paid minor bureaucrats in the larger *zavods* and towns did a thriving business selling forged identity papers. The problem was Jack's American accent. There was no way, short of being silent in the extreme, that he could pass himself off as a native.

That night Ali resorted to a new tactic.

Looking down on his naked, unresponsive captive, he said, "You will keep your eyes open, Mrs. Sandt." He pried her thighs apart. "I said, 'Open them.'"

She kept them tightly closed.

"I want them open."

She refused.

He grabbed her by her hair and yanked her to her feet. He slugged her in the stomach. She dropped to her knees gasping for air. When she recovered, he said, "On your back, eyes and legs open."

She did as she was told.

He was into her.

She kept her eyes open, unblinking, but she did not see Ali. She looked straight through him, unblinking, unseeing.

Jack on a horse, spurring hard, his face determined, was riding hard, coming for her.

WITH THE TREES GETTING LARGER, JACK AND PARSHA CONTINUED their descent of Cholsoun Pass. At length they entered a forest of magnificent cedars, with foliage so thick they couldn't see the mountain above them. Then a cloud moved into the cedars, and they rode slowly through an eerie fog. Jack could barely see Parsha in front of him. The branches were loaded with water from the storm, giving them a shower every few minutes. Soon they were sopping wet.

Suddenly, Parsha stopped his descent and turned his horse to the east. Jack said, "What's up?"

Parsha turned in his saddle. "I'm not sure. I think I made a mistake."

"Mistake?"

"I don't think this is the Cholsoun Pass, but I'm not sure."

They continued on through the dense fog. A sighing breeze began high in the trees and the fog swirled about them. Jack thought he heard water coming from somewhere below them. Parsha heard the same thing. Again he stopped.

"We wait," he said, and dismounted, looking concerned.

Jack dismounted as well. "What is it?" he said.

"We'll see. Let's wait for the fog to clear."

They sat waiting. Jack heard the sound of water again, sounding like it was coming from below.

Slowly the fog lifted, swirling in wisps among the branches above them. Finally it cleared, and Parsha eased downhill. He knelt, looking down at something. Jack knelt beside him, and they looked down the face of a steep cliff. The bottom was nearly three hundred feet below them. Jack quickly backed up and lay on his stomach. He inched up to the edge and tentatively peered over, but even that was unsettling. Parsha seemed amused by this, although Jack noted that the Cossack got down on all fours. They looked to the right, and to their mutual astonishment, they realized that they had been traveling through the fog at the very edge of the precipice, at times within ten feet or less of the chasm.

Seeing his astonishment, Parsha smiled lazily. "I told you it wouldn't be easy finding your wife."

Jack said, "We couldn't see anything. I could barely see the ground. What happened?"

"We overshot the pass when we were escaping the storm. This cliff is on the far side, I remember."

Jack burst out laughing, relieved to be alive. "Now you remember!"

Parsha gave him a lopsided smile. "Cliffs and fog come in many forms, Jack. We spend our lives walking on the edge of invisible precipices. How many other cliffs are we walking on at this very instant that we can't see?"

ALI'S BAND CIRCLED THE SILVER *ZAVOD* AT ZIRIANOVSKY, SITUATED near a morass at the base of the eight-hundred-foot-high Revnevaya Gora, the source of the silver. A great plain, nearly devoid of vegetation save for an occasional birch and flowering shrub, extended to the edge of the mountain, giving the area a sterile, desolate appearance. Sonja could see the purple profile of the more imposing Eagle Mountain in the distance.

Three days later, the Kyrgyz marauders passed Little Narym, an outpost of Cossacks stationed on the plain within a few versts of the Chinese frontier, and two days after that they circled Great Narym, a fortress of Cossacks. The Cossacks grew wheat and rye as well as cucumbers and watermelons in the valley of the Narym, and they had the exclusive right to all the fish in the Nor-Zaisan, the Irtysh, and the other streams running into them. This was the crown's way of buying their loyalty. Sonja saw a few Kyrgyz living in yurts near Great Narym; they wintered there, feeding their flocks and herds on the plains.

TWELVE

Bouchtarma Station

AT DUSK ON THEIR SIXTH DAY OUT, TRAVELING through a light rain that had them soaked and cold and miserable, Jack and Parsha saw the light of a station on the Bouchtarma River. This was close enough to Ali's haunts in the Kourt-Chume that the locals might have heard rumors of his comings and goings.

Bouchtarma station was a small hut on a high bank overlooking the river, built of logs flattened on each side with the cracks plugged with moss and mud. The flat roof, made of squared timber, was covered with six inches of grass-covered earth. The station was surrounded by a wicker fence to protect the household animals from the wolves, and it had a shed in the rear.

Upon entering, Jack and Parsha discovered that the hut had two rooms. Six men, three women, and two children inhabited the first room, about fifteen feet by twelve feet; the roof was leaking and the earthen floor was covered with wet grass mixed with mud. Jack and Parsha nearly gagged at the odor, caused by an accumulation of various bodily fluids and wastes ground into the mud and grass and by the steam from clothes drying above a stove.

The stationmaster ushered them into the second, smaller room— also with a leaking roof—about twelve feet by five feet, which had a stove by a wooden bench. The stationmaster lit the stove, which took up nearly a third of the space.

As the fire got going, a storm moved in. The wind battered at the side of the hut and water began streaming down through the many cracks in the roof. The stove leaked smoke. Soon their eyes were burning and they could hardly see. They retreated to the larger room, never mind the stench and the fact that they were stuffed like cordwood with the other inhabitants.

All things considered, the men looked like they were in fair enough condition. But the women, barefoot and with blue handkerchiefs tied on their heads, were dressed in filthy coverings tied about their waists with a piece of twisted hemp. One thin, emaciated child, looking sorrowful and not a little desperate, was about four years old. A baby of about two, staring at them with large brown eyes, was filthy.

Here was a scene that would make Karl Marx gnash his teeth, and Jack found it unnerving.

As Parsha and Jack warmed their joints, which had been stiffened by the cold, Parsha asked, discreetly, if any of the men had heard of the comings and goings of the Kyrgyz bandit Ali, but they had not. They suggested that Jack and Parsha proceed to the Tschinimschanka River, where they could float downstream to Werchnayan Pristan. There a detachment of Cossacks was bent on ridding the area of Ali and his band of thieves. The authorities there would almost certainly give them the latest report on Ali's whereabouts.

Jack gave their hosts some rubles for a supper of boiled meat and boiled potatoes. And by way of thanks for the fire, hospitality, and information, Parsha and Jack retrieved one of their dwindling supply of bottles of vodka. Their hosts responded with a bottle of *nalifka,* made from wild berries, and they sat in the flickering light of the candles and drank. After a while, amazingly, Jack got used to the stench.

THIRTEEN

The Attentive Lover

AFTER RIDING THE GRASSY STEPPE FOR NEARLY SIX hours—crossing several dry streambeds in the process—Ali's marauders proceeded across a stony, barren plain. They aimed at some dark ridges on the horizon. They came upon a depression that was devoid of living things yet held a lake about eight or ten versts long. The bleak lake had no outlets; even its shores were black and sterile.

The Kyrgyz tried unsuccessfully to circle the lake counterclockwise, but ran into another riverbed cut into a ravine about fifty feet deep and three hundred feet wide. A small stream was trickling along the rocks at the bottom. It was impossible to cross the steep ravine on horseback, so they had to retreat and go clockwise. This was slow going because the terrain was covered with jagged rocks the size of eggs.

Having negotiated the stones on the lakeshore, they proceeded into dark ridges that turned out to be masses of stone, some several versts high, separated by small, sandy steppes with occasional tufts of rough grass. Ali and one of his men climbed atop one of the stony ridges to see what lay ahead. Sonja assumed they were trying to spot a Kyrgyz camp where they could eat and feed their horses.

Sonja rode each day with one constant companion. Guilt. Her capture by Ali had not been her fault. She could do nothing at all to prevent his sexual attention. That was not her fault either. Every night, she put all her emotional resources into her passionate trances. She did her absolute, very best to remain an unresponsive, unfeeling vessel. And she knew that Jack would understand her plight.

Despite all that, Sonja was racked by terrible guilt for having yielded to Ali before her wedding night with Jack. She felt guilty. She couldn't help it. Such awful, gnawing, terrible guilt it was. It wasn't fair that she should feel guilty. She didn't understand why she should feel any guilt over something she could not prevent. But she did.

And she felt an implacable hatred of the vile Ali that grew every time she set eyes on him. There would come a day, she vowed, when Ali would pay dearly for doing this to her.

Eventually the Kyrgyz band came across a wide, grassy depression that signaled another river. Then Sonja saw the river itself on the far side of the valley. The Kyrgyz headed for the river with the sun sinking fast, which made them anxious. None of them wanted to spend another cold night on the steppe with nothing to warm them but a single cover. Finally, they saw some horses on the far bank of the river and knew that they must be close to an *aoul*.

They retreated. Something was up, Sonja knew. "What are you going to do?" she asked.

Ali shrugged. "We are going to steal some horses from a small *aoul* belonging to a Kyrgyz named Mohammed. And some women too if there are any worth having."

"Women?"

"To join you in my harem. The women in a harem become lifelong friends. They form a bond. I'm told the mutual suffering has something to do with it, but there are pleasures as well. You will wait here without a horse. We could bind you, but you're not going anywhere. If you are so foolish as to try to escape, and we have to waste time tracking you down, you will regret it. Do you understand?"

Sonja said nothing.

With that Ali and his men rode off in the direction of the *aoul*.

Sonja looked back to the northwest, half expecting to see Jack riding in her direction. There was of course nothing. For the moment, she was alone. It began to rain.

TIPSY FROM THE VODKA, JACK AND PARSHA SAID THEIR GOOD nights to the residents of Bouchtarma station and retired to the shed to spend the night. The roof of the shed leaked badly, but Jack hung a towel under the drips above his head. The howling wind slapped the rain hard against the shed. He lay there, listening to the rain and wind. Soon the towel would be soaked, then what? There was no escaping the water.

After a while, Parsha said, "Going to be a wet night."

"I think so."

"Thinking of her, are you?"

"Yes," Jack admitted.

"If we get the rubies, that would be nice, but that's not what I'm after. Ali has been raiding isolated Cossack families and villages for years. He told you the story about what Koslov did to his cousin. That's nothing to what Ali did to me. Six months ago he and his band killed my entire family. My mother and my father. My grandfather. An aunt and an uncle. Three brothers and two sisters. A nephew and a niece. All gone. And what had they done to him? Nothing."

Jack squeezed the water out of his towel and poked the plug back into place.

"They took two muskets and some knives, and burned down every building on the farm. I am alive today because I was out hunting. From the edge of the woods, I saw Ali and his men, but I could do nothing. I felt helpless. If I had fired on them, they would have run me down and killed me as well. The only thing I could do was remain silent, vowing some day to have my revenge."

The wind suddenly began blowing harder. Still the rain came. *Whap! slap! whap! slap!* against the shed.

Jack said, "At least we didn't have to sleep inside with that smell." He waited. Parsha would tell his story at his own pace.

—————

WITH THE RAIN SLAPPING AGAINST HER IN COLD, HARD SHEETS, Sonja walked in the direction she calculated was northwest. It was as though she were on a vast, earthen sea. Ahead of her somewhere were mountains. In this part of the world mountains rose from nowhere. Everywhere, eventually, there would be mountains. In the mountains there would be water. There would be food.

Ali and his Kyrgyz warriors had raided a camp for horses. That would take time. There would be the inevitable fighting. The stolen horses would have to be tended to and possibly defended. More time. And when they went back for her and discovered she was missing, what could they do? They couldn't possibly track her until morning, and if she was lucky, the wind would blow away all traces of where she had been.

Sonja refused to accept her fate like a docile cow, drooling and chewing her cud. Let the Kyrgyz catch her if they could. If they caught her, let them do to her what they would.

There was a price to be paid for freedom. Jack Sandt's countrymen had paid it. In 1848, people across Europe had rebelled. They were paying the price still.

Sonja's countrymen had come to believe in her as a kind of symbol. She could not let them down. She would never yield. She would not. No.

Sonja kept a steady pace, swinging her arms.

MEANWHILE, IN THE LEAKY SHED WITH JACK AT BOUCHTARMA station, Parsha continued matter-of-factly. "Ali took my family by surprise. They were at his mercy. He shouted at his men, telling them what to do. He was excited. He likes killing. He killed every one of them, every one, my parents, my brothers and sisters, my aunts and uncles, my cousins."

Jack now understood why Emil said he should let Parsha tell his story in his own time and in his own way.

"Ali did it because of what a unit of the Tsar's Cossacks did to a Kyrgyz family last year. The Kyrgyz family hadn't done anything to the Tsar except live in an area claimed by the crown. It's a circle of violence that seems never to end."

Jack rearranged the grass under him, trying to remove a lump that was poking into his shoulder.

"Russia runs red with blood, I'm sorry to say. It has always been that way. It is our inheritance."

It was impossible to stay dry. Jack knew that in the early hours of the morning, when the temperature dove, he would wake up freezing.

"Tell me about America, Jack."

"I sat through some wicked storms in the mountains out west."

"No, no, not the storms. The people. The government. Tell me about that."

"We're an experiment," Jack said.

"Oh?"

"The British colonists had enough of George the Third. So after they drove the British out, they decided that their government should be by consent of the governed."

"You vote for your leaders."

"Correct. The men who wrote our Constitution believed that wherever there is power, there is a potential for mischief. They deliberately separated our Congress from the courts and from the president so that one branch of government might check the excesses of the other two."

"Does your president have gendarmes that ride at night?"

"No, we do not, I'm pleased to say. This is in large part due to the wisdom of our first president, George Washington, who set an example. He did not want to be called His Majesty or His Highness or any of that. He settled on Mr. President. The president is in charge of the government, yes, but he is still one of us, a citizen. Washington even set a precedent by declining to run for a third term in office."

"And you don't have serfs."

"We use African slaves for labor in the South." Jack sighed. "An abomination which will ultimately cause us much pain."

"As will the owning of serfs in Russia. This can't continue. Eventually there will be rebellion."

"I can't speak for Russia." Jack thought of Karl Marx in his pathetic London flat, struggling on behalf of revolution.

"There will one day be a great upheaval in Russia, believe me. The Cossacks, Kyrgyz, and Kalmyk all suffer from the Romanovs."

They lapsed into silence.

"I want Ali's head. That's why I'm with you. I'll help you get your wife, but it's Ali's head that I'm after."

"His head?"

"Yes. And his cock and balls to stuff in his mouth. I want to take it back so all my relatives can get drunk and piss and shit on it, and we can send a rider to drop it off in a Kyrgyz camp so they will know what happens when one of them slaughters a Cossack family for the sport of it." He fell silent.

Now Jack understood Parsha's motive. Listening to the rain slapping against the hut, Jack fell asleep.

Sonja's clothes were rags. She was filthy. Her eyes were forlorn. She called out to him, "Jack! Jack! Help me, Jack!"

Jack woke up. He was cold. It was still raining. Sonja was still in Ali's hands. He was letting her down.

SONJA KNEW HER BEST CHANCE FOR SURVIVAL WOULD BE TO MAKE it to the mountains before dawn, but she also knew that was impossible. She was wet and miserable; the frigid wind knifed through her. After an hour of walking, she developed burning spikes of pain in her shins. She pushed through the pain until her shins were on fire, and she was forced to stop to relieve the agony.

She sat with her back to the wind, trembling from fatigue. After the pain in her shins subsided, she continued walking.

Thirty minutes later, the pain returned.

She again rested until it subsided.

When the pain returned a third time, Sonja ignored it. Her only chance was to widen the territory Ali would have to cover to find her.

The pain!

She kept walking.

The awful pain!

She clenched her teeth.

Out here, Sonja knew, the demonic Shaitan, the devil, was said to rule. As she walked, she began to compose a poem in her head, pushing the words this way and that to take her mind off the pain.

THE HANDS OF SHAITAN
Alone at night
on the Kyrgyz steppe,
in the shadows of the Altai
Shaitan is my attentive lover,
faithful, wicked Shaitan.
His blowing fingers
feel my body,
slide around my neck,
slip inside my blouse,
caress my breasts,
and travel up my thighs.
Love me, Shaitan,
Keep me awake,
Keep me moving.

FOURTEEN

The Crossing of the Tschinimschanka

AT THE STATION ON THE TSCHINIMSCHANKA RIVER there was no bark large enough to carry their provisions and them downriver to Werchnayan Pristan, but Jack and Parsha were told they could have one built if they wished. It was clear that the poor wretches at the station were eyeing the American, wondering how much Jack would be willing to pay. Jack and Parsha had little choice, so the Cossack negotiated for the construction of a new bark. They were told that their craft would be ready for them in the morning.

They ate a supper of black bread and tea, determined to make their voyage at dawn.

Jack and Parsha awoke with the rising sun, eager to see their new boat. The peasants manning the station, encouraged by dreams of Jack's money, had done their best to fashion what they generously and persistently called a bark. They had taken two canoes, each carved from a tree trunk, and spaced them five feet apart, joining them with beams over which they nailed a platform of broken, rotting boards. The result was a floating platform of sorts, about fifteen feet long and ten feet wide. This craft or raft looked capable enough floating at the edge of the water, but on closer inspection the aged canoes looked extremely suspect. No, more than suspect. They were flat rotting.

The eager peasants, having sold them this dubious bark, then offered their services as guides to steer it downstream to Werchnayan Pristan. Since the locals knew the river and Jack and Parsha didn't, Jack paid them their exorbitant fee. He had to do what was necessary to survive. To guarantee that they wouldn't take off once they were paid, Parsha insisted on paying half at the start, half when they made it to their destination.

AT DAWN THE KYRGYZ HAD NOT YET FOUND SONJA. SHE WAS BONE cold. Her clothes were sodden. She was exhausted. Her feet were swollen. Was this it, then? Could she go no longer? The sky above her was slate gray. A hard wind started blowing.

To stop now would be lethal. With the orange sun rising to her left, she continued on, her legs wobbly.

She entered an eerie zone of pain and resolve. She remembered a poem she had written when she was sixteen years old.

IN THE POTATO CELLAR
In late March, snowing outside,
my mother sent me to the potato cellar.
Dank and dark it was,
smelling sour from the mold and mildew.
I brushed back the cobwebs.
I crossed the packed, earthen floor.
The potatoes, turned soft, were sprouting.
When the sun returned and the ground thawed
my mother would plant the sprouts
and grow more potatoes.
One day, she said, I would grow potatoes too.
As she said this, I saw a Cossack outside
riding through the snow.
Where was this man going? I wondered.

What adventures would he have?

What adventures might I have were I not a woman?

Sonja smiled grimly. Each painful step was a triumph.

THE PEASANTS HELPED JACK AND PARSHA LOAD THEIR GEAR FOR the crossing of the Tschinimschanka River and, bearing paddles no larger than a child's spade, confidently took their places at the bow and stern. They were now, officially, steersmen. They assured their passengers that the paddles were for guiding only, not propelling the bark. The current would take care of that.

The Tschinimschanka at that point was broad and wide. Like the Ob and the Ouba, the Tschinimschanka was cut into several streams or channels that were separated by islands overgrown with thick stands of willow. The shores were lined with swampy patches of reeds. Using their little oars, their guides confidently paddled them into the current, and they were away, sliding grandly downstream. In the beginning, it was a tranquil voyage. Although it was ill-advised to put too much weight on a single board, Jack's concerns about the rotten deck and canoes began to wane with the passing of time. Why was he worried? This was a simple matter of floating downstream.

The Tschinimschanka bore an amazing volume of water. Not a breeze ruffled the surface. There was not a sound to be heard. They floated along in a vast, wonderful calm. It was a nice break after the hard travel on horseback.

Suddenly they were in the middle of a howl of shrieking, as though demons had risen from the lower regions. The screams were followed quickly by a rush of flapping wings, and thousands of ducks rose from the reeds on the shoreline. Up the fowl came, more and more of them, until they nearly blocked out the morning sun. Ducks, ducks, ducks! Jack had never seen so many ducks since the fall migrations on Chesapeake Bay.

The ducks behind them, they continued their serene drift downriver.

Jack noted the encounter with the ducks in his journal, watched the passing islands through his telescope.

When one of their steersmen began muttering in Russian, Jack was unconcerned. But he noticed a look of concern on Parsha's face. "What's wrong?"

Parsha cleared his throat.

Jack felt an ominous shift in the raft. "What?"

He pointed toward one of the canoes.

What was wrong was clear enough. A rotten spot in one of the canoes had collapsed, and the canoe was taking on water. The canoe was sinking at an alarming rate. Everything Jack had brought with him was at risk—all his daguerreotype supplies and equipment, not to mention his compass, sextant, barometer, thermometer, and weapons. If the canoes went under, the rotten boards were insufficient to serve as a raft.

Jack's mouth turned dry and a stab of anxiety coursed through his stomach. "What do we do now?"

"We paddle for shore," Parsha said.

The steersmen, finding the second half of their fee at risk, leaped to their task. With one half of the raft listing dangerously, they paddled toward shore for all they were worth, a task hampered by their insufficient paddles.

Jack and Parsha each ripped a board off the deck, which they used for paddles. Jack's broke immediately, and he tried another. It too snapped. On his third try he got a sturdy piece of wood.

They were in a stretch of channel where the current quickened. The reeds seemed as far away as the moon as the raft sank lower and lower on the water. Jack paddled so hard that his arms and shoulders burned with pain and his hands were rubbed raw.

Would they make it?

Jack didn't think so. No way.

He was almost right. The water was up to the rotten deck as they reached the edge of the reeds. As both canoes filled, they leaped out, discovering to their relief that the water was only waist high. They were able to save the cargo by holding the deck on top of the water and pushing it through the reeds, struggling through the muck.

Jack plopped on the ground, wet, cold, disconsolate, and exhausted, feeling he'd like to use the so-called steersmen for target practice. While apologetic about what had happened, they seemed unconcerned, however. After powwowing with them in excited Russian that was too fast for Jack to comprehend, Parsha calmed down as well.

"What now?" Jack asked.

Parsha said, "We'll have to spend the day here while they fix the bark."

Jack was still sore as hell, and he could not imagine how they proposed to fix anything. The canoe that had caved in was beyond repair, and the other was equally rotten. "Fix it? How, pray tell?"

Parsha grinned. "These people know how to make do. It's how they survive. Watch."

"Watch what?"

"They used the rotten canoes for the bottom of the bark because that's what they thought we expected. It's more European. They had their doubts it would survive, so they brought along what they need to make a proper Tschinimschanka River bark."

Jack stared at him, disbelieving. "What we expected? More European?"

"Right. They wanted us to be confident. Otherwise they might not have gotten the job. Now they'll build a bark that they themselves use to float dried meat or fish to market at Werchnayan Pristan."

Using sharp knives and an outsized ball of twine, the Tschinimschanka boatmen proceeded to construct what was a sensible, inexpensive peasant solution to travel on the river. The hollow reeds along the shore of the river were about an inch thick and closed every six or eight inches, forming a string of tubes. The steersmen cut these reeds in five-foot lengths and used the twine to tie them into bundles. This was no easy chore because the reeds seemed as hard as steel and cutting enough for six large bundles took several hours.

While their helpers labored with the reeds, Jack and Parsha tried their hand at finding something for supper. Parsha took the shotgun and Jack took a revolver and some fishing gear, thinking they would try to catch some grayling. They hiked downstream past the reeds to a point where the channel eddied toward shore in a deep pool. Without a word Parsha pointed quickly at the water below them.

He had spotted several *talmane,* or sturgeons, from four to six feet long basking in the water. Jack drew his Colt revolver and fired quickly at one of the forms.

The fish scattered, but one remained, floating on the water.

Parsha grinned broadly. "Good shooting!"

"Lucky."

He laughed. "No matter. Our friends are going to like this, and so will we." Parsha waded quickly into the water and grabbed the giant fish by the gills. He dragged it to shore, and they discovered that it was nearly six feet long.

Jack described the incident in his journal while Parsha set about cutting the giant fish into large steaks. The sun set slowly over a magnificent vista. Upstream, the river flowed through purple peaks and ridges. Beyond that lay the brown, gray, and green ridges of the Cholsoun Range, the jagged granite peaks dusted with snow. Farther north lay the snow-covered giants of the Altai. To watch the colossal, ethereal mass of those great, brooding mountains at sunset was nearly a religious experience. The Altai were mysterious, forbidding. Awesome.

In the dim light of dusk Sonja could barely make out the silhouette of the mountains that lay dead ahead. She could also see the dim forms of mounds that turned out to be piles of stones.

The farther she walked, the larger were the stone mounds.

At length Sonja came upon large rocks scattered on the steppe, followed by a large enclosure surrounded by a wall, seven feet thick and four to six feet high, made of large stones with smaller rocks fitted in between them. None of the stones had been cut. She knew this was probably a place forbidden by the Kyrgyz. The evil Shaitan lived here.

She could go no farther. However strong her resolve, her body no longer responded.

She found a place where the wall had collapsed to less than two feet tall and climbed over it. Inside she found a crumbling obelisk of basalt stones about fifty feet high. She collapsed on the cold ground, curled up against the base of the wall facing the wind. If her body recovered, she could continue on to the mountains in the morning.

THE STEERSMEN COMPLETED THEIR LABORS SHORTLY AFTER DARK. Their Cossack craft rode high and dry above the water. Nothing was going to sink bundles of hollow reeds. Jack's gear was safe, and he had changed into dry clothes, so he calmed down. Parsha smothered the sturgeon steaks with wild onions and garlic and fried them in deer tallow. He dug out some bottles of vodka by way of celebrating their survival.

Such a celebration it was. The moon was high and bright. The sturgeon was delicious—more than they could possibly consume—and they ate until they nearly burst, with Parsha plopping more steaks on to fry as needed. To say they got drunk is to understate their condition. They got drunker than louts. Then some wolves began howling in the distance as though serenading them. About midnight, when they were drinking and laughing at their misfortune, adding details and drama with each retelling of the tale, the howling seemed to grow closer. They drank some more vodka and laughed even louder. Let the wolves bare their teeth and bay if they pleased. They were not frightened. They were invincible. Nothing could harm them.

SONJA WAS AWAKENED BY THE SOUND OF HOOVES. THEN VOICES. Kyrgyz. Shivering, she pressed herself against the base of the crumbling wall. Maybe the shadows would save her.

The voices got louder. They were getting closer.

They stopped just outside the ancient temple.

She heard the word "Shaitan" in their conversation. Maybe they were fearful of coming inside.

No. They were dismounting.

She curled up into a ball, resolving to remain absolutely still. In the dim light, maybe they would mistake her for a boulder. Such was her desperation.

Then they were above her, looking down. One of them kicked her in the ribs. She lay there inert. Maybe they would think she was dead.

The Kyrgyz kicked her harder. She cried out. The Kyrgyz spoke her name.

"Mercy," she said in Russian. "I'll do anything you want. Anything. Please don't take me back. Tell him you couldn't find me."

A hand grabbed her by the hair. She winced. "What would it hurt?" she asked.

He yanked to her feet. She was almost too weak to stand. "Mercy," she said again.

In Russian that was surprisingly good, the Kyrgyz said, "There is no mercy on the steppe, Mrs. Sandt. Here pain rules."

IN THE MIDDLE OF THE DRUNKENNESS, one of the steersmen mentioned, casually, that Jack and Parsha might try crossing the Irtysh onto the Kyrgyz Steppe. Somewhere close to the Mantilla Rocks, near the Monastery Mountains, they would find a wealthy Kyrgyz named Mohammed, who had repeatedly been raided by Ali's bandits. Mohammed might be in the mood to help them.

Parsha said, "Why didn't you tell us this before?"

"I didn't think of it," he said.

Parsha cocked his head. "Because you were so busy calculating how much money you could make from building a bark that wouldn't float."

The steersman gave them a self-deprecating grin. "Probably," he said.

FIFTEEN

The Price

 THE KYRGYZ WARRIOR WHO HAD FOUND SONJA REINED in his horse at Ali's yurt. He untied Sonja, who lay on her stomach behind his saddle, and dumped her onto the earth with a thump, her ankles and wrists still bound. Sonja had not slept. She was exhausted. Her feet were swollen.

She looked up at Ali and the faces of the Kyrgyz watching her. Among them was a brown-eyed Kyrgyz girl, a real beauty.

Ali said, "I thought you might try that. Never mind. Little tired, are you?" He gestured at the brown-eyed girl. "We stole this girl Fatimeh along with the horses." He studied her, thinking. "So what do we do to you to teach you a lesson?" He chewed briefly on his thumbnail, then brightened. He said something to one of his warriors.

The man knelt with his knife and unceremoniously cut Sonja's clothes off with vicious strokes of the blade, leaving her naked on the ground with bound wrists and ankles. A second warrior grabbed two lengths of rawhide, then spread a length of harsh *voilock* on the ground. The first man pushed her onto the edge of the *voilock* with his boot, then rolled her up. She felt the ends of the *voilock* being tied.

Somebody kicked her in the ribs. Inside the bag, she could hardly breathe.

Above her, Ali said, "I am the Mahdi. You should feel privileged to be mine. How long you stay in there is up to you. When you're ready to accept your fate, just let me know."

He waited for an answer, then said, "The question is how long you will suffer before you yield."

Sonja felt herself being pulled, bumping, on the ground.

THE STEERSMEN HELPED JACK AND PARSHA SECURE MOUNTS AND packhorses from a settlement on the east bank of the Tschinimschanka. They rode southwest across a level plain that extended about eight versts before it rose to a range of low hills. When they reached the hills, they discovered that these were made of quartz that sparkled like snow in the sun and were the site of several score of ancient Kyrgyz tombs in the shape of pyramids about ten to twelve feet square.

The steppe was no place to sleep on a starry night. The temperature became bitter cold. With the Monastery Mountains rising in a mist before them, they pushed on through the wind that cut right through them. At dusk they saw a large Kyrgyz encampment, with at least three dozen yurts, on the shore of a small lake, with great herds of horses and camels moving slowly toward it. This must be Mohammed's camp at the Mantilla Rocks, the foothills of the Monastery Mountains.

They drove their horses down the bank. Jack had never seen anything like the vista before them. It was dusk, time to milk the camels and cows, and there were animals everywhere, amazing living streams of animals being guided toward the lake.

As they rode through a din of bleating sheep and grunting camels, Parsha explained the habit of the Kyrgyz to keep moving to find fresh grazing for their animals. The women did the milking. The men drove the herds to and from the pastures. "They herd the horses and camels the greatest distance each day, perhaps ten to fifteen versts. The oxen are taken five to ten versts away. The sheep remain nearest the *aoul.* They'll stay in one spot for eight or ten days, then move on, looking for more grazing. When the fall is coming on, as it is now, they'll move their herds well south of here, returning in the spring."

Jack did his best to count the animals, but except for the camels, that was impossible. He counted 115 camels, including their young. He estimated there were about a thousand cows and oxen, two thousand horses, and six thousand sheep and goats. As they drew near the yurts, a pack of savage-looking dogs met them, growling and with teeth bared. Then, suddenly, three fierce-looking Kyrgyz confronted them, bearing whips.

Jack and Parsha stopped, holding up the palms of their hands to show they came in peace. This struck Jack as foolishness; two men were not about to attack this camp by themselves.

Beside him, Parsha murmured, "I know their ways. Do as I do. If you're uncertain, catch my eye."

The oldest of the whip-bearing trio, the apparent leader, had a formidable black beard and a deep scar on his forehead. He wore red high-heeled boots and a coat made of brown horse skin, tied at the waist with a red shawl. The makers of the coat had left the black mane of the horse intact, and the mane extended halfway down the center of his back. His fox-skin cap, lined in crimson, fell over his ears and rose to an odd cone on top, serving what purpose Jack couldn't imagine.

Making no attempt to introduce himself, he motioned with his hands that they should dismount. They did. Jack had his Sharps in a saddle scabbard. Parsha had his shotgun slung across his back. They both had one of the Colt revolvers holstered on their belts. Jack's stash was in his saddlebag. An old man appeared to take care of their mounts. Jack didn't want to be separated from his weapons or money. He glanced at Parsha, feeling anxious.

Remarkably, Parsha seemed unconcerned. He smiled. "Relax, Jack. We're their guests." Holding up his hands to show they were empty, Parsha quickly retrieved a loaf of sugar from one of their packhorses and gave it to him. "We'll need a gift."

For the first time, the man with the horse-skin coat spoke. "You will unload your weapons, please."

They did as they were told. As they unloaded the weapons, two young boys appeared and began unsaddling their horses.

THE HORSE DRAGGING SONJA STOPPED.

Sonja heard Ali's voice above her. "How are you doing?"

Sonja felt like she was going to explode from the pain. She wanted to scream to the heavens. She didn't.

Ali laughed. "You can stop it anytime. All you have to do now is yield."

She remained silent. She tried to block him out.

My name is Sonja Sankova Sandt. I am of the valley. My husband is Jack Sandt. He is of the mountain. Together we come full circle. We will never yield.

"Another couple of hours and we'll be stopping for the night. You think you can make it that far? I want you alive. No fun for Colonel Koslov to cut the ears off a corpse."

A bolt of pain shot up Sonja's spine. She started to speak, then closed her mouth. She refused to give him the satisfaction.

"Resist if you will. I'll fuck you hard when we get back. You'll feel better then." Ali yelled at his warriors, and they continued on.

Sonja had never imagined that pain could be so obscene. She wept silently, willing herself not to cry out and beg for mercy.

My name is Sonja. My husband is Jack Sandt.

"If you want mercy, all you have to do is ask."

Whatever the price of freedom and human dignity, I will pay it.

"Speak up. I can't hear you."

My man is Jack Sandt.

"Are you sure you won't change your mind?"

We will never yield.

SIXTEEN

In the Yurt of Chief Mohammed

BEARING THEIR UNLOADED FIREARMS AND A SMALL box of daguerreotypes and trailed by the boys with their saddles and saddlebags, Jack and Parsha followed the man in the horse coat to a large yurt. A spear was stuck in the ground beside the entrance, and a tuft of horsehair at the top of the spear blew in the wind. Next to the spear with the horsehair, a hawk was chained to a perch stuck in the ground. Jack followed horse coat into the diminutive entrance, which was covered by *voilock*.

They were met by a stout, square-built man, about sixty years old, with a broad face, a fine, flowing gray beard, and intelligent brown eyes. He wore a close-fitting silk cap embroidered with silver. His long yellow-and-pink-striped robe, or *kalat*—tied at the waist with a white shawl—was made of silk. He wore high-heeled red leather boots that looked too small for him, causing him to walk with difficulty.

They introduced themselves. This was indeed Mohammed, the chief of this camp. He spoke Russian, although not well. Jack was later to learn that this ability to speak Russian was unusual among the Kyrgyz, who despised the language.

Mohammed invited them to sit on a beautiful Bokharan carpet. The boys with their saddles and saddlebags placed them at the sides of the entrance and disappeared.

Mohammed's wife watched demurely from the edge of the yurt. She was twenty-five or thirty years younger than he was. She wore a black *kalat* of *kunfu,* Chinese satin, tied at the waist with a red shawl. Her boots were the same make and color as her husband's. She wore a white muslin cap, pointed, with lappets hanging almost to her waist. She had a broad face with high cheekbones, a wide mouth, a small nose, and large, black eyes. She was not beautiful. Neither was she bad looking. A bath would have helped, but baths did not appear to be part of the Kyrgyz regimen.

There were three children in the yurt as well, playing on a sheet of *voilock.* A five-year-old boy was dressed in a yellow-and-red-striped *kalat.* Two little girls, perhaps three and four years old and naked, rolled about playing with a young goat.

Jack and Parsha were not told the name of the wife or the children.

The yurt was a circle about thirty-five feet in diameter and twelve feet high at the center. For walls, the Kyrgyz wove five-foot-high panels of willow, a wood that could be peeled from a bough in strips. They fastened the panels together with rawhide, allowing them to be folded up. To keep the yurt watertight and warm, they stretched sheets of *voilock* over the willow panels and willow rib skeleton of the dome. They tied the ribs to the tops of the panels and bent them upward, fastening them into holes drilled into a four-foot ring, forming a circle that let in light and released smoke from the fire in the center of the floor.

Parsha said, "My companion is an American. He has never been inside a Kyrgyz yurt."

Mohammed looked surprised. "No?"

Looking about, Jack cleared his throat. The furnishings were simple. Decorated wooden boxes sat on *voilock* on the far side of the fire.

"Please, let me show you my modest house." Mohammed was a wealthy Kyrgyz, and it was with some pride that he made his offer.

"I would be honored," Jack said.

Stepping past his naked daughters, Mohammed led Jack to the decorated boxes. "These contain my family's clothing, some bolts of Chinese silk, dried fruits, tea, and a modest number of *ambas.* Our humble belongings."

Jack felt he was supposed to be impressed by *ambas,* but he had no idea what Mohammed was talking about.

The Kyrgyz chief could see that, and opened a box filled with squares of silver about two and a half inches long, an inch and a half wide, and maybe three-tenths of an inch thick.

Persian and Bokharan carpets were stacked on top of the boxes, and Mohammed's personal saddle was stacked on top of those. As befitted the chief of such an impressive *aoul,* Mohammed's saddle was inlaid with silver and had velvet cushions. His battle-ax lay against the pommel of his saddle, its blade inlaid with silver; its handle, about four feet long, had a leather thong at the end for the owner's wrist.

Common saddles, saddle cloths, horsehair ropes, and *tchimbars* were fastened around the sides of the yurt with leather straps. A *tchimbar* was large, billowing costume so fashioned that a Kyrgyz could travel with three or four *kalats* tied around his waist when he rode. This form of carrying one's belongings gave Kyrgyz horsemen an odd, globelike appearance. With tiny head and legs protruding from a bulging middle, they looked like unwieldy horsemen; in fact, they were excellent riders.

To the left of the fire was a decorated leather bag or bottle with a tube in one corner, a stack of enameled Chinese wooden bowls, and a metal cauldron.

Mohammed stopped there. He tapped the leather bag. "This is the most important piece of furniture in my *yurt.* Do you know about koumiss?"

Jack shook his head.

"It is made of fermented mare's milk. It is not ready to drink until it has set for two weeks." He said something to his wife, and she inserted a wooden rod into the tube at the corner of the bag and stirred the contents vigorously. "It's a woman's work to stir the koumiss as my wife is doing now. This has to be done frequently. A koumiss container is never washed, by the way—it would spoil the contents. You may have seen the small leather bags carried by Kyrgyz riders. Those are for the koumiss.

"We will have some now. A proper welcome to my yurt." He clapped his hands loudly and a young man stepped through the door. He had apparently been waiting outside in the cold in case his services were needed. Mohammed said, "Kill a lamb. Bring it quickly."

The young man disappeared without a word.

TURNING HIS BACK TO THE DRIVING, COLD RAIN, ALI WAVED HIS hand and motioned to the Kyrgyz pulling the roll of *voilock* containing Sonja Sandt. He slipped off his horse, walked over to the roll, and gave it a kick. In Russian, he said, "You in there! Sonja! We have work to do tonight. Are you ready to come out?"

No answer.

He kicked her again, harder. "Do you yield?"

Nothing.

"Speak!"

Ali frowned and said something to the Kyrgyz. To the lump in the *voilock,* he muttered, "Are you dead or just stubborn? Bitch!" He used his knife to cut the rawhide binding, then unrolled the *voilock* with a violent push of his foot. Sonja's body, glistening with blood, rolled out into the rain.

Ali muttered something in Kyrgyz, then knelt to see if his captive was unconscious or dead.

My name is Sonja Sankova Sandt. I will pay whatever price.

In Russian, he said, "You were dragged because you tried to escape. I cannot allow my women to flee. When you've healed you will be responsive in my bed or there will be consequences of a kind that you never imagined in your wildest nightmare."

SEVENTEEN

The Comfort of Laudanum

 SONJA AWOKE AND WINCED FROM THE PAIN WHEN she tried to move. She was lying on a carpet with a pillow under her head. Above her knelt the young Kyrgyz girl she had seen moments before she had been rolled up in the *voilock*. The girl looked relieved. In Russian, she said, "Ah, you're awake. I was beginning to wonder if you were going to make it. My name is Fatimeh."

Sonja looked around the yurt. "Where am I?"

"I'm not sure. Ali was afraid he'd killed you. We've stopped long enough for you to recover. I think we're headed for his *aoul* in a valley of the Kourt-Chume."

"I'm thirsty."

"I bet you are." Fatimeh cradled her head and dipped some water from a bucket with a wooden cup.

Sonja accepted the cup and took a sip and quickly finished the rest. "Are we in the mountains?"

Fatimeh looked surprised. "Why yes. How did you know?"

"The water was cool and sweet. How long have I been unconscious?"

"For about ten hours now. Since I speak Russian, I've been given the job of seeing to your health. Ali says if you die, I die too. When you get well we'll both be moved into the yurt with the rest of the harem."

"The harem?"

Fatimeh nodded. "Ali has older women to milk his animals and cook. We're to be part of his harem."

"The younger ones and those he likes."

Fatimeh sighed. "I've been massaging you with oil. I didn't know what else to do. You're bruised all over, but your hips and knees are the worst. And your shoulders."

Sonja tried to move and stiffened from the pain. "When I was taken I had an embroidered bag with some medicine in it. I don't suppose I still have that."

Fatimeh checked the entrance to the yurt. Speaking softly, she said, "Yes you do. Full of small bottles plus there is a . . ." She glanced at the entrance.

"A pistol. The pistol is still there?"

Fatimeh nodded. "Ali just glanced inside the bag. The pistol was underneath the bottles."

Sonja smiled. "Mention it to no one. I'll need one of the bottles, please, and a spoon."

Fatimeh fetched a blue bottle from the bag and poured out a yellowish brown solution.

As she took the spoonful of medicine, Sonja said, "This is laudanum."

"Laudanum?"

"A solution of alcohol mixed with opium. It kills the pain. You know about opium?"

Fatimeh shook her head.

"It's made from the juice of the unripe poppy."

"I see."

"This is part of the unused supply I had for my Russian father. He died a couple of weeks ago from a tumor growing in his chest. I would like to sit up. Can you help me sit up?" Sonja felt the warming laudanum begin spreading through her body.

"Of course." Fatimeh took her around her shoulders.

Sonja cried out from the pain. "You're Kyrgyz. How is it you speak Russian?"

Fatimeh dipped her some more water. "My father, Mohammed,

speaks Russian. So does my brother Hasan. We learned so we could better deal with the Tsar's tax collectors and for bargaining with the Cossacks."

"We will be patient. My husband will be coming for me. And perhaps your brother as well."

Fatimeh had a faraway look in her eyes. "Yes, I suppose he will one day, although I'm not sure I'm looking forward to it. Hasan has the family's honor to maintain."

"Its honor?"

"Tell me, do you know a lot about the ways of the Kyrgyz?"

Sonja looked puzzled.

Fatimeh told her about women and honor.

Sonja was disbelieving. "You're telling me your family is honor bound to kill you because you slept with a man who kidnapped you?"

"Because I slept with any man other than the husband chosen for me."

"Well, we won't let that happen. Jack will be here. We have to prepare. The first chance we get we need to steal weapons. Muskets. Battle-axes. Knives. Whatever we can lay our hands on."

Fatimeh leaned forward, her eyes serious. "Please, Sonja. You don't know what you're talking about. If they catch you, they'll have you stoned. The harem is guarded constantly by Ali's eunuch."

"His eunuch?"

"His name is Raj. He's a Turk. While you were unconscious, I had a chance to talk to the other members of the harem. They tell me Raj was a scholar before Ali captured him and had his testicles removed. He speaks Kyrgyz, Arabic, and Russian. His job is to see to it that nobody enjoys the harem except Ali. He sleeps at the entrance to the yurt of the harem. He tells the girls who is to sleep with Ali and what they should wear. He, uh, prefers his girls in pairs. One to hold the other down."

"Meaning you and me."

"Very likely," Fatimeh said. "They tell me that to go too long without being chosen is not a good sign. When Ali grows tired of a female, she is moved to another yurt, where she milks horses and camels and makes koumiss."

"We do what we have to do to survive."

Fatimeh said, "We wait for Jack."

"Yes, we do."

Fatimeh smiled at Sonja. "You're very lucky to have such a man to believe in."

The entrance to the yurt opened and a handsome man entered—tall, square-jawed, with piercing brown eyes and a full black beard. "I see that milady is feeling better. My name is Raj." He bowed politely.

EIGHTEEN

In Appreciation of Koumiss

JACK AND PARSHA RETREATED TO THEIR PLACES ON the carpet. The wife set a lacquered bowl before each of them. She removed the koumiss container from its stand and filled each of their bowls with the fermented liquid.

Catching Jack's eye, Parsha drank his in a single pull.

Jack did the same. The koumiss had an odd, sour taste.

Mohammed looked pleased. "Is it good?"

"Very good," Jack said. "I've never had better."

Mohammed appeared uncertain.

Parsha said, "He speaks the truth. It is good." He gave Jack a meaningful look. They had drunk Mohammed's koumiss. It was time to give Mohammed the sugar.

Jack produced it quickly. "We bring sugar for your family. Perhaps your children would enjoy some."

"Ah, sugar!" Mohammed was delighted.

At that moment, the young man entered the door with the carcass of a freshly butchered lamb, which he fastened onto a spit above the fire. A second young man had dried horse and camel dung, which he added to the fire, after which he retreated from the yurt without a word. The first young man began turning the lamb.

"Perhaps the girls would like some sugar," Jack said.

The wife glanced at Mohammed. Mohammed nodded.

The wife gave each of the children a small ration of sugar, which they sucked on with delight, their brown eyes sparkling.

If Jack and Parsha were to find Ali and his band, they had to get on the good side of the Kyrgyz. The little boy and his sisters were watching the proceedings with awe. Jack said, "In one of our packhorses, I have a machine that takes images like this." He withdrew his daguerreotype of Karl Marx and showed it to Mohammed.

He waited while Mohammed admired it. "Would you like me to capture an image of your family?" He turned the dag to show it to the wife.

She looked at her husband with dark brown eyes that said she wanted the portrait.

Mohammed said, "*Da.*"

His wife hurried to the boxes and retrieved fresh *kalats* for her children. She dressed her son in a pink-and-yellow-striped *kalat* like his father's, and the girls in black.

Jack motioned with his hands that he wanted the children closer together and with the boy at the rear. Mohammed's wife grabbed them by the shoulders and pushed them together, looking at Jack for approval.

"That's just right," Jack said. "Thank you. I'll need lots of light, some torches perhaps. It will only be for a few seconds. And you will have to remain perfectly still. Perhaps some more sugar would help them sit still."

THE DAGUERREOTYPE OF MOHAMMED AND HIS FAMILY WORKED like magic. While Parsha made small talk, Mohammed's wife retreated to the edge of the yurt, where she admired the daguerreotype in silence, taking great care to handle it only by the edges as she had been told. The children were destined for a hard life on the steppe. One day they would look like their mother, or close to it. Jack wanted to give them something to look back on. That's how they looked when they were children.

The icy wind thumped against the side of the yurt.

The cooking lamb smelled good. Jack let Parsha do the talking.

Mohammed was most curious about Jack. "What are you doing way out here?"

Jack said, "I was in the Urals taking daguerreotypes when I met and married a beautiful young woman, a poet who offended Peter Koslov at a Christmas party."

Mohammed grinned broadly. "Ah, so you are the one! Sonja Sankova's American husband. The story of your ambush precedes you. A ball to Koslov's ankle. Too bad it wasn't his heart, but congratulations anyway."

Jack said, "A bad shot. I apologize. Ali took Sonja as bait for Koslov."

Parsha interrupted. "That's why my friend is here, to retrieve his wife."

Mohammed's face darkened. "Colonel Koslov has troops out here in the steppe after you both. Did you know that?"

"Bad ankle and all?" Parsha asked.

"His ankle is in a plaster cast, but he can still ride. His rage masks the pain." Mohammed studied Jack with clouded eyes. "He saw you clearly, Mr. Sandt. It is not only your wife's ears that he wants."

Jack blinked.

"More satisfying than merely killing you is how he sees it. Let you regret firing your pistol for the rest of your life. For destroying his ankle, you surrender your feet. He has vowed to take both your feet and make you walk on stumps. Colonel Koslov knows Ali has your wife. He wants her. He knows you want her too. If I were you, Mr. Sandt, I would be very, very careful."

NINETEEN

Black Wind

 ALI'S SCOUTS RETURNED TO REPORT THAT COLONEL Koslov and the Wolfpack were pursuing him onto the steppe, leading a battalion of Russian soldiers. Ali was anxious to reach the safety of his *aoul* in the Kourt-Chume. He wanted to ride. The Kyrgyz rode.

The swelling in the purple bruises that covered Sonja's body had subsided, but riding was still painful. Were it not for Sonja's supply of laudanum, continuing would have been unbearable. For Ali, his captive was still alive, which was all that mattered to him. He was indifferent to her suffering.

After riding the grassy steppe for nearly six hours, crossing several dry streambeds in the process, Ali's band of Kyrgyz proceeded across a stony, granite-strewn plain barren of all vegetation. Sonja had never imagined such a vast waste. They traveled slowly, stopping periodically to check the horizon for any sign of Cossack patrols. They ascended a small ridge and spotted a Cossack picket in the distance. They circled the picket, passing around the margin of a crater that had granite blocks and fissures radiating from the center. After passing a lava flow that had oozed from a crack, then hardened, they continued in the growing heat, then entered undulating terrain dotted by small brown hills.

A few versts later Sonja saw a fearful dense black mass, about a verst wide, rolling straight at them.

Ali and his warriors knew what to do. With Ali shouting instructions, they quickly dismounted, an anxious eye on the approaching blackness. Working swiftly, taking no nonsense from any of their mounts, the Kyrgyz guided their horses onto their knees in a semicircle with their sides pointed in the direction of the wind. When the horses were in place, Ali demonstrated what Sonja was to do next.

They all lay down in the middle of the semicircle, each behind a sheltering horse, with their arms over their heads and their hands over their eyes, noses, and mouths.

Sonja was no sooner in place than she heard a thunderous, impossible roar.

She braced for the wind.

The sun disappeared as though in a full eclipse.

They were plunged into blackness.

The stinging wind was upon them with a fury. The air was so filled with sand that it was nearly impossible for Sonja to breathe. It got worse, if that was possible. They were trapped in a shrieking, terrible howl. Their clothing filled like balloons.

They endured five horrific minutes of howling violence before the storm passed on. The Kyrgyz got up, laughing, glad to be alive, and dusted themselves off.

Ali said, "And here you thought the storm on the mountain was something! You're learning how to be a Kyrgyz woman." He tapped her between the legs. "You will wash yourself well tonight. You will have sand everywhere."

TWENTY

The Smoking of Hashish

MOHAMMED, AMAZED, GLANCED FROM PARSHA TO Jack, then blinked. "Rescue your wife? You two alone? Against Ali?" He looked disbelieving.

Parsha said, "My friend Jack is a man of honor. If someone steals his wife, he will do whatever is necessary to get her back. He will sacrifice his life if necessary. He believes that life without honor is a life not worth living."

Jack thought that was a bit melodramatic, but it obviously impressed the chief. Mohammed gestured to his wife, who unpacked an intricately carved brass pot with a small bowl on top and a wooden box about twice the size of a man's fist. The box too was carved, and had ivory and mother-of-pearl inlays. A tightly woven tube tipped by ivory ran from the bottom of the pot.

"We will smoke," he said. "Good for the appetite." He placed the instrument in front of them. He opened the box and retrieved a chunk of brown substance.

The brown substance didn't look like any tobacco Jack had ever seen. Smoke? Puzzled, he glanced at Parsha.

Parsha said, "It is pressed from the pollen of a kind of hemp that grows along the rivers. The Kyrgyz use the fiber for twine."

"Should we offer him a bottle?"

Parsha shook his head. "He doesn't drink."

Mohammed took a stick and put the end of it into the fire until it burst into flame. He briefly held the flame under the brown chunk, then rubbed some of the chunk into the small brass bowl at the top of the pot. Jack noticed that the brass vessel had a small hole in it.

"Have you never smoked hashish?" Mohammed asked.

"Never," Jack said.

Mohammed grinned and gave the ivory-tipped tube to Parsha. "You show him, then?"

Parsha gave him a small bow. To Jack, he said, "You watch. There is water in the brass vessel. The smoke will travel through the water, cooling it down. You put your thumb on this small hole." He did. "Then you draw through the tube." He did that, too. The hashish in the bowl began to glow. "And then you release your thumb from the hole." He released his. Then, talking without exhaling, he said, "And the cool smoke shoots into your lungs. You hold it there."

Jack waited.

Finally Parsha released the smoke from his lungs. "Very nice," he said.

Mohammed looked pleased. He set about reloading the bowl. "Your turn," he said.

Tentatively, Jack tried to do as he was told, but the smoke burned his lungs, and he wound up in a fit of coughing that he could scarcely stop.

Both Parsha and Mohammed seemed amused. Parsha said, "Not so much smoke until you get used to it."

Jack knew it would be impolite to decline another turn, so he tried it again, but with less gusto. He took a moderate, measured draw on the tube. He released his thumb. The smoke rushed into his lungs. He held it. It had a remarkably pleasing taste and odor. He liked it.

A mild glow descended over him. Mohammed took a turn. Then Parsha had a second turn. Then Jack. He entered a drifty, optimistic state.

TWENTY-ONE

The Fate of Mohammed's Daughter

BY THE TIME THE PIPE CAME AROUND AGAIN, JACK
Sandt had finished. He suddenly began to get very hungry. His stomach growled. The lamb browning over the
fire smelled wonderful.

Mohammed said, "I should tell you that Ali and his band raided one
of my small *aouls*. They left with all their food and firewood and my
eldest daughter, Fatimeh. The oldest sister of these three."

Parsha caught his eye. "Took your daughter?"

Mohammed nodded. "She was there to be observed by her prospective
husband, who was killed in the raid. Ali has been telling the Kyrgyz that
he is going to build an army and drive the Russians off our land north of
the Altai. Some believe him. Others do not. He either didn't know the
aoul belonged to me or he was trying to show that he is afraid of no one.
Most likely he picked on me to impress the smaller *aouls*. He accuses
me of cooperating with the Tsar because my sons and I speak Russian. A
lie. We learned Russian to make trading with them easier and to deal with
the Tsar's tax collectors. In fact, Ali himself speaks a little Russian. Guaranteed, Ali doesn't know he captured my daughter. If it were not for the
coming of cold weather, Ali and everybody in his camp would be dead by
now. We will be moving south shortly and need all our men to herd our
animals. He counted on that."

Jack asked, "Did any of your people see my wife?"

Mohammed shook his head. "If she's with him, she and Fatimeh are now part of Ali's harem. He keeps five or six concubines in his main camp in the mountains. He pretends he is a sultan." He spit into the fire. "I must say, respectfully, that trying to rescue your wife with just your Cossack friend is suicide, Mr. Sandt. He has far too many warriors. You would never make it past his pickets. That's if you managed to avoid Colonel Koslov and his troops. I am only the chief of a modest *aoul.* Your only hope is convincing a sultan to help you."

"Do you have any suggestions?"

He nodded. "I do. My friend Sultan Azziz has far more animals than I do and more warriors. Sultan Azziz long ago tired of Ali's talk, but until recently it was only that, talk. Now Ali's bandits have struck the sultan's smaller *aouls* several times in recent weeks. But I should warn you, Azziz is no fool. He will never commit his warriors to battle unless he's convinced there's a likelihood of victory. For Azziz to attack Ali and fail would be to put every Kyrgyz *aoul* on the steppe at Ali's mercy. Better the Russians than him."

"Hmm. And how would I gain an audience with Sultan Azziz?"

Mohammed smiled. "My son Hasan can introduce you. Hasan has his sister Fatimeh to avenge. He has vowed that after he kills her, he will take Ali's head."

The statement startled Jack. "What?" After he killed his sister? What the hell was this?

Parsha took Jack by the arm and said mildly, "If a Kyrgyz woman sleeps with another man, she must be killed to preserve the family honor. As long as Fatimeh remains alive, Mohammed's clan will be shamed."

"But it . . ." Being kidnapped was hardly the same as running off with someone.

Parsha could see Jack was horrified. He squeezed Jack's arm tightly, meaning the American should shut up.

Jack did, but he was still stunned by the barbarity.

"He can have Ali's head if he can beat me to it," Parsha said.

Mohammed arched an eyebrow. "So you want his head too, eh? Are you willing to compete with Hasan?"

Parsha grinned. "May one of us succeed."

Mohammed said, "Hasan is a good shot and a hard rider. Plus he can serve as your interpreter. The nights are getting longer and colder. Hasan knows the location of most of the Kyrgyz *aouls*. Sleeping in a warm yurts is far better than freezing on the ground. He'll keep up his end, never fear." Mohammed motioned to his wife, and she popped to her feet and left the yurt.

A few minutes later Mohammed's wife returned with the oldest of his three sons, the man wearing the horse-hair coat with the mane in the back. Here was probably a fighter. He had the swagger.

"My son, Hasan," Mohammed said. He introduced them.

"I'm honored," Hasan said.

Mohammed bade his son to sit.

Hasan did and accepted a turn at the water pipe.

Mohammed said, "Ali has kidnapped Mr. Sandt's wife, and he wants her back."

There was a question in Hasan's eyes. He was curious but said nothing.

Mohammed said, "Yes. His wife is with Ali. You are to go with them to Sultan Azziz's *aoul.* Perhaps Azziz has had enough of Ali's raids on his animals."

Jack said, "Will we encounter a camp allied with Ali?"

Mohammed said, "You might. But as long as you're with my son, there's no need to worry. Kyrgyz will want to be hospitable. If you run into Colonel Koslov, that is another matter. But then again, Hasan knows the steppe far better than the Russians do."

Parsha said, "You should know, Jack, that for our Kyrgyz friends, a reputation as a good host is a requirement for survival. A Kyrgyz never knows when he will need food and shelter. Turn away a traveler, and you may one day be turned away yourself."

Mohammed looked pleased. "Your Cossack friend is right. He understands our ways. When in the company of a Kyrgyz allied with Ali, you merely avoid talk of him. They are Kyrgyz, so they'll be gracious hosts. They may believe in Ali's boasts, but they'll let him do his own fighting. And one thing they would never do is turn you over to the Russians. They all hate the Russians."

Mohammed fell silent for a moment, thinking. Then he said, "Incidentally, you should also know that the Kalmyk despise Ali as much as I do. They're a hateful, uncivilized people, but they're tired of Ali raiding their *aouls*. They suspect his grand ambition includes expanding Kyrgyz territory south toward China as well as north of the Altai." He stopped, then added. "You should be warned that the Kalmyk are hardly more than animals. Trust them this much." He squeezed his thumb and forefinger tightly together. "If you succeed in retrieving your wife, good for you. Let Ali be the conquering hero from the grave. Say, the lamb looks ready. Shall we eat?"

Jack was tired of talk. He was starving.

TWENTY-TWO

Journey Across an Earthen Sea

JACK AWOKE THE NEXT MORNING TO A BABBLE OF shouting, grunting, neighing, bleating, and barking. What a racket! He stepped outside the yurt to take a look and found that the camp was a confusion of animals being prepared for the journey to their pastures. There were horses, camels, cows, goats, and sheep everywhere. Animals, animals, animals.

With the noise continuing outside, Jack and Parsha had a breakfast of leftover lamb and tea with Hasan and his father. When they were finished, Mohammed gave his son a hug and wished them well, and they were on their way to visit the estimable Sultan Azziz.

There were now three of them, Jack, Parsha, Hasan wearing his coat with the mane down the back. Hasan seemed friendly enough, and it made sense to have a Kyrgyz traveling with them into Kyrgyz territory—especially the son of such a wealthy and powerful man as Mohammed.

The weather was wet, cold, and windy, with clouds obscuring the distant Mantilla Rocks and beyond them the Monastery Mountains. Out there on the vast, rocky plains that stretched as far as the eye could see there were no visible means of getting one's bearings, and Jack was forced to use his compass as a sailor on an endless earthen sea.

They rode for five hours before the sun began burning off the mist. Looking back, it was as though they had made no progress at all. In the midafternoon they passed through some unusual formations of rocks, some in the shape of churches, fortresses, and ruined castles. A few huge columns rested on small bases as though they were pedestals. Hasan led them down a narrow ravine through these gigantic forms of granite, saying that legend on the steppe had it that this was the residence of Shaitan, which Jack took to be the Islamic corruption of Satan.

Hasan said few if any Kyrgyz would remain near this place after dark. Passing through the bizarre and grotesque shapes, it was easy for Jack to see how that belief had come about. After taking nearly two hours to negotiate the labyrinth, they came upon crumbling walls of basalt stone built by an ancient people—possibly to protect a temple in the center which had long since fallen into ruin.

As the haze lifted, Jack, Parsha, and Hasan could see the snowy summits of the Kourt-Chume Mountains extending to the southwest, and behind them the higher summits of the Altai shone like burning gold. They bore to the southwest and ascended a high ridge covered with mossy turf and bare rock. They passed a seven-hundred-foot-high pyramid of red and gray porphyry on a brown, grassy slope. The pyramid had small mounds of red porphyry near its base. Then came a small salt lake bordered by orange and crimson plants.

An hour past the pyramid they passed through a gap in a mountain that seemed to rise out of nowhere, like an island poking out of the ocean. They rode along the base of a rock precipice about two hundred feet high. It was striking how much the rock wall resembled a cliff at the seashore. The scattered rocks and gravel lacked only seaweed and shrieking seagulls to give it the appearance of a beach at low tide.

They rode past what Jack imagined as headlands and small bays, some running to the high ridge that they had passed earlier. How remarkable it was that an arid desert should so resemble the ocean, as though the water had simply disappeared, leaving the landforms behind. Striking out across the empty sea with his remarkable companions, Jack thought of Ulysses, pushed off on his many adventures, separated from his wife, longing to see her again. But he forbade himself to dwell on the thought of Sonja. Ahead of them, they saw another small chain of mountains rising as islands above the sand.

On the far side of the barren ocean, they came upon what for all the world looked like a cove in one of the island mountains. High cliffs flanked the cove. Neither Parsha nor Jack could see any path through the mountains, but Hasan knew the way. He got off and led them up what looked like an impossible trail. Jack was afraid one of the horses might slip and break a leg, but Hasan seemed unconcerned. They negotiated the trail safely and eventually came to a steep, mossy slope on the far side of what Jack had come to view as an island in the middle of the steppe.

On seeing the hill, Hasan said, "It won't be long now, Jack. We're nearing one of Sultan Azziz's smaller *aouls*. His main *aoul* has far too many animals."

As the sun began set, the bitter wind started sweeping across the wasteland, and within minutes Jack Sandt felt like a block of ice, his layers of clothing notwithstanding. Parsha was used to the steppe and sat stoically atop his mount, his shoulders hunched against the cold. Hasan seemed oblivious of the cold, although he knew Jack was suffering.

About twenty minutes later they came upon the spot where Hasan had expected the sultan's camp, but it was gone. There was not an animal or yurt in sight, although the ground had recently been trampled by horses and camels, and their waste was everywhere. The camp had apparently moved in great haste.

There was nothing to do but push on. With Hasan providing directions, they did just that.

TWENTY-THREE

Amulets for Tenders of the Flame

JACK, PARSHA, AND HASAN ENTERED ROLLING TER-
rain. They passed hill after hill with no sign of animal
life. Hasan was perplexed. On they rode. As the sun set, it
got colder, and colder still. It was a cloudy night. The wind
kicked up. Another storm was obviously brewing over this vast land of
storms.

An hour later, they saw the flickering of fires in the distance. Suddenly, armed riders appeared from nowhere, blocking their way.

Hasan began palavering with them in their language, and after a
minute he turned and said, "They were attacked last night by what
they think was part of Ali's band. They lost seventy horses and five
camels. They moved the *aoul* today but are bracing for another attack
tonight. They have pickets out to give warning."

Parsha said, "Surely Ali's men will be alert for pickets."

Hasan shrugged. "They do all they can. Azziz's main *aoul* is another
fifteen or twenty versts from here. They do the best they can under the
circumstances."

Jack, Parsha, and Hasan rode through the gusting wind to the camp,
which turned out to be ten yurts set in a defensive semicircle at a tiny
water hole. The herd of this *aoul*, mostly camels and horses, numbered
in the hundreds, not the thousands, as Mohammed was able to boast.
They were gathered around the water with guards posted on the flanks.

As the travelers entered the camp, a cold rain began lashing the ground. Before they could dismount and follow Hasan's friends to the shelter of a yurt, hail the size of small eggs began hammering the earth.

After some more brief palaver, it was decided that Jack, Parsha, and Hasan would sleep in a yurt whose owner had been killed in the raid the previous night. His wife and children would sleep in another camp. Leaving their mounts and packhorses to be taken care of by Azziz's Kyrgyz, they retired quickly to the yurt, cold and exhausted from their long day in the saddle. As they changed out of their wet clothes, the hail continued to rattle against the *voilock*-covered dome. After ten minutes the hail turned to sleet that pounded against the yurt in loud, slapping waves.

No sooner were they in dry clothes than two middle-aged women entered the yurt with bundles of brushwood, which they added to the fire. They put a samovar on a hook above the fire to boil water for their tea, then left without a word, returning shortly with a blackened pot containing boiled mutton, which they put over the fire to heat. They retreated a second time and returned with more firewood.

Hasan attempted to stir the pot of mutton but one of the women grabbed the ladle from him, giving him a look. She said something Jack couldn't understand.

Hasan said, "They've been assigned to take care of us for the night. They'll be staying to take care of the fire."

Jack eyed the hole at the top of the yurt. When the hole was closed, the fire warmed the yurt, yes, but the smoke also collected, burning the eyes of those inside. When it was open, the icy wind blew rain inside.

Hasan, as though reading his mind, said, "They'll close the hole to keep the yurt warm. When the yurt gets too smoky, they'll open it long enough to clear. This is women's work. While one naps, the other tends the fire and opens and closes the hole as necessary."

Jack blinked. "You're telling me that we get to sleep while they keep the fire going and vent the smoke."

"Women's work."

The women made them tea, and Jack, Parsha, and Hasan gathered around the fire prepared to eat Kyrgyz style, directly out of the pot, but the women insisted on serving them in wooden bowls. They were famished after such a hard day, and the mutton was delicious. By the time they finished their meal, the yurt was warm and cozy, and the women pulled a sheet of *voilock* over the hole at the top of the yurt.

Hasan and Parsha immediately curled up in their blankets, and Jack lit a candle, determined to write some notes on the day's adventures for his *Tribune* stories. The women stared at Jack, transfixed, as he wound his watch. He held it to the ear of one of them. She was immediately excited.

"It talks!" she said, her eyes wide.

Her companion obviously wanted to hear it too. Jack gave her a turn. She listened. Her eyes widened. "Yes," she said.

Jack took out his notebook, trying to remember the day's events so he could record the details. There was much to tell. Using the compass to navigate on the steppe. The hills that looked like islands in an ocean. The ancient ruins. The pyramid. The women leaned toward him, curious. The book was an obvious wonder to them.

Hasan, who had not yet fallen asleep, said, "They can't read or write. They think that's a book filled with amulets, and you must be a wealthy mullah."

"What?"

"A mullah will trace a few characters on a piece of paper and exchange it for a sheep. They can write anything and these people won't know the difference."

"I see." Jack retrieved a piece of red sealing wax and heated it until it dripped on a piece of paper and traced JS in the wax for Jack Sandt. He did the same thing on a second piece of paper and gave one to each of the women, who were delighted. "These are for keeping the yurt warm. They will give you health and good fortune. It will protect you from harm."

They smiled shyly. A nice thank-you.

With Jack's audience of two staring at him with wide brown eyes, he finished his notes. He snuffed the candle and lay back. Despite the wind and rain, the yurt was warm and cozy. His belly was full. He was at least making some progress in his search for Sonja. Thinking of her, he fell asleep, dreaming.

When the squall hit with fury, they had pulled the stern plugs and flooded the aft tanks, lowering their junk low in the water. There she weathered the swells that washed across the decks. Now with the bank of black clouds receding in the distance, a diminishing memory, they were safe. Jack toiled hard at the rotary handle of the bilge pump. He and Sonja took turns pumping water from the aft tank. With each passing minute, the junk rose higher in the water. Turning the handle was hard work, but a pleasure.

Now, from the helm, Sonja called, "It's empty! Coming about. Watch your head."

His shoulder still aching from his chore, Jack squatted on the deck as the boom at the bottom of the lateen sail passed overhead. The breeze felt cool on his sweating back and chest.

"Look ahead! Look ahead!" she called.

He joined her at the helm, where she was checking their chart. She was right. Ahead and slightly to their port was the profile of an island with a ridge of mountains in the interior.

She said, "Hard to make out which island it is." She leaned against him. "But never mind, we'll find out shortly, won't we?"

"I say there'll be friendly people there and good food, and we'll have a wild night together on a proper bed."

SONJA AND FATIMEH HAD NO SOONER SETTLED INTO THE YURT occupied by the harem— still strangers to the other women—than Raj appeared and said quietly, "The master desires that Madame Sonja and Lady Fatimeh grace his yurt tonight." The harem, glancing at Sonja and Fatimeh, watched with interest while Raj opened one of the trunks containing the *kalats* worn by the women on their visits to the master's yurt. He selected two translucent black silk *kalats* with red sashes.

Raj held one up to the candlelight. "One can see right through these. Very sexy. If you would disrobe please, Lady Fatimeh. Let's see what we have to work with."

With Raj watching with interest, Fatimeh slipped out of her *kalat*.

Raj looked pleased. "A classic Kyrgyz girl! Full breasts. A nice plump behind." He took her by the elbow and turned her sideways, the better to examine.

"And now you, madam, if you please."

Sonja too removed her clothing. She stood naked, aware that she was being inspected by everybody in the yurt. There was competition in the harem. Nobody wanted to have to get up at the crack of dawn to milk horses and sheep.

Raj circled her, saying, "Fine boned and slender. Small. Wonderful face. You could use a little more meat for the master's usual taste, but you're still quite nice. I see why he admires you. And you seem to be healing fast." He brushed his hand lightly between her legs, causing the startled Sonja to stand on her toes. "Small down there, I bet. The master likes that in his women," Raj said. "Are you still sore from your painful journey, madam?"

"A little stiff, but I'm getting better."

He poked her on the hip. She winced. He frowned. "Still bruised, but it can't be helped." He handed Sonja and Fatimeh the black *kalats*. "You will wear these, please." As Sonja and Fatimeh dressed, he said politely, "He found you and your husband near Kolyvan Lake, as I understand it, Mrs. Sandt."

Sonja nodded.

"The pleasure you offered Master Ali on the trail was quite different from your duties as a member of his harem here in his main *aoul*. Tonight you will be initiated into your duties and responsibilities as pleases the master. You'll find they are quite different than the trail. The two of you will do what you're told. You will please the master or be flogged." He sighed. "I'm afraid the wielding of the whip would be my unpleasant duty. I hate it, so please, please, ladies, do us all a favor . . ." He let the sentence drop.

When they were dressed, Raj escorted them to Ali's yurt. As they walked, he said to Sonja, "I have read your poetry, madam. You're quite good. Passionate. And unafraid."

Sonja smiled. "Well, thank you."

"A shame this had to happen to you. By the way, the master has informed me, Mrs. Sandt, that with you so far, he has entertained himself only in the sexual manner usual among Western men and women. He has saved for tonight your pleasure of receiving him into the more painful lowermost of your two orifices, which he enjoys with boys when he is on a campaign. Miss Fatimeh will hold you by the wrists or ankles. You understand."

"I think I get the idea," Sonja said.

Raj said, "The master tells me you were singularly unresponsive on the trail, which has offended him greatly. It is his desire that you learn humility and entertain him in a manner that pleases him. If I were to offer some advice, Mrs. Sandt, I would suggest that you submit to his wishes. I guarantee, you will not want to suffer the consequences of continued resistance. Eventually, you will do as he asks."

Fatimeh said, "She's right. Don't be foolish. Remember Jack."

Raj paused by the entrance to Ali's yurt. "Listen to your friend, madam. I take it Jack is the name of your husband."

"Who is coming after me this very moment."

"Ah, yes, Mr. Sandt. A lucky man. If he is smart, he will retire from this part of the world and go back to America. As I understand it, Colonel Koslov is after the both of you. His vow to remove your ears is well known. They tell me that he has designs on your husband's feet."

TWENTY-FOUR

The Meaning of Two Legs

IN THE EARLY HOURS OF THE MORNING JACK WOKE TO a loud rumbling. The ground shook. He could hear shouting. It was a herd of horses thundering through the *aoul* at a full gallop. Women began screaming. One of them shouted, "Ali! Ali! Ali!"

Jack grabbed his shotgun and threw a Colt revolver each to Hasan and Parsha. The women, seeing they needed light, stoked the fire. As the shouting and shots continued outside, he showed Hasan how to cock the revolver by pulling back the hammer. As he did, he cursed himself for not having shown him earlier.

He stepped out into the cold wind. Women were screaming, children shrieking, dogs barking. Everything was confused. It was impossible to see who was who or what was what. He saw men on horseback not ten yards away, but it was impossible to tell whether they were friend or foe. They brandished swords and battle-axes. If they had muskets, he didn't hear them.

One of the women who had been tending their fire poked her head from the entrance of the yurt. Jack glanced at her. She understood his predicament. She shouted, "The men on horseback are robbers, sire. Robbers. Shoot them!"

As she said that, several of Azziz's men arrived with battle-axes, ready to take on the riders. So this was to be it then, combat Kyrgyz style with men on horseback and men on the ground, blade to blade. Limbs would be severed. Blood would flow.

The cylinder of the shotgun held six rounds. Each of the Colts was loaded with six rounds. If the raiders had muskets, they were empty by now, and reloading them in the dark on horseback was difficult if not impossible. But muskets weren't the weapons of choice for the Kyrgyz.

Jack, Parsha, and Hasan, joining Azziz's warriors carrying battle-axes, advanced on the horsemen. Those on foot would chop at the legs of the horses, hoping to bring their enemy to earth. Those on horseback would chop down on those on foot, aiming for heads, chest, shoulders, back, whatever target presented itself. A ghastly, bloody prospect. Jack had never imagined such brave fighters as the Kyrgyz. Or foolhardy.

At the feet of the raiders, not three or four feet from their targets and a heartbeat before the axes drew blood, Jack, Parsha, and Hasan began their grisly chore of introducing Mr. Colt's latest inventions to the steppe. Cock. Point. Pull the trigger. Cock. Point. Pull the trigger. Even though the horses were rearing above him, the targets were impossible to miss. With the recoil punching his shoulder, Jack fired all six rounds from his shotgun, knocking a rider from a horse with each shot. Hasan and Parsha seemed to be having nearly equal success with their Colts. When his shotgun was empty, Jack stepped inside and grabbed his Sharps.

The surviving raiders, startled at having encountered such a lethal barrage, shouted at one another and retreated into the night. One rider lingered momentarily, trying to see who had such remarkable weapons. They had fought the smooth-bored, muzzle-loading muskets of the Tsar's soldiers and gendarmes, but this shocking rapid-fire assault was of another order. Jack saw him clearly, silhouetted against the night sky, his battle-ax raised.

Jack knocked him off his horse with the Sharps. "Curious were you?" he muttered.

Azziz's warriors erupted in cheering and clapped him on the back.

As they stood over the fallen raiders, the rain returned. With water running down his face, Jack stepped among the bodies of the dead Kyrgyz raiders. Jack, Parsha, and Hasan had killed nine of Ali's men and wounded four in an encounter of less than thirty seconds' duration. To the cheering of his companions, one of Azziz's men served up the coup de grâce, severing the survivors' necks with his battle-ax.

Behind him, Jack heard one of the women in their yurt talking excitedly to her friends.

Hasan burst out laughing.

"What is it?" Jack said.

Hasan said, "The women believe the amulets you gave them protected us from Ali's warriors."

They retreated inside their yurt, and Parsha retrieved a bottle of vodka from their packs. Azziz's men had suffered no casualties and lost no animals. It was clear there would be no sleeping for the rest of the night. It was time for laughter and relief that they had survived and retelling the story of their close-up slaughter of bandits who had gotten far more than they had bargained for. Soon their yurt was crowded with excited Kyrgyz warriors. They got out hashish, but did not use a water pipe. Instead they smoked from a long, elaborately decorated wooden pipe that fastened together in the middle and with a small clay bowl at the tip no larger than the end of a man's thumb. The hashish pipe, green, crisscrossed with yellow and black, was remarkably similar to "peace pipes" smoked by the Indians out west.

Jack took a turn on the pipe and handed it to Hasan, who gave him a half smile as he accepted it. Softly, he said, "This night is very good, Jack."

Jack didn't understand.

He said, "We drove off Ali's raiders with no loss of men or animals. If we need help in the future, we've only to ask Azziz."

The pipe was passed to Jack. He took a draw, watching the glow of the hashish in the small clay bowl. Parsha gave him the bottle of vodka.

He took a hit. The combination of vodka and hashish made him drifty. It felt good to be alive.

A voice floated by him. It was Hasan's.

"What?"

Hasan said, "They will take us to Sultan Azziz's main *aoul* tomorrow. If we need help in rescuing your wife, they're certain the sultan will want to help us. This is the third attack on one of the sultan's smaller *aouls* in two weeks."

Parsha said, "They all want amulets."

"What?"

"Amulets like you gave the women. They think the amulets gave us victory. Can you make more?"

"Of course. No problem." Jack tore off a sheet of paper and folded it smaller and smaller, then tore off squares about two inches on each side. He smoked some more hashish and dripped a small ration of red wax on each square, carefully writing JS on each, and gave this invincible protection to each of the pleased warriors in the yurt.

RAJ OPENED THE *VOILOCK* ENTRANCE AND MOTIONED FOR SONJA and Fatimeh to enter. They stepped onto a Persian carpet. The walls of the yurt were covered with silk *kalats* and *tchimbars* hanging on pegs, as well as finely decorated saddles inlaid with silver, beautiful saddle blankets, plus battle-axes and a collection of jeweled knives on either side of the entrance.

Ali waited, leaning against a pile of cushions beside a pile of trunks. Watching them, he took a draw on a brass hashish pipe. He wore a white *kalat* of Chinese satin tied at the waist with a pink sash. Exhaling, he said, "You have told them what to expect, Raj?"

Raj bowed. "Yes I have, master."

With a languid flip of his wrist, Ali sent Raj on his way. When Raj had disappeared, he pointed at Sonja. "Take off your *kalat*. You are not to look at me directly."

Looking at the carpet, Sonja undressed.

"Turn around." Ali put his right hand at his crotch.

She turned, amazed that he was already hard.

Ali handed Fatimeh a small beaker. "This is olive oil. You will use your fingers to lubricate her backside. No talking."

Sonja caught Fatimeh's eyes momentarily. No talking was needed for Fatimeh to say she hated what she had to do. Sonja blinked, telling Fatimeh it was okay.

She felt Fatimeh's oily forefinger inside her.

Ali said, "On your knees. Spread them wide. Wrists above your head."

Sonja winced as she felt his finger test the lubricant.

"Hold her wrists."

Sonja felt Fatimeh grasp her wrists.

Ali said, "In St. Petersburg you may have been a poet, but here you are two legs supporting two holes that are mine to use as I please. You are that and nothing more. I own you. I am the Expected One. I *will* be shown proper respect. I *will* be obeyed. You *will* respond when I enter you. You *will* call me master. You *will* worship me properly. Do that and your visits will be more pleasant. After you were dragged across the steppe, I warned you there would be consequences to continued resistance."

Sonja bit her lower lip. There would be terrible consequences if she continued to resist his harm. It was foolish to challenge him, she knew. She would do her best to grant him his wishes. *Forgive me, Jack,* she thought. *I do what I have to do.*

"Do you understand?"

"Yes, master."

Ali said, "Ah, you're learning. That's better." He entered her.

Beneath him Sonja, wincing at the pain of his thrust, twisted and moaned and cried out, pretending to be maddened with pleasure, her senses overwhelmed by the powerful Kyrgyz stud. "Oh, master, master!" she cried, doing her best to be convincing.

When he finished, he rose, his face hard. "You were pretending.

If there is anything worse than an unresponsive woman who resists, it is a woman who fakes passion. I gave you proper warning. I will give you one day to think about your punishment. After tomorrow, you will love me with all your heart and soul, Mrs. Sandt."

TWENTY-FIVE

The Aoul of Sultan Azziz

 JACK, PARSHA, AND HASAN AWOKE AT DAWN AND ATE a breakfast of boiled mutton and tea. They departed with Sultan Azziz's riders, destined for his main camp. Five hard hours later, shortly after ten o'clock, they rode through a herd of camels and horses. Hasan said they were Azziz's animals. Every Kyrgyz they met had a battle-ax hanging from his saddle. Hasan said that in peaceful times the herdsmen of a sultan as powerful as Azziz would think such a display unnecessary, but following Ali's assaults on their animals, his herdsmen now rode armed.

A few versts after they encountered the first animals, they passed through a small arroyo and ascended the crest of a hill, which looked down upon a camp of seventy to ninety yurts sprawled along the bank of a small stream that flowed from a lake about four versts wide and five versts long. Cattails and reeds bordered the near side of the lake. Thousands of sheep and goats grazed on the grassy far side of the lake. Jack had thought Mohammed's camp was amazing. He hesitated to think what this camp must be like come milking time. All those mares and ewes and cows to be milked! The poor women. It was easy to understand why Mohammed was in league with Sultan Azziz.

The pickets had sent word ahead of their pending arrival, and as they drew close to the yurts, they were met by several riders brandishing battle-axes.

One of them, recognizing his comrades from the smaller camp that had been raided the night before, placed his hand on his chest and said, "Aman."

"Say 'Aman,' " Hasan murmured.

"Aman," Jack repeated.

Two of the riders rode ahead at a gallop, while a huge Kyrgyz led them at a slower rate down the hill toward the incredible *aoul*. What a problem in logistics it must have been to keep constantly on the move with so many yurts to dismantle, move, and erect again!

Riding beside him, Hasan could see Jack was impressed. He said, "See. Didn't I tell you Sultan Azziz was a powerful man? If we are to receive help in our mission, it is he who will give it to us."

As they neared the edge of the camp, there was much commotion. Dogs barked. Women bearing bundles of firewood scurried into yurts.

The huge Kyrgyz led them to the largest yurt in the camp. A spear was stuck into the ground at the door with a long tuft of black horsehair blowing in the wind. A tall, polite man met them at the entrance. He held out his hand to help Jack dismount and led them inside, with Jack bearing his box of magic daguerreotypes.

They were met at the door by Sultan Azziz, a strong, ruddy-faced man in a black velvet *kalat* edged with sable and tied at the waist with a crimson shawl. He had a red cap, conical in shape, trimmed in fox fur and with an owl's feather attached to the tip of its cone.

Beside Jack, Hasan said, "The feather at the top of his hat signifies that the sultan is descended from Genghis Khan."

The sultan seated Jack and his two companions on a Bokharan carpet inside the wide entrance to the yurt, then sat down opposite them. Behind them ten advisers and warriors squatted to watch the proceedings and listen to the conversation. Outside the entrance, women with black, curious eyes gathered to watch the proceedings.

With everybody in his court place, the sultan snapped his fingers and two sons appeared, one about ten and the other maybe twelve. They were dressed in pink-and-yellow-striped silk *kalats* with green shawls around their waists. He bade them to bend close with a motion of his hand, and then they disappeared.

Hasan kissed the sultan's cheek, and the sultan kissed Hasan.

Azziz said something in his language. Hasan translated. "He says these are his two sons, Yusef and Ahmad. He says the sultana is on a visit to the *aoul* of another sultan three days distant. He extends his apologies. He knows she would have been pleased to welcome a visitor from the United States of America. A faraway place indeed."

Yusef and Ahmad returned with tea, dried figs, and dried apricots. They placed the tea and dried fruit before Azziz and his guests, then disappeared.

Jack took a sip of tea and looked around at the enormous yurt. The sultan's sleeping place was obscured by silk curtains and flanked by two birds chained to perches. One was a large black eagle, locally called a *bearcoote,* and the other was a falcon. He noted that everyone in the yurt, the sons included, kept their distance from the raptors, especially the *bearcoote,* a ferocious-looking bird.

In addition to the *bearcoote* and the falcon, three goat kids and two lambs were secured in a pen.

Jack showed the sultan a daguerreotype he had taken of the old man and his family in the mountains. "Would you please tell him that with his permission, and as a gift, I would like capture his image that he might hang it in his yurt. Tell him it would be better if we did this outside in the daylight, where I can have him stand with his musket."

Hasan passed on this offer. Azziz murmured something in return and bowed slightly in Jack's direction. The answer was yes.

"Tell him I have a small chore to complete first. I must polish the small plates to prepare them for my machine."

Hasan relayed his instructions, and Jack set about the chore of polishing and buffing two small plates. As before, he would give one to the sultan and keep a second for himself as a record of his travels.

As he polished, Hasan and the sultan, watching, continued to talk.

Hasan said, "The sultan says the enemy of his enemy is his friend. He begs you not to judge all Kyrgyz by the criminal Ali."

Jack said, "Tell him that with the exception of Ali, I find the Kyrgyz to be a generous and civilized people."

Hearing that, Azziz looked pleased.

Hasan said, "The sultan says his warriors were amazed by the performance of your repeating pistols and shotgun at the raid last night."

"Ask him if he would like me to give a demonstration after I capture his image. Tell him I have one weapon that his warriors didn't get to appreciate last night. After he sees what these weapons can do, I have a proposal for him with respect to Ali."

Azziz watched Jack with his dark eyes as he listened to Hasan. Then, hand at his black beard, he gave his reply, which didn't have to be translated. Yes, he would like to see Jack's weapons in action.

Jack said, "I'll need a goat kid as a target. If they are to be butchered anyway, two lambs as well. Tell him the plates are ready. I can take his image and show him my weapons whenever he would like."

Jack's request was relayed to Azziz, who began shouting instructions as he rose from the carpet. Three men scooped the kid and two lambs out of the pen. He took a small sheet of paper and drew a circle in the center, and they all went outside.

RAJ, BEARING A FLOGGING WHIP OF TWENTY LEATHER THONGS ON the end of a handle, led the naked Sonja by a slender rope tied to a collar around her neck. He walked slowly around the communal fire so Ali's warriors could see what she looked like in the flickering light.

From the shadows, Ali watched.

When Raj stopped, Ali said, in Russian, "Stand closer to the fire and turn, Mrs. Sandt. My warriors want to see what you look like."

She did not budge.

"Raj!" Ali called.

Raj struck her hard on the butt with the whip.

She stepped closer to the fire and turned.

"The other way."

She turned before the thongs fell.

"Ah," Ali said. "See, she is stubborn, but not stupid. My warriors would like to see more of your breasts. Face them. Weigh them in your hands. Turn."

She did.

"Drop your hands. Strike her breasts, Raj. One blow on each. Make them bounce. And make them sting."

Raj struck her sharply twice.

Sonja, hands at her side, flinched, but suffered the blows in silence. She would not give them the satisfaction of crying out.

"Show them your backside, Sonja. Arch your back. Turn."

She turned, back arched, bracing herself.

"Give her ten hard ones, Raj. I want welts. You will count each time the whip strikes, Mrs. Sandt."

The whip fell. "One," Sonja said. The pain took her breath away. Another blow. "Two."

When Raj had finished, Ali strolled from the shadows and ran his hand over her burning rump. "Sonja's sin is that she is determined to show me no pleasure in bed. She lies there like a log, no doubt thinking of her husband. I have decided that you all will have her each night until she has a change of heart. She needs to understand that she is now a member of my harem. I require her to admire me and respond to me as the khan, not just give me her body. When she shows me proper respect as her master, her duty of entertaining you in number will end. In the meantime, enjoy."

Ali started to leave, then stopped. "When they're finished with her, give her forty more strikes, Raj. Turn her ass purple. Welts are fine, but no scarring later on. That will give her something to look forward to when they're inside her."

"I understand, master," Raj said.

"I want to hear her screams from my yurt. They must be genuine. If I don't hear her or think she's faking the screams, I'll make you do it again." With that he stalked off.

Only then, when the warriors pinned her to the ground, did Sonja begin to weep. After all she had been through, one more test. As the first warrior entered her, she murmured, "Forgive me, Jack."

Sonja did her best to imagine that the warrior inside her was her husband, but she couldn't do it. After they were finished, she was to be flogged. Ali was right. Her mind was on the whip. She had never felt so hopeless or close to defeat.

BOOK THREE

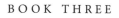

*At
Monko~seran~Xardick*

Laconic He Was

THANKFUL THAT HE WOULD GET TO TAKE THE DAGS of his host outside with good light, Jack Sandt posed the sultan, a handsome bearded figure, standing erect with one hand on his hip and the other holding the muzzle of his musket with the butt resting on the ground. After he completed developing the images in his diminutive tent, he emerged with a daguerreotype in each hand, holding them carefully by the edges.

The sultan was most pleased.

Jack told Hasan that he wanted the paper target attached to the top of a string and placed at twice the range they considered right for a normal handgun. The Kyrgyz had few muskets to begin with and even fewer pistols. What they had were smoothbore and accurate for only ten or fifteen feet. One of Azziz's warriors obliged by mounting the stick atop the paper about thirty feet away. Thirty feet wasn't a whole lot for a pistol with a seven-and-a-half-inch barrel. He put a holster on each hip, with the left pistol facing the rear, since he was right-handed. He secured the caps and slipped the pistols into place. A Colt dragoon weighed a little over two and a half pounds, so this was a real load.

Sultan Azziz and his warriors gathered in a semicircle at Jack's back.

Jack was dry-mouthed. He concentrated on the target for a moment, imagining the pistol in his hand and the flight of the bullet. He took a deep breath and exhaled slowly. He thought, *This is for you, my darling.*

Jack knew how to shoot a pistol, maybe not as well as a cowboy out west, but still . . .

He wiped the sweat from his forehead with the back of his arm. He drew the left revolver with his right hand, cocked it with the heel of his left hand, and squeezed off a round. The bullet slapped the paper. As quickly as he could, he recocked it and fired again. He worked as fast as he could, concentrating on the target for all he was worth. When the left pistol was empty, he switched to the right revolver and continued firing until it too was empty.

Behind him, Sultan Azziz and his warriors burst into applause. When Jack turned, they were staring at him literally openmouthed.

Jack didn't need a target to demonstrate the shotgun. He just fired off six shots into the ground as fast as he could recock the gun. Each blast of shot ripped a huge hole in the ground, leaving dust to linger in the breeze. Let them imagine the damage that could be done to human targets in a short space of time.

That done, he picked up his Sharps. He said, "Hasan, would you tell them I would like the kid staked out at a range of three, no, make that four times the range of their best musket. You go with them. On your return, I want you to count your paces. I want to know exactly how far away the kid is staked. No need to tell them you're counting."

Hasan nodded and passed on Jack's request. And momentarily he and a small party of Kyrgyz warriors took the kid and two lambs and began walking. As they did, Jack turned to Parsha. "Would you please tell the sultan I will need a staff or post about this high?" He held his hand up at eye level.

A boy was sent to oblige his request as they watched Hasan and the sultan's warriors stake the kid and two lambs out at what seemed like an obscene distance. They finished their chore and began walking back as the boy returned with a length of pole that was just about right.

When Hasan got back, he said, "Four hundred paces, Jack. Nobody can hit a kid that far."

Parsha grinned. "You watch."

Jack unfolded his telescope and took a look at his targets. The kid was in the middle, flanked by the lambs. To add to the drama, he decided to try for the lambs first and finish with the kid. He gave the telescope to Hasan. "Would you please show Sultan Azziz how to use this if he doesn't already know? I want him to see the action close up."

It turned out that Sultan Azziz had looked through a telescope before but never one as powerful as Jack's. He focused the telescope and his eyes widened. The remaining Kyrgyz all squinted their eyes, straining to see his targets.

Jack set the peep for four hundred yards. He set the bottom of the Sharps atop the pole to steady it and concentrated on the left lamb. The Sharps was nice and steady. He took a deep breath. He let it out slowly, then stopped. In the stillness of a heartbeat, motionless, he pulled the trigger. The Sharps bucked hard against his shoulder. Without waiting to see if he had scored, he quickly loaded another cartridge as Mr. Maynard's remarkable tape moved another detonator into place. He took the right lamb. Again he reloaded. He fired again. The goat dropped. All three animals lay dead. Jack wiped the sweat from his brow with the back of his hand. Laconic he was, not cocky.

Sultan Azziz was amazed. Watching Jack, he said something to Hasan.

Hasan said, "The sultan says you are the best shot he has ever seen and your weapons are wonderful. He would like to go inside to continue our talk."

Jack said, "Tell him that would please me very much."

On the way inside, Jack murmured into Parsha's ear. "Tell Hasan I will be talking of rubies. Neither of you should show any surprise at anything I say."

TWO

What Jack Would Do

THEY ALL WENT INSIDE AND TOOK THEIR PREVIOUS places in council with Sultan Azziz. Jack said, "The revolvers and shotgun I demonstrated for the sultan were designed by a man named Samuel Colt, a resident of the American state of Connecticut. In 1836 Colt took his revolvers to the Department of War in Washington, hoping to sell them to the army. But the officers turned him away, claiming they could imagine no conceivable use for a pistol with a revolving cylinder. It was possible they were merely stupid, but it was more likely that their current arms suppliers were paying them under the table. Colt took his revolvers to the Republic of Texas, where Texas Rangers were having to defend isolated settlements in the western part of their nation from attacks by Comanches."

Jack nodded to Hasan, who translated.

Jack said, "The Texas Rangers hit upon a simple tactic. They would draw the attention of Indians, who were armed with bows and arrows and a few muskets that required up to a minute to reload. After the Comanches had fired their arrows and a round of musket balls, the Rangers counterattacked quickly and used their rapid-firing Colt revolvers to blast the Indians off their horses at close range."

Azziz obviously understood the import of that tactic.

"Ask the sultan if it is not the practice of the Tsar's Cossacks to establish pickets just beyond the range of muskets."

Azziz listened, then nodded yes.

Jack said, "Easy matter to use my Sharps rifle to shoot the pickets from the safety of distance. To defend themselves, the pickets will chase their tormentors, going farther and farther from the camp. The farther out they are, the more vulnerable they become. The sultan should think of the possibilities. Tell him I can buy him both Colt pistols and the Sharps rifles in quantity. I can even help him earn the money necessary for the purchase."

The sultan listened, then ran his fingertips down his jaw without taking his eyes off Jack. Azziz gave a short reply to Hasan.

Hasan said, "The sultan begs you, please, Mr. Sandt, tell him how."

Jack said, "I'm after my wife, Sonja, who is being pursued by Colonel Peter Koslov of the Tsar's gendarmes. Ali captured her to use as bait to draw Koslov into ambush. Ali is bent on avenging the death of his cousin, whom Koslov blinded and released into the steppe to starve to death. You may have heard the story." He paused for Hasan to translate.

Hasan said, "The sultan says yes, he has heard the story of what Koslov did to Ali's cousin. He has also heard that Ali has captured the woman who bloodied Koslov's nose at the Tsar's Christmas party. And he knows that you shot the colonel in ambush, destroying his ankle. The colonel has vowed to have both your feet in addition to your wife's ears."

"Tell him I need warriors to help me rescue my wife from Ali before Koslov gets to her. Koslov will get neither ears nor feet."

Hasan rendered the request and translated the sultan's reply. "He says his warriors are reporting that Koslov and the Wolfpack have arrived on the steppe with a force of Russians three times as large as Ali's bandits. Koslov himself is leading the force, riding with his foot in a cast. All who have seen him say he is in constant pain that has rendered him furious. His anger grows by the hour. The sultan begs to speak without offense, but the idea of rescuing your wife is foolishness. What can you possibly offer that would cause him to send his warriors into doomed battle?"

Jack said, "Tell him a fortune in rubies, wealth beyond his wildest dreams—enough to buy thousands of horses and tens of thousands of camels and sheep."

Hasan translated.

Azziz perked up.

"The Tsar has ordered that a new throne be made for the Romanov dynasty. The craftsmen will use gold and gems from the Urals. All have been collected save for rubies to be transported from a mountain in eastern Siberia."

On hearing of the rubies, Sultan Azziz inadvertently licked his lips.

Jack said, "My wife knows the name of the mountain where the rubies are awaiting transport. I don't. If Ali learns of the rubies, he would have the means to buy all the muskets he needs to fulfill his ambition of controlling the Kyrgyz Steppe and the Altai."

Hasan translated.

Never once taking his eyes off Jack, Azziz asked a question.

Hasan said, "The sultan wants to know the name of the mountain with the rubies."

Jack said, "I say again, my wife knows the name of the mountain. I don't. I do know that the rubies are to be picked up soon."

"And their destination?" Hasan asked. He too was curious.

Jack flipped one of his Chihuahua spurs with his finger, sending it spinning. "To Yekaterinburg, where the throne is to be made."

Sultan Azziz stroked his beard. He spoke quietly to Hasan.

Hasan said, "Yekaterinburg. The sultan says he has heard the same rumor."

"But he doesn't know their origin."

Hasan shook his head.

"We all know it's the origin that counts, not the destination."

"The sultan wants to know what you propose."

Jack said, "That I lead a party of the sultan's warriors against Ali with the purpose of rescuing my wife and stopping his raids on your animals. We need to do this before Koslov's force finds him. After that we will go after the rubies. The sultan stands to eliminate the scourge of Ali, who has been raiding his smaller camps."

The sultan listened gravely to the translation, looking slightly disappointed, and gave his reply.

Hasan said, "The sultan said if you had come to him with this proposal six months ago, he would have agreed. Now Ali greatly outnumbers
his warriors. It would be foolish to attack him. It would take months to
arrange the necessary alliances with the other *aouls*. Most of them are
afraid to take on Ali, even with a superior force. And they will want to
stay well clear of Koslov."

Jack said, "I'm curious. If the Sultan's warriors were to attack Ali,
how would they do it?"

Hasan blinked. "They are brave Kyrgyz. There is but one way. They
would attack full strength with battle-axes, crossbows, and such muskets as they have. The most skilled and determined fighters will win. He
has enough warriors to defend his main *aoul* against Ali, but not to attack him directly. A major defeat would leave his people at Ali's mercy."

"Tell the sultan that in America I am known as Apache Jack. I would
lead an attack in the manner of the Apaches." Jack didn't have any idea
how Apaches fought, but he wasn't about to let the truth get in the way
of getting Sonja back.

Hasan relayed this to an obviously puzzled Azziz, then translated his
reply. "The sultan says he has heard of the Turks and the Prussians and
the Spanish and the French and the English, but not the Apache. Who are
the Apache?"

"Indians," Jack said.

Azziz looked puzzled. "Indians? India?"

Jack said, "It's what we call the natives of the New World. Not to be
confused with India. Tell the sultan my grandmother was an Apache,
which is why I am known as Apache Jack. The Apache are treacherous,
cunning fighters who know how to win when they are outnumbered.
They are brave, yes, but they are also smart. For them there is no honor
in dead warriors. Only victory matters."

Hasan translated. The sultan looked interested, but not satisfied.

Jack said, "Tell him I don't want to die either. I don't propose to en-
gage Ali in direct battle against impossible odds. I would rely on stealth
and treachery. I would accept one of the sultan's men as my second-
in-command, with authority to withdraw his warriors any time at his

discretion. If we rescue my wife, I will share the rubies with him half and half. Furthermore, I would help him buy and ship Colt revolvers and Sharps rifles from America."

Hasan translated.

Azziz blinked. "Ninety percent for me," he said in Russian.

So Azziz did speak some Russian after all! Jack bet he was fluent with numbers and percentages. "My weapons and the information from my wife will make it all possible. Sixty percent for you, forty for us."

Azziz listened, frowning slightly. The possibility remained that Jack could find himself another sultan with the necessary warriors. He said, "Sixty-five, thirty-five."

"My friends Parsha and Hasan get the first shot at taking Ali's head."

Hasan relayed the request.

Sultan Azziz nodded yes.

"I agree."

Azziz rose from the carpet.

Hasan said, "Stand, Jack."

Jack stood and Sultan Azziz embraced him, kissing him on both cheeks. He had never been kissed by a grown man and felt uncomfortable.

Quickly, Parsha said, "Kiss him back. Do it."

Sonja's life was at stake. Jack did what he was told. A sultan he might have been, but he smelled like a goat.

Azziz stepped back and began giving instructions to the council behind, and in seconds people were scurrying everywhere in a hubbub of activity.

Hasan said, "The sultan told his people that the American will lead them into battle against Ali. Tonight we will rest. Tomorrow we will have a feast to celebrate, then we will ride."

THREE

Women Before Dogs

 THE SUN SHONE BRIGHTLY OVER ASIA, AND THERE was but a gentle, gusting breeze on the steppe. It was characteristic of that part of the world—so dry and so far from bodies of water—that the temperature rose quickly during the day and plunged during the night, a phenomenon Jack had experienced in his adventure as a drover out west. It was just eleven in the morning, so the midday warmth lay ahead. By two or three o'clock it would be blazing hot.

The proposed feast was far too large to hold inside the yurt, so Sultan Azziz ordered carpets to be spread outside. Azziz sat, gesturing that Jack should take a place on his right and Parsha on his left. To facilitate his duties as a translator, Hasan sat with Jack. A small space in front of the sultan was left empty, and in front of that, in a semicircle, sat a group of about fifty Kyrgyz, including distinguished advisers, trusted warriors, elders, and relatives, including both males and females. The men sat up front, followed by the boys. Females were relegated to the rear.

Azziz then called for his brass smoking pipe, which was larger and more elaborately decorated than Mohammed's had been, and they smoked while they watched the feast being prepared.

The Kyrgyz lit a large fire under a cauldron. When the water was boiling, the two lambs and the goat kid Jack had killed, having been butchered and chopped into chunks, were dumped into the cauldron.

Then more meat was added. In a few minutes the cooks were skimming scum off the water and flicking it onto the ground, where it was devoured by ravenous dogs.

They smoked while the meat cooked. The sultan and Jack made such small talk as was possible through translation. At length two men entered the circle bearing what looked like a cast-iron coffeepot. In fact this was filled with hot water that they poured on their hands so that all might wash. The two men returned as necessary so that all the men got to wash their hands. The women had to pour their own water.

When that was done, large wooden platters filled with boiled meat and rice were brought out. The sultan was served first. He beckoned Jack, Parsha, and Hasan to join him around his platter.

Hasan murmured in Jack's ear. "You will need your knife. As the sultan's guest, you will eat first. He will give you a chunk of meat. When it is given, accept it without hesitation, and eat it with gusto. Praise the food."

Azziz used his knife to cut off a chunk of meat from the steaming platter. He placed the meat into Jack's hand. Jack began eating. Azziz immediately did the same, followed by the rest of the company.

"It is delicious!" Jack said. That wasn't a lie.

Looking pleased, Azziz wiped his mouth with the back of his hand.

As guests of the sultan, they were treated to the choicest parts. For those who sat in the semicircle a different custom was followed. The advisers, elders, and relatives sitting nearest the sultan chose what they wanted from the platter in front of them. They grabbed, say, a joint, took a couple of bites from it, and passed it to the man behind them, who ate some more. The second rank of males passed the remains to the third. Then the boys got their turn. The women and girls in the rear got to gnaw on bones. When they had consumed every scrap of sinew and gristle from the bones, they threw them to the dogs.

As the feast progressed, Jack noticed three naked urchins steal silently up toward the sultan's platter. While his relatives and advisers immediately in front of him presumably occupied his attention, their hands shot out quick as an adder's tongue and snatched food from his tray. They rushed behind a pile of *voilock* to devour the take. When they did this a second time, Jack watched the sultan from the corner of his eye. Azziz knew what they were doing, but pretended not to notice.

Jack saw a naked boy of about four station himself among the dogs, armed with a dry bone that he used to whack the dogs on the snout and steal the bones being tossed their way by the women. The Kyrgyz lived in a harsh world, and the children learned at an early age to survive by any means possible.

When the meat was finished, some men brought around bowls of broth, which they drank. This done, they returned with the pot of warm water for them to wash their hands.

Then Azziz raised his hand for silence. He spoke briefly, seeking no reply. He looked around. There were no objections.

Hasan translated. "The sultan said tomorrow you will lead his warriors into battle against Ali's camp using the tactics of the Apache tribe and the Texas Rangers. His warriors are to obey you as one of their own and follow you to their death if necessary. He said Ali's ambitions are getting out of hand. It is dangerous to let him continue. He must be stopped. He says his warrior Omar will be second-in-command."

Having informed his camp of his will, Sultan Azziz retired to his yurt. The feast was over. There were no speeches. No proclamations. No posturing. No predictions. No exhortations to bravery. No pleading of grand causes. None of that. The sultan had made the decision and that was all that was required. The next day, the visiting American, Jack Sandt, would lead them into battle. On his word they would pick up their battle-axes and lay down their lives for the camp if necessary. Such was the way of the Kyrgyz.

A large, fierce-looking Kyrgyz stood from the front rank of the semi-circle and stepped forward. His horsehide coat had a flowing mane down the back just like Hasan's. Watching Jack, he asked a question.

Hasan said, "This is Omar, the sultan's most trusted warrior. He asks if you require any special preparations."

Jack thought a moment, then said, "Tell him I would like to have hot tallow poured over several sheets of *voilock*. After the fat has hardened, I would like the *voilock* cut into strips about this size." He held up his hands indicating a rectangle about eight inches long and three inches wide. "All his warriors should have knives in addition to their crossbows and battle-axes."

"Consider it done," Omar said.

"So you speak Russian?" It was good that Omar spoke Russian. It would not have been good for Jack to be unable to talk directly to his second-in-command.

"I speak it a little," he said. "I'm best at lying. I'm the one who deals with the Russian tax collector."

Jack grinned. "We're all good at lying when it comes to the tax collector."

"But with you I will speak the truth," he added quickly. "It is the sultan's wish."

"Would you like to learn to shoot the Sharps?"

"I would like that very much."

"Where is Ali's camp now?"

"In the Kourt-Chume." Omar told Jack that Ali's camp was located in a valley that was about four hundred yards wide at the mouth. The valley narrowed to less than two hundred yards in about a verst. It was protected on the sides by high cliffs. Ali kept his animals in this valley at night. Ali's yurt was in the center of the valley about a half verst from the entrance. His warriors lived in a compound of yurts at the base of the eastern cliff. The only way to mount a frontal attack was from the mouth, which Ali could easily defend.

"What kind of animals and how many?"

"Horses mostly, maybe two thousand."

"Is it possible to circle around the valley and ride down from above?"

"Well, I suppose it could be done." He frowned. "With some effort," he added quickly.

"I see. I want two dozen bowmen to ready the arrows tipped with fat." Jack stopped. "Their quarrels," he added quickly. A crossbow shot a quarrel, not an arrow. It was hard for him to get used to the different terminology. "I want the rest of your warriors to fashion some loose straps to go around their horses. They should practice riding while slung under the bellies of their mounts. The way to do it is to cross the reins over the neck of their horse's neck. They should start practicing immediately and not quit until sundown."

"Sir?"

"I have my reasons. You'll see."

"Sir?"

"Yes, Omar."

"My warriors tell me they admire your pistols very much."

Jack said, "Tell them that if we are victorious against Ali and steal the Tsar's rubies, I will send to America for a shipment of pistols so that each warrior might have one."

"Is that a promise, sir?"

"It is."

"For pistols like that, they will follow you anywhere, sir."

FOUR

To Be a Coward

JACK, PARSHA, AND HASAN SPENT THE NIGHT IN A yurt vacated for them and with two old women attending the fire. The next morning the women delivered a breakfast of boiled mutton. When they were finished with breakfast, Jack spotted a feather from the tail of a *bearcoote* or falcon on the *voilock* that covered the floor and stuck it in the band of his hat. Jack Sandt was ready to lead a war party.

They stepped outside, where a stiff, cold wind was gusting across the steppe. A band of about a hundred Kyrgyz warriors armed with battle-axes, crossbows, and a sprinkling of muskets was waiting on horseback. Omar was waiting for his instructions, and seconds after he emerged from their yurt, Sultan Azziz joined them.

Hasan said, "The sultan asks if you are ready for battle, Jack."

Jack turned sideways to a gust of wind. "I'm ready to ride."

"The sultan will speak to his warriors."

As Azziz talked, Hasan translated. "The sultan is telling his warriors that you will be leading them into battle against Ali with Omar as your second in command. They are to follow your orders as though you were a Kyrgyz. He says they will fight Ali in the manner of Apache warriors and the Texas Rangers, which you will now explain."

The sultan stepped back. It was Jack's turn. He said to Omar, "Tell me, do the Kyrgyz fight at night?"

"At night?" He blinked. "We are brave men."

He'd answered Jack's question. Jack took a deep breath. He had no idea how Apaches fought. Loudly and forcefully, he said, "The Apache believe there are just two kinds of fighters. Smart winners and dumb losers. An Apache does not die foolishly. Remember, the winners get to tell the tale, so they are never cowardly. Only the losers are cowardly. If the tactics of the Apache work, they are heroic. If they fail, they are cowardly."

As Omar translated, Jack noticed that Sultan Azziz looked amused at the truth of his observation.

"For the Apache no path to victory is cowardly," Jack said. "There is nothing more barbarous than to die or become maimed yourself. To be a coward is to die stupidly and leave your wives widows and your children without fathers." Jack had no idea what an Apache warrior might think of his spiel, but he thought it sounded good. He drew his Colt dragoon and held it high, waving it back and forth. "If we win, I promise revolvers for each heroic survivor. You will be storied throughout the steppe."

Jack wasn't so foolish as not to know what was uppermost on Azziz's mind. He wanted to rid the steppe of the scourge of Ali, yes. But most of all Azziz coveted the Tsar's rubies. Jack wasn't sure he could trust the Kyrgyz to keep his end of the bargain when it came to sharing the booty, if that came to pass. But one thing at a time. For Jack, Sonja was the treasure of a lifetime. Once he got her freed, the rubies, if there were to be any, would be a bonus. His and Sonja's share of rubies would buy them a grand junk and then some. Maybe even a tavern in Hong Kong. If he didn't get them, there were other ways to earn the money.

Sultan Azziz had smiled benignly throughout Jack's exhortations to victory. It seemed as though he genuinely did have confidence that Jack would carry the day. Looking at it another way, if Ali's marauders were left at large to plunder whatever they fancied, what did the sultan have to gain by torturing Jack to find the village with the rubies? Logically, Ali should come first. It was in both their interests that the question of the rubies should be postponed.

Omar said, "Sir, would you like to see the riders under the bellies of their mounts?"

"Yes, I would."

Omar raised his hand and a half dozen riders thundered past, riding easily under the bellies of their horses.

"Good work, Omar."

Omar looked pleased. He had demonstrated that he was a competent and trustworthy second-in-command.

Jack was forced to leave his daguerreotype gear behind. He could not lead pack animals on a war party. Nevertheless, he took the precaution of slipping his boxes of daguerreotype images into his saddlebags. He could replace his camera. If he lost the images, they were lost forever.

Jack had never imagined in his wildest dreams that he would be leading a war party of Kyrgyz warriors on the Asian steppe, but there he was. The sultan had arranged for him to ride a strong stallion of a beautiful gray, nearly silver color—a breed much favored by Arabs. Jack knew by looking at the horse that he would be fast. In his adventure as a drover Jack had ridden the descendants of mustangs that had originally escaped the Spanish invaders of Mexico. They were good horses, very fast at short distances and quick stopping and starting, which made them good for herding beeves. For thousands of years the Arabs and Kyrgyz had bred their gray horses for endurance over long distances.

Jack put a calming hand on the horse's soft nose. "This horse's name is Andy Jackson." He put his Russian saddle on Andy Jackson and slid his Sharps into its sheath.

Jack gave Hasan and Parsha each a Colt revolver, and the shotgun to Omar. He knew that the gods of fortune were with him, having delivered such a congenial trio of comrades in arms. Their only hope against a force three times their size was the element of surprise. Surprise he hoped to deliver.

"Let's butt 'em up," Jack shouted in English.

"Butt 'em up?" Omar had no idea what Jack was talking about.

Jack swung atop the stallion. "Let's ride," he said in Russian. He dug his heels into Andy Jackson's flank.

They rode.

Parsha eased his mount alongside Jack as they loped across the steppe, headed for the distant mountains. Softly, he said, "You should never forget, Jack, that by nature the Kyrgyz are a treacherous people. We are not one of them. Once we get your wife, we truly should consider escaping these thieves at the first opportunity."

"I had that figured," Jack said mildly.

They rode all that day; as dusk approached, dark clouds roiled and boiled across the horizon. Soon one of those periodic, bizarre storms that thundered across the steppe was full upon them. The Kyrgyz warriors knew all about the rain; each warrior carried a sheet of *voilock* that he could pull around his shoulders in the rain or sleep under at night. These were now put into use.

With the sun sinking low in the western sky, the foothills of the Kourt-Chume Mountains rose before them. Omar told Jack that they were within a few versts of their enemy. The rain was annoying but also a stroke of good fortune. Their approach over the steppe was much traveled by Ali's herdsmen and animals going to and from the camp. With the heavy rain having destroyed any distinction between new and old tracks, Ali would have no way of knowing he was in any danger.

To make sure Ali's herdsmen didn't accidentally spot them, Jack and Omar led the warriors into a narrow valley parallel to the one occupied by Ali's camp.

FIVE

With the Rising of the Sun

 ABOUT THREE VERSTS UP THE NARROW VALLEY, THE
party of Kyrgyz warriors pulled into a stand of cedars,
where they split forces. A larger body of warriors, led by
Parsha and Hasan, continued up the valley to begin the
laborious chore of getting their horses into place at the upper reaches of
Ali's valley. Jack and Omar led a party of twenty-four archers up the
ridge parallel to the valley where Ali had established his camp.

Parsha and Hasan were to use a mirror to signal their arrival in place
for the attack. If they saw smoke, they were to withdraw immediately.

The rain stopped but water continued to drip from the wet branches
of the cedars. When Jack and Omar emerged from the trees, an icy, cutting wind buffeted their backs. They picked their way through loose
rocks scattered among rugged boulders.

An hour later they reached the edge of a fifty-foot-high cliff overlooking a narrow valley that contained Ali's sprawling *aoul.* Jack sat on
a rock and used the telescope to survey the valley below him and study
the possibilities. A river wound through the valley, twisting and turning
like a serpent. Two thousand horses, a thousand each of cattle and
sheep, and several hundred camels grazed along the river.

Ali's warriors were billeted in thirty yurts at the foot of the cliff, immediately below them.

The grandest yurt, presumably Ali's, lay in the center of the valley, surrounded by a semicircle of six smaller yurts. Ali's yurt was well out of range of a musket fired from either cliff. But it wasn't too far away for a .50-caliber Sharps with a rifled barrel.

As Jack studied the valley, Omar said, "Ali's herdsmen take the animals out onto the steppe to graze during the day and return them to the safety of the valley at night. When there's not enough grazing to support his herds, he'll move his *aoul* to another valley. It's impossible for an *aoul* to keep large herds without staying on the move. Ali's greatest fear is that several sultans will put aside their differences long enough to unite against him. To prevent that, he keeps the envious chiefs of the smaller *aouls* in constant agitation, posing as their ally and refusing to move his *aoul* out onto the steppe, where it would be vulnerable to attack."

"I take it this limits how many animals he can keep."

"Yes it does, but Ali's ambition is conquest, not more horses and sheep and camels. The smaller chiefs are blinded by their envy of the sultans. They either don't see his treachery or ignore it. When he has enough power, he'll venture back onto the steppe and take over the smaller *aouls* one by one. Sultan Azziz is descended from Genghis Khan. Ali wants to *be* Genghis Khan."

As Jack studied the valley, the camp began to stir. Herdsmen began arriving from the steppe, driving their animals before them. Women set out for their evening milking of mares and ewes. Watching through the telescope, he said, "How do I tell the leaders?"

Hasan said, "They will have manes down the backs of their coats like Omar and me."

"Got it," Jack said. He didn't want to pick anybody off until he had a chance to catch a glimpse of Sonja, if she was still alive. "No dogs," he said. "Where are the dogs?"

Omar scoffed. "They're warriors. Warriors don't take dogs. They need the women to milk the animals and . . ." He left the sentence unfinished.

"For the other," Jack said.

"For the other, yes."

Good that there were no dogs. But where was Sonja? Was she still alive? A stab of anxiety coursed through Jack's stomach.

Then he saw her. Sonja emerged with a good-looking young woman from a yurt next to Ali's, and they headed toward the river with leather buckets.

Jack gave the telescope to Omar. "She's there with the young Kyrgyz girl headed for the river."

"I see her. A beauty. Your wife?"

Jack sighed. "She's still alive at least."

Jack took the telescope again, watching Sonja collect water and begin the long trudge back to the yurt with the heavy bucket pulling at her shoulder.

As the dimming sun disappeared over the ridge on the far side of the valley, Jack and Omar and their archers retreated from the edge of the cliff. They built a small fire and the bowmen set about the task of securing the pieces of fat-soaked *voilock* to their arrows with twine. Jack had no idea if shooting burning arrows would work, but he had been told by drovers on the Chisholm Trail that Apaches did that with arrows. Everything he was doing was based on the tales of his fellow drovers. How much of it was true and how much apocryphal or fanciful, he had no idea. It sounded good.

He had put Sonja's life on the line with his fast talking. He was beginning to have second thoughts. Chewing on his lower lip, he studied the valley below him.

PARSHA AND HASAN LED THE KYRGYZ WARRIORS DOWN THE UPPER reaches of the canyon. The sky was clear and the night was cold although passing clouds periodically obscured the moon. They rode bareback with ropes around the withers and flanks of their mounts. The headwaters of the river rippled on their left.

An hour later the main river, slowing into lethargic folds, flowed silently at their feet.

A half hour after that, they encountered the first animals, a herd of sheep folded onto the ground to keep warm.

They passed camels.

Then they came upon Ali's huge herd of horses.

Parsha checked his mirror to make sure it wasn't broken, then raised his hand. The Kyrgyz warriors slipped to the underside of their mounts. Slowly, they eased their horses into Ali's herd and began working their way down the valley, blending in with Ali's herd. They needed to be in place by dawn.

BEHIND JACK THE FIRST EDGE OF THE MORNING SUN BEGAN WORK-ing its way through the trees. On either side of him the crossbowmen waited with quarrels tipped with wads of fat-soaked *voilock*. These were anxious moments. To wait too long was to squander the element of sur-prise. Ideally the sun should be directly behind them, blinding the Kyr-gyz looking up from below.

Squatting on the lip of the cliff, Jack focused his telescope on the val-ley, hoping to spot Parsha and Hasan and their warriors easing down the valley slung under the bellies of their horses. Behind him Omar and one of the crossbowmen wrapped wads of fat-soaked *voilock* on the end of sticks to form torches to light the quarrels.

As sun rose higher, Jack spotted something at the bottom of the valley. He yelled to Omar, "Russian cavalry and the Wolfpack! If Hasan is to stand a chance of retrieving Sonja, he has to ride now. Send up the smoke! Send up the smoke! Now, now, now! Do it now! Send up the smoke!"

As the smoke billowed up, a flash of reflected light flashed at him from Hasan's mirror. Jack yelled, "Hasan is riding! Fire the quarrels! Fire at will!"

SIX

Fate of a Man Without Mercy

HEARING THE SHOUTING AND HUBBUB AND THE booming echo of a rifle shot across the canyon, Sonja hurried toward the entrance of her yurt, which was suddenly on fire. Directly outside, she saw one of Ali's warriors facefirst on the ground, then heard an echo that reverberated off the cliffs on either side of the valley. *Ka-boom-woom-woom-woom!*

Two warriors bent to help the first.

A musket ball knocked a warrior sideways, followed a second later by the echoing report from the weapon fired from the top of the cliff. *Ka-boom-woom-woom-woom!*

The second warrior, alarmed, turned in the direction of the report. He stiffened. Silence. *Ka-boom-woom-woom-woom!*

Sonja motioned for the frightened Fatimeh, who was lying flat on the carpet of the yurt along with the other six members of Ali's harem.

Fatimeh shook her head no. "It's not safe, Sonja."

"Come here. Quick, quick." She motioned with her hand.

Reluctantly, Fatimeh did.

"He's here," she said.

Fatimeh looked disbelieving. "Your husband? Are you sure?"

Sonja grinned. "He said he'd come for me. We can't just sit here passively. We have our stolen knife, and we have a derringer." She stepped outside to see what was happening.

At the top of the cliff, backlit by the morning sun, crossbowmen were lobbing burning quarrels down on Ali's camp. Mixed in among them, a sole marksman was picking off Ali's warriors.

Jack!

But, unaccountably, Ali's warriors were ignoring the attack from the top of the cliff. Their attention was directed farther down the valley. Sonja turned and saw gray-and-scarlet Wolfpack uniforms mixed in among Russian cavalry.

CONCENTRATING, SHOWING NO EMOTION DESPITE HIS ANXIETY over who would get to Sonja first, the Russians or Hasan, Jack set about the chore of picking off the warriors milling in confusion among the burning yurts. Equally calm, the bowmen continued to shoot flaming quarrels downward on the tops of the yurts fifty feet below them.

In the burning confusion at the base of the cliff, Ali's warriors, simultaneously under attack from Russian cavalry and the Kyrgyz at the top of the cliff, milled about in confusion, shouting and squinting up at the flames arching down on them.

A yurt exploded.

"There goes his powder," Omar said.

Jack shouted, "Switch to regular quarrels! Hasan needs help. Continue firing at Ali's warriors. When the Russians are in range, fire on them."

The crossbowmen pulled quarrels from their quivers and rained arrows down on Ali's warriors. At that range and angle their crossbows were more accurate than smoothbore muskets.

Jack let the bastards have it, shoving one brass cartridge after another into the breech of his Sharps. *Ka-boom! Ka-boom! Ka-boom! Ka-boom!* He buckled a body with each shot.

"A Texas turkey shoot," he called to Omar. He pulled down on another target.

A Texas turkey shoot? Omar didn't understand.

Jack had never imagined that he could do anything so ghastly or completely cowardly. But these sons of bitches had taken Sonja, and he didn't have any sympathy whatsoever. He was in little danger from return fire; his victims, under simultaneous attack from the Russians, had to fire up into the sun. The .50-caliber bullets were huge, producing a stunning recoil. Jack casually picked the fleeing warriors off, *Ka-boom! Ka-boom!* Each shot kicked hard against his shoulder.

He looked through the Sharps's peep sights, targeting the large yurt in the center of the valley. He saw Sonja and a Kyrgyz girl running for it.

WEARING THE CLOTHES SHE HAD BEEN CAPTURED IN, SONJA HAD A knife tucked in her belt and her derringer in hand. Fatimeh bore the knife she had stolen. When they got to the entrance of Ali's yurt, Raj blocked their way, musket in hand.

Derringer in hand, Sonja confronted him. "It's his turn, Raj."

"I cannot allow it."

"He did that to you, didn't he?" She pointed at his crotch.

Raj clenched his jaw.

"You've had no choice but to serve him. There was no escape. Now there is."

They heard screaming coming from the mouth of the valley. Russian soldiers with swords held high were riding hard up the valley, overwhelming Ali's warriors as arrows rained on the camp from the top of the cliff.

Raj needed no further persuasion. He ripped open the entrance.

Sonja and Fatimeh stepped inside. There the mighty Ali stood, shocked, bewildered, unable to comprehend what was happening. He had expected that his camp would be safe from the Wolfpack. Sonja found it curious that Ali had not joined the battle. Why wasn't the heroic khan on his way toward the entrance of the valley to repel the invaders? The saying was The bigger the bully, the bigger the coward. Was there something to that gem of folk wisdom?

Sonja tapped Ali's crotch with the end of her derringer and without a word pulled the trigger.

Ali screamed and fell to his knees.

"Does it hurt?" she said mildly.

Ali looked up, wide-eyed, clutching himself. Blood seeped through his fingers.

Sonja gave Raj the knife and began reloading her pistol. "I want you to make sure I got it all. And I do mean everything."

Raj knelt before the stricken Ali and set to work with his knife, saying, "You richly deserve this, sire."

The shocked Ali looked up at Sonja, his eyes wide with pain.

Sonja said, "Foolish to expect any sympathy from a woman you dragged in a roll of *voilock* all day and later turned over to your warriors for their amusement. That's not to mention the flogging." She ran her free hand over her bruised backside, wincing as she did. "How many Kyrgyz warriors do you suppose will follow a man who has to squat to pee? Some khan that would be!"

THE VALLEY WAS A CONFUSION OF RIDERLESS HORSES AND HORSE-less riders, popping muskets, yelling, and the screaming of wounded and dying men. Hasan arrived at Ali's yurt as Sonja and Fatimeh stepped out.

He raised his battle-ax and rode hard straight at Fatimeh.

Fatimeh looked up at him, mouth open, eyes wide.

Sonja too saw the oncoming warrior.

The blade of the battle ax flashed downward.

In a single motion, Sonja aimed and fired the derringer.

The impact of the .50-caliber bullet knocked Hasan off his horse. He landed at the feet of his sister, who dropped to her knees beside him. Hasan had blood squirting from a severed artery in his neck. Fatimeh grabbed the artery and squeezed, stopping the pumping of blood. She looked into the eyes of the dying man. "Hasan! Hasan! My God, Hasan!"

"Where's Ali?" Hasan asked.

Sonja said, "In his yurt. Justice is done."

"Justice is to take his head."

She grabbed her crotch with her left hand and used the edge of her right hand to demonstrate the grisly nature of the justice.

Hasan smiled faintly.

"Taking his head would be showing him mercy," Fatimeh said. "He didn't show anybody else mercy. A proper fate."

"I die now, little sister."

"If I dishonored my family, it was not my doing. Ali took me against my will. There was nothing I could do. Please forgive me, Hasan."

"I die. You live. You go now."

Sonja grabbed her by the hand. "He's right, Fatimeh. We run."

"To where?"

"Somebody is at the top of the cliff. I don't think they're Russian. We run up the valley."

Leaving Hasan behind, they ran as hard as they could.

SEVEN

Captured!

 AT THE EDGE OF THE CLIFF, JACK SANDT AND THE
Kyrgyz warriors looked down on the Wolfpack and the
Russian soldiers riding through a ghastly field of broken,
bleeding, screaming, and dying Kyrgyz warriors. Drifts
of red turning pink rolled out in lazy whorls from the shores of the
river.

Through the telescope, Jack had watched Sonja shoot Hasan as he
started to swing his battle-ax at the Kyrgyz girl, who he suspected was
Hasan's sister, Fatimeh. Now he watched, helpless, as Sonja and Fatimeh
ran up the valley, seeking refuge.

Behind them, he spotted Colonel Peter Koslov leading the Wolfpack.

He aimed his Sharps at Koslov and pulled the trigger. Koslov's horse
plunged forward, sending Koslov sprawling.

Jack had hit the horse in the neck, and it lay dead.

He quickly reloaded the Sharps and fired again. This time a gendarme stepped in front of the bullet and pitched forward.

Two more gendarmes, glancing up in Jack's direction, dragged Koslov
to cover while their companions kept riding after Sonja and Fatimeh.

Jack, unable to fire for fear of hitting his wife, could do nothing as
the gendarmes scooped up the two women.

Through his telescope, he watched as the gendarmes took Sonja and
her friend back to Koslov. His mouth dry, he watched Koslov receive his

captives. They talked, glancing up in Jack's direction. Finally, a gendarme raised a white cloth and rode in the direction of the cliff.

Jack lay at the edge of the precipice, waiting.

When the gendarme got to the base of the cliff, he yelled up, "Are you Jack Sandt?"

"I am."

"Are you the man who destroyed Colonel Koslov's ankle."

"I am."

"The colonel says his ankle is more important than his pride. He will trade her ears and her life for you."

Jack chewed his lower lip. "Tell him if he takes her ears, I will destroy his other ankle and he will never walk again."

The gendarme glanced briefly back in Koslov's direction, then back up at Jack. "As you wish, Mr. Sandt. I am instructed to tell you that the colonel will give you time to think it over. He has to retrieve the rubies for the Tsar. He says you know where to find him. You have two weeks to show up, after which he will remove her ears and release her." Saying no more, the gendarme rode back to Koslov.

Jack noted that Koslov, knowing that Kyrgyz were listening in on the conversation, had wisely directed his subordinate not to specifically mention Monko-seran-Xardick. Unfortunately, Omar would now report to the sultan that Jack knew full well the location of the rubies.

Jack and the Kyrgyz warriors waited until the Russians had retreated from the valley with their captives. Then Omar assigned warriors to steal everything worth having and round up Ali's scattered herds.

EIGHT

Hunting Wild Boars

SULTAN AZZIZ, SHOWING POLITE CONCERN FOR SONJA'S safety, was elated by the destruction of Ali and his private army and the capture of his animals. The destruction of the upstart Ali had been accomplished without the loss of so much as a single Kyrgyz warrior. Further, the sultan did not appear to be surprised or concerned that Jack had known the destination of the rubies all along. The sultan was a Kyrgyz. In Jack's boots, he would have lied too.

He said the victory called for a celebratory hunt. During the amiable atmosphere of the hunt, he said, they would discuss the destination of the Romanov rubies and how they might best separate the gems and Jack's wife from Colonel Peter Koslov and his detachment of gendarmes. What did Jack think of that?

Jack said a hunt sounded fine, knowing it was an occasion for congenial man-to-man talk. He knew that Azziz would first try to charm Jack to get what he wanted. He would offer a share of the gems for Jack and Parsha's voluntary cooperation. Later, he would steal their share. Hence the sociable hunt.

Jack had hunted deer as a boy in Maryland. He looked forward to hunting with the sultan and especially seeing the *bearcoote* and falcon in action.

Jack and Parsha knew the hunt would be their only chance to escape.

After a good night's sleep atop sheep's pelts in a private yurt the sultan had thoughtfully provided them with, they stepped outside to see the camp in a buzz of preparation for the hunt. They had a breakfast of boiled mutton with the sultan, and they were ready to depart. To complete the ruse of being an amiable hunter, Jack left his daguerreotype gear behind, taking only the boxes of developed images in his saddlebags.

Three hunters led the caravan, followed by Sultan Azziz and two of his younger sons, flanked on either side by Omar and another guard bearing muskets. The sultan and his sons wore large, billowing *tchimbars* made of black velvet embroidered with silk. They had three of the most beautiful mounts Jack had ever seen, sleek, long-legged Arabian stallions. The oldest boy carried the hooded falcon, which was used to hunt fowl. Two Kyrgyz hunters bearing the hooded *bearcoote* chained to a perch followed them. Then came Jack and Parsha, followed by a party of twenty Kyrgyz hunters in bright *kalats* and carrying battle-axes. At the rear were ten Kyrgyz packhorses carrying food and gear. For the sultan, a caravan was a form of grand entertainment—combination sport, spectacle, and celebration.

The party headed due east toward mountains that had lately harbored Ali. They would spend the night at one of the sultan's smaller camps.

Hearing this, Parsha said mildly, "A deal is a deal. I wanted vengeance against Ali. I got it. We now go for your wife and the rubies."

"It never occurred to me that you wouldn't live up to your word, Parsha."

"It is dangerous to wait too long to make our move."

"Better sooner than later. I agree," Jack said.

Three hours later they arrived at a stagnant river fringed with bushes and reeds. Several of the hunters went ahead to look for sign. They rode slowly along the marshy edge of the river. Jack began to feel that giddy rush of expectation that he always had on the hunt.

Thirty minutes later one of the hunters rode back to confer with Sultan Azziz.

The sultan motioned for Jack and Parsha to join him.

As the American and his Cossack companion came up, Azziz's sons stared intently ahead, looked eager.

Although Parsha's knowledge of the Kyrgyz language was not as good as Hasan's had been, he was able to serve as a translator. "The sultan says the hunters have spotted earth recently dug up by the snouts of wild boars. The hunters will spread out in hopes of flushing one."

"A razorback!" Jack said.

"A razorback?" Parsha asked.

"What they call a wild boar in the United States."

Parsha grinned. "I see. The wild boars here have large tusks and are dangerous when they're cornered. You should be very careful when you're near a wounded one."

"The ones in the United States are pretty ornery too," Jack said.

"The sultan invites us to join him and his sons up front. He says it would be a treat for them to see an American marksman at work with such a fine weapon."

Jack unslung his Sharps, and he and Parsha joined the sultan and his two sons. They moved slowly forward, keeping their eye on the marsh along the river.

Half a verst later, four large deer burst from the reeds about three hundred yards in front of them and bounded over the plain. Even a Sharps wasn't much use with a running deer at that distance, but it turned out the Kyrgyz didn't rely on muskets or crossbows in such circumstances. The keepers, seeing the deer, immediately unhooded and unshackled the *bearcoote*. The great black eagle sprang eagerly from the perch and soared aloft. He circled high above the steppe, then stopped, floating grandly in the air with his great wings outspread. Thus poised, he searched for his prey. Having spotted the deer, he folded his wings against his body and shot straight down at incredible speed at the fleeing deer.

The lead hunter shouted. The party sprang into action, riding after the deer in a full gallop.

At the front of the group, riding hard, Jack saw the *bearcoote* strike his prey, grabbing its neck with great talons. The deer pitched forward and sideways onto the ground. The eagle grabbed the deer's neck and back and began ripping and tearing in an effort to get at his victim's liver.

The *bearcoote*'s keeper arrived within a minute. The eagle still gripped the deer by the neck, ensuring that it did not escape. Upon a signal from the keeper, the eagle released its grip. The keeper slipped the leather hood over the bird's head, reshackled his legs, and put him back on his perch. Amazingly, the bird made no effort to resist.

They returned to the river in search of the boar. As they rode on, Parsha said that no dogs were taken on the hunt because the *bearcoote* would kill them. The *bearcoote* was used to hunt wolves, foxes, wild goats, antelopes, and several kinds of smaller deer.

An hour later they spotted a bristly back moving through the tall grass and reeds. It was a boar! They saw two more bristly backs, slightly smaller than the first. They ran them for about twenty minutes, losing sight of them several times. Finally, they lost them for good. Or so they thought. They slowed their mounts, looking for a bristly back moving through the grass.

Suddenly, all three boars burst into the open about four hundred yards in front of them. The large boar went one way. The two smaller ones took a different tack.

Being given the lead on the sultan's instruction, Jack and Parsha set after the large boar. The horses were as eager for the hunt as the *bearcoote* had been, and galloped with enthusiasm toward the fleeing boar. Soon they could see the boar's formidable tusks. Foaming at the mouth, he gnashed his teeth in rage.

When they were twenty yards away, Jack fired at him, wounding him. Hardly flinching, the boar rushed on. Jack had never realized a wild boar could be so fast. Crazed with pain, the beast literally flew along the ground, bounding this way and that.

About fifteen yards from the boar, matching its speed, Jack fired another round with his Sharps, but riding atop a horse at full gallop made accurate shooting difficult. His aim was high. Although he drew blood, his bullet barely grazed the beast's shoulder. The enraged boar suddenly wheeled, its feet digging into the ground. He charged at Jack's mount. The horse sidestepped him. The boar continued its blind charge, slashing the air with its huge tusks, finally ripping them into the neck of Parsha's horse. The horse crumpled onto the ground, pitching Parsha over its head.

Parsha scrambled to his feet and dove for safety behind his horse, which was twisting and crying out in pain, its hooves pawing frantically at the air. Blood squirted from its neck in crimson ropes.

Another hunter shot at the boar but missed.

Parsha was in mortal danger from the frenzied boar.

The Kyrgyz hunters, trying to stay calm atop their panicked mounts, swung down at the boar with razor-sharp battle-axes. Jack drew a Colt and rode alongside Parsha, hoping to snatch him out of harm's way. But Jack's horse, wild with fear and nearly uncontrollable, leaped and bucked this way and that.

The boar continued its feral slashing.

Jack fired a shot.

The boar stopped, stunned by a bullet lodged in its innards. It looked up at Jack with hateful, wild eyes, mustering its energies for another charge.

Jack grabbed Parsha by the wrist. He yanked, and Parsha scrambled up behind him.

Breathing bubbles of blood, the boar slumped to the ground.

One of the other hunters rode up and spit on the boar. "Shaitan!" he said.

Indeed. A devil boar it had been, a fighter to the end.

They rode back to the main party, where the sultan waited. The hunters there had killed one of the smaller boars. The second had reversed itself, successfully entering the shelter of the reeds. The hunters lost it, concluding that it had likely swum to the far side of the river.

The sultan gave Parsha a new horse, relegating its rider to one of the packhorses. A half hour later, still pumped with excitement and retelling the story of the killing of the huge boar, they reached a small herd of camels that belonged to Sultan Azziz's camp. Azziz called Jack forward and used his hand to indicate that this was where they would spend the night.

Jack had the sultan alone. He drew and cocked one of his revolvers, aiming the muzzle at the sultan's head. He said to Parsha, "Tell the sultan we'll be taking him with us to guarantee our safety. If his men try to stop us, he dies. When we're far enough away, we'll let him go. We won't have any use for him. Tell him we gave him victory over Ali. He'll have to be satisfied with that."

Parsha translated this.

No rubies? Sultan Azziz frowned and gave his reply.

Parsha said, "He says do what you think you can get away with."

"Tell him I caught up with my wife twice, at Bagodat and at Ali's camp in the Kourt-Chume. I will catch up with her again. To me, her ears are more important than rubies." He paused, then added, "Of course, if Parsha and I can get the rubies, we'll take them, too."

Parsha translated for the sultan, then said, "Your wife intact and the rubies. We'll have both, my friend."

With that, Jack and Parsha rode out of the camp with the sultan as their hostage. Although there were only two of them, all they needed was a good head start. They would get as large a lead from Azziz's party as possible before they released him.

As the sultan's hunting party grew smaller and smaller behind him, Jack said, "Tell him that the hunt was fun. I had never seen a trained eagle in action before."

The sultan listened, repressing a hint of a smile.

Parsha relayed his reply. "The sultan says he is pleased that you enjoyed the hunt. But you should know that he will send his warriors after us, and you will regret your treachery for many painful hours before you die. He says there is no place on the steppe where we can hide."

NINE

Bedu the Kalmyk

JACK SANDT AND PARSHA RELEASED SULTAN AZZIZ shortly after dark. At two o'clock in the morning, totally exhausted, they pulled into a stand of willow trees along the river. They couldn't light a fire for fear it would be spotted by their pursuers.

They fell silent. The moon was full. The stars were out. The night was bone cold. Wolves bayed in the distance.

"After all that, Koslov got her. I can hardly believe it."

"He wants both of you, not just her. He wants her ears and your feet. For the moment, she's safe."

A spike of anxiety coursed through Jack's stomach.

"We'll get your wife, and we'll steal the Romanov rubies. We'll do both."

Jack took a deep breath.

"You'll see," Parsha said.

The next day they galloped across the grassy steppe, heading to the southwest toward Kalmyk territory, the blue sky above them turning to a purple haze on the horizon. At length they arrived at a narrow lake that lay parallel to the river. On the shore of the lake they came upon a small wooden temple where Kalmyk came to make sacrifices. The Kalmyk were from Mongolian territory, bordering China, and although those in this region had lately taken to Islam, they still revered their ancient gods. They burned offerings of butter and animal fat on a stone altar inside the temple. They had traced some crude figures on a large rock beside the temple, which was flanked by rods flying small silk flags with inscriptions on them.

With the sun disappearing in the west, they descended the steep bank of the river. Seemingly from nowhere, several Kalmyk horseman rode up to meet them. When Parsha saw that they were Kalmyk, he looked relieved.

Parsha palavered with them in their language. He said, "They're from Chief Bedu's camp. They've been watching our approach for several hours now. They've sent a rider ahead to tell of our arrival."

"We follow them then?"

"Chief Bedu doesn't like Sultan Azziz any more than we do." They followed the Kalmyk down the riverbank toward Chief Bedu's camp.

THE WOLFPACK'S HORSES NEARLY DROPPED FOR LACK OF WATER as they pushed across the saline plain. Then, as the sun was sinking low, they came upon a sandy ridge; in crossing the ridge they saw a lake extending eight or ten versts across the steppe. Colonel Koslov's lieutenant sprang from his horse to sample the water, but he spit it out and made a face. *"Gorkie."* Bitter.

The horses apparently didn't find it bitter, because they sucked it up with gusto.

"We'll camp here," Koslov said. He dismounted, wincing as his bad foot struck the ground. He limped to the edge of the lake and stood, the pain etched on his face. He turned mildly to Sonja and said, "Be thankful your husband shot me in the ankle. Otherwise you'd be minus your ears now."

"Perhaps he is more clever than you think, Colonel."

Standing with his weight on his good foot, Koslov said, "He loves you. He'll come. And when he leaves, it will be on stumps. Whether he lives or not will be his choice. *Then,* I remove your ears."

The gendarmes decided the only way for them to drink the awful water was to make some tea. It was still hardly palatable. But their bodies were dehydrated. They had to drink. They spent the night at the side of the bitter lake, which had swamp grass for their horses to eat.

As they sat by the campfire, Koslov, eyeing her, said, "Which is it to be tonight, little one? Your ears or the other?"

She didn't have to be told what 'the other' meant. She said, "I thought you told my husband that you would spare my ears if he showed up to . . ."

"Surrender his feet to pay for destroying my ankle. What's the difference if I take your ears now or later? The never-quit Jack Sandt will still show up. He's in love with you, and judging from his attack on Ali's camp, he's not lacking courage."

No, he doesn't lack courage, Sonja thought.

Koslov unsheathed his knife. He leaned over and pushed the hair back from Sonja's left ear. He put the blade against her ear. "Remember the blow at the Christmas party?" He clenched his teeth. "With the Tsar watching. You recall that?"

"I remember," she said.

"Then you know better than to challenge me. Now then, I want you in my tent, naked. Do it now."

It was dark by the time Jack and Parsha saw the distant silhouettes of the Kalmyk yurts. They were met by Chief Bedu, a tall, thin man in his fifties with small black eyes, a prominent nose, and a scanty beard. He had high cheekbones and darker skin than the Kyrgyz. He was dressed in a long, dark blue *kalat,* made of silk and buttoned across the chest. He hung his flint and steel for making fire and his knife on a leather girdle around his waist, fastened with a silver buckle. He wore red high-heeled boots similar to those worn by the Kyrgyz. Jack realized this was the steppe equivalent of cowboy boots. His helmet-shaped headdress, made of black silk trimmed with black velvet, had two broad red ribbons hanging down the back.

Bedu took Jack's horse in hand and led him to a yurt where women were spreading fresh carpets on the floor. The yurt would be theirs for the night.

After stowing their belongings, they adjourned to their host's yurt, where two women stood ready to attend to their needs. Bedu had ordered that a sheep be put on to boil in another yurt, where they would eat supper. One woman wore a green-and-red silk *kalat*. The other wore a black velvet robe. Both garments were tied at the waist with broad red sashes. They wore short high-heeled boots that weren't good for walking, and they hobbled about awkwardly.

The Kalmyk yurts were similar to those of the Kyrgyz and likewise covered with *voilock*. A small low altar table opposite the doorway held several small metal vases plus the Kalmyk's copper idols. One vase held millet. The others held milk, butter, and koumiss. The family stored its valuables, domestic utensils, and the koumiss bag in boxes to the left of the altar table, while they slept on the right atop piles of *voilock*.

They all sat in a circle in front of the altar table. The two women began dipping into an iron kettle, serving up bowls of tea mixed with salt, butter, milk, and flour, giving it the appearance of a thick soup. As they drank this unusual brew, which tasted far better than Jack would have thought, Parsha told Bedu that they were fleeing Sultan Azziz's warriors, which, judging from the expression on his face, was a good recommendation as far as Bedu was concerned.

After the tea, they adjourned to the yurt next door, where the fatted sheep was boiling for the welcoming feast. As they sat eating the mutton, Parsha and Bedu had a lengthy conversation. Both men became quite animated at times, sometimes laughing, at other times rolling their eyes. When they had finished, Parsha said, "Bedu knows who we are."

"He does."

"News of Ali's defeat has spread rapidly. The larger camps are relieved to be rid of the ambitious Ali. And while the smaller camps had been thinking they would end up with some animals from the rich sultans, they had begun to distrust Ali."

"So everything is as it was before."

"Yes, something your Western diplomats would call . . ." Parsha searched for the right phrase.

"A balance of power," Jack said.

"A return to old ways, yes. Jealousy, envy, greed, bickering, stealing from one another's herds. The larger camps may have learned a lesson about the consequences of excess greed, but Bedu says he doubts it."

"A wise man," Jack said.

"Bedu says Azziz's warriors are claiming victory over Ali. They said the American who pretended to lead them had a cowardly battle plan so they ignored him. Although they were outnumbered four to one, they stormed past the pickets at the entrance to Ali's valley. They took on Ali's warriors blade to blade. They killed every one of Ali's warriors."

Jack smiled.

Parsha said, "I told you the Kyrgyz are famous liars."

"Sounds like it."

"But Chief Bedu says some of Ali's warriors escaped and claim that the Wolfpack and a brigade of Russian soldiers took them by surprise and overran them, not Azziz's warriors."

"And whom does Chief Bedu believe?"

Parsha laughed. "Outnumbered four to one, Azziz's men fought blade to blade and killed every one of Ali's warriors? Bedu says that's camel manure. He says everybody knows the Kyrgyz are liars. Nobody is a bigger liar than Azziz." Parsha spat on the ground in disgust.

After Bedu's wonderful feast Jack and Parsha spent a quiet night in the yurt. As was the practice in the Kyrgyz yurts, the Kalmyk fire was attended by two women who took turns sleeping and periodically removing the cover to let the smoke escape.

Parsha seemed to have developed an odd ability to read Jack's mind. He said, "Your wife is still in one piece. We will get her. We will. Sleep."

"Thank you, Parsha."

"You can't get your mind off her, I know, but you have to try."

TEN

The Meaning of Friendship

THE NEXT MORNING JACK AND PARSHA HAD A BREAK-fast of the leftover boiled mutton. Accompanied by a party of twenty Kalmyk warriors, they sat out on the first leg of their journey, headed east, destined for faraway Monko-seran-Xardick. The range of mountains before them, the Tangnou, was enveloped in clouds. But as the sun rose, the vapor dissipated, and the Tangnou turned out to be splendid, awesome mountains with startling white caps poking up into the deep blue sky.

At midmorning, Parsha leaned to Jack. "The Kalmyk tell me our progress is being monitored by a small party of riders who have a tele-scope."

"Watching us from a distance?" Jack said.

Parsha nodded.

"Who do the Kalmyk think they are?"

"They don't have any idea."

"People working for Koslov?" Jack asked.

"Could be," Parsha said.

They soon reached a sandy plain, covered in parts with coarse red-dish gravel.

Parsha rode alongside Jack and said, "The Kalmyk are telling me that whoever is out there with the telescope is gone now."

SHORTLY AFTER DAWN, THE KALMYK SCOUTS WORKING FOR THE Wolfpack arrived in camp and had an animated conversation with Colonel Koslov, through Koslov's interpreter. Koslov, questioning the scouts at length, looked pleased. When the scouts left, Koslov ordered the gendarmes to break camp.

To Sonja, he said, "Gather your belongings. Help out."

Sonja said, "Was that about Jack?"

"Yes, it was. Good news. Your husband and a Cossack companion have broken free from Sultan Azziz. They spent the night with a Kalmyk named Bedu and are at this moment apparently headed for Monko-seran-Xardick." Koslov grinned. "See. What did I tell you? He loves you. A man of courage. Also a fool."

"You'll be waiting for him at Monko-seran-Xardick."

"If one of our Kalmyk friends doesn't capture him first, yes, we'll be waiting. A Kalmyk will do anything for money, and the word is out." He stopped. "We've made it clear that we will pay for him alive only. Any Kalmyk delivering him dead loses his own feet." With that, Colonel Cut turned and tended to the chore of breaking camp.

A half hour later, the Wolfpack proceeded across a sandy desert that had no water and were forced to drink the brackish contents of their canteens.

AFTER TWO DAYS OF HARD RIDING, JACK AND PARSHA REACHED THE summit of a stony ridge, and below them lay Kessil-bach-noor, a lake about a hundred versts long and twenty to thirty versts wide. Extensive beds of reeds and bulrushes grew along its shores, plus some good grazing, although they saw no Kyrgyz or Kalmyk camps.

Later that morning they encountered some Kalmyk riders returning to their camp from a visit to their kinsmen farther east. After some palaver, during which time the Kalmyk glanced at Jack several times, Parsha reported the conversation.

"They're being told that Colonel Koslov and the Wolfpack are half a day north of here, also headed east."

"To Xardick."

"It appears that way. They say Koslov has offered ten thousand rubles to anybody bringing you to Xardick as a captive. The Kalmyk hate Koslov, and few of them would trust Koslov to actually pay the reward. But they say there might be a few Kyrgyz who might try. They think we should avoid all Kyrgyz, who they say are mostly dishonorable."

"Of course the Kyrgyz say the same thing about the Kalmyk."

Parsha laughed. "Correct. They'd be bored if they didn't have somebody to distrust."

"Where did you tell them we're going?"

"To Lake Baikal, which is east of the Syan-Shan Mountains and Monko-seran-Xardick. They advise us to stay as close to Mongolia and China as we can. We'll have to dodge bandits and patrols of the Chinese army, but better that than allowing some rogue to go for the reward."

Jack glanced at the Kalmyk and gave them a tip of his hat by way of a thank-you. "I think we should give them some sugar."

Parsha grinned. "So do I. It's always smart to stay on the good side of the Kalmyk, and word of a grateful traveler spreads fast on the steppe."

They gave the Kalmyk a small loaf of sugar and continued on their way.

THE WOLFPACK CONTINUED PAST THE TARBOGATAI RIVER, circling north of Tchoubachack, a desolate, ramshackle Chinese town that Sonja could barely see through the telescope that Colonel Koslov let her use. Avoiding Chinese pickets stationed outside the town, they reached a valley with rocks of deep red jasper. A crimson mountain to the north of them gave off an odd, luminescent glow in the late-afternoon sun.

They camped near the high conical tombs of sunburned bricks where the Kyrgyz established their camp once a year to pay homage to their ancestors. Once again, a Kalmyk scout arrived. As before, Koslov listened with interest to his report, at one point glancing at Sonja with a crooked smile.

When he was finished with the scout, Koslov said, "There is no doubt now. Your husband and his friend are behind us. They were last seen at Kessil-bach-noor. There is one more thing that I find of interest, a mutual interest in a manner of speaking."

"And that would be?"

"Ali eluded us in the raid and escaped up the draw. Now we're told the full story of what happened to him. You got your revenge, pretty one. They call me Colonel Cut. What does that make you?"

She didn't answer.

"Perhaps now you understand what drives me."

She thought, *Only a madman would equate what I did to you and what Ali did to me.* She said nothing.

IN FRONT OF JACK AND PARSHA, PAST SOME SANDY RIDGES, LAY THE vast unbounded plain over which Genghis Khan had marched his savage hordes more than six hundred years earlier. As the sun settled over the Tangnou, the sky turned yellow, then a deep orange. The light, fleecy clouds scattered about the silvery peaks were streaked with crimson on their undersides. Jack rode thinking that Mongols had seen the exact same scene as he. The same snowcapped mountains. The same crimson on the underside of the clouds.

They passed the remains of ancient carts, or barrows, abandoned on the steppes. Jack wondered if some of the crumbling barrows might not contain relics pillaged by the great khan's conquering hordes. He wanted to stop and take a look, but they needed to find a decent place to camp for the night.

Just as it got dark, they found a small stream of pure water surrounded by good grass for the horses and wood for the fire. They filled their bellies around the crackling fire. They did not talk about the man with the telescope. They both knew they were being watched; Colonel Koslov was biding his time, monitoring their progress.

As he pulled his single blanket over him and curled up for sleep, Jack wondered if his wife was still alive. Did she still have her ears?

One of the luckiest things Jack had ever done was destroy Colonel Cut's ankle. Peter Koslov would want nothing less than for Jack to witness the removal of Sonja's ears before he surrendered his own feet. Yes, he told himself again and again and again, Sonja was still alive, and yes, she still had her ears.

Each night when Jack and Parsha lay down for some rest, Parsha sought to reassure him.

"I know what you're thinking over there. Sonja is still in one piece. We will retrieve her."

"And steal the rubies," Jack said.

"That goes without saying," Parsha said. "We're friends. We made a deal. Your wife first, then the rubies. It is dishonorable and unthinkable for friends to go back on their word. Without friends where would we be, Jack? Nowhere."

ELEVEN

The Nature of the Vessel

THE WOLFPACK RODE ACROSS A SANDY STEPPE. BE-
fore them lay the fourteen-thousand to fifteen-thousand-
foot-high Alatou (Variegated Mountain) and the snowy
summit of the Actou (White Mountain), which were
dwarfs compared to the giants of the Altai behind them to the west.
Hate him as she did, Sonja was amazed at the terrible pain being endured by Peter Koslov. She knew the fury was growing within him at
each stab of pain. He never tired of telling her that for having destroyed
his ankle, he would have both of Jack's feet. Never mind that it was a
lucky shot in a thunderstorm; the damage had been done.

The Wolfpack encountered the first of several rocky ridges that rose
about three hundred feet above the flat steppe. They climbed to the top
of the third ridge and saw the distant Ala-kool, which was actually two
lakes, one larger than the other. Soon after, they came onto the deep,
rapid Tarsakhan River, a dangerous stream that rushed like a torrent
between high, sandy banks. They followed the current of the river for
several versts until it slowed, meandering through reedy curves.

That night at their campfire, Colonel Koslov showed her his ghastly
necklace of dried ears. "I've always thought they look like dried mushrooms. What do you think, Mrs. Sandt? Here, touch them!"

Sonja recoiled.

Koslov put them away. "I'll give your ears special treatment. I've been thinking of having a craftsman at Granilnoi Fabric string them on a gold chain separated by a garnet. That's your birthstone isn't it? A garnet. If I have it right, you were born in January."

"Please," she said.

"I've vowed to take your husband's feet, but I'm not so sure what I can do with them. The toes might do it. Perhaps I can have his toes dried." Watching her reaction, he grinned broadly. "You shouldn't have acted so impetuously at the Christmas party. Okay to write your silly poetry, but striking me was going too far. If we don't set limits, however are we to rule?"

AT THE VILLAGE OF ATCHINKS, JACK AND PARSHA TURNED SOUTH-east toward the Sayan Mountains, passing the headwaters of the Yenisey River in a high valley between the Tangnou and Sayan Mountains. They eventually entered the valley of the Oka River, traveling along its banks until they came to a tributary, the Djem-a-louk, that raced down a bed of jagged lava that stretched up the mountains as far as they could see. They passed a small camp of Bouriat who warned them that the great lava flow was inhabited by Shaitan.

From the Bouriat explanation of Shaitan's alleged haunts, they took it that Shaitan resided in the cone of the volcano that had spilled all this lava. They rode until sundown, entering the dreaded lair of Shaitan. They camped that night on jagged lava.

At the end of each day Jack studied the daguerreotype of Sonja and him on their wedding day at Kamenskoi Zavod. Sonja had looked so sweet and happy and hopeful on her wedding day. As he held the precious image each night, he felt buoyed, his confidence renewed. Sonja was still out there, still intact. He would retrieve her. He would take scores if not hundreds of daguerreotypes of her over the years.

THE WOLFPACK CROSSED THREE RIVERS BETWEEN THE LAKES OF Ala-kool, finally reaching the main lake, about sixty versts long and twenty-five versts wide. A narrow rock reef ran from shore to shore about ten versts from each end of the lake. Two versts from the north shore a small, rocky island rose a hundred feet out of the water. A ledge of rock ran from the shore, nearly joining the island. Eight rivers emptied their contents into the main lake, which had no outlet; the wildly hot summers evaporated the water.

Sonja had read an account by Baron Humboldt, who claimed that one of the islands of the Ala-kool contained a volcano. There was none. She had no idea where Humboldt had got that notion, unless it had been passed on to him by hyperbolic Tatar merchants who had crossed the steppe in caravans. Perhaps the travelers mistook the rocky island for a volcano. Humboldt had a reputation as a great explorer, but after Ala-kool, Sonja began to wonder.

After Koslov finished with her on that night on the eastern shore of Ala-kool, Sonja fell into a deep gloom. She was no longer able to escape into fantasy. The junk that she had first imagined had been clear in her mind's eye, and she could see the detail. As her ordeal continued, the image had become fuzzy and indistinct. No matter how hard she tried to resurrect the vision, it remained a blur. Then one night, as hard as she tried, it was impossible to imagine the junk for even a fleeting second. It was gone. Would it never return?

The disappearance of the comforting junk sent her into a deep gloom.

THE NEXT MORNING JACK AND PARSHA CONTINUED UP THE FAR side of the Djem-a-louk, which at one point disappeared, running underground for nearly fifteen versts. The river passed beneath cliffs fifteen hundred to two thousand feet high; in places the ancient volcanic explosion had hurled great chunks of lava into the narrow ravine where the river flowed, filling the valley with ragged boulders to the bases of the surrounding cliffs. They passed a waterfall about twenty-five feet wide that plunged thirty feet, was wafted by the wind until it looked like a fine piece of gauze before plunging another thousand feet, lost in swirling vapor before it hit the ground. At the bottom it regenerated it-self and became a stream again.

They traveled for three days, passing through chasms sixty to ninety feet deep and sleeping on hard lava at night. At sundown of the third day, they came upon the lip of the huge elliptical crater about two thou-sand feet from the summit of the mountain. The crater contained an eight-hundred-foot-high cone at the northern end and a thousand-foot-high cone at the southern end. The gray, purple, and deep red col-ors in the crater and on the mountain above were spectacular in the setting sun.

Watching Jack study his wedding daguerreotype that night, Parsha, who had seen the image many times, said, "May I see it again?"

"Certainly. You know how to hold it." Jack handed him the precious daguerreotype.

Holding the plate by the edges, Parsha turned it to the light. "Sonja is a little beauty. I envy you. No wonder you love her so."

Jack said, "Just looking at it gives me courage and resolve."

Parsha handed it back. "As well it should."

"One way or the other, this will all end soon."

With the firelight flickering against his face, Parsha said, "I think you're likely right, my friend."

COLONEL PETER KOSLOV AND HIS GENDARMES TRAVELED ON across red and orange sand containing an occasional clump of yellow-ish green grass. The lower mountains immediately in front of them, the Karatou, were formed of deep purple rocks that receded into the multi-colored ridges of the Alatou farther east. Above the Alatou loomed the glaciers and snowy flanks of the Actou. Seven rivers flowed from the north side of Alatou, three emptying into Lake Tengiz.

The Wolfpack came upon a tomb that Koslov told her was the Great Tumuli, which the Kyrgyz believed was built by Shaitan, who had super-vised the moving of rounded rocks from the Lepsou River, eight versts distant. The Great Tumuli, a domelike mound, was 33 feet high and 364 feet in diameter.

Soon after, they encountered a smaller tomb—shaped roughly like a blast furnace—built by a people who had preceded the Kalmyk. The tomb, built around two graves covered with large blocks of stones, had a hole on top and a two-by-four-foot door on the bottom. They calculated that it was twenty-five feet in diameter and fifty feet high, with walls four feet thick.

Sonja had fought Ali to the bitter end, but faced with Colonel Cut's knife, ever within his reach, her ability to resist suddenly evaporated. Under the covers with her hated enemy each night, Sonja was compliant, if listless, letting Koslov have his way. When her chore was over, she felt overwhelmed by a never-ending, oppressive guilt that she had somehow betrayed her husband. Such ghastly, awful, terrible guilt!

Unable to write anything approaching poetry, Sonja decided one night that if she could not dream the junk, she would draw it. By way of pushing back the guilt, she used a nub of pencil to begin sketching the broad outlines of a lateen sail.

LEAVING THE VOLCANIC REGION BEHIND, JACK AND PARSHA RODE southeast toward the higher parts of the mountain chain that extended into Mongolia. Eventually they descended the mountains, encountering a shelf of ice over the Buch-a-Sou River, which ran through a deep valley. The ice ranged from twelve to twenty feet thick with subterranean channels of water flowing in every direction; they passed over an ice bridge, a dangerous crossing with ice crashing into the river below.

Five days later, they reached Nouk-a-daban (A Mountain Over Which It Is Possible to Ride). They circled the flank of the mountain in a hard rain, and rode through yet another morass, at times struggling through mud and water up to their saddle flaps. It was now late September, and the cold rain, pushed by hard blasts of wind, turned intermittently into sleet and snow.

That night Jack did not remove his precious daguerreotype from its case.

Watching this, Parsha said, "Just remember what I tell you night after night because it's true. Your wife is okay. We will retrieve her."

"And we will steal the rubies."

Parsha laughed. "We will also steal the rubies, but I'm not sure you understand, my friend, that rubies or not, I would still risk my life helping you get Sonja back. I am a Cossack warrior. I made a pledge. I will honor my word. Please, believe me when I tell you, Jack. You need to look at your daguerreotype." He waited. "Do it."

Jack did. He smiled at the sight of his wife.

Parsha said, "See. You need it."

THE NEXT MORNING THE WOLFPACK BEGAN A THREE-DAY ASCENT of the Alatou. At the summit of a high pass, they could see north across the plain of Karatal to Lake Tengiz and south to China. They passed over the Alatou through a ravine formed by the Tchim-Boulac (Pure Spring). Their wild trip took them two and three hundred feet above the raging torrent below them. The reddish brown porphyry along the way was flecked with white veins.

After she had finished her chores each night, Sonja worked on her junk by the flickering light of the fire. She had only a few minutes alone, but she put those minutes to good use. She put knotholes on the planking of the junk. She drew the twists on the rope. She included small patches on the sail.

Koslov, curious, watched her in silence.

The Wolfpack rode hard for a week, sometimes passing three or four stations a day with as much as three hundred versts between stations. They came upon sandy soil covered with pines and swamp covered with birch. A vast, vast place were the steppes; travelers were swallowed up by the incredible space. At length they came to the Russian frontier at Semipolatinsk.

That night in a rough lodging at Semipolatinsk, Sonja began sketching in the broad outlines of a tropical island on the horizon beyond the junk. The gas lantern gave off a better light than their usual campfire, and Sonja wanted to take advantage of it.

Watching, Koslov said, "You've been working hard on that drawing every day. It's a Chinese junk, I believe."

"I'm half Chinese," Sonja said mildly.

"And its meaning? It must mean something for you to work on it with such obvious passion."

"It's a vessel," she said.

"A vessel. No more?"

It's hope, she thought. *Hope is a kind of vessel. It buoys us.* She said, "Forcing myself to imagine details of the junk keeps my mind occupied."

"Have you ever seen such a vessel yourself?"

She shook her head. "I've seen a crude drawing of one."

Southeast of Nouk-a-Daban, the majestic Monko-seran-Xardick loomed before Jack and Parsha, an incredible mountain rising to the heavens. The rushing torrents of water following storms high on Xardick had cut numerous deep ravines down its steep flanks, exposing the minerals underneath.

They entered a narrow valley of beautiful transparent and opaque green talc with beautiful pieces of nephrite lying on the surface. Jack found a fabulous deep green piece with yellow veins, and Parsha found a light green specimen streaked with white metallic veins. Higher up, they found handsome crystals of lapis lazuli and aquamarine.

The rubies destined for the Tsar's new throne were to be found at the headwaters of the Black Irkout on the eastern flank, facing Lake Baikal. On the trail around the southern face of Xardick, they found themselves again being watched by someone with a telescope.

They pushed on.

As they rode, getting nearer the lair of the Wolfpack, Parsha said, "Repeat after me, Jack: She's okay."

"She's okay."

"We'll get her."

"We'll get her." They rode in silence. Finally, Jack said, "No rubies? What happened to the rubies?"

"The treasure is your wife," Parsha said.

TWELVE

Where Dead Men Hang from Trees

AT LENGTH JACK AND PARSHA LOOKED DOWN ON Kossol-gol, a lake some hundred versts long and thirty versts wide, stretching south toward Mongolia and beyond. Through his telescope Jack studied a large wooded island toward the northern end. In the middle of the lake, toward the southern end, a conical island looked volcanic in origin. Jack counted three more volcanic hills around the shores from which lava had at one time issued. One of these domes, at the northern end of the lake, was huge.

They continued on, crossing several ridges of pines and cedars. They started down a narrow draw with a small stream tumbling down the steep pitch. A bank of low clouds enveloped the mountain as they approached the headwaters of the Black Irkout.

Parsha saw a flash of red. Jack took a closer look through his telescope, and there, far below them, was a Wolfpack picket. He gave the telescope to Parsha, who studied the area some more and spotted a second picket.

They retreated higher up the mountain to a pine grove and tethered their pack animals. All gems found in Siberia were officially the property of the crown, but everybody knew that was a joke out here, so far away from European Russia. The word in Yekaterinburg was that representatives of the Tsar had hired a body of workers to scour the area for rubies.

Was there a village down below or just a campsite? They had no way of knowing.

They went down the mountain on foot to have a closer look. As they eased through the pines, it suddenly turned cold, and a wind began blowing through the tops of the trees. Small flakes of dry snow began twisting and swirling through the branches.

Parsha yanked Jack to the frozen ground.

As he hit hard, Jack saw the danger.

Not fifty yards away, a gendarme picket was looking straight at them. Had he seen them? Or was he looking at something else, and they just happened to be in his line of sight?

"Lie completely still. Don't show your face," Parsha whispered.

Jack did as he was told, his heart pounding like a kettledrum.

At length the picket, who either had not seen them or had orders not to do anything if he had, went on his way.

Careful that they were not entering a trap, they continued, only slower than before.

Parsha spotted him first. Or it. He gave Jack a nudge with his elbow. He whispered, "Look there."

Jack saw it. The corpse of a peasant hung upside down from a tree. A gust of wind caught the body, swinging it momentarily.

Downhill on the far side of the valley, Jack saw another hanging corpse. And another and another. Using the telescope they counted seven such hanging corpses.

They heard somebody shout somewhere downstream from the camp.

They retreated back into the trees and continued downhill. At last they were able to see the main camp. A dozen older yurts apparently housed the workers at the gem site. A half dozen newer yurts had been built for the Wolfpack.

Then Jack spotted Sonja and Fatimeh as they bent to enter the second of the newer yurts. "See there!"

"I see them," Parsha said.

"We need to see the rest of the camp," Jack said.

As Jack and Parsha circled wide of the camp, they heard another shout. They lay on their stomachs and inched closer over the cold ground. The sun was going down. It was getting colder. The orange sun, setting over the summit of the mountain, turned slowly purple. The wind continued sighing in the treetops above them.

They saw the source of the shouting. A dozen of Koslov's Wolves were supervising about fifty peasants who were digging into the hillside with crude spades and short, sharp sticks. How they could see anything in the remaining light was beyond Jack, but they were working like there was no tomorrow.

Jack and Parsha continued downhill. Fifty yards later they came to a clearing. The spitting snow stopped. They hunkered down in the cold wind. They used the telescope to study the terrain below them. Three hundred yards downhill, the creek entered a larger stream that was likely the headwaters of the Black Irkout. Two versts farther on the river slowed for a small meadow in which they counted the shadows of a dozen crude huts that likely called themselves a village, probably a settlement that had appeared after the discovery of rubies.

Jack said, "What do you think, Parsha?"

Parsha sighed. "I think it's an easy matter to shoot pickets with your Sharps, but if the snow returns and sticks, the Wolfpack will be able to track our comings and goings up and down the mountain. If they get on our trail, they'll eventually run us to ground. Getting your wife out with her ears intact will be hard enough. Getting our hands on the rubies will likely be impossible."

Jack glanced up at the dark bank of clouds above them. "Will it snow or won't it?"

Parsha looked up, squinting. "Hard to say. But if it doesn't return tonight, it soon will. Tomorrow maybe, or the day after that. It's that time of year."

On the way back uphill, they decided to have another look at the work crew. It was now too dark for the workers to make out the details on the ground.

An officer with a bad limp arrived on the scene, surrounded by subordinates. Jack didn't have to be told who that was.

"Koslov," Parsha whispered.

"Has to be."

One of Koslov's subordinates shouted an order, and the peasants quickly abandoned their places on the side of the hill and formed a line.

Jack and Parsha took turns watching the ensuing ritual through Jack's telescope.

Each peasant had a small leather bag tied at his waist. The peasant at the head of the line stepped up to two waiting gendarmes and emptied his bag into a small tray held by one of Kostov's subordinates. Having done this, he stepped aside. The next peasant did the same thing, then stepped behind the first peasant, beginning another queue. The next peasant followed and the next until all fifty peasants had emptied their bags onto the tray.

When this was done, one of the subordinates shouted again and one peasant stepped from the line, shoulders slumped, head hanging. Without a word, he turned and put his hands behind his back. The gendarme tied his wrists. The work party began marching up the hill in the direction of the camp. They stopped at a mature pine tree. Two gendarmes took out a length of rope and threw it over the sturdy lower branch of the tree. They tied the bottom end to his ankles and hoisted him up so that he hung there like the corpses higher up the draw.

Koslov pulled out a pistol and shot the peasant in his shoulder, the impact of the bullet sending him spinning. When he finished spinning, Koslov took a knife from a scabbard at his hip and removed the peasant's ears.

Koslov stashed the ears in a small leather bag and casually reloaded his pistol. He shot the peasant again. The earless peasant cried out. His body spun on the rope with renewed energy.

The commandant Peter Koslov thought spinning the worker with bullets was funny.

"He's laughing," Parsha said.

Koslov put a third bullet in the worker's face. Accompanied by subordinates, he limped back up the trail toward the camp.

The remaining peasants and the gendarmes walked up the trail toward the yurts and their supper.

Nobody looked back.

"Jesus!" Jack said.

"Low producer for the day. An incentive to the others to dig harder tomorrow."

"We need to find their horses."

"No place for them to graze up here," Parsha said.

Jack and Parsha continued downhill until the hill flattened out into a swampy meadow just before the creek emptied into the Black Irkout. The river flowed past the village they had seen from higher on the hill. The Wolfpack kept their horses in a corral made of thin pine poles stacked end to end in a zigzag pattern, a method of construction common in the American West, where the slender trunks were called lodgepole pines.

Careful not to spook the horses, they circled the corral until they spotted the pickets, two of them.

"Just two guards. They apparently feel safe enough up here," Jack said.

"Who up here would be crazy enough to take on the Wolfpack?"

They began their trek back up the mountain in the dark. The cold wind keened in the branches of the trees. They paused to catch their breath.

Parsha said, "To be honest, what worries me is that they don't appear to be worried about us. It seems like business as usual. I don't understand."

Jack looked troubled. "I don't either."

"If I were Koslov, I'd have ambushed us by now. Are we overlooking something?"

"Good question. What you don't know is what kills you."

A wolf began baying in the distance. Another wolf joined the howling, then another, until every wolf in the pack had turned its throat to the moon. Abruptly, the howling stopped. An unnerving, single wolf yipped and yelped. Another began baying. Another joined the howling, and the cycle was repeated.

THIRTEEN

A Gathering Storm

 JACK SANDT AND PARSHA GOT UP AT FIRST LIGHT THE next morning. The spitting snow continued on and off as they made their morning tea, but an ominous bank of black clouds began moving in from the northeast as they mounted up for what they knew would be a long day of hard work.

There was no way of knowing the Tsar's instructions to Koslov. If the snow returned and began coming in earnest, would the Wolfpack be forced to fold its operation and take what rubies it had to Yekaterinburg and the craftsmen at Granilnoi Fabric? The odds of two men successfully ambushing the Wolfpack and rescuing Sonja would diminish with each passing verst.

Or did Koslov have time to wait for Jack and Parsha to show so he could complete his revenge against Sonja and her husband?

Trailing their packhorses, Jack and Parsha rode downhill and circled wide of the Wolfpack camp and the village until they came to the trail about a verst southeast of the settlement. The trail followed the course of the Black Irkout. Three versts farther on the trail split. The left fork followed the Black Irkout east to Lake Baikal. The right fork turned southwest, going down the steep south face of Xardick toward Kossol-gol and the steppes. Lake Baikal was Russian turf. Mongolia and China lay south of the Kossol-gol. Not smart to ride east.

They took the right fork to see what was down there. They quickly discovered that the trail looped and turned back on itself. In places it was possible to ride east and from atop the horse see the lower trail heading west.

Finally, Jack stopped his horse. "You think the Wolfpack had any reason to explore this trail?"

"I don't see why," Parsha said.

"Nor do I. I say we take this trail."

"And do what?"

"Ambush them. In their beds is best. Then we grab Sonja and Fatimeh, hightail it, and see how much damage we can inflict on them. We finish them off down there." Jack pointed downhill.

"On the steppe."

Jack grinned ruefully. "If any of us are left by then and we're lucky."

JACK AND PARSHA SET ABOUT SLASHING A PATH THAT ZIGZAGGED downhill, cutting through a stretch of trail that looped back twelve times in a hundred yards. Each time the path intersected the trail, they blazed a marker on a tree. They pushed logs aside, cut back overhanging branches, and removed loose rocks and rubble that could cause a horse to lose its footing. After four hours of hard work they had a functional, if barely visible, shortcut down the mountain—a dangerous trip, but safe enough if a rider knew the way and concentrated.

They cut three dozen sharp stakes about six inches long and buried them in the trail with the tips sticking up, and covered them with a little dirt.

After they had finished their shortcut and buried the stakes, they rode back up the trail again, circling wide of the village. Their chore this time was to mark a series of stations about two versts apart where they would exchange their exhausted mounts for fresh ones that they would somehow have to steal beforehand.

They completed their work as the sun sank low over Xardick, and pitched camp well back into the cedars. When they were finished the next day, they would retrieve their pack animals and gear.

They had themselves a nice supper of tea and dried venison, rehearsing their plan as they ate. The earlier snow, spitting and intermittent, disappeared, replaced by a full-blown storm.

IN A SNOWSTORM GROWING MORE VIOLENT BY THE MINUTE, IT WAS not easy spotting the gendarmes guarding the horses. Jack and Parsha, patient, concentrating, understood the shift. One gendarme guarded the entrance to the corral. A second was posted at the door to the yurt containing the tack. Jack and Parsha circled quietly through the night. Communicating with their hands, each chose a guard. Jack would take the guard by the corral; Parsha got the one by the yurt.

Watching each other, pointing with their hands, they struck as one.

Jack's guard sensed him and turned, alert. Jack dropped the knife and grabbed him tightly by the throat before he could cry out, squeezing as hard as he could. They rolled.

The horses in the corral began to stir.

Jack kept his grip.

His victim struggled.

Jack squeezed so tightly that his hands ached. The guard struggled desperately. He glared at Jack in ragged desperation. It was him or Jack, a furious, feral moment. Who was the strongest? Who was the most determined? Jack put every ounce of energy he could muster into the effort.

The picket went limp.

Parsha appeared at Jack's side. "Easier using the knife."

"He was strong. I almost blew it."

"But you didn't."

"Let's get on with it," Jack said.

Parsha gave two short whistles. They hurried into the yurt and began grabbing saddles, saddle blankets, and bridles. They quickly saddled horses, ten in all. Leaving two saddled horses tethered to the corral, they set out on the trail to the village, each leading a string of four saddled horses. They tethered four mounts to each of the two stations they had prepared. Having thus prepared fresh horses for their retreat, they returned to the corral. In the blackness of the snowy night, wolves bayed. Restless and hungry they were.

FOURTEEN

Whiteout

JACK AND PARSHA EASED UP THE TRAIL TO THE Wolfpack camp in a storm that had turned into a blizzard. The trail itself had already disappeared under a mantle of snow. The whiteout forced them to grope and feel their way slowly up the hill in the direction of the Wolfpack camp.

Suddenly, Parsha gripped Jack's shoulder.

Uncomprehending, Jack stopped.

Parsha pointed to a form in front of them.

Jack thought it was a large rock at first, then recognized it as a human form, a gendarme picket squatting to keep warm and with his back to the wind.

Parsha motioned for Jack to stay in place, using the edge of his hand to mimic a knife. He pointed at Jack and himself. Jack understood. Parsha was to circle behind the picket. If he was forced to, Jack was to rush the gendarme with his own knife.

Jack readied his knife as Parsha disappeared.

A few minutes later, Parsha stepped from the shadows like a ghost and swiftly ran his knife across the picket's throat. The picket soundlessly toppled forward, spurting blood.

The appearance of the Wolfpack yurts also caught them by surprise. Parsha saw them first and grabbed Jack's shoulder. They squatted side by side, considering their next move. Parsha's face said, *Where are the guards? Even in this storm there should be more guards than a single picket down the trail.*

Parsha looked concerned. *Yes, something is wrong.*

Jack held up the palm of his hand. *Should we continue?*

Parsha bunched his face. *What the hell?*

Parsha stopped by the entrance to the first yurt. Jack halted by the *voilock*-covered opening of the second yurt. They cocked their Colts.

Jack raised and lowered his free hand. Once . . . Twice . . .

Each threw open a cover.

Parsha stepped into the first yurt. Jack entered the second.

Parsha fired at a sleeping figure and cocked his revolver.

In the next yurt, Jack yelled, "Sonja! It's me!" He yanked Sonja from under her blanket. She was completely dressed, as was Fatimeh. "You come too," he said to Fatimeh.

Sonja started to say something, but before she could open her mouth, Jack yanked her outside.

Parsha fired at a man who sat up. He cocked again. He aimed at the torso of another gendarme and fired. His targets were so close it was impossible to miss. He cocked and fired, cocked and fired two more times. In a matter of seconds it was over.

Jack and his wife and Fatimeh emerged from the yurt simultaneously with Parsha.

They were surrounded by eerie figures in the fury of the snow. Wolfpack. Ambush.

Kismet in a heartbeat.

Jack grabbed both Sonja and Fatimeh by the hair and hurled them to the ground behind the stack of firewood at the rear of the first yurt, pitching himself on top of Sonja as he did. Parsha dove onto Fatimeh. Jack and Parsha pulled the stack of cordwood tumbling onto their backs.

About them the infuriated gendarmes milled about, unable to see in the blinding snowstorm. They'd had the American and the Cossack surrounded at close quarters, then—

Gone!

How had they managed to escape?

The collapse of a pile of firewood went unnoticed in the confusion.

A man with a terrible limp stopped less than a yard in front of them. Colonel Peter Koslov was in a rage. "This was supposed to be an ambush. A simple ambush. It was carefully planned. We let them come for the women. We surround them. It was easy to execute. How could you not get them? Where are they?"

Hesitantly, a voice said, "We followed your orders, sir. We were ready. But in this snow we—"

"We what?"

"They must have—"

A pistol cracked. Koslov screamed, "I don't tolerate excuses. Members of the Wolfpack do not make excuses. And they do not fail. 'Must have, must have . . .' Must have what? I want the Sandts, both of them. Go, go, go!"

The disconsolate Colonel Cut leaned briefly against the cordwood, swearing as he toppled more chunks onto his unseen quarry. Under the firewood, the dag man and the Cossack, pleased that they had thought as one at the critical instant, hardly dared to breathe. Jack found Sonja's left hand with his own, and they gripped one another as tightly as they could.

AFTER A FEW MINUTES, KOSLOV LEFT TO DIRECT THE IMPOSSIBLE search in the blinding snow. When they were sure the way was clear, Jack and Parsha crawled from under the firewood. With Parsha leading the way, they groped their way downhill. Their progress was torturously slow, out of concern that they might inadvertently bump into a gendarme before they got to their horses—if their horses were still there.

Jack was elated that at last he had Sonja's hand in his. Even if the night ended in tragedy, he had at least caught up with her. She held his hand so tightly, he thought she was trying to break it.

Jack, Sonja, and Fatimeh could only trust that Parsha, a skilled and experienced woodsman, would somehow be able to maintain his bearings. Did Parsha have any idea where he was going? They had no idea. They followed him, trusting.

At length, as the billowing snow began to thin and the first glow of the morning sun appeared in the east, they came upon the ghostly forms of their waiting horses.

The next question was whether the gendarmes had already found the horses and were once again waiting in ambush.

Jack, Sonja, and Fatimeh lay on their stomachs while Parsha circled the horses checking for gendarmes.

In a few minutes, he was back. No gendarmes.

As they mounted their horses and rode off, they heard shouting behind them. They spurred their mounts, galloping hard. At the first station they leaped from their horses and threw their saddles onto the backs of the waiting animals. They rode their fresh mounts hard between the first and second stations, where they again switched horses.

Behind them, the Wolfpack rode in hard pursuit but without a change of mounts began to fall slowly behind. The difference, for Jack and his wife and their companions, was critical.

They rounded a bend in the trail. The sharpened points were coming up. On their right, the blaze marking the first leg of the new trail. Jack pulled up, motioning for Sonja to do the same. Parsha yelled to Fatimeh, and she did the same.

"What's this all about?" Sonja said.

"Fresh mounts alone won't do it. Parsha and I have arranged a series of ambushes. We have to cut down their number. It's our only chance." He stopped. "I forgot about . . ." He relaxed.

Grinning, Sonja pulled back her hair. "I've still got 'em. He was waiting for you. He wanted to take both ears and feet at the same time."

"Good that you and Fatimeh were already dressed."

"There was a reason for that," Sonja said. "Koslov and his men have been planning and rehearsing the ambush ever since we got here. Every night, they lay in wait. Every night Fatimeh and I went to bed fully clothed just in case. We never dreamed you would actually get to us."

"Much less get you out."

Sonja laughed. "There's that, too. You wouldn't have if there hadn't been a whiteout."

JACK FINGERED THE COOL METAL OF THE LEVER THAT TURNED THE cylinder of his shotgun. If he had feared that Sonja would somehow be too emotional for what had to be done, he had been wrong. Sonja, remarkably calm, ran her fingers down the barrel of her Colt dragoon.

Jack waited. A minute passed, two. Then he heard it, a faint, distant rumble. That would be the hooves of the Wolfpack's horses.

Again he readied the shotgun.

The Wolfpack rounded the bend, riding hard.

Sonja whispered. "Do it now, Jack. Shoot!"

"We wait."

"Jack?" Sonja's anxious voice rose in pitch.

"Shush."

The Wolfpack's horses hit the pointed stakes and began bucking and rearing.

Shooting slightly uphill, Jack aimed at a Wolfpack torso and pulled the trigger.

Boom! Jack cranked in another round. *Boom!*

He heard the sharp *crack* of Sonja's revolver.

Boom! Crack! Boom! Crack! Boom! Crack!

"Ride, Sonja!" Jack turned his horse and followed Sonja down the freshly blazed downhill trail.

PARSHA AND FATIMEH LISTENED TO THE DIMINISHING SOUND OF Jack and Sonja's horses as they continued down the mountain. The heavy snowfall had returned, but the wind had abated. They waited. Seconds passed as hours. The entrance to their escape route was obscured by the falling snow, fog, and the branches of the trees. No Wolfpack. Either the surviving gendarmes were continuing down the main trail with extreme care or they had retreated.

Parsha whispered to Fatimeh in the Kyrgyz language. "We'll count them before deciding how many rounds. Foolish to take chances."

"I agree."

A wind from the steppe picked up, whipping the snow up through the trees.

At last the Wolfpack slowly rounded the bend in the trail with muskets at the ready. The rider on point leaned over his horse's neck, studying the trail in front of them. Parsha counted twelve gendarmes. He whispered, "We each take three quick shots, then ride."

Fatimeh, who had never in her life fired a weapon and never imagined that she would, nodded her head in agreement.

The gendarmes rode closer.

Parsha saw Koslov. This was not the time to kill Koslov. If they did, the others would grab the rubies and retreat. He whispered, "Save the colonel."

Fatimeh nodded.

The gendarmes drew closer, the details of their faces becoming clear.

Parsha cocked the pistol and whispered, "You take the left. I'll take the right. On three."

Fatimeh cocked her Colt.

Parsha whispered, "One. Two."

Parsha and Fatimeh fired *boom-boom-boom, boom-boom-boom,* then headed down the mountain to catch up to Jack and Sonja.

Remember Us

JACK, SONJA, PARSHA, AND FATIMEH RODE IN THE DI-
rection of Kossol-gol, their horses leaving hoofprints in
the deepening snow. About a half verst out, still at the
base of Mono-seran-Xardick, they found some rocks for
cover and waited. Through the fog and snow, Sonja counted the silhouettes of nine gendarmes, although it was impossible to tell one rider
from another. She saw that Koslov was riding in the middle. Or at least
a man in his uniform. She couldn't see his face. She adjusted the telescope, but she still couldn't see him clearly.

Beside her, Jack adjusted his peep for distance. He sighted the lead
figure. *Ka-boom!* The Sharps's recoil rocked Jack's shoulder. The lead
gendarme hit the snow with half his neck blown away, carotid arteries
squirting crimson.

The Wolfpack stopped.

Jack reloaded quickly. He picked another gendarme and *ka-boom*
dropped him, too.

The gendarmes retreated to the safety of a small pile of rocks.

Sonja refocused the telescope. "They're sending two to the right and
two to the left."

"Leaving three in the middle."

"That's right. Don't you think there should be more of them?"

"I was wondering that." Jack tracked a gendarme through his sights. *Ka-boom!*

"Got him," Sonja said.

The remaining scouts retreated to the sheltering rocks.

Sonja heard the howling of wolves.

"They know people are dying," Parsha said.

Sonja shushed them. "Listen. Horses!" She turned.

Gendarmes thundered at them from the fog, firing ball-and-cap pistols.

Sonja fired the shotgun and hit a horse, which almost landed on her. Beside her Fatimeh cried out.

Sonja levered the cylinder and swung the shotgun at Koslov. His horse reared as she pulled the trigger, but he and his men rode on.

Sonja, Jack, and Parsha watched them disappear into the snowy murk. How many were there? Six? Eight? It was hard to tell. The gendarmes had lost one of their own, plus one horse down, and one or more of them had been wounded.

Fatimeh too lay dead from a round in her heart.

SONJA HELPED JACK AND PARSHA ROLL FATIMEH'S BODY UP IN HER blanket. Sweet Fatimeh, dead. Sonja could hardly believe it. One moment she was fighting for her next breath, as they all were. Now she was staring into the falling snow through unseeing brown eyes. Sonja closed her eyelids. They had been so successful that they had nearly believed they were invincible. Now this.

Shaken, they reassessed their situation. The Wolfpack, gathered behind the rocks, outnumbered them perhaps thirteen to three, but they had the Sharps, the shotgun, and the Colt dragoons. The long-barreled dragoons had far greater range than the gendarmes' stubby pistols, which also had to be reloaded between shots.

Jack said, "Suggestions anyone?"

Sonja said, "How about that Texas Rangers tactic you told me about. That's why they bought Sam Colt's revolvers wasn't it? To use against the Comanches. What if I ride out to draw their fire, then you go straight at them with your Colts while they're reloading?"

Jack turned to Parsha. "What do you say, Parsha?"

"If you two are willing, so am I."

Jack said, "Don't ride too close, Sonja. We want them to shoot at you, not knock you onto the snow."

Saying no more, Sonja mounted her horse and spurred him in the flank. She rode hard through the snow, heart thumping, screaming as loud as she could, hoping Koslov could hear her. "Remember Oblinsk! Remember Oblinsk! Remember Oblinsk!"

Nearer, nearer.

"Remember Oblinsk!"

She suddenly turned, whipping the flanks of her horse. The horse slipped on the snow but kept its balance. Sonja heard the pop of muskets. Here was the moment of danger.

She rode on unharmed. She turned, looking back over her shoulder.

Jack and Parsha charged out of the snow and fog, spurring their mounts toward the gendarmes, who were frantically pouring powder down the barrels of their muskets. The American and his Cossack friend galloped past the Wolfpack, fanning the hammers of their long-barreled dragoons. The gendarmes dropped their muskets and grabbed their inaccurate, stumpy pistols.

Sonja counted eight shots fired and saw several gendarmes go down. How many shots had been lethal was unclear in the confusion. She could make out Koslov, who was clearly stunned by the turn of events. She rode back and rejoined Jack and Parsha, who had taken a ball in his chest from one of the Wolfpack pistols, a lucky shot. She and Jack helped him from the horse. He was bleeding internally and in terrible pain. Sonja dug out her last bottle of laudanum, and he took a slug.

Parsha was unable to move. "I'm likely going to die here." He looked at some drops of his blood in the snow. "Look here. Precious little rubies at the foot of Xardick." He grinned ruefully. "Koslov's out there with seven gendarmes. You need to do something while I can still help."

———

SONJA TOOK THE RIGHT FLANK WITH TWO COLT DRAGOONS AND the shotgun slung over her shoulder. Jack took the left with two Colt dragoons and the Sharps slung over his shoulder. They both lay on their stomachs on the snow and pushed themselves forward with their knees and elbows. The ground beneath the snow was frozen hard as a rock. Behind them, breathing with a gurgling, cracking sound as his lungs filled with blood, Parsha had the derringer and Jack's pocket watch.

It was like crawling on cold bricks, but Sonja was determined. With Jack, she had fought woman beside man and held up her end of the bargain. She wasn't about to weaken now.

Sonja inched along the ground, her face cold, her fingers numb. Her knees and elbows ached. She could barely see the silhouette of the rocks that protected Koslov and his remaining gendarmes.

She and Jack had given themselves a half hour to get in place. Parsha had the only watch, so they had to wait for the signal.

When she could see the figures of the soldiers from the side, she stopped. She had gone far enough. The longer she remained in place, the greater the odds of her being discovered. Staying as flat as she could, Sonja cocked the shotgun. She would fire at bodies in general. A wounded or weakened gendarme was as good as a dead gendarme.

She waited.

She heard the muffled pop of Parsha's derringer.

She aimed the shotgun at a crimson tunic in the fog and fired. *Whump!* A miss. She heard Jack's Sharps. *Ka-boom!* She levered the cylinder. *Whump!* Got one. She could hear Jack fanning shots from his Colt dragoon. *Crack! Crack! Crack!* She levered in the third of her allotted three rounds. *Whump!* Got another.

She slung the shotgun over her shoulder and, knowing one well-placed shot would bring her down, sprinted back into the cover of fog and falling snow.

She stopped, unable to catch her breath. Her chest was on fire from the frigid air that had ripped into her lungs. She eased back toward the rear of what was left of the Wolfpack, listening for Jack's whistle.

Silence.

Had Jack been taken down?

She heard the whistle. She whistled in return. Another whistle. She whistled back.

When she found him, Jack was bleeding from his left side where a Wolfpack musket ball, ricocheting from the barrel of the Sharps, had grazed his ribs. He touched the wound with his fingers and winced. "Smarts a tad, but I'll be okay," he said.

Jack and Sonja reloaded their weapons and circled back to Parsha, who was dead.

Jack, numb, looked down on his friend's corpse. "I've never seen such courage. And after all that we have been through. Poor, poor Parsha."

Sonja gripped him by the shoulder. "We're not finished yet, Jack."

"I know. I know." He took a deep breath.

Jack and Sonja rolled Parsha up in *voilock* and placed him alongside Fatimeh. The advantage was shifting once again. They were still out-numbered, but Jack could now see well enough to pick off the gendarmes from beyond the range of their muskets.

Hooves.

The thunder of hooves.

They crouched behind the dead horse.

Jack took the lead rider with the Sharps. *Ka-boom!*

As the attacking gendarmes rode past, Sonja pointed and pulled, pointed and pulled, pointed and pulled, the shotgun bucking against her shoulder. *Whump! Whump! Whump!* She blasted three gendarmes off their saddles. Beside her, Jack was fanning Colt dragoons as fast as he could.

When the smoke cleared seven gendarmes were down, four dead and three badly wounded. One member of the Wolfpack remained, Colonel Peter Koslov. In the distant, whirling snow, Koslov watched them from atop his mount.

Jack removed the weapons from the wounded gendarmes while Sonja focused the telescope on Koslov, who sat astride his horse, a determined but defeated figure. He wasn't going anywhere. He was at their mercy, but they were in no hurry to end his predicament.

Behind Koslov, Sonja saw the dim figures of the wolves that had been howling earlier. Eyeing their prey, they were closing in. "What will he do next?"

"He's trapped. A trapped animal will bare its teeth and charge. A human animal will try to negotiate first."

"His horse is bleeding from the neck."

Jack gave her the Sharps.

"Take my time?"

"This is your action, Sonja. You've earned it. Play it however you want. Your call."

Sonja waited as Koslov rode toward them in the billowing snow. He was a grim, hateful figure, determined to prevail.

His horse crumpled from beneath him.

He dismounted and began limping toward them, carrying a saddlebag. Behind him, the wolves edged closer to their prey.

Koslov shouted, "The never-quit Mrs. Sandt, the lady with the hard right hand!"

"Me. Ready to knock you down again. Permanently this time."

"What now, are you going to quote from Sun Tzu? Wait for the fortuitous blinding blizzard, then strike!" Koslov continued forward, his face and features becoming clearer.

Sonja said, "You want Sun Tzu? Sun Tzu says, 'By persistently hanging on the enemy's flank, we shall succeed in the long run in beating the commander in chief.'"

Koslov looked disgusted. "Or perhaps this is how Americans fight. Always from ambush or from a distance. Never face your adversary. Isn't that what they did to George the Third? Cowards firing their Pennsylvania long rifles from the woods. Where is your honor?"

"Honor? What kind of nonsense is that coming from a man who entertains himself by removing other men's ears?"

Wolves, ghostly figures in the falling snow, began gathering around Koslov.

Sonja eyed Koslov through the peep sights.

A wolf appeared from the misty gloom, running straight at Koslov.

Ka-boom! Sonja dropped it on the spot. She inserted another cartridge into the breech and levered up another Maynard cap.

Another wolf raced out of the snow.

Ka-boom! Sonja knocked it off its feet. "It's not rubies I'm after, although I'll take those, too."

Koslov glanced down at the dead wolf, then back at Sonja. "You're Russian. Is this what you learned from your American friend? Killing from ambush!"

Another wolf raced out of the snow, its paws digging into the frozen steppe.

Seeing it, Koslov fell on his stomach and covered his neck with his arms.

The wolf was upon him, ripping at his back. Koslov screamed in pain.

Ka-boom! Sonja knocked the wolf off Koslov's back.

Jack murmured, "You're standing tall, Sonja. The serfs of Oblinsk and all the Jews he's pushed around are pulling for you."

Koslov struggled to his knees. "You couldn't have done it without that musket of yours."

Sonja sad, "It's not a musket. It's a breech-loading fifty-caliber Sharps rifle. My husband says it's the weapon of choice for hunting buffalo in America."

"And the pistols?"

"Colt dragoons. Also American."

Koslov said, "I have the rubies. My life for the rubies."

Sonja smiled grimly. "The rubies? You want to bargain? The rubies are ours anyway, Colonel."

Koslov glanced about. More wolves were gathering behind him. "What then? What do you want?"

"I want your ears. You're lucky you're not the man who dragged me behind a horse all day."

"What?"

"You heard me. Your ears for your life. It's your ears that I'm after. Remove your ears, sir."

The wolves drew closer. Sonja counted five of them, malevolent shadows lurking in the snowstorm. Then more, six, seven. There were more behind them that she couldn't count.

"My father was born a serf. I stand here representing the serfs at Oblinsk and all Russians who suffer under the tsars. The revolution begins here, now, at Monko-seran-Xardick. We will melt the ice atop the summit."

"What revolution?"

"The one that started in the rest of Europe five years ago. It may take us a few years, and a lot may go wrong, but eventually we'll bring all of you down. All the princes and princesses. All the tsars and tsarinas. There'll be no more masters and serfs, only free men and women. I want your ears. I want you to cut them off to show you're sorry for what you did. It's that or the wolves. Your choice."

Koslov looked disbelieving. "You can't mean it."

"You don't think so?"

Another wolf tried its luck.

Ka-boom! Sonja knocked it off its feet. "If I don't get my way, the next wolf gets you." She inserted another cartridge and cranked the Maynard strip. "I want your ears, Colonel. Your ears to show you're truly sorry for what you did at Oblinsk. Your ears for atonement and for justice. A small victory, but all victories count. Remove your ears now, or I let the wolves have their way."

Koslov retrieved his knife from his pocket. He hobbled closer to them. "You're a poet. A writer. Be civilized."

Then she saw. Koslov was wearing his necklace of dried ears. "What's that around your neck?"

He didn't answer.

"Civilized?" she said, astonished. "You want *me* to be civilized? Did you show mercy at Oblinsk? Were you civilized? I want your ears."

Koslov took the end of his left ear with his left hand, but couldn't bring himself to act.

"Your ears for your life. Both of them. I want them strung on your necklace with the others."

"Please."

Evenly, she said, "Do it if you want to live, Colonel. Small price. Your ears to join those you took. The necklace will be incomplete without your ears. Fair enough, wouldn't you say?"

Koslov glanced back at the circling wolves.

"Cut upward with the knife. Take it off. Now! Then the other. Don't throw them away. Hold on to them."

Koslov ripped the blade upward. Ear in hand, he stood facing them, blood running down the side of his head.

The wolves rushed him again.

Glancing at them, his face stricken, he shouted, "You promised! My God."

She shot one wolf, and the rest retreated. "Both ears. The necklace won't be complete without both ears."

He stared at Jack and Sonja with wide eyes. "Mercy!"

"I want the second ear," she said evenly, her voice hard.

Koslov took the second ear. He stood in the falling snow, holding his ears in his left hand, with blood streaming down both sides of his head.

"What do you think, Colonel? You like the cut?"

Again the wolves attacked. The lead wolf knocked Koslov down. He screamed in agony as the wolf gripped him by the shoulder and ripped. She pulled the trigger, *ka-boom*, shattering the wolf's skull.

The remaining wolves retreated.

Koslov got to his knees, gripping his left shoulder with his hand. "Help me."

"They'll be back," she said.

Koslov turned, looking for the pack. Were the wolves re-forming for another charge?

"Throw us the rubies," Sonja said.

Koslov threw them the saddlebag, then stemmed the flow of blood from his bleeding ears and tended to the wound on his shoulder where the wolf had clamped its jaws.

Jack retrieved the saddlebag and gave it to Sonja.

Sonja opened the saddlebag and scooped out a handful of rubies. She examined them close up, then poured them back into the saddlebag. "See the flow. Running rubies. They're the blood of Russians."

Jack said, "How many, Colonel?"

Koslov said, "Six hundred and twenty-four, weighing a little more than two kilos in all. What are you going to do now?"

Mildly, Sonja said, "We're riding south with the rubies."

"And me? What happens to me?"

"Now it's your turn to run from a wolfpack. Maybe the wolves will be back. Maybe not. If they don't get you and you don't bleed to death, maybe you can make it back to the village. I wish you luck in that regard. Fun if everybody in St. Petersburg and Moscow gets to tell the story of the unstoppable Colonel Peter Koslov. Colonel Cut chased a half-Chinese female poet halfway across Russia in an effort to remove her ears and returned without his own."

"I like it," Jack said.

Sonja said, "Remember Oblinsk, Colonel Koslov!"

"I—" Koslov closed his mouth. Hands on the sides of his bleeding head, he turned, peering into the snow to see if the wolves were returning.

JACK AND SONJA PILED ROCKS OVER THE BODIES OF PARSHA AND Fatimeh. Jack knelt in the fallen snow, remembering his Cossack companion. Finally, Jack stood, looking down on Parsha's makeshift grave. He took a deep breath. "I'll never forget you, old friend. Never. I swear. Remember that foggy day when we were trying to find the Cholsoun Pass. Turned out we were walking on the edge of a cliff. You told me that cliffs and fog come in many forms. We spend our lives walking on the edge of invisible precipices. You had that right."

Carrying with them the storied rubies of Monko-seran-Xardick, Jack and Sonja abandoned the stricken Koslov and rode south.

Sonja said, "It's a constant struggle keeping a balance between the hot and the cold, the feminine and the masculine, the loving and the violent." She rode in silence, then added, "Maybe I should have put a bullet through his heart. If he survives, he'll pursue us to the ends of the earth."

"It was your call," Jack said. "And I agree. I hope he makes it back so all of Russia will know. If he shows up again, we'll do what we have to do."

Soon Jack and Sonja Sankova Sandt were alone in the swirling snow. Their run together had hardly begun. Ahead lay vast reaches of the Gobi, then China. Not once did Sonja look back at the earless Colonel Cut, commandant of Tsar Nicholas's Detachment One, alone, bleeding, cold, surrounded by wolves.

AN HOUR BEFORE SUNSET, JACK AND SONJA STOPPED BY A SHELTERing outcrop of rocks that poked up from the vast white sea of snow-covered plain that stretched before them. They built a fire and fashioned an enclosed lean-to to protect them from the wind that rushed down the flanks of the mountain that had yielded the Tsar's rubies. They made tea, and Jack got out his boxes of daguerreotypes.

One at a time, he shared the images with Sonja and remembered. In London, the determined Karl Marx in his flat at 28 Dean Street. In St. Petersburg, the pompous Count Vladimir Chermerkov, who had arranged his travel documents. At Nijni Novgorod, thoughtful Russians, the writer Ivan Turgenev and Jack's hosts, Prince and Princess Onkifovich. From Yekaterinburg there were the artisans at Granilnoi Fabric, proud of their work. Also at Yekaterinburg, the fine lady in her greenhouse, oblivious of the barbarities of such obscene wealth. And in Yekaterinburg too, the cold-eyed Colonel Peter Koslov in his uniform with all his medals. From Ilmskoi, the resolute warriors Irina and Tamara, with their knowing smiles, looking grand and proud. From Maias, near Lake Chirtanish in the Urals, the exuberant Baroness Marya Borisovna, the lady who would not yield to the years. From the chapel at Kamenskoi Zavod, their wedding picture. From the foothills of the Altai, Ali, the Expected One, exuding preposterous ambition. From the Altai, Emil and his charming family, and Parsha, the brave Cossack hunter and warrior. On the Asian steppe, Sultan Azziz, with his watchful, ever treacherous eyes.

All those figures stared out at the viewer, frozen in a moment in time. *Here we are,* they said, *this is what we looked like in Russia and the Urals and Siberia in the spring and summer of 1853.*

Leaning against one another, feeling good, Jack and Sonja returned to the daguerreotype of their wedding day. Sonja unfolded her drawing of the junk. "Working on this is what kept me going."

"Really?" Jack told her about his dream of the two of them on a junk that had survived a terrible storm. The sun was out. The wind was balmy. And ahead of them lay an island with the promise of adventure and good times.

"What do you think, does it look anything like a junk?"

He studied it. "It's a grand junk, Sonja. When we get to Hong Kong, we'll sell some rubies and hire some boatbuilders to duplicate it."

Sonja was pleased. "One just like it? Really?"

"If you're going to build a junk, you have to start with a sketch, right. We'll work from your drawing and build a superb junk and find that island that I imagined."

Sonja grinned broadly. "It's out there, has to be."

"When the storms come, we'll flood the aft hold and wait it out."

Sonja took another look at the daguerreotype of the brand-new Mr. and Mrs. Jack Sandt at the wedding chapel. "It's been a long journey from that day in Kamenskoi Zavod."

Jack began packing the images back in the slotted boxes. "My daguerreotypes capture the exterior and the eyes of the people I encounter. But in here and up here"—he tapped himself on the heart and the side of his head—"is the writer's territory."

"Let's do it then," Sonja said. "Let's put our story on paper."

Jack and Sonja decided to put their adventure on paper, recording the details as they saw and felt them, alternating episodes and chapters. Hers. His. Hers. His.

They wanted their story to say this:

From St. Petersburg to Monko-seran-Xardick we fled, wolves in pursuit, fangs bared. Run, run, run. We crossed snow and ice and mountains and steppe. We survived. This is how we felt. This is what we endured. Truly, let it be said that compared to the treasure of human dignity, the Romanov rubies are little balls of dung.

LATER, SONJA SLIPPED UNCERTAINLY UNDER THE COVERS WITH HER husband. Ordinarily, their coming together for a delayed wedding night would have been a reunion of passion and joy. But Sonja still bore the burden of guilt. Should she tell Jack what had happened to her at the hands of Ali and Koslov? She knew that he surely must know that they had not treated her with any kind of respect.

Did he really need to know the details? And if she told him, how would he bear it? Would he understand her torment? Or, despite his best intentions, would he be put off by what had happened to her at the hands of other men?

Even worse was the question of her own ability to respond to him. Yes, she had survived physically intact; she had recovered from her ordeal of being dragged across the desert, and the marks of her flogging had disappeared, and she still had her ears. But had she been emotionally crippled by her experience? Would the touch of a man, even her husband whom she loved, cause her to recoil?

Sonja hardly knew where to start.

Beside her, Jack, holding her hand, said, "I don't think now is the proper time for you to tell me what happened to you, if ever. You decide, Sonja. If you choose not to tell me, that's fine by me. I understand. As far as I am concerned you are the same young woman I married at Kamenskoi Zavod."

She moved against him. "I—" She couldn't continue.

"I know it couldn't have been good. I was tormented every day just thinking about what you must have been going through."

"Someday maybe," she said. "If that's okay by you."

"Fine by me." He sounded relieved. "To be honest, I don't know if I could handle it now either. The other can wait as well. We've waited this long. We can talk about our junk if we want. Or whatever."

Sonja could smell him beside her. She loved him, and she wanted him. "A kiss wouldn't hurt," she said. "It's been a while. Thinking of you each night kept me going. I knew you were out there coming for me. I never gave up hope, Jack."

"Me either. I had the advantage of having the daguerreotype of the two of us together." Jack kissed her softly.

She felt him grow hard against her hip. Sonja's doubt about her ability to respond emotionally to Jack quickly evaporated. She took him in her hand and squeezed.

He moaned softly. "You!"

She felt his hand slide onto her breast. She sucked in her breath and shuddered. "Oh!" she murmured.

"You like that?" he asked. He was teasing.

She made a sound in her throat.

"Does that mean you want me to stop?"

She turned and they kissed passionately, their tongues a tangle.

Coming up for breath, she said, "You better not stop!"

With those four words, Jack and Sonja Sankova Sandt began their long-delayed wedding night in a snowstorm at the edge of the Gobi. Their bodies were warm. Their spirits were high. Their future together lay ahead.